THEY WERE TRAPPED BETWEEN RITUAL AND REBELLION, CHILDREN OF AN ANCIENT FAITH WHO DARED TO BREAK THE RULES.

DAVID, THE ELDEST SON—He bought the family line, married the family's choice—and gave his heart and soul to the business at the expense of his faith.

NATHAN, THE YOUNGEST SON—He was born to be The Doctor, sacrifical offering on the twin altars of religion and family—until he broke all the rules for love.

MARIANNE, THE GRANDDAUGHTER—She was the rebel who asked the unthinkable questions and dared to find the answers on her own.

SARAH, THE MATRIARCH—Master manipulator, she wanted too much for her children and never stopped expecting more. Reluctant realist, hers was the force that built a mighty family, the cement that held it together when all else failed.

SCATTERED SEED

Maisie Mosco

BANTAM BOOKS
TORONTO • NEW YORK • LONDON • SYDNEY

Acknowledgements:
Ethel Bernstein for assistance in research
H. R. Gouldman for guidance in compiling
the glossary

SCATTERED SEED
A Bantam Book / November 1981

First published in Great Britain by New English Library

ISBN 0-553-20106-9

Published simultaneously in the United States and Canada

*Bantam Books are published by Bantam Books, Inc. Its
trademark, consisting of the words "Bantam Books" and
the portrayal of a rooster, is Registered in U.S. Patent
and Trademark Office and in other countries. Marca Reg-
istrada. Bantam Books, Inc., 666 Fifth Avenue, New York,
New York 10103.*

PRINTED IN THE UNITED STATES OF AMERICA

0 9 8 7 6 5 4 3 2 1

To the memory of
Dr Frank Rifkin,
an irreplaceable friend and mentor

Children of the martyr-race,
Whether free or fettered,
Wake the echoes of the songs,
Where ye may be scattered.
Yours the message cheering,
That the time is nearing,
Which will see all men free,
Tyrants disappearing.

from a *Chanukah* hymn

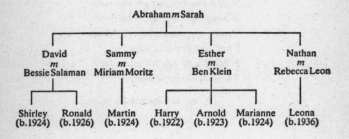

The Sandberg Family

Abraham *m* Sarah

- David
  m
  Bessie Salaman
  - Shirley (b.1924)
  - Ronald (b.1926)
- Sammy
  m
  Miriam Moritz
  - Martin (b.1924)
- Esther
  m
  Ben Klein
  - Harry (b.1922)
  - Arnold (b.1923)
  - Marianne (b.1924)
- Nathan
  m
  Rebecca Leon
  - Leona (b.1936)

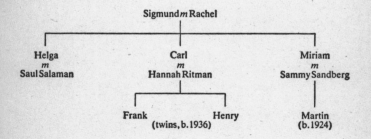

The Moritz Family

Sigmund *m* Rachel

- Helga
  m
  Saul Salaman
- Carl
  m
  Hannah Ritman
  - Frank
  - Henry
  (twins, b.1936)
- Miriam
  m
  Sammy Sandberg
  - Martin (b.1924)

PART ONE

Relative Values

Chapter One

Sarah stood by the window waiting for Abraham to arrive home from work. On weekdays, there was no fire in the parlor grate to warm the chill air, and she had slipped her faded shawl around her shoulders. She preferred its comforting folds to the smart cardigans her children bought for her. And in a way it was like an old friend—from the days when she had not owned a coat and it had been her outdoor garment.

She could hear the wild, autumn wind tearing the few remaining leaves off the tree by the garden gate, and the angry crackle of the bare branches as they were whipped this way and that. How quickly the seasons passed. Another winter approaching. Another year gone by. She rarely paused to think about it, but this morning the calendar had brought her up short.

She and Abraham had been in their twenties when they left Russia. Now, they were in their fifties. But she hadn't noticed her aging appearance until the date reminded her that the Sandbergs had stepped ashore in England thirty years ago today.

Her neighbor's grandfather clock chimed on the other side of the wall, intruding upon her thoughts. Usually, she was busy in the kitchen at this hour, but she had prepared the evening meal early and had put on her best frock. She smoothed the box-pleats which fell from her still-slender hips and adjusted the white, lace jabot she had pinned to the neckline to give the simple, gray serge a festive touch.

The frock was not new, but she took care of her clothes and would probably still be wearing it five years hence. Not like her daughter-in-law, Bessie, who discarded things the moment they were no longer fashionable, Sarah thought as her eldest son's car pulled up outside and she went to open the door.

3

The cat joined her in the lobby and she bent down to fondle its marmalade fur. Tibby was pregnant again, but when had she ever had a cat that didn't keep having kittens? And they'd all been called Tibby. Except the first one, the ferocious black tom named after the Tsar by the friends who'd given him to her. The calendar had reminded her of those friends, too, whom she hadn't seen for years and rarely thought about; but the Berkowitzes had been part of her first weeks in England.

"Hurry up and come in before it starts to rain, Abraham!" she called, watching her husband ease himself out of David's car. The night sky had a sullen look about it, with clouds the color of dead cinders scudding across the surface of the moon. It's a Manchester night, she thought, comparing it with the crisp, starry nights of her youth, which she had not done for a very long time. A sudden memory of riding in a sledge through snowy streets with a strong young man at her side assailed her.

"Turn up your coat collar," she instructed the frail figure he had become.

"You think I'll have time to catch pneumonia walking up the garden path?" he retorted spiritedly.

Everyone knows how delicate his chest is except him, Sarah said to herself exasperatedly. Would he bother to wear a muffler if I didn't wind it around his neck myself every morning before he left the house? But at least he didn't have to wait in the cold for a tram, like most people. Working for his son was a blessing: David drove him to the factory and brought him home.

"You're not coming in for a minute, David?" she called as he stretched across the car to shut the door, which his father always neglected to do.

"Not tonight; I'm late already and we're going to a card party," he shouted back.

"So enjoy it. Give Bessie my love, the children also."

"Such a busy life they lead, those two. Never an evening by their own fireside," Abraham muttered when the car had moved away. He wiped his feet on the porch mat, then followed Sarah inside the house and wiped them again on the extra one she had placed in the foyer to preserve the new carpet David had bought for them. "Every night with the card parties!"

"And where do the winnings go?" Sarah replied. "To the

refugee fund, in case you've forgotten. A card player for the sake of it David isn't."

Abraham took off his hat and coat and put on the shabby black *yarmulke* he always wore on his head indoors. "It's someone's birthday?" he asked, pausing in the kitchen doorway.

The table was covered with a lace cloth instead of the usual darned linen one, and it had been set with the best china and cutlery. A bowl of the Michaelmas daisies, which grew in profusion in the back garden, decorated the center.

Sarah smiled at Abraham's mystified expression. "My birthday is in March, and yours you had two weeks ago. Do you see anyone here but you and me?"

He gave the table another perplexed glance, then went into the scullery to wash his hands.

When he returned, Sarah was sitting by the hearth. "All he noticed is the table," she said to the air. "That his wife is dressed in her finery, he doesn't see."

"I see that you haven't got on the nice link of crystal beads David and Bessie brought you from Blackpool. A person could give you diamonds and you'd still wear that brooch you brought from Dvinsk!"

Sarah fingered the small, gold filigree oval pinned to her collar. "So it's my favorite. But even if it wasn't, I'd wear it to mark the occasion. Thirty years ago tonight, you weren't driven home in a motor car, Abraham. We had no home, and a horse and cart took us from the railway station to the Berkowitzes' house."

Abraham stared into the fire for a moment, then a long sigh escaped him. "It's really that long?"

"In 1905 we fled here from the pogroms. You can't add up any more? All day I've been thinking about it. And how we arrived in Manchester with only a shilling to our name." Sarah's smile grew reminiscent. "Which David wanted us to spend on a cab, remember? Such big ideas he had."

"He hasn't changed." Abraham got up from his rocking chair and went to eye his reflection in the sideboard mirror, as Sarah had done that morning. "Red hair I had when we came!"

"Mine has gone gray, too."

"But otherwise you don't look much different," he said, turning to survey her.

Sarah laughed and rose to bring a dish of sweet and sour

mackerel to the table. "Put on your glasses and look at me again!"

"So we're not what we used to be, is that what we're celebrating?" Abraham asked dryly as they sat down to eat.

"Thirty years of freedom's what we're celebrating," Sarah answered quietly, dishing up the fish. "For Jews that's something to celebrate. Especially now."

Abraham contemplated the sprig of parsley garnishing his plate. "Maybe one day we'll drink to Hitler's downfall, like we did when the Tsar got what was coming to him."

"The Tsar was toppled by his own people. Who is going to topple Hitler when the Germans believe in him as if he's God?"

"So what can you do?" Abraham sighed. But it was the age-old Jewish question, to which he expected and received no answer. "A nice celebration we're having, with what you've just reminded us of."

"A person can rejoice in his own good fortune without forgetting those who aren't so lucky," Sarah informed him. "You had a good day at the factory? I didn't ask you yet."

"I haven't had a good day since David put in those Hoffman presses."

Sarah shook her head disapprovingly. "Something to make things easier for him my husband doesn't like. He prefers those heavy flat irons, from which he's got stooping shoulders and still gets pains in his arms after using them all those years."

"So I'm old-fashioned."

"And if David was like you, where would the business be?"

"Still in his father-in-law's house in Southall Street, and he wouldn't be having sleepless nights about his big overheads," Abraham replied.

Sarah squeezed some lemon juice onto her mackerel and kept her thoughts to herself. She could not change her husband's nature, and saying too much would hurt his feelings. Abraham had never thought it necessary for people to strive for more than they had.

"How many meals can a person eat? How many clothes can he wear?" he asked as though he had read her mind. "But David is never satisfied. He's got too much ambition."

Too much is better than none, Sarah thought. When David had told her he was moving to new premises, she had been anxious about his extending his business when others were cutting down their expenses. But he had said the time to do it was while property was cheap because times were bad. In good times a factory building would be beyond his resources, he'd explained. That had been two years ago, and now trade had begun to pick up and Sarah was no longer worried. What David set out to do he always did; he was the only one of her four children who took after her.

"Fruit and cream on a week-night?" Abraham said when they had eaten their fish and Sarah brought the dessert to the table. "We really are celebrating!"

"But don't mention we had a party to the children," Sarah said guiltily. "We never had one without them before; they might be upset I didn't invite them."

"I'm surprised you didn't."

Sarah licked the cream off her spoon and smiled at him. "I wanted it to be just you and me. The children would make fun of me; they take freedom for granted." Her expression clouded as memory carried her back. "To value it, you have to know what it's like to be oppressed, Abraham."

Chapter Two

When David arrived home, the house was unusually silent. Generally, Bessie's voice shrilled from the kitchen the moment he opened the front door, upbraiding him for being late, and his children rushed into the foyer to greet him and share a wink because their mother was behaving true to pattern and it had become a secret joke between him and them.

"Where is everyone tonight?" he called.

The maid's voice answered him mournfully, from the kitchen. "Summat's 'appened, Mr. Sandberg."

David saw his reflection pale, in the hallway mirror, as he thought of some nameless catastrophe having befallen his children or his wife, in that order. Then Shirley and Ronald appeared at his side and his knees felt weak with relief. "Where's your mother?" he asked them.

"It's Mom it's happened to," Shirley replied and Ronald burst out laughing.

"If you're having a lark with me, I'll lam the pair of you!" David barked though he had never laid a finger on either of them, and knew he never would. He stalked through to the kitchen, where the angular Yorkshire housemaid, whose hands were never still, was seated on the overstuffed sofa, crocheting a white, rabbit-wool scarf for Shirley. "Where's my wife, Lizzie?"

"At the 'airdressers, 'avin a perm, Mr. Sandberg."

"At this time of night?"

"Summat went wrong wi' t'solution'n 'er 'air's fell out."

"What!"

"It's true, Daddy," Shirley said. "She phoned up to tell us not to wait supper for her."

"I don't think I feel like any supper," David muttered, trying not to imagine Bessie's pudgy countenance without a frame of hair.

"Thi're doin' what thi can, ah expect, Mr. Sandberg," Lizzie consoled him. "I expect that's why t'missis 'asn't come back yet."

"I don't see what they can do if there's no hair to do it to," Ronald said practically.

David controlled a shudder. "You and the kids sit down and eat, Lizzie. I'll wait for Mrs. Sandberg."

He went into the parlor and sat tapping his fingers on the arm of the chair, edgily, then fished in his jacket pocket for his packet of Goldflake cigarettes. Some of his friends smoked cigars, but he had never learned to enjoy them. Not in the way his late father-in-law had once prophesied he would, he thought as his mind swooped irrelevantly into the past.

Why had he suddenly remembered that? A picture of Isaac Salaman offering him a Havana swam before his eyes as he lit a cigarette. "I don't smoke, Mr. Salaman," he heard his own voice echo nervously down the years. Well, he smoked now; couldn't open his eyes and start the day without one. Why had he ever started? he asked himself, stubbing the cigarette out. Was it living with Bessie that'd made him need something to calm his nerves? No, the need had been there before then.

He sat cracking his knuckles for a moment, then another voice echoed in his mind. "I wish you'd stop doing that, David. It sets me on edge!" Miriam's voice. He'd begun smoking to stop cracking his knuckles, he recalled with a wry smile, and lit another cigarette absently, thinking of the heartache he could have saved himself if he'd known then what he knew now.

That there was no such thing as a love you couldn't recover from. That Miriam would marry his brother Sammy and the passion he'd once felt for her would die away and be replaced by uncomplicated affection. That he could share his life with Bessie, though their marriage was founded on nothing more than a bargain—a business partnership coupled with Bessie's hand, offered by Salaman the day he'd said David would learn to enjoy cigars.

Maybe the recollection hadn't been irrelevant. Hadn't the early years of his marriage been beset by Bessie's anxiety about her plainness, compared with Miriam's beauty? She had doubted that David could really care for her and had made him miserable because of it. Her self-doubt hadn't been in evidence for some time. Would it return because of what had happened to her hair?

It's how it'll affect me I'm thinking of, David admitted to himself as he got up to find the beauty salon's number in the telephone directory, and was shocked because he had never considered himself a selfish man.

"What've you done to my wife, Ruby?" he said as lightly as he could when the hairdresser answered the phone.

"I hope you're not going to sue me," she replied nervously.

This had not entered David's mind. "Don't be daft!"

"My parents would have a stroke. The Cohens and the Sandbergs came over on the herring boat together," she reminded him as if she were not convinced.

"What would I want to sue you for?" he asked impatiently.

"Money. Revenge, maybe."

"Stop talking nonsense and let me talk to Bessie."

"She left here nearly an hour ago. Perhaps she called somewhere on her way home."

But David knew his wife would have done no such thing. He lit another cigarette and began pacing the room, eyeing Bessie's collection of cut-glass ornaments which filled every nook and cranny and wondering where she could be. Losing her crowning glory would devastate any woman. It was enough to make one of Bessie's mentality jump into the Irwell river. Appearance was all to her; it always had been.

His fears were cut short by the sound of the front door opening. He rushed into the entrance hall and found Lizzie and the children there, too.

"It's not the end of the world, love," he said comfortingly as his wife removed her coat, but not the scarf swathed around her head.

"It is to me," she replied in a quivering voice. "I've been walking the streets. I couldn't even bear to come home."

Shirley touched her own, carroty ringlets self-consciously. "Your hair'll grow again, Mom. Don't be upset."

" 'Course it will," Lizzie said encouragingly.

"We'll still love you even if it doesn't," Ronald declared. "But let's see what you look like now, without your scarf. In case it does."

His mother gave him a withering glance. "Nobody's going to see what I look like, Ronald." She glared at David as if he were responsible for her plight. "Nobody at all."

David watched her walk upstairs, leaning heavily on the banister, and smiled reassuringly at the children. But an ominous sense of *déjà vu* had settled like lead in the pit of his stomach. Another stormy passage in his marriage had just begun.

Chapter Three

Marianne watched the high school boys and girls alight from a No. 11 tram. How she wished she was one of them, but next year perhaps she would be. If she'd been born a few months sooner, she'd have sat for the scholarship exam last winter when her cousin Martin did.

Her brother Arnold's red head, under his Manchester Grammar School cap, and then her brother Harry's dark one, capless, appeared in a noisy crush of lads jostling each other onto the pavement.

"What're you doing here, our kid?" Harry inquired, loosening his Central High School tie.

"Where's Martin?" she asked Arnold, ignoring Harry's question.

"I'm not glued to him just because he goes to my school now. Maybe he couldn't find his way out of the building; it takes the new boys ages to find their way around," Arnold answered with the superiority of a sophomore.

Marianne peered down Cheetham Hill Road to see if another tram was approaching.

"You'd better come home with us; it's getting dark," Harry said to her.

"I'm waiting for Martin."

Arnold grinned. "It's no use arguing with that one, Harry. She's only little, but she knows her own mind."

Marianne flicked her black bangs away from her eyes and glowered at him. "What if I am little? Cousin Shirley is bigger than me, but she never comes top of the class."

"Like you do," Arnold said teasingly.

"Leave the kid alone," Harry instructed him with big brotherly authority. "You know she hates being reminded of her size."

"I don't appreciate being called the kid, either," Marianne said in a dignified voice. "And kindly don't consume all the scones before I arrive home, you two."

"How can you have room for scones when you've just swallowed a dictionary?" Arnold quipped.

Marianne opened the exercise book she was clutching in her hand and pretended to read, but she was listening to her brothers' chortling as they strode away. Martin didn't make fun of her because she liked big words. He didn't make fun of her about anything. If only he was her brother and Harry and Arnold her cousins! But her life was full of if-onlys and she sometimes wondered if anyone else's was.

Martin seemed perfectly happy with his, but Auntie Miriam was his mother and she wasn't strict, like Mom. Anyone would be satisfied if they were allowed to read in bed and stay up late to hear grownup programs on the wireless, instead of nothing but *Children's Hour*.

She gazed pensively into the drug store window at the brightly colored liquids in fat-bellied flasks labeled "poison," then averted her eyes with a shiver. How could something that looked so pretty be deadly, too? A figure was looming towards her out of the evening mist that had fallen patchily on the main road and she hoped it wasn't Mom, coming to fetch her. Usually she went straight home, but she wanted to talk to Martin on his own, which she was hardly ever able to do now that he went to a different school. Whenever she popped across the backyards to see him after tea, Auntie Miriam and Uncle Sammy were there. And Martin was always doing homework, or practicing his *Bar Mitzvah* portion though he wouldn't have to say it in *shul* until he was thirteen.

Thank goodness she was a girl and didn't need to have that on her mind as well as her other worries. Like not being good at arithmetic, even though her English made up for it. And having that awful period-thing to look forward to; and the terrible agony of having babies, which, Lizzie had told her and Shirley, was a woman's lot.

The figure emerged from the mist into the pool of lamplight near the streetcar stop and Marianne sighed with relief; it wasn't Mom after all. Then a tram trundled into sight and clanked to a halt.

"Martin!" she shouted as he leaped off the step.

"There's nothing wrong, is there?" he called, hurrying towards her.

"Trust you to ask that!"

Martin tugged the peak of his cap sheepishly. Why was he always expecting something bad to happen?

"If there were, d'you think I'd be the one the family'd send to tell you? Honestly, Martin! I just fancied walking home with you, like we used to."

He flashed her a smile which animated his pale face, and hitched his leather satchel higher on his shoulder. "So come on then."

They trudged along in companionable silence until they had turned off Cheetham Hill Road into a street of terraced, lace-curtained houses.

"I've got something to tell you," Martin said. "About my grandfather."

"What's Zaidie Sigmund been up to now?" He was not Marianne's grandfather, but she and her brothers had always looked on him as one and she smiled, thinking of how he was always in hot water with Martin's Auntie Helga who kept house for him.

"He's courting a lady."

Marianne gaped. "Who is?"

"Grandpa."

"Why're you calling him that, when we've always called our grandparents Zaidie and Bobbie?"

"I'm trying to stop using Yiddish words."

Marianne thought of their mutual Sandberg grandparents who used Yiddish words more often than Sigmund Moritz did. Zaidie Abraham had never learned to read English and enjoyed reading the *Yiddish Gazette* every week.

"Bobbie Sarah and Zaidie Abraham won't like it," she declared emphatically.

"They'll just have to lump it," Martin replied.

Marianne gave him a shocked glance. "I don't know what's come over you, Martin."

"You would if you were in my class," he said moodily. "They're nearly all Christian and I feel a right idiot when I forget and call someone a *shlemiel* or something. It's not like Temple School, Marianne—half-and-half. Where there aren't any stuck up devils who say things that make you feel like something in a glass case," he added heatedly.

Marianne was eyeing him with dismay.

"They're not all like that," he admitted, simmering down. "But how many does it take?"

"Why don't you punch them on the nose?"

Martin kicked a tin can which was lying on the pavement into the gutter, then slowed his pace, thoughtfully. "Remember what we used to sing to Shirley when we were all little and she was always saying horrid things to us?"

"Sticks and stones may break my bones, but words will never harm me," Marianne chanted softly.

"Well that's my philosophy," he told her, quickening his step again.

"What's philosophy?" she asked, skipping to keep up with his long-legged stride.

"It's time you began reading books like the ones in my grandfather's library, instead of stuff like *What Katy Did*; then you'd know. Look it up in the dictionary when you get home."

"I can't," she giggled. "Our Arnold said I've swallowed it."

Why must she start giggling in the middle of a serious conversation? Martin thought exasperatedly.

"Made up any poems lately?" she inquired out of the blue.

Her mind jumped about like a grasshopper, too. From one subject to another. But she was his favorite cousin all the same. "Poems don't get made up. They get written," he corrected her.

They had reached the cobblestoned passage where the back doors of their homes faced each other and halted prior to parting. Martin stood stirring some mud with the toe of his boot. Marianne watched his long fingers playing with the buckle on his navy gabardine jacket, then scanned his face uncertainly; the thick eyebrows, a shade or two darker than his light brown hair, drawn together in a thoughtful frown above the small nose; the thinnish lips and the tapering chin. He looked the same, yet somehow he wasn't. She could feel something different about him, as if he was suddenly a lot older than her. But if she worked hard, next year she'd be at a high school and catch up with him, learn all the new things he was learning.

She had yet to discover that catching up with Martin intellectually would not be easy. They had been reared from birth in the same close family ethos and an extraordinary rapport had always existed between them; but Martin was Sigmund Moritz's only grandchild and Sigmund had implanted in him a love of learning and literature, as he had with David and Nathan Sandberg when they were boys. Paradoxically, Martin's father, Sammy, was the only one of the three Sandberg brothers who had had no taste for scholarship, and he had never read a book in his life.

"All right, Martin," Marianne conceded with something akin to respect in her voice. "I won't say 'made up' any more. So have you written any poems lately?"

Martin surveyed the thin little figure leaning against the wall and smiled amusedly. One of her fawn bicycle socks had slipped down to her ankle, the top buttonhole of her blazer was fastened to the second button, and there was a smudge of ink on her olive cheek.

"I wrote one this morning, on the tram, as it happens," he said fishing a scrap of paper out of his pocket and slipping it into hers. "Have you written any more stories?"

Marianne nodded and handed him her dog-eared exercise book. "You can read them in bed tonight. What's your mom got to say about Zaidie Sigmund courting a lady?" she inquired irrelevantly.

"I don't think she's very pleased."

"Your Bobbie Rachel won't let him marry the lady unless she's nice, Martin. She'll fly down from Heaven when he's asleep and whisper in his ear that he mustn't."

"There's no such place as Heaven."

Marianne felt as if a cold hand had touched her heart. What was the matter with him? "How can you say such a dreadful thing? It'd mean there's nowhere for all the dead people to go, wouldn't it? And if there's no Heaven, why would the grownups tell us there is?" Something was prodding her memory. She was sitting on the grass under a tree, watching Martin chew a blade he'd just plucked from beside her. "The day of Bobbie Rachel's funeral, we went to Bellott Street park and you told me you'd dreamed about Heaven!" she accused him. "You even described the angels and now you're saying there's no such place."

"That was ages ago." he said dismissively. "In some ways you're still very childish, Marianne."

Marianne watched him stride across the entry and disappear through his back doorway, then turned and entered her own yard. When she walked into the kitchen, her mother was turning over some clothes which were drying on the fireguard.

"Is it true there's no Heaven, Mom?" she demanded taking off her blazer and tossing it on to the sofa.

"Twenty minutes late she comes home from school and right away she's asking questions!" Esther Klein exclaimed. "Hang your blazer up, my lady!"

Marianne took the blazer to the lobby and hung it on the low peg reserved for her garments.

"Now she's asking me about Heaven," her mother snapped when she returned. She cast a harassed look around the disordered room, which she had not had time to tidy since she arrived home from her husband's shop an hour ago. "Why doesn't somebody ask me about Hell?"

Marianne took the buttered scone her brothers had left on the plate for her and stood nibbling it. Arnold had gone to Hebrew school, but Harry, who no longer went because he had been *Bar Mitzvahed* a few months ago, was seated at the table doing his homework and shrugged when Marianne exchanged a glance with him.

"Mom never used to be in a bad temper all the time, did she, Harry?" Marianne said voicing their thoughts.

"I had no reason to be," their mother retorted rolling up some garments that were dry enough for ironing.

"Shall I do that for you?" Marianne offered.

"It wouldn't do any harm if you did."

Marianne fetched the clothes basket from the scullery. "Sit down and have a rest, Mom," she said taking over Esther's task.

"Don't be *meshuga*, love," Esther replied with a weary smile. "How can I, with all I've still got to do? Your dad's entitled to find his home nice and shipshape when he gets back after a hard day's work, not looking like a rag bag." She began sorting out the jumble of odds and ends which had accumulated on the dresser, putting them away in the cupboards and drawers.

"But you've been working at the shop all day, too," Marianne reminded her.

"I know I have. But I'm a woman and it's a woman's job to keep the house nice."

"Why should it be?" Marianne demanded.

"Because it always has been!" Esther exclaimed impatiently, brushing some crumbs off the sofa. She fetched the carpet sweeper and began running it over the rug. "Nobody seeing the state of this room would believe I'm really a neat and tidy person," she told her son and daughter. "But I can't be in two places at once, and I'm not going to be for much longer."

"Are you going to stop helping Dad in the business?" Harry asked her. "I'll be fourteen soon, then I can leave school and work for him," he added, putting down his pen, which he wished he could do permanently.

"The while you're still thirteen," Esther answered. "And there's good living accommodations behind the shop."

Marianne stopped folding a shirt. "You don't mean we're going to live there?"

"We shouldn't have waited this long to do it," Esther nodded. "Why should I tear myself in two like I've been doing? It'll be easier for me when the house and the business are both in one place."

"Mom's right," Harry said.

"But what about us?" Marianne blurted. "You and Arnold and me?" She knew she should be considering her mother, but a feeling that her world was turning topsy-turvy filled her with alarm. "We'll have to leave all our friends and the shop's miles away, near the docks where the people aren't Jewish."

"They're the people your dad makes his wages from," Esther told her sharply. "And they're nicer than some Jews. They've always got a smile for you, though most of them are much poorer than us. Dad was going to tell you about this when he comes home and Arnold's back from *Cheder*, but now you know."

Marianne sat down on the padded lid of the coal scuttle, looking the picture of misery.

"Buck up, kid!" Harry jollied her. "We can come to Cheetham and see everyone on the weekends, can't we, Mom? It won't be that bad."

"There's a sensible boy!" Esther applauded, patting his head approvingly on her way to stir the pan of split pea soup she had put to simmer on the blackleaded hob at the back of the fireplace. "One of you kids'll have to come after school once a week, as well, to fetch the chicken and meat. There's no kosher butcher in that part of Salford. Our Marianne can do it if she likes, and have her tea at Bobbie Sarah's."

"I won't need to come to Cheetham after school, Mom," Marianne pointed out. "I'll still be at Temple School until I pass the scholarship exam. I'll be coming here every day."

Esther was tasting the soup. "Of course you won't, you silly girl," she said distractedly, adding more salt to it from the jar she kept on the kitchen mantelpiece because the scullery was damp. "After we move, you'll be going to Stowell Memorial School, Marianne. Near the shop."

Harry looked shocked. "But that's a church school, Mom. Dad told us when he took us to see how he'd dressed the shop windows all in white for Whitsun and we passed it. He said all the little girls who go there'd be buying their Whit Walk frocks from him. Don't you remember, Marianne?"

Marianne did not reply.

"Our Marianne can miss the scripture classes when they're reading the New Testament; nobody'll mind," Esther answered. "And it's no use you sitting sulking, love," she added briskly to Marianne. "We're moving because it's best for us and that's that. I've always been a good saleswoman.

Remember me telling you I worked in a gown shop when I was a girl? With me there all the time, the business'll do a lot better and we'll be able to afford a lot of things we haven't got now."

"Will Arnold and me be able to have bikes?" Harry asked eagerly.

Esther glanced around the shabby room, at the threadbare purple carpet which was not her taste, but that of her sister-in-law Bessie who'd passed it on to her, the darned upholstery of the sofa and the blue chenille curtains faded to gray from years of laundering. "After we've bought a few other things, Harry," she told her eldest son whose ideas were as big as his Uncle David's.

"I'd rather stay here and not have any new things," Marianne whispered.

Esther surveyed her tense expression and the little clenched fists which meant she was trying not to cry. How do I come to a kid like this, who gets worked up over everything and nothing and doesn't want to see reason? she asked herself with the surge of exasperation and love combined that her daughter so often aroused in her. Who did Marianne take after? It had to be something in her blood that made her as different from Harry and Arnold as chalk was from cheese, because all her children had received the same upbringing. Marianne had a will of iron, too, but she'd got that from her grandmother, who seemed to understand her better than anyone else did. The rest of her troublesome nature must come from those relatives of her father's who'd been writers and artists in Austria. And here am I having to deal with it, Esther thought wryly.

She went to kneel beside the coal scuttle on which Marianne was still hunched, and stroked her silky, black hair for a moment, enjoying the feel of it.

Marianne looked up at her with surprise; her mother was not given to such demonstrativeness. Harry seemed surprised too.

"I don't have much time for you kids these days, do I?" Esther said, aware of their reaction. "But it doesn't mean I don't love you. And things'll be different after we move, you'll see."

"I don't want them to be different," Marianne declared, deliberately missing the point. "And I don't want to leave Temple School until I've sat for the scholarship exam, even if we are moving. They're teaching us special things to make sure we pass."

The love and exasperation rose in Esther again, with the latter well to the fore. "You'll do as you're told; you're only a little girl," she snapped, going to give the soup an angry stir.

Marianne got up and went to fetch her blazer.

"It's nearly teatime; your dad'll be home soon. Where d'you think you're going?" Esther demanded, watching her put it on.

"To tell Bobbie Sarah what you're doing to me!" Marianne said hotly as she fled into the scullery and out the back door.

Chapter Four

Sarah was preparing pastry when the door-bell rang. She took off the old blue, wrap-around overall she wore to protect her clothes from flying flour and went to see who the caller was. At noon on a Thursday, her Jewish neighbors would be busy with their pre-*Shabbos* cooking as she herself was. There were so many different things to prepare, it took her two whole days. Her Christian neighbors would be getting their dinner ready, or eating it; most of them made themselves something hot and thought it strange that she couldn't be bothered to do this just for herself.

"Sigmund!" she exclaimed with surprise when she opened the door. "You've got no customers for try-ons today?"

Sigmund Moritz followed her into the kitchen and lowered his short, plump frame into Abraham's rocking chair. "Let them wait," he answered nonchalantly.

"So what brings you here, when my husband isn't home?" Sarah joked. Sigmund was like a brother to herself and Abraham and his wife had been like a dear, sweet sister. Rachel had been dead for four years, but a day never passed without Sarah thinking of her.

"There has to be a reason?" Sigmund said unbuttoning his coat and avoiding her eye.

"With you, yes," Sarah replied bluntly. "In all the years we've known each other, whenever you've paid me a morning visit it's been for something." She had a good idea what the something might be and Sigmund's demeanor was confirming it. "Remember when we lived in Strangeways and our children were young, how you used to walk in through the back door when I wasn't expecting you? In those days you were like a mouthpiece for David, always encouraging his impossible ideas," Sarah smiled though she had not smiled at the time.

"So here I ring the front doorbell; coming the back way is a longer walk. And David doesn't need me to speak for him any more," Sigmund said brusquely, swallowing his regret that his mentorship of the young David Sandberg had led to nothing.

Sarah put on her overall again—with Sigmund Moritz she did not stand on ceremony—and began the delicate process of pulling her pastry to make it paper thin.

"When Helga does that it always breaks," Sigmund remarked.

"It has to have just the right amount of oil in it." Sarah stretched the dough carefully with her small, strong fingers. "So?" she said questioningly. "To watch me make strudel for the *Shabbos* tea party you haven't come."

Sigmund's gaze roved casually to the brass candlesticks on the mantelpiece and the gleaming mortar and pestle that matched them, but Sarah could feel a sudden tension emanating from him, as if he were steeling himself.

"Maybe I came to ask you to make an extra piece," he said quietly.

He's going to ask if he can bring his lady friend, Sarah thought. And he hadn't yet mentioned her to his own children, though Helga and Carl live in the same house with him. Tell me about her already, she wanted to urge him. Get it off your chest and you'll feel better. Did he really believe that none of the family knew about the woman? But he had always been a man who contained his deepest feelings, hiding himself behind a book, losing himself in music. When she and Abraham had first met him they'd thought him eccentric and rude. Time had proved them right about his eccentricity, but they'd learned long ago that the rudeness was part ego and part absentmindedness, never personal.

"There's someone I'd like you to meet and *Shabbos* after noon, when everyone comes here, would be a good time," he said.

Beating about the bush was not Sarah's way. Until he himself broached the subject, she would not have dreamt of doing so; he was entitled to his privacy. But now that he had, she spoke her mind. "Someone you'd like to marry, maybe?"

Sigmund looked startled and then guilty, fidgeting with his watch chain, his pinkish complexion reddening, as if he were a small boy caught with his hand in the biscuit tin.

"It isn't a crime," Sarah said gently. "But why did you wait so long to tell us?"

"My son and daughters know, too?" he said resignedly.

Sarah nodded. He had been seen in Mandley Park with the woman, during the summer. It was not a park the Sandbergs and Moritzes frequented, but one of the small, grassy retreats in Salford, which was probably why Sigmund had selected it as a meeting place, the family had surmised. David and Bessie's maid used it as a short cut to Higher Broughton when she went there to visit a friend and had loyally reported her observations, which had included that she had not liked the look of the lady.

"Listen, who can keep a secret round here?" Sarah jested swallowing her misgivings. "But why did it have to be a secret?"

Sigmund took off his pince-nez and studied her. "Nobody minds?"

"All they mind is the way you've kept it to yourself," Sarah lied. But sometimes a person had to lie because the truth would cause trouble. Helga who hadn't shed a tear in public when her soldier husband, Saul Salaman, was killed in the Great War, had wept on Sarah's shoulder at the prospect of some unknown woman taking over the household she had run from the time her mother's illness began. Miriam was concerned for her elder sister, but more so for her father when she heard Lizzie's description of his lady friend.

"Her name is Gertie Fish and she lives in Salford," Sigmund supplied. "I met her when I was looking for fancy buttons for Paula Frankl's spring coat and I couldn't get them at my usual place."

So Paula Frankl's to blame! Sarah thought irrationally. Rachel Moritz had not liked her.

"Gertie's got a trimmings shop," Sigmund went on. "Before her husband died, they had one in Sheffield."

"How come she moved to Salford?" Sarah inquired.

"To be near her family. Mrs. Radinsky is her twin sister."

Sarah could not conceal her consternation. Mr. Radinsky was a lovely man. She and Rachel had bought their fruit and vegetables from him when they lived in Strangeways. But his wife!

"I know what you're thinking," Sigmund said defensively. "But identical twins they're not."

"I didn't say a word."

"Your face was enough."

Sarah began filling the pastry with apple and raisins, trying to check her flustered feelings. "Perhaps you should mention her to your children before Saturday?"

Sigmund replaced his pince-nez on his nose and mopped his brow, which was noticeably perspiring. "And go through with them what I've just been through with you?" He sprang up and laced his stubby fingers behind his back. "Once is enough!" he snorted irascibly. "I'm my own boss; I can please myself what I do! My children are adults; who I marry won't affect them."

"Miriam, maybe not; she doesn't live with you. But Helga and Carl—"

"A lot of companionship I've had from those two since Rachel went," Sigmund cut in with a bitter smile. "Helga's across the street at Miriam's every evening. And Carl—well you know what he's like. I might as well be in an empty house as living with him." He stood staring into space morosely.

"You should have told them how you feel," Sarah said softly, distressed by the sadness in his eyes.

"Should my own flesh and blood need telling?"

"You can't blame them, Sigmund. All their lives you've let them think books and music were all you needed."

"Maybe I thought that myself," he admitted grudgingly. "When Rachel was alive."

A man needs a woman's presence, Sarah thought. Even one like Sigmund, capable of being so wrapped up in his own interests he'd forget his wife was there. But a deep love had existed between him and Rachel and had made what most women would find intolerable tolerable to her. Would Mrs. Radinsky's sister be the same?

"So you'll bring Gertie to the *Shabbos* tea party," she said forcing a smile which belied his misgivings. "And I'll tell the family she's coming."

Sigmund's expression suffused with relief. "From you it would be better than from me," he said gratefully. "Then on *Shabbos*, there'll be no need for any discussion. Everyone will just wish us *Mazeltov* and we can arrange the wedding date."

Sarah saw him to the garden gate and watched him head back towards his house where he had his tailor's shop, noting the spring in his step. Unloading his burden had done him good. And now it was up to her to pave the way for him with his children. But hadn't it always been like that with the Sandbergs and Moritzes? Feeling and doing things for each other, their lives woven together by time and events, joys and sorrows shared.

She waved to her neighbor, Mrs. Watson, who was cleaning the upstairs windows. Then as she gathered up some sheets of newspaper that had blown on to the path, she reflected that Mrs. Watson had a lot of relatives, too, but they weren't always running to her with their problems, like Sarah's did. Today it was Sigmund. Last night it had been her granddaughter Marianne; then her son-in-law Ben Klein, still not sure it was right to take his children to live near the docks. Who would it be next?

She thought about her son Nathan and the pain he had caused her and smiled down at the cat which had come to rub itself against her lisle-stockinged ankles. "Everything passes, Tibby," she told it. "The trouble is there's always something else around the corner to take its place."

Chapter Five

Mrs. Kaplan shuffled into the surgery and sat down on the edge of a polished oak chair, her manner suggesting she was not sure if she would be staying. "Not a bad place you've got here, Nat," she said grudgingly to the darkly handsome young man seated behind the desk.

Nathan Sandberg glanced around his prison and managed to smile.

The shrivelled-looking little woman fanned her beady gaze along the glossy cream walls, holding it for a moment on the framed certificate as if to satisfy herself that Nathan was qualified to attend her. "I want you should take me for a patient, Nat. A desk with a leather top must have cost something," she added as though this were a deciding factor in her choice of practitioner.

"And what can I do for you?" Nathan inquired in his bedside voice, which at times sounded to him more like a shop assistant's.

"Plenty, I hope!"

Nathan controlled the urge to laugh. Wait till he told his partner who the latest addition to their list was. "She'll expect two bottles of medicine instead of one," Lou would groan. Mrs. Kaplan had been called the meanest woman in Strangeways when they were boys. She hadn't been the cleanest either, he recalled, eyeing the stains on her rusty black coat and trying not to wrinkle his nose as a mixed waft of moth balls and body odor drifted from across the desk. Would he ever become oblivious to the unsavory side of his work? Others said you did, but it hadn't happened to him yet.

"So, Mrs. Kaplan," he said, collecting himself. "You're not feeling too well, eh?"

Mrs. Kaplan inserted a black-rimmed fingernail beneath the man's flat cap she habitually wore and scratched her head vigorously. "I'm only middling," she shrugged, producing a sniff and then a cough. "How else can I be with my layabout sons?"

Nathan had not been in practice long, but he had already learned that a GP's work included listening to his patient's woes, as well as to their hearts and chests, and that often the therapeutic process of unburdening themselves did more good than pharmaceutical remedies. Mrs. Kaplan was not the first old acquaintance from Nathan and Lou's Strangeways childhood to defect from another doctor's care and place herself in theirs; and it sometimes embarrassed Nathan to find himself hearing the family secrets of people for whom he had run errands when he was a youngster.

Who am I to be advising them? he would ask himself. And why should they think I'm the oracle all of a sudden? "It's because 'doctor' is a magic word," Lou had said when they discussed this. "It puts you in a class apart." Nathan was well aware of this phenomenon, but still found it difficult to associate its manifestations with himself and Lou. Especially when they walked along Lower Broughton Road to where their cars were parked, and men old enough to be their fathers touched their caps to them.

"Your sons're giving you aggravation, are they?" he said sympathetically to Mrs. Kaplan who had stopped scratching her head and was coughing again. He picked up his stethoscope. "We'll just have a listen to your chest, shall we?"

Mrs. Kaplan recoiled against the chairback and crossed her arms over her sagging bosom. "It's really necessary?"

Nathan was as reluctant to look at it as she was to reveal it, but it had to be done. "I'm afraid so." He averted his eyes to some papers on the desk whilst she prepared herself for the ordeal and told him about her sons' gambling debts.

After he had sent her away with some soothing words for her aggravation and a bottle of Mist. Expect. Sed. cough syrup for her cough, he pressed a bell to summon the next patient and went to scrub his hands with carbolic soap, marveling that there was still skin on them, the way they got scrubbed a hundred times a day.

"Sit down, will you?" he said without turning from the washbasin when someone entered. "I won't be a minute."

The tall, pleasant-faced man who had limped into the surgery smiled to himself and did as he was bid, running a

hand through his curly red hair which was still damp from
standing at a tramstop in the rain.

"Sammy!" Nathan exclaimed warmly when he reached
for a towel and saw him. "Don't tell me you've been sitting in
the waiting room?"

"Sure I have, Nat. Why shouldn't I?"

"Because my family don't have to." Nathan perched on
the edge of the desk and smiled at him. "You should've
knocked on the surgery door to let me know you were here."

"I don't expect special treatment."

A surge of affection for his self-effacing brother welled
up in Nathan. You wouldn't catch David waiting with the patients! But they were direct opposites in every way. "What's
the trouble?" he inquired.

"My leg."

Nathan was momentarily surprised, then wondered why
he should be. Perhaps because he was used to Sammy being
lame and had never heard him complain about it.

"Also my hip," Sammy added. "But don't say anything
to Miriam. I don't want to worry her."

"You'd better undress and let me look at it."

"Anyone'd think you'd never seen it before!" Sammy
grinned as he lay down on the couch. "That we didn't share a
bedroom for umpteen years."

"I wasn't a doctor then." Nathan felt the mangled shin-
bone with gentle fingers.

"That Cossack did a good job when he galloped his
horse over it," Sammy said lightly.

How can he smile about it? Nathan thought. Most
people would spit whenever they heard the word "Cossack" if
they had had this deliberately done to them by one. But
Sammy was too good-natured to bear even a brute like that
any malice. "How old were you when it happened, Sam?" he
asked.

"It was a few years before we left Russia," Sammy said
thinking back. "I must've been about two."

"Who set your leg, afterwards? Or tried to, I should say,
because it looks as if it was done by a carpenter! No wonder
there's arthritis there and this leg's shorter than your other
one."

"Mother must have taken me to a doctor, but how can I
remember?" Sammy studied his brother's thoughtful face as
Nathan continued examining him. Was this calm young doc-

tor in the starched, white shirt and navy pinstripe suit really little Nat who used to throw tantrums for no reason? But he'd always been clever, never without a book in his hands. "Miriam thinks our Martin gets his brains from their Carl," he smiled. "And I let her think it, but in my opinion he takes after you."

Heaven help him if he ends up like me, Nathan thought cynically.

"But David's Ronald is the one who looks like you," Sammy added.

"Yes, he does, doesn't he?" Nathan agreed with a stiff smile. "Like that snap of me someone took when I'd just started at Manchester Grammar and I was showing off my school uniform." He went to sit at his desk. "All right, you can get dressed now, Sam. I'll give you something to help the pain and arrange for you to see an orthopod."

"What's that?"

"Medical slang for an orthopedic specialist."

"David said I might have to see one, when I told him about my hip before I left the factory."

"He's an amateur physician now, is he?" Nathan replied crisply. "As well as everything else he sets himself up to be."

"Now, now, Nat," Sammy said awkwardly.

"You still think he's Jesus Christ, don't you?" Nathan answered with a little bitterness he could not disguise.

Sammy tried to laugh it off. "A nice thing to say about a Jew from Cheetham Hill!"

"But he can't put a foot wrong so far as you're concerned, can he?" Nathan sat twiddling his fountain pen in an uncomfortable silence whilst Sammy finished dressing.

"David's very good to me," Sammy said quietly.

"Sure he is; who could deny it? He's too good by half! To all the family."

Sammy fiddled with a button on his raincoat, an unhappy expression in his deep blue eyes.

"That's why we're all so indebted to him," Nathan added flatly as if his sudden burst of emotion had left him drained.

"Whatever David's faults are, his generosity makes up for them," Sammy declared sincerely, thinking how strange it was to have to defend someone because they were too kind and remembering a similar conversation he had once had with Miriam about David.

"If you say so," Nathan replied in the same tone. He was gazing at the photograph of his wife which Lou had deemed was a standard requisite on a doctor's desk. The first time he had seen it, David had sat quietly smoking while their mother showed it to Nathan, after she had got it from a matchmaker.

"How's Rebecca?" Sammy asked glancing at it, too.

"She's fine, thanks."

Sammy winked knowingly. "All things considered."

"She's over the morning sickness now." Nathan turned from the photograph to his brother and assumed his role of physician again. Sammy hadn't come to the surgery to rake over old coals. "I'll send you to see Mr. Latimer, Sam. He's a very clever man."

"David said if I need to see a specialist I should go privately and he'll foot the bill," Sammy said and saw Nathan's lips tighten. "Look, you know me; I wouldn't mind sitting and waiting at a hospital," he added uncomfortably. The coldness between his elder brother and his younger one upset him, and he was beginning to feel like a bone between two dogs, even though one of them was not present.

"Sure I know you," Nathan smiled, then the smile disappeared. "And I know David, too. But there'll be no bill to foot and you won't have to sit waiting, either. Mr. Latimer's son Paul was at medical school with me and we're good friends. Paul was at my wedding."

"I noticed there were some *goyim* there," Sammy recalled.

Nathan laughed abruptly. How typical this was of the Jewish attitude. The Gentile one, too, only the other way round. "Anyhow, Paul's his father's house surgeon now," he said to Sammy. "I'll get him to fix it up."

After he had finished the evening surgery, Nathan remained seated at his desk, enjoying the silence and the feeling that the pressure was off him for another day. Perhaps he'd be lucky tonight and not get any calls from patients to disturb his sleep. Oh sweet oblivion! he thought, then told himself to stop couching his thoughts in the lyrical language he'd indulged in his youth. He was a professional man, engaged in matters of life and death, not the carefree classics scholar he'd wanted to be.

He glanced at his watch and saw that it was nine o'clock. He was later than usual because Lou had been called to a confinement whilst seeing his patients and Nathan had had to see them as well as his own. Most evenings, they chatted about their cases before they went home. About personal things, too. That's when Lou keeps my feet on the ground, Nathan reflected wryly. As he'd promised to do when they were students. Only all Lou's dreams had come true for him, and Nathan's had not.

"Dreams shmeams, life is what you make it!" he heard Lou say in his mind's ear. It was a sound philosophy, but you had to be Lou's kind of person to adopt it.

He got up and put on his coat and let himself out of the terraced house, his eye falling on the brass plate bearing his name and qualifications, as he shut the door. As usual, looking at it evoked a sense of unreality—enhanced the feeling that he was watching himself play a part. The feeling remained with him whilst he drove home. Even the word "home" seemed unreal when applied to the house where he now lived.

"Home is where the heart is," David's maid Lizzie had embroidered on the framed sampler she gave to him and Rebecca for a wedding gift, Nathan recalled with irony, heading towards the place where his heart was not. Was it talking about David with Sammy that had set his mind on this track? Most of the time he avoided it, aware of its futility. He had chosen his path, if chosen meant allowing something to happen to you. And reflections like those he'd just indulged in were links in the chain that bound him to the past. From which he was still trying to unshackle himself.

He drove along Bury New Road, past the darkened shops on Market Place, and stopped the car near the corner where Broughton High School for Girls stood secluded discreetly behind a clump of trees. Hunger pangs were attacking his stomach; he had not eaten since noon, yet he was reluctant to go home.

"If we have daughters, maybe they'll be pupils there," Rebecca had said when they bought the house not far from the school. Their first child was due in February, but the prospect of fatherhood seemed unreal to Nathan, too. It was as though he had been plucked from one life and replanted in another which included career, marriage and children. Commitments which caused most of his peers to flourish with pride, but to which he seemed unable to relate.

On his left was a short stretch of road known as The

Cliff, which people said was liable to subside and crumble one day. He sat hunched over the steering wheel, gazing at the vast, industrial panorama below, its distant streetlights twinkling like an illusory fairyland, the tall factory chimneys poised against a sky rendered crimson along the horizon line by the hot glow from the furnaces in Trafford Park.

By day, the view was bleak and unwelcoming, as much of Manchester and Salford was, and David had not wanted Nathan to set up practice in a working-class district. "Why spend your life in seedy surroundings?" he had argued. But Nathan and Lou wanted to help alleviate the suffering of people still existing in the penurious conditions from which they and their own families had escaped, and had bought and refurbished the surgery of an elderly overworked doctor who wished to retire.

Everything's relative, Nathan mused, gazing down at the lights which lit the path of weary men returning each night to their smoke-grimed little houses, after toiling in the factories. Some of them were his patients and did not even have hot-water taps, or own a towel worthy of the name to offer him when he washed his hands. His daily rounds sickened him with its ever-present squalor, but at least he was able to go home to Salford's pleasant residential suburb of Broughton Park; he didn't have to live that way.

It's time you stopped kicking and screaming about your lot, Nat! he told himself as he started the engine and drove to the tree-lined avenue where his house was situated. But it was easier said than done.

A chink of light between the front-room curtains meant Rebecca was at home. Some evenings, she went with Lou's wife, Cora, to a meeting of young women who were raising funds for German Jewish refugees and left Bridie, their maid, to serve Nathan's meal. He let himself in and hung up his coat in the cloakroom which led off the hall, pausing to scan his fatigue-lined face in the mirror above the washbasin. When he emerged, Bridie was rubbing a thumbmark off the half-moon table with a corner of her starched white apron.

"Good evenin', Doctor-surr," she smiled.

Nathan had asked her not to address him that way, but her habit of doling out a double dose of respect each time she spoke to him seemed unbreakable.

Bridie straightened her cap, which was on at a lop-sided angle as usual, and put a thick forefinger to her lips as Na-

than was about to reply. "Herself's asleep on the sofa, Doctor-surr," she whispered glancing at the front room door.
"Lookin' ivery bit of it like that picture o' the blessed
Madonna me mother sent me at Christmas," she added rever-
ently. " 'Twud be a pity t'disturb her. 'Tis cold cuts y're gettin' t'night, Doctor-surr. Oi've laid 'em out f'ye."

"Thank you, Bridie."

Nathan went into the parlor, which his wife called the
lounge, and stood with his back to the fire looking down at
her. The smooth, oval face and heavy eyelids fitted Bridie's
description of her. But the rest did not. Madonnas didn't
have sensuous lips darkened to an inviting mulberry-red, nor
long-legged voluptuous bodies like Rebecca's which fired him
with desire when she lay in his arms. A crude remark David
had once made drifted into his mind. A man can enjoy a
woman without loving her, his brother had brutally implied
and Nathan had been shocked, had thought this could never
apply to himself. But now he knew differently and the knowledge had diminished him in his own eyes.

Rebecca stirred drowsily, brushing away a lock of ebony
hair that had strayed from her chignon to her cheek, then
rested her hand upon the swell of her belly, and Nathan felt
ashamed of the hardening in his treacherous groin as he
watched the gentle rise and fall of her full breasts.

The photograph provided by the matchmaker had not
prepared him for her breathtaking loveliness in the flesh. Nor
for the sweetness of her nature. Why did he feel no love for
her, though she had shared his life and his bed for more than
a year? But the chemistry that people called love could not
be analyzed like the contents of the bottles in his dispensary,
nor was there any antidote for its painful effects. Living with
Rebecca had not made him forget Mary.

Rebecca opened her eyes and gave him a welcoming
smile. And then a quizzical look from their tawny depths.
"What're you standing there thinking about, darling?"

"You."

She laughed with pleasure. "What're you thinking about
me?"

"How beautiful you are," he said telling her half of the
truth.

"I don't feel beautiful, with a stomach the size of a foot-
ball and all done up in maternity clothes!"

"You always wear shades of brown," he remarked, eye-

ing her chocolate-colored skirt and the beige Shantung blouse
which would make most women look drab, but somehow enhanced her dusky complexion.

"Don't you like brown?"

Nathan smiled at her anxious expression. But his amusement was tinged with guilt because she was always so eager
to please him. There's never a strident note about her, he
thought, or about anything she does. The way she had furnished their home was the essence of subtlety. The curtains
and upholstery in this room were sage green and the carpet a
dull gold which complemented the oak-panelled walls. A silver candelabra stood graciously alone on the mantelpiece and
the only other ornament was a big Chinese vase, at present
filled with bronze chrysanthemums, on a pedestal by the window. David's house had just been refurnished and Bessie had
been lavish with the money she inherited after her father's
death last year. But you can't buy good taste, Nathan reflected, comparing his brother's over-adorned parlor with his own.

"I like everything about you," he told his wife sincerely.
But liking, even coupled with admiration, was not love.

Rebecca held out her hand to him and he went to sit
beside her on the sofa, breathing in the fresh soapy fragrance
which always surrounded her.

"I felt the baby move today," she said in the husky voice
with a London accent that still sounded foreign to him.

"Well, you're five months on, aren't you?" he replied
clinically, wishing he could react like a prospective father instead of a doctor.

"At first, I thought a fly'd got under my clothes and was
crawling about on my tummy. It felt as if something was fluttering its wings against me, Nat, and I even got undressed to
have a look," Rebecca went on excitedly. "Then I phoned
Cora and she said the first time hers moved it felt like that.
So faint you couldn't tell whether the movement was on your
inside or your outside."

"You'll know when it lands you a hefty kick!"

Nathan got up and went to a small mahogany table where
some thick slices of salt beef and a leg of roast chicken
awaited him. Rebecca's excitement and his own inability to
share in it had heightened his feeling of playing a role. The
Crown Derby dinner service and monogrammed cutlery did,
too.

How did an ordinary chap like him, the son of poor immigrants, come to all this? The elegance that he admired, but felt strange with. The tasteful trappings of wealth. He began eating, but a great surge of resentment had welled up inside him and he could hardly swallow the food. He'd succumbed to his brother's emotional blackmail, that was how he'd come to it! Sacrificed himself on the twin altar of religion and family, abandoned his Gentile sweetheart and allowed himself to be sold in the marketplace. To a Jewess whose family had the wherewithal to buy him for her, he thought, casting a smoldering glance at Rebecca and suddenly not liking her at all.

"What's the matter?" she asked.

Nathan stared down at the table. The cutlery and china were wedding presents from her relatives, whose affluent life-style made him feel like a pauper in their midst when he visited them in London. "I was just thinking that your background lived up to the matchmaker's information about you," he said, wanting to wound her.

Rebecca looked as if he had slapped her face.

Chapter Six

"Tell your father we're not going to the *Shabbos* tea party tomorrow," Bessie said to Shirley.

Shirley looked disappointed. "Why not, Mom?" Her grandmother's Sabbath gathering was the highspot of the week, when the children heard exciting bits of grownup gossip and were allowed to play hide-and-seek all over the house.

"Harry and Arnold and me were going to look through all the old things in the attic," Ronald put in.

"How can I go among people looking like this?" their mother demanded, fingering the black scarf enveloping her head, which she had worn all week as if to emphasize her plight.

"If you want to be a prisoner in the house till your hair's

grown again, please yourself," David said from behind his
Manchester Evening News. "The kids and I'll go to my
mother's without you."

"Tell him I don't care what he does," Bessie commanded
the children, though her tone implied otherwise. "And if he
doesn't sue that Ruby Cohen for damages, I'll never speak to
him again."

"You're not speaking to me anyway," David retorted.

"Tell him he doesn't deserve me to."

Shirley and Ronald exchanged a long-suffering glance.
Their mother's temperament was nothing new to them, but
her latest method of punishing their father for they-knew-
not-what had brought them into the thick of it. She had not
addressed a word directly to him in their presence since Monday night, when she retired to bed after returning from the
hairdresser's.

"Why don't you tell him yourself, Mom?" Ronald asked
bravely.

"Because she's playing silly buggars," David declared
lighting a cigarette.

"You can tell him it's a sin to smoke on *Shabbos*, too, as
he seems to have forgotten," Bessie said sharply.

David glanced at the flickering candles on the table. Lizzie had just cleared away the dishes after the evening meal,
which was eaten in the dining room on Fridays, instead of in
the kitchen. The goblet from which he and his family had
sipped wine after he recited the *Kiddush* prayer was still
standing beside the silver candlesticks and he experienced a
pang of nostalgia for the Friday nights of his youth.

His mother's candlesticks were brass and there had been
times when *tsimmes* and gravy had been all she could afford
to give them to eat. But the simple carrot stew had somehow
sustained them in devoutness more than the large portions of
roast chicken seemed to now, when the menu had assumed
more importance than the religious ritual. Once you take one
step, it's easier to take the next, his mother had warned him
the first time he broke a Sabbath law, and it was true.

He had slipped into the habit of going to the factory on
Saturday mornings, instead of to *shul*, without it troubling his
conscience. All he observed nowadays were the dietary laws
and the High Holy Days. But he had never smoked in the
same room with the *Shabbos* candles before. He averted his
eyes from them, but did not put out the cigarette.

"I wonder if Mom writes Dad a note when we're not there to tell him things for her?" Ronald whispered snidely to his sister whilst shaking the dice for their game of snakes and ladders.

They oughtn't to be playing the game on *Shabbos*, David thought. But what was the point of not allowing it? When he let them switch the lights on and off and ride instead of walking; spend money, too. His mother's warning had really come home to roost!

"That's what you get for being a horrid boy, our Ronald!" Shirley sniggered as the red counter he was sliding along the board arrived at the head of a very long snake.

"Don't you believe it, love," David said to her, watching his son reluctantly slide the counter down the reptile's tail. "You know in some ways life's like a game of snakes and ladders, Shirley."

"Ask him what he means by that," Bessie shrilled.

David saw her claw at her triple-string pearl necklace, as if some emotion that she was struggling to contain were choking her, and the buttons on the bodice of her blue crêpe dress were wobbling about on her heaving bosom.

She's gone right back to how she was when we were first married, he thought. Building things up in her mind and thinking everything I say is some kind of criticism of her. His premonition that this would be the outcome of losing her hair had soon been followed by the reality. But it had not really been a premonition. More a logical conclusion based on the events of the past which his wife's inherent insecurity would not allow her to bury forever beneath the present. The most she was capable of was brushing the past temporarily aside, like dust swept beneath a rug which would rise to confront her again whenever the rug slipped from under her feet.

David lit another cigarette from the stub of the old one and watched the smoke disperse the way his hopes of domestic stability had done, aware of Bessie eyeing him anxiously and of his children watching both of them. Much more of this and his kids would end up as neurotic as their mother!

"I've been up a few ladders and down a few snakes in my time, that's all I meant," he told them, though what he had really meant was that a person doesn't necessarily get what they deserve. "The trouble is the snakes are easy to slide down, but the ladders are hard to climb," he added and was relieved to hear them laugh.

"The one he climbed when he married me wasn't," Bessie informed the children. But she was in effect reminding David, as the look she gave him illustrated. "One day he was just a worker and the next he was boss of poor Zaidie Salaman's business," she said nastily ."Because Zaidie was ill with a broken heart after my brother died in the war."

"That was our Uncle Saul that we never knew," Shirley told Ronald, who had less interest in the family history than she had. "He was married to Auntie Helga."

"And if he hadn't been killed, he'd have been running the factory now, instead of your dad lording it there on his own," Bessie declaimed, continuing her vendetta against David.

Shirley ignored the reference to the factory. Long ago love affairs were much more intriguing. "It's a bit like a story I read in Lizzie's *Peg's Paper*," she said with a dreamy smile. "The way Dad's brother married Auntie Miriam and your brother married her sister, Mom. It's very romantic."

"You shouldn't be reading such drivel," David rebuked her. "We've got lots of good books in the house."

Bessie had stiffened at the mention of her old enemy Miriam and he found this hard to relate to the way the two of them had sat chatting amicably at his mother's, last Saturday. But his wife could change with the ease of a chameleon and needed nothing tangible to color and recolor her attitudes. A convenient memory was another of her attributes; the idea of her dead brother running the business if he'd lived was ludicrous. Saul had been David's closest friend and his nature had been the direct opposite of Bessie's. But his business acumen was negative and his interest in the factory nonexistent.

"Watch out, Dad!" Ronald piped.

A long cylinder of ash was teetering on the end of David's cigarette. He felt the glowing tip sear his fingers and dropped it hastily. "I forgot I was smoking," he muttered retrieving it and putting it into an ashtray.

Bessie rushed to examine the carpet and succeeded in finding a minute singe on its brand new, raspberry-and-custard pile. "Tell your father he'll set the house on fire one of these days with his carelessness!" she rasped to Shirley. Then her headscarf slipped off and they saw her for the first time without her hair.

Shirley gasped and burst into tears, and Ronald had one of his fits of laughter.

David did not know whether to cry with his daughter or laugh with his son. His wife looked pathetically funny and was gazing at him with a hunted expression in her curranty eyes, rooted to the spot by the humiliation of being seen like this by her husband and children, the fingers of one hand twitching against the other in a nervous spasm, as if she were caught in a trap.

Pity tightened his throat as his brain sought the right words to comfort her. The anger she had aroused in him had fled away, as it always did when she suddenly seemed ridiculous and vulnerable. But there were no right words. His sympathy would be misunderstood and rejected; she had turned a deaf ear to it all week, and he had finally lost patience with her.

"Put your scarf on again, Mom," Ronald spluttered. "Before you catch cold."

Bessie emerged from her trauma and covered her head. "Now you know I wasn't exaggerating, David," she said dispiritedly. "I bet you thought I was making a fuss about nothing, that it was just a little bald patch."

"Hurray! Mom's just spoken to Dad!" Ronald yelled.

"And tomorrow we'll get her a wig to wear till her hair grows again," David smiled.

Bessie was tucking in the ends of her scarf in front of the mantelpiece mirror. "I wouldn't be seen dead in one!" She turned around to glare at David, then shrieked with horror. Her elbow had caught her best crystal vase, sending it to shatter in the hearth.

David knew what her next words would be before she uttered them.

"Now look what you've made me do, David!"

"You always say that to Dad if he's there when you break something," Ronald accused her. "Doesn't she, Shirley?"

Shirley nodded reluctantly.

They know her as well as I do, David thought and wondered if they had noticed his own quirks and failings, too.

"You're always getting at Dad when it isn't his fault, Mom," Ronald said moving close to David.

"Shut up, Ronald! Leave Mom alone!" Shirley flashed and went to link her arm through Bessie's.

So Ronald's on my side and Shirley's on Bessie's, David

saw with a sense of shock. It was probably normal for them to identify with the parent of their own sex, but even so— What're we doing to these kids? he asked himself remorsefully. A lovely childhood they'd have to look back on! What could be worse than a divided family? And how easy it would be to foster partisan feelings, he thought as Ronald's warm little hand crept into his.

"Go and kiss your mom and apologize for what you said," he instructed Ronald, though every word the boy had spoken in his defense had been correct. "And you come and give me a hug, Shirley. You can give your brother one, too. He's just as sorry for Mom as you are."

Plenty of time for things to divide them when they grow up, he reflected, watching the children shake hands solemnly. But God forbid it should be the kind of thing that had come between himself and his brother Nat.

Bessie was staring mournfully at the splinters of expensive glass in the hearth, which had momentarily taken precedence over the loss of her hair. "That vase cost my poor dad a fortune, David."

"Anything that can be replaced by forking out cash isn't worth getting upset about," David replied.

"Why not, Daddy?" Shirley asked him.

He sat down in his wing chair and cradled her on his lap, then settled Ronald on the chair arm, thankful for the comfort of these two youngsters who loved and trusted him. "Because the things that can't be bought are the ones that really matter."

That night Bessie let him make love to her and afterwards he stroked her scarfed head—which she had doubly protected by the addition of a bonnet-style hairnet—grateful that she had not rebuffed him, pondering on the way her stupidity aroused tenderness in him—though her barbed tongue, which sprang from it, caused him so much pain.

It's you I care about, Bessie, not what you look like, he wanted to tell her, but he knew she would not believe him; her conception of married love had not matured with their years together, as his had. He had never loved her in the romantic sense, but marriage had taught him that love is many-sided and multi-dimensional, that children and troubles shared add depth to a shallow beginning.

His wife had fallen asleep and was snoring loudly, though she complained that his snores kept her awake. Marriage! he thought, and smiled in the darkness as Bessie wriggled her icy feet between his. As if a bald head could stop him caring about her after twelve years! Or was it thirteen? He was beginning to lose count. But to Bessie, his feeling for her was still only skin deep.

The next morning, he rang up Ruby Cohen from the factory to ask her advice about a wig.

"Maybe you should get a blonde one?" Ruby suggested.

"No," David said hastily. If he went home with a blonde wig, his wife would put her own brand of interpretation on it and think he didn't love her because she was a brunette. "I want one exactly like Bessie's hair, Ruby."

"So I'll go to town myself and get it for you. I'll even stand the cost, seeing you're not going to sue me. You're not, are you?"

"Just get me the wig, Ruby! I'll pick it up from your place on my way home for dinner."

Moishe Lipkin, David's traveling salesman, was in the office when he made the call.

"Why didn't you think of getting Bessie the wig right away? You'd have saved yourself a week of *tsorus*," he smiled.

Moishe was not just an employee, but an old and trusted friend in whom David often confided.

"I could also cause myself trouble by taking one home, so keep your fingers crossed till she's agreed to wear it," David replied.

"When I look at you married men, I'm happy to be miserable on my own!" Moishe joked, eyeing David's weary expression. Then his own grew wistful. "I proposed to Helga a couple of times, you know."

David looked surprised. Most things reached his ears over the family grapevine, but Helga had always kept personal matters to herself. "I've often wondered why you've stayed single, Moishe."

Moishe shrugged philosophically. "I meet plenty of nice girls on my travels. There's one in Cardiff who's been trying to catch me for years. But what can you do? Helga's the only one I've ever wanted. The first time I asked her, she wouldn't leave her sick mother, and after Mrs. Moritz died she said her father needed her."

He got up and paced about, opening a drawer in the file cabinet and shutting it again, picking up a bottle of ink from

David's littered desk and moving it to a different position absently, a wiry little man immaculately groomed in a well-tailored dark suit. With the same monkey-face and restlessness he had had as a small child, David recalled, watching him.

"Remember how you nearly fell overboard when we came to England, Moishe?" David smiled.

"My mom's never let me forget it!" Moishe paused to stare through the window at the slate-roofed factories across the street. "I also remember your dad and mine tramping around Strangeways together when we first got here, looking for work. And how we all used to grumble about the rain. But it's rain that's given us our livelihood, isn't it?"

"It was far from a livelihood in those days. When I look back on them, it seems miraculous that we survived."

Moishe sighed. "Doesn't it always, one way and another? But Jews as a race are great survivors."

"Let's hope it stays that way," David said, thinking of the tales he had heard recently of jackbooted bullies hammering on doors in the middle of the night in Hitler's Germany. Which gave him a troubling sense of "There but for the grace of God go I." He pushed the distant specter away. What good did it do to dwell on it?

"So tell me how you did with the new line last week," he said to Moishe shifting his thoughts to business. Saturday mornings were the only time he saw his salesman.

"I'll go through the order sheets with you afterwards, David. Right now, I want to talk to you about designing a label. One that people will connect with our coats the minute they see it. At the moment, all we put on is the cleaning instructions. The customer doesn't know who makes our garments."

"What does that matter, so long as she likes what she sees and buys it?"

Moishe smiled shrewdly. "You'd be surprised what a name can do. When a firm's got a smart reputation, the customer's as good as bought one of their coats before she sets eyes on it. How are we going to get a reputation like that if we've got no label?"

"Hm," was David's thoughtful reaction.

Moishe pressed home his point. "We're making beautiful garments, but without a name they'll never be in that class."

David sat doodling on his blotting pad. "Let me think about it, Moishe."

"What's to think about? I spend my life in those smart shops watching women choose, while I'm hanging around waiting to see buyers. I know what I'm talking about, David."

"You're the only person I know who's more go-ahead than me, Moishe," David smiled. "Remember how I took you aside at our Sammy's wedding, when the business was still on the floor, and offered you a job? I knew then I was doing the right thing. All right, we'll have some labels made with Salaman printed on them."

"No," Moishe replied adamantly. "I think the firm needs a new name, too."

David stopped doodling. "What're you talking about?"

"Salaman smacks of a little Jewish factory."

"You're getting anti-Semitic all of a sudden?"

"What I'm getting is clever. We're not making coats for Jewish housewives to wear when they're shopping for fish. Most of our business is done with *goyim*, as I don't have to tell you."

"Bessie'd kill me if I used a label that hadn't got her father's name on it," David said. "You know how close she was to that old miser."

"He wasn't miserly with her," Moishe recollected. "She was the only kid in Strangeways who had two *Shabbos* coats and money to buy toffees."

And it didn't end there, David thought. His first car had been bought by the father-in-law he'd despised, so Bessie could be driven around in one. Everything she'd wanted that David couldn't afford to give her she had asked for and got from her father. "No, he wasn't," he said brusquely to Moishe retasting the bitterness of past humiliations. "And if I change the firm's name, too, she'll double-kill me."

"She won't if your bank balance goes up because of it," Moishe answered astutely. "And believe me, it will. So will my commission; I'm not being entirely unselfish," he grinned. "So let's start thinking of a new name."

"If I brought part of my own into it, it might help Bessie not to mind," David said thoughtfully. "Especially as our Ronald'll be coming into the business one day. How does Sandberry strike you?"

"Too like Burberry."

"Sandgarments, then?"

"Coats for the deckchair assistants at Blackpool he thinks he's promoting!"

"We could combine my two kids' first names. Shirlron doesn't sound bad."

"For one of those factory houses where the people aren't satisfied with just a door-number."

David threw down his pen. "You'll have to leave it to me, Moishe. Let's deal with your orders now; then you can go home and I can get down to doing the books."

"It's a pity Sammy can't take that job off your hands."

"Sammy knows nothing about bookkeeping," David bristled.

He still can't bear the slightest criticism of his brother, Moishe thought with a silent sigh. When was David going to come to his senses and stop carrying Sammy? "He could go to night school and learn, couldn't he?" was all he dared say. "I'm going to his house tonight. Why don't I suggest it?" he added carefully.

"I'd rather you didn't," David said curtly. He lit a cigarette and puffed it edgily. Why did nobody but himself make allowances for Sammy? Moishe was Sammy's best friend, but even he considered him a shirker. And Bessie had wanted David to fire him for years. "Sammy's got to see a specialist about his leg," he said as though his brother's disability mitigated his deficiencies.

"I'm sorry to hear that," Moishe replied, only too aware that in David's eyes it did.

"Sooner or later I'll employ a bookkeeper," David said stiffly.

Moishe smiled to ease the strained atmosphere. "The new label will help you to afford one." That the business was run on a shoestring was no secret to him. His interest in it was as personal as if he were a director, which he hoped to be one day. Meanwhile, he was content to work hard to bring that day nearer. "Sanderstyle would be a good name for the firm," he said with a flash of inspiration. "And it's got the first half of Sandberg in it," he pointed out to add weight to the suggestion.

David looked up from the order sheets Moishe had just handed to him. "I like it," he said after a moment. "It's got class."

"So you'll buy me a bottle of *schnapps* for thinking of it for you," Moishe grinned.

David arrived home for lunch with Bessie's wig, and the name Sanderstyle buzzing like a friendly bee in his mind. But the wig had to come first. He would tell her about the name later.

"I'm not even going to open the box," she said.

Shirley opened it for her. "It looks just like your own hair, Mom. Be a sport and try it on." She took it out of the box and held it up for Bessie to see. "Look, it's even got marcel waves."

David stood by the window, carefully saying nothing. Fortunately, Ronald was not yet back from *shul* to put in a wrong word at the right moment!

"If it suits yer, Mrs. Sandberg, yer can wear it'n go to t'tea party at Bobbie Sarah's," Lizzie said. "Then yer'll see what Zaidie Sigmund's sweet'eart's like, along o' t'rest o' t'family."

Bessie hesitated, then went upstairs to put on the wig. When she returned, Shirley told her how lovely she looked.

"I've never looked lovely in my life," she said with desperate honesty. "How do you think I look in it, David?"

"Like Bessie Sandberg again," he smiled, relieved that she did.

"You wouldn't lie to me? Let me make a fool of myself?"

"Yer know as I wouldn't," Lizzie declared before David had time to reply. "Yer look a treat, luv. Yon's a much nicer *sheitel* than 'er next door wears an' yer'll not 'ave ter wear it all that long. It's not as if yer'll 'ave it on yer 'ead forever, like she will, 'er being very *frum*."

"Your Yiddish gets better and better, Lizzie," David grinned.

"If I don't know by now as a *sheitel*'s a wig religious Jewesses wears after they've wed, an' *frum* means religious, Jesus 'elp me, Mr. Sandberg! An' who were it lit t' *Shabbos* candles when t'missis were ill in bed?"

"You, Lizzie love," Shirley said kissing the maid's freckled cheek.

"Aye. Even though it were on a Good Friday."

Bessie kept on the wig while they ate their meal and Ronald came home and was halfway through his before he noticed, which convinced her that her appearance was passable.

David heaved a grateful sigh and allowed himself to toy in his mind with a design for a Sanderstyle label, while spooning his *lokshen* soup. He was still preoccupied when they walked the short distance to his mother's house, that afternoon.

"Oh God, it's blowing off!" Bessie shrieked as a gust of wind greeted them at Sarah's garden gate.

Shirley and Ronald had the presence of mind to each clamp a hand on the top of her head to hold the alien hair in place, whilst David propelled her to the porch and Lizzie pressed the doorbell.

Sarah, who had witnessed the incident through the parlor window, was the essence of tact. "What a lovely coat you've got on, Bessie," she said when she opened the door and did not raise her eyes above the level of its silver fox collar.

Sarah's Sabbath tea party was a tradition begun in 1905 when she invited Sigmund and Rachel Moritz and their children to share a simple repast in her home in Strangeways.

The Sandberg-Moritz clan nowadays could not have fitted into that tiny house, nor would the refreshments she served then have satisfied the newest generation's anglicized appetites. Egg and cress and tomato sandwiches, jam tarts and buttered scones were served along with the plain sponge cake and strudel. And even the elders took their tea with milk instead of lemon, though Sarah and Abraham still slipped a cube of sugar into their mouths, Russian-style, rather than stir a spoonful into their cups.

In earlier years, the gathering had begun at three o'clock, but the family now arrived at four-thirty and stayed until eight, so that Esther and Ben Klein could join them for a couple of hours after closing their shop.

Saturday afternoon was the happiest time of Sarah's week and reminded her of her childhood in Dvinsk, when all her relatives had gathered for *Shabbos* tea in her grandmother's house. She would sit behind the two enormous willow-patterned teapots her son-in-law Ben had given her when his living came from a pot-and-pan stall on Flat Iron Market, surveying her brood with satisfaction.

This particular Saturday, she was unable to relax. Several of her grandchildren, who had heard their Auntie Bessie had lost her hair, were staring at the wig. Why hadn't David told her his wife would be wearing one, then she could have warned the children not to pass any remarks about it? It wouldn't take much to cause Bessie's tense expression to erupt into something worse.

And Nat was eyeing David so coldly Sarah could not pretend she was imagining it. She glanced at Rebecca, who was unusually subdued, and at Miriam and Helga, seated tight-lipped side by side on the sofa, awaiting the arrival of their father and prospective stepmother. So quiet it was in the room, so different from the usual noisy chatter—enough to make even Sarah feel nervous!

"So," she smiled issuing her habitual opening gambit. "And what has everyone been doing this week?"

Marianne was seated cross-legged on the rug, fiddling moodily with the garters that held up her white *Shabbos* socks. "You know what I've been doing, Bobbie," she declared passionately. "Crying my eyes out, that's what."

"But it won't make any difference, will it?" Sarah replied kindly.

Marianne got up and left the room. Martin, who had been seated beside her reading, followed her as everyone knew he would. They had been following each other that way since they were toddlers.

Sarah sighed and sent Arnold after them with a plate of cakes; food was always a comfort. She would have sent Shirley; handing round food was a girl's place. But her younger granddaughter might say something to make Marianne feel worse. The way they seemed to dislike each other was a source of distress to Sarah. "Marianne's upset about moving to Salford," she told the family.

"I wish that was all I had to be upset about!" Bessie snorted.

"You can't expect a child of ten to understand why it's necessary," Sarah answered. "If she didn't have to change schools before she sits for the scholarship, she'd feel better. But what can you do?"

David stopped musing about his Sanderstyle label and thought of all the adult things his mother had expected him to understand and accept when he was a child: like working in Mr. Radinsky's store every night to earn fruit and vegetables, and having to leave school to slave in Salaman's sweatshop, when he'd hoped to be a solicitor. But thank God the children in the family didn't have to sacrifice themselves for economic reasons any more.

"Why can't Marianne stay where she is until then, Mother?" he asked. "Traveling to Cheetham by tram every day isn't going to harm her."

"Esther and Ben think she's too young to do it."

"I'll have a word with them about it," David said as if the result was a *fait accompli*.

"Isn't it up to them to decide what's best for their own child?" Nathan asked curtly.

David helped himself to a slice of the Viennese Sachertorte Miriam brought every week and bit into the rich, chocolate confection without replying.

Sarah could feel the animosity bristling between them, but Rebecca went on sipping her tea and seemed unaware of it, though she was seated beside Nathan. God forbid that lovely girl should ever find out she's the cause of it, Sarah said to herself. If Nat had had his way, a *shiksah* would have been sitting in Rebecca's place. But the danger had passed. David had not let it happen. Sarah would have known nothing about it if she hadn't found a snapshot of a Gentile girl wearing nurse's uniform in Nathan's pocket when she was pressing his jacket. David had wanted to protect her from even the knowledge and she hadn't told him or Nat that she knew.

"I don't think it's for you to interfere, David," Nathan persisted.

"What you call interference, I call advice," David said calmly. His young brother's rancor was hard to take, but he would not make things worse by allowing himself to be provoked. "We'll just have to agree to differ, won't we, Nat?"

Further exchanges were prevented by the doorbell and a chorus of "Good *Shabbos*, Zaidie Sigmund!" from the lobby as the children opened the front door.

Carl Moritz put down his *Manchester Guardian* and rose to his feet nervously. Abraham and his sons had risen, too. But it was left to Sarah to bridge the awkward moment when Sigmund escorted his lady friend into the parlor.

"Welcome to my house, Mrs. Fish," she said hoping her stiff smile did not belie the greeting.

"Call me Gertie. I won't be Mrs. Fish much longer," the bride-to-be responded coyly.

"With Gertie's looks, it's a wonder she's stayed a widow until now," Sigmund declared after he had introduced everyone to her.

The family surveyed the dumpy little person clinging to his arm and remained silent.

"She reminds me of Mary Pickford," Sigmund added confirming his besotted state.

Young Ronald Sandberg's gaze moved slowly from the lady's too-short pink coat to the black patent bar-strap shoes on her chubby feet before turning contemplatively to the fat, golden curls below her powder-blue halo hat. "You mean Shirley Temple, don't you, Zaidie?"

David and Bessie exchanged an embarrassed parental glance. But Mrs. Fish preened herself as if she had received a compliment, and Sigmund chuckled and pinched her rouged cheek.

Had he gone blind—or mad? his nearest and dearest were asking themselves. Lizzie had described his companion in the park as "mutton dressed up as lamb" and the family had envisaged an aging woman trying to look like a young one. This elderly-little-girl travesty was a shock. Ronald had spoken the brutal truth, as usual.

Mrs. Fish sat down by the fire and took a mirror from her handbag to check that the lipstick cupid's bow she had added to her tiny mouth was still there. "People in Sheffield nicknamed me Dolly," she revealed whilst admiring her reflection.

Sarah was not surprised. The painted dolls with stuck-on yellow hair that David had given to Shirley and Marianne last *Chanukah* were what Mrs. Fish resembled. How could a man as clever as Sigmund Moritz also be so stupid? But everyone knew that men who were getting on could sometimes be foolish about women, even intelligent men. Hadn't the Sandbergs' old and respected friend Rabbi Lensky just taken a girl younger than his own daughters for his third wife? Sarah cast a surreptitious glance at her husband to see how Gertie had affected him and was relieved that he was carefully not looking at her.

"My brother-in-law Maxie Radinsky sent you his regards," Mrs. Fish said while Sarah poured tea for her and Sigmund.

It did not strike Sarah as strange that his wife had not done so. Mrs. Radinsky had never addressed a friendly word to the impoverished housewives who shopped at the store, but had sat smugly behind the counter recording their purchases in an account book, licking her indelible pencil between one entry and the next as if it tasted of gold. With the same false smile on her long face that was on her twin sister's round one now. Alike in appearance they weren't. But they were peas from the same pod, and Sarah noted that Gertie's ready smile did not soften her china-blue eyes.

She shooed the children out of the room. The way they were gaping at Gertie was setting her on edge.

Sigmund went to sit on the arm of his beloved's chair. "So let's make the wedding arrangements, while everyone is here."

"I've already spoken about it with my sister," Gertie declared. "The reception will be in her house." She smiled up at Sigmund. "We'll be married the first Sunday in November."

"As soon as that?" Sarah said before she could stop herself. November was next month; there wouldn't be enough time to talk Sigmund out of it.

Mrs. Fish's smile disappeared as if she had flicked a switch to remove it from her face. "For what reason should we wait, Mrs. Sandberg? You've got a friend of yours up your sleeve for him to marry instead of me?"

Sarah wished she had. "A nice sense of humor you've got, Gertie," she countered with a chuckle, though she knew the woman had not been jesting. Sarah had in fact summed her up as having no sense of humor whatsoever.

"Like Gertie says, what is there to wait for?" Sigmund demanded, scanning the doubtful faces of those who cared about him.

Mrs. Fish put her hand on his. "A home we don't need to fix up."

"We've got two to choose from," he endorsed.

"And mine is where we'll live," she informed him.

Sigmund looked taken aback. "You want to move into that flat above your shop?"

His son and daughters shared a hopeful glance. Their father had evidently not yet discussed such practical matters with his lady friend and was fond of his own home. There could be a difference of opinion about it.

"All of a sudden you don't like my flat?" Mrs. Fish challenged him.

"It's very nice," he said placatingly, though he found the over-furnished living-room claustrophobic and the sound of the mainroad traffic intrusive. "I'll have to think about it, Gertie."

"When we're on our own, the Viennese comes out in him; he calls me *liebchen*," she confided archly, stroking his fingers. But she could sense the sudden doubts filtering into his mind. She held up her left hand for everyone to see and indicated a small cluster of diamonds on the third finger, which looked lost among the large ones she was wearing on the others. "You've seen the engagement ring he gave me?" she said to remind him and them that a contract was a contract.

Sarah heard Miriam and Helga gasp. To remarry was natural, but to plight his troth with their dead mother's ring! How could Sigmund have done such a thing?

"He took it out of his pocket and showed it to me one day, and I said how I'd always wanted one like it," Mrs. Fish said, supplying the answer. "But that's how my darling is. He can't deny me anything." She patted Sigmund's blushing cheeks. "What is there to think about, Siggie? You'll move in with me and help me in the business. There's no need to kill yourself with work being a tailor any more."

Sarah watched her gaze into Sigmund's eyes and saw the mesmerizing effect it had upon him.

His next words confirmed it. "Whatever you think is best, Gertie my dear."

Miriam found her tongue. "Hasn't my father told you his earnings pay most of the household bills, Mrs. Fish? My brother only gets a small wage. Bookshop assistants don't get paid very well."

"Your brother should have found a job where the money is better."

"He's happy where he is and Father's never minded," Miriam replied.

"My Siggie is too softhearted. But when he's married to me, I won't let people take advantage of him. I will be his only responsibility," Mrs. Fish declared, and any pretense of affability left the atmosphere.

Two bright spots of color appeared on Miriam's pale cheeks, and Sammy got up to put a restraining hand on her shoulder.

David recognized the danger sign, too. Carl and Helga would not raise their voices; it wasn't in their natures to do so. But Miriam would not contain herself much longer. He sat cracking his knuckles in the uncomfortable silence, longing for a cigarette but unable to light one in his mother's house on *Shabbos*, wanting to tell the dreadful woman a thing or two himself. But Miriam might order him to keep out of it.

He'd have to leave it to her to try to stop Sigmund from putting his head in the noose.

Sigmund was staring down at the carpet, aware of his godson Nathan watching him and his old friend Abraham fidgeting with his moustache as he always did when upset. The family's disapproval of Gertie was very evident, but it was he who was lonely, not them. Why couldn't they understand? Realize the things she'd just said meant she cared for him?

"It's disgraceful how his grownup children have sponged on him all these years," he heard Gertie declaim. But her soft hand on the back of his neck stopped him from saying it wasn't like that.

Sarah was fingering her brooch and almost crushed the delicate filigree as her anger mounted. "Sponging isn't a word we use in this family," she said sharply.

"Me, I believe in calling a spade a spade," Mrs. Fish retorted.

Miriam brushed off Sammy's hand and leapt off the sofa to confront Sigmund. "Can't you see what's happening, Father? Are you going to let a conniving woman cut you off from your children who've loved and respected you all their lives?" She eyed Mrs. Fish with undisguised contempt. "That's what she's trying to do and she hasn't even got you yet!"

Sigmund glanced hesitantly at his son and his other daughter, whose faces were stiff with humiliation.

Then Mrs. Fish produced a sob and a square of white lace to wipe away a crocodile tear. "The way your Miriam speaks to you, Siggie darling, I'm glad I never had any children. Me she insults also."

"Look how you've upset Gertie!" Sigmund flared, quelling his inner conflict and glaring at Miriam. "And nobody is cutting anybody off! Marriage arrangements always get everyone rubbed up the wrong way. When Nat married Rebecca, half the *shul* committee fell out with the Sandbergs because they weren't invited to London for the wedding."

"It's true," Abraham sighed, unable to bear the furor taking place in his home, wanting only peace.

Sigmund clutched at the slender straw his friend had held out to him. "It's always the same, Miriam. People say things they don't mean at times like this. Your father-in-law agrees." He placed a comforting arm around Gertie who was still sobbing. "Afterwards, we'll all be friends and the way your mother brought you up, you'll show respect for your stepmother," he told his children.

"Like my own I'll treat them," Mrs. Fish promised glibly, switching on her smile again now she had won.

There isn't a motherly bone in her body, Sarah thought grimly. Or a grandmotherly one, either. She had barely glanced at Sarah's lovely grandchildren—not even at Martin, who was Sigmund's grandson, too.

"Come, Siggie darling. It's time we went," the interloper said as if he were already her husband.

The family watched him follow her out like an obedient schoolboy.

"It's on his own head!" Miriam stormed after they had gone.

"At least Helga and I won't have to live in the same house with her. It's as well Father's agreed to move into her flat," Carl said with relief.

David waited for him to add that he would leave the bookshop and find a job that would support him and Helga. If this didn't jolt Carl from his disinterest in money, nothing ever would.

But Carl said nothing more, as if what happened to himself and his sister were not his responsibility, and neither Helga nor Miriam suggested to him that it was. They knew he would not be happy doing any other kind of work and to them this was all that mattered.

David controlled the urge to say something to Carl. Doing so would bring Miriam's wrath upon his own head. The Moritzes had always been the same—satisfied with the proverbial crust, with no desire to better themselves. But Carl seemed unconcerned about where even the crust was to come from, though his earnings would do little more than pay the rent.

Sarah's thoughts were similar to David's. How wise she had been, years ago, to advise Esther to break her engagement to Carl. And David had been right to do likewise with Miriam. A wife who had no respect for ambition was fine for Sammy, but would have been disastrous for his elder brother.

"Helga and Carl will manage," she declared breaking the contemplative silence. But Carl did not ask how and she wanted to give him a good shaking. Nobody had the right to

be that complacent! "You'll do what we did in the old days
when money was tight, Helga," she said, recalling the numer-
ous transients who had lived in her Strangeways house.
"You'll take a lodger."

"But how could Father put them in this position?"
Miriam exclaimed.

David thought of the hundreds of times her green eyes
had blazed at him that way and was thankful he did not have
to suffer her passionate outbursts anymore. Even though he
sometimes had to suffer Bessie's.

"There's no fool like an old fool," Bessie quoted.

"And everyone knows why your father didn't behave like
one," Miriam said acidly.

"What do you mean by that?" Bessie flashed.

"I mean you wouldn't let him. Every time he met someone he fancied marrying, you said you'd finish with him if he
did. Saul heard you say it and told us, when we were kids.
But I don't doubt you held that threat over him till the day
he died."

Bessie touched her wig, Miriam's stare was piercing
enough to see through it, and glared back at her.

Sarah held her breath. The old hatred between these two
had surfaced the way she had hoped it never would again.

"To make sure nobody else got his money," Miriam
added cruelly.

"You'll have to forgive her; she's upset, Bessie," Sammy
apologized for his wife.

"But there's no need to take it out on me, is there? Did
you hear what she said to me, David?"

David took her hand in case she doubted whose side he
was on. "You'd better say you're sorry, hadn't you, Miriam?"

Miriam smiled contemptuously. He and Bessie were a
good pair! They worshipped money the way some people
worshipped God. She had lost respect for David a long time
ago and wondered how she could ever have been in love with
him. She saw Sarah eyeing her pleadingly and knew she must
make some sort of apology for her sake. With Sarah, her
relationship had been the opposite. The longer Miriam knew
her, the more she respected her. And Sarah wanted peace in
the family.

"All I meant was I wouldn't finish with my father for
any reason," she shrugged. "Or even threaten to. No matter
what he did I'd stand by him."

"Then you're the one who's a fool," Bessie told her witheringly.

"We'll all stand by him, of that there's no question," Sarah interceded hastily. "So if anyone's thinking of not going to his wedding, let them forget it," she pronounced in the voice she sometimes used that made people wonder how such a tiny woman could possess such strength. She sat down in the chair Mrs. Fish had vacated and stared at the flickering flames in the grate, fidgeting absently with the heavy, silver bun at the nape of her neck, her aquiline profile regal in the firelight.

"If Ma wore a crown, she'd be just like the pictures of Queen Victoria," Miriam remarked.

"The way she lays down the law, also!" Abraham endorsed.

Sarah responded with good grace. "Somebody has to, or where would we be? And if we turn our backs on Sigmund now, how will he be able to come to us when that Fish woman makes him miserable?"

"For goodness sake, Ma!" Rebecca exclaimed. "Why meet trouble halfway?"

It was the first time she had spoken and everyone turned to look at her.

"By the time it reaches you, it could be too late," Sarah replied.

Rebecca rose from her chair, her lovely face puckered with weariness. "But like Miriam said, it's on his own head. I've never spent such a dreadful afternoon! My relatives don't get themselves worked up about everything. In our family, if someone won't listen to good advice, we reckon it's their lookout."

"That must be because your family's so English," Nathan said snidely. "All those generations they've been here."

"I've had enough of your cracks, Nat!" Rebecca retorted. The only other one he had made was about the matchmaker, but she had not yet recovered from it. "And I don't think I'll ever get used to how your people behave. If everyone will excuse me, I'd like to go home."

Sarah watched her go sullenly to the lobby to get her coat. Until now, Rebecca had seemed placid; this sudden flare-up was a surprise. She caught Abraham's eye and knew he was thinking the same. Another temperamental daughter-in-law was all they needed!

Chapter Seven

Sigmund married Gertie Fish in November, as she had decreed. A General Election returned the Conservatives to power the same month, and Carl said that England, as well as his father, was now on the road to trouble.

"Why'd you think that, Uncle?" Martin asked him.

Helga had invited Miriam and her family for Friday night supper to meet the lodger who had moved in that day, and Carl was thoughtfully breaking up the extra *knedl* his sister had just plopped into his chicken soup.

"That power-drunk maniac in Germany isn't going to limit his activities to the Third Reich," Carl predicted. "But all we'll get from Baldwin's government will be the politics of appeasement."

"And appeasement doesn't prevent war," the pleasant-faced young woman opposite him added. "It just allows more time for the other side to build up their armaments."

"You're making me go goosey, Miss Ritman," Miriam shuddered.

"But it's no use having one's head in the sand, is it?"

"That's what Father used to say before the last war," Helga recollected. "He saw it coming long before it happened."

Miriam looked troubled. "Father prophesied what's happened to the German Jews, too, but he didn't limit it to Germany."

"He's obviously a clever man," Hannah Ritman, who had not yet met Sigmund, concluded.

"I shouldn't think there's a book he hasn't read," Martin told her. "Well, not one that's worth reading, Miss Ritman."

"I wish you'd call me Hannah," she smiled.

Martin indicated the crammed bookshelves lining the

54

walls of the homely little room. "All those are his. I bet you've never seen so many before."

"Well, certainly not in anyone's kitchen."

"He used to sit in here when he wasn't in his work-room," Helga explained. "His wife wouldn't let him take them to her flat; she said they'd spoil the decorations."

"She wouldn't let him take his gramophone and records, either," Martin said with disgust. "She can't bear classical music."

"Not like you, eh, Martin?" Hannah laughed. "Maybe I'll take you to hear the Hallé Orchestra."

"Uncle Carl takes me."

"But you're welcome to join us, Hannah," Carl put in.

"Thank you." Hannah got up to examine some of the book titles. "Proust, Plato and Goethe, and I haven't even begun looking yet!" she exclaimed with delight. "Am I allowed to borrow them?"

Carl looked surprised. "Of course. But I've never met a woman who'd want to."

Hannah's hazel eyes twinkled. "Really? I understand you work in a very highbrow bookshop."

"I meant an ordinary woman."

"Oh dear," she said returning to her chair with mock chagrin. "So that's how I strike you!"

"I just meant—well, you're not a blue-stocking," Carl mumbled confusedly, aware of his family watching the exchange with interest. He averted his gaze from Hannah's ribbed, wool sweater which emphasized her small, high breasts. "At least you don't look like one."

"Some people would say I am," she replied getting on with her meal.

"Well, it's unusual for a woman to be as interested in politics as you obviously are," Carl said.

"But it shouldn't be, should it?" Hannah smiled. "A woman's brain is no different from a man's. Why shouldn't she use it?"

Miriam laughed. "She's too busy frying the fish."

"Because she's let men convince her that's all she's fit for," Hannah answered heatedly. "It's a very convenient arrangement for the male sex to be waited on hand and foot, and women ought not to accept it."

"You sound like Mrs. Pankhurst," Helga said in a shocked voice.

"Mrs. Pankhurst was the best thing that ever happened to the English female," Hannah declared. "We wouldn't have had the vote without her."

Sammy chuckled. "It's no wonder people think you're a blue-stocking!"

"I took a degree in political science, as it happens."

Carl stopped eating. "There's more to you than meets the eye, isn't there?"

Miriam and Helga were regarding Hannah with something akin to awe, but she appeared not to notice and went on spooning her soup.

"For a while, I lectured on it," she added. "But it was like living in a world of theory. What I want is to see the right theories put into practice."

"You mean the left ones, don't you?" Carl joked. Something about this lively woman told him she was a Socialist.

"Touché," she smiled.

Miriam and Helga got up to take the empty soup plates to the scullery.

"Can I help?" Hannah offered in her brisk, yet easy manner. "I'm not domesticated, but I'll try not to break anything."

"Stay here and entertain the men," Miriam instructed her. There was no doubt that Carl was in his element in Hannah's company, though the opposite was probably the case for Sammy! "Tell me all about her," she said to Helga when they were alone in the scullery.

"All I know is she was brought up in an orphanage in London, and she's just got a job teaching poor kids in Ancoats. The headmaster saw our ad in the *Manchester Evening News* and told her about it," she said. Helga began dishing chicken and *tsimmes* onto dinner plates and smiled. "Carl wasn't keen to take her. He would've preferred another man in the house."

"If he shuts his eyes, he can pretend she's one, with that deep voice and those intellectual ideas!"

"But when he opened them he'd know she wasn't, with that long, fair hair. Not to mention her figure."

"He's noticed that all right." Miriam smoothed down her tailored, gray dress. "She must be about my age, but she makes me feel matronly."

"Me too," Helga declared.

Miriam surveyed her sister, who was thirty-eight but

looked ten years younger. "There's nothing matronly-looking about you, love. Nobody'd guess you're older than me; it must be marriage that ages a woman."

Helga laughed. "In that case, I'll look young forever!"

"Aren't you ever going to say yes to Moishe?"

"I doubt it." Helga poured gravy onto the heaped plates. "But even if I never remarry, I'm not alone in the world, like Hannah is. It must be terrible to have no family."

Miriam smiled dryly. "Sometimes I'm not so sure."

When they returned to the kitchen, Sammy was listening politely to something Hannah was saying. But Carl and Martin had their elbows on the table and their chins cupped in their hands, their eyes riveted to her face.

"Your son's very interested in hearing how Hitler came to power," Hannah told Miriam whilst the plates of food were distributed.

"My brother seems to be, too," Miriam smiled. "Which is rather surprising as I'm sure he already knows."

"Then why hasn't he told Martin?" Hannah asked, eyeing Carl reprovingly.

"He didn't ask me," Carl said.

"In future you must," Hannah counseled the boy. "And you can always ask me anything you want to know. If I can't supply the answer, I'll find a book that will."

"That's an invitation for him to drive you daft!" Miriam laughed.

"I shan't mind," Hannah reassured her. "Childhood is the time to form the habit of questioning everything. If you don't start then, it's on the cards you never will. But parents discourage it. They think their kids are clay to be molded in their own image."

Miriam exchanged a glance with her husband.

"If you ever have any, you'll find there's more to being a parent than that," he told Hannah.

"I don't intend to."

"Don't you like children?" Martin inquired, looking crestfallen.

"Of course I do, love. But who'd look after them while I'm busy with my career?" Hannah tasted the *tsimmes* and pronounced it delicious.

"I'll show you how to make it," Helga offered.

"What's the point when I'm never likely to do any cooking?"

Hannah's vibrant personality dominated the rest of the meal.

"My mother-in-law'd have a fit if she heard some of Hannah's ideas," Miriam said to Carl when he came into the scullery to see why she and Helga were taking so long to make the coffee.

"I wish I hadn't asked her to go with us to the tea party tomorrow," Helga said.

Carl grinned. "It'll be like an irresistible force meeting an immovable object."

Chapter Eight

The clash of personalities Carl foresaw did not take place the following day. Nor did Sarah's *Shabbos* gathering. Martin was taken ill early in the morning and by the afternoon, tea parties were far from the family's thoughts.

Miriam found him seated on the edge of his bed clutching his stomach when she went to waken him, and his ghastly color told her the pain was no ordinary cramp. If only Esther was here, she panicked. But the Kleins had moved to Salford two weeks ago, and she could no longer dash across the back entry to fetch her practical sister-in-law as she had often done in the past.

"Sammy!" she shouted. "Go next door and bring Mrs. Hardcastle, right away!"

"I don't want Mrs. Hardcastle," Martin groaned. "I feel sick."

Miriam gathered him close. His face felt hot and dry to her touch, but his hands were cold and clammy. "Martin ate too many prunes last night," she said trying to smile as Sammy came in from their bedroom, half-dressed. "Hurry up and go next door, will you?"

"I'll go to the phone box and give our Nat a ring, as well."

The way his wife went to pieces if anything was wrong with their son had always troubled Sammy. Everyone loved their kids, but not in the obsessive way Miriam did. If Martin so much as pricked his finger, she would panic in case he got blood poisoning. Sammy, too, wished his sister was still at hand as he limped downstairs and went to fetch their neighbor. Mrs. Hardcastle was a kindly woman, but full of old wives' tales and would probably work Miriam up instead of calming her down.

"Do you think a hot water bottle'd help?" Miriam asked anxiously when Mrs. Hardcastle entered Martin's bedroom bringing with her the smell of the bacon she had been frying.

"Lawks-a-mercy no, lass! 'Eats' t'last thing ter put on a bad stomach ache, in case it's appendicitis. Best wait for yer brother-in-law, Miriam."

"Is that what I've got, Mom?" Martin asked. "Will they have to cut me open?"

Miriam could not reply. Her tongue had cleaved to the roof of her mouth.

Mrs. Hardcastle sat down beside Martin. "Now don't you fret, lamb." Beads of sweat had appeared on his forehead, and she wiped them away with a corner of her flowered overall, her homely face crinkling into a reassuring smile. "Me grandson Albert 'ad 'is took out, but they put 'im ter sleep. 'E knew nowt about it." She glanced at Miriam. "Yer mam looks a sight worse'n you do, Martin. Ambulance men'll be cartin' 'er off on a stretcher'n if they only fetches one wi' 'em, you'll 'ave ter walk!"

Nathan had left on his rounds when Sammy telephoned his home, but Rebecca said Lou was at the surgery and she would ring up and ask him to call.

"Get a grip on yourself, Miriam!" Lou instructed when he arrived and found her sitting tying knots in her dressing gown cord, her thick, black hair in violent disarray as though she had run her fingers through it a hundred times.

"That's what me'n Sammy's kep' tellin' 'er, Doctor," Mrs. Hardcastle said. "Poor Sammy doesn't look too good 'imself. I don't know which 'e's worried about most, 'is son or 'is wife."

Lou sent the neighbor downstairs to make some strong tea while he examined Martin.

"I wish I 'ad ten bob fer every cup me'n Esther's 'ad ter

make 'er since Martin 'ad 'is first tumble when 'e was knee 'igh t'a grasshopper," she said as she departed.

It did not take Lou long to complete the examination. "I'll take you to hospital in my car, chuck," he told Martin, hiding his grave thoughts behind a smile. "You've never had a ride in it, have you?" The boy's soaring temperature indicated the presence of peritonitis, and waiting for an ambulance to be arranged could mean the difference between life and death.

Miriam slumped to the floor as Lou and Sammy left the room carrying Martin wrapped in a blanket.

"Mrs. Hardcastle'll take care of her. I can't spend all morning with you Sandbergs," Lou said.

But his expression told Sammy this was not the reason he had not turned back.

"I'm taking you to the Royal Infirmary, chuck," he smiled to Martin. "Where your Uncle Nat and I trained to be doctors."

By one o'clock, Martin was in bed on a surgical ward, minus his appendix. But the deadly infection was rampant.

Lou telephoned Nathan.

"You'd better tell Miriam. I'm glad it isn't me who's got to," he said gruffly. "Give her a good talking-to and bring her to the hospital. I'll stay with Sammy until you get here."

Nathan stood gazing through the hall window at a clump of laurels in the front garden that were eternally fresh and green. If God could create plants that living didn't diminish why hadn't He created Man that way? And why had He allowed diseases to scourge mankind, so that chaps like Nathan had to spend their lives battling against them?

Sometimes Nathan wondered if there was a God, but his religious conditioning would conflict with his reason as it was doing now, and he'd expect to be struck down for his treacherous thoughts. Saturday morning always depressed him. It was the time that he set aside to visit his housebound geriatric patients. To check on the progress of their decay, he thought cynically, though his compassion for them was boundless.

Who wouldn't be cynical after being confronted with all those senile smiles and wrinkled faces? The shrunken, bent-over bodies and gnarled, liver-spotted hands. The eyes dimmed by cataracts. And the abject gratitude for ten minutes of a young man's time. But Man was not a laurel bush, Nathan reflected bitterly, and there was no medicine to halt the ravages of old age. He replaced the telephone receiver which was still in his hand after Lou's call. Or to wipe out infections like his nephew had.

Rebecca had come out of the parlor and was standing behind him. "What is it, Nat?" she asked quietly.

"It's possible Martin's going to die."

Her hand flew to her throat. "What's the matter with him? Can't you and Lou save him?"

"We're doctors, not miracle workers!" Nathan exclaimed angrily as the limitations of his profession hit home. "And the same goes for the surgeons at the Infirmary, who are a damn sight cleverer than we are. People seem to think doctors are endowed with magic powers; they won't accept it when there's nothing we can do."

He went to fetch his coat from the cloakroom. "And now I've got to try to make Miriam accept it. Tell her she's just got to hope Martin will be one of the lucky ones whose body can fight the infection."

"I'll come with you."

"What for?" Nathan said venting his feelings on her. "She's bound to take it badly, and you've made it plain you don't approve of the way my family behave in a crisis." He left the house without giving Rebecca time to reply.

Miriam lay on the kitchen sofa trying to draw a veil over her mind. It was only a dream; she had not really emerged from a faint to find Mrs. Hardcastle waving smelling salts under her nose. And Martin gone, not downstairs reading at the table, not anywhere in the house, but whisked away to an operating theater. She opened her eyes and saw Nathan standing with his back to the fire looking at her.

He had entered the back way and had sent the neighbor home. Miriam had seemed to be asleep, but he realized now that she had just been lying with her eyes closed, shutting everything out. How was he to tell her what he must? He made himself do so, and her lack of response chilled him more than if she had screamed.

"We'd better go now," he said gently.

"I'll have to get dressed first. I'm still in my dressing gown."

"You're wearing a sweater and skirt, Miriam."

She glanced down disinterestedly and saw that she was.

"Don't you remember putting them on?"

Miriam shook her head. She did not want to remember anything.

Nathan brought her gabardine jacket from the hallway and bundled her into it. She made no attempt to help him, letting her arms fall limply to her sides after he had put them into the coat sleeves, sagging like a rag-doll while he fastened the buttons and pulled out a pocket flap which his meticulousness would not allow him to leave tucked in.

When they got into the car, he opened the windows wide so that the cold air would blow in her face. But her cheeks remained chalk-white and her demeanor lifeless.

"I think we should take Mother," he said pulling up outside his parents' home. The need for Sarah's strong and comforting presence had suddenly assailed him.

"Take anyone you like," Miriam answered indifferently, as if they were going to the cinema and not to where her child lay perilously ill.

Nathan bounded up the path and kept his finger on the bell until Sarah opened the door. He glanced back at the car before entering the house, but Miriam had not so much as turned her head and remained silent when he returned with both his parents. What's going to happen to her if Martin dies? he asked himself. If just the possibility of it is enough to reduce her to this?

"Get out and sit in the back with Mother, Miriam," he said, opening the door for her. Having Sarah beside her might help.

Nathan had warned Sarah and Abraham that Miriam was in a state of shock, but they had difficulty in suppressing their own when they saw her appearance.

"No tea party today, Ma," she said in a brittle voice as they set off. "What will you do with all the cakes?"

Abraham invoked an old Yiddish curse to blight the jam tarts and strudel instead of his grandson. "Let the cakes be a *kapora* for our Martin."

Miriam's lips trembled, but she said nothing.

Sarah took her hand and remained silent, too. Sometimes contact could say more than words. She wanted to tell Miriam not to worry, that her neighbor's grandchild had recovered from the same illness Martin had. But it wouldn't be the truth. Little Tommy Evans had been spared the terrible complications. It was no use saying anything; all a person could do was pray.

They passed through the town center, across Market Street thronged with shoppers laden with parcels. Sarah had never seen it so busy before; but she had never been to town on a Saturday before. Or ridden in a vehicle on *Shabbos*. She hoped the Almighty would understand why she and Abraham had broken His law——that any Jewish grandparents would have to in such circumstances.

"Martin likes reading the *Manchester Guardian*," Miriam said tonelessly as they passed the newspaper's office on Cross Street.

"He'll be reading it on Monday," Abraham assured her. "God won't let a good boy like him die."

Miriam remembered her gentle mother whom He had allowed to die after years of suffering, and her sweet-natured brother-in-law Saul Salaman who had met death brutally on a battlefield. I don't trust God any more, she thought, and it was as if a rock which had always been there to lean upon had been taken away.

When they reached the hospital, Nathan put a firm arm around her while they traversed a long, covered way leading to the wards.

"A big important place like this can't afford corridors with windows?" Abraham muttered.

"Turn up your coat collar," Sarah ordered him. A person could catch pneumonia from the icy blasts here instead of getting better! She eyed a couple of hurrying nurses and hoped they were wearing wool vests under their thin uniforms.

They found David, Esther and Ben waiting near the entrance to the surgical unit, with Sammy.

"Rebecca phoned me and I rang Esther," David said.

"A nice *Shabbos* gathering, eh?" Abraham said sounding choked.

Seeing them all there affected Sarah, too. Then Lou came out of the ward and told Nathan to take Miriam and Sammy inside.

Sammy had been alone in the corridor when Lou went to have a word with the house surgeon. "What're you all doing here?" Lou asked the family.

They looked at him wordlessly.

"All right. You don't have to tell me; I know," he said

with feeling. "But this isn't the Jewish hospital where the staff
are used to having patients' relatives cluttering up the place.
If Sister Reilly finds you all hanging about here, she won't
like it."

"Is that so, Dr. Benjamin?" a soft brogue inquired from
behind him.

Lou turned and saw the silver-haired angular woman
eyeing him. "I was explaining they can't stay, Sister," he said
respectfully.

"An' I'll be after telling them meself, if I see fit, thank
you." She surveyed Sarah thoughtfully. "It's young Dr. Sandberg's mother isn't it? And the little lad who's so poorly'll be
your grandson, though he doesn't favor you, nor his mammy
and daddy neither."

"He looks like his other grandma, rest her soul," Sarah
explained.

Sister Reilly's starched features creased into a smile,
which Sarah would not have thought possible.

"Let me think where I can put you, Mrs. Sandberg," she
said as if her survey of Sarah had brought her to a favorable
decision. "You can't be standing here for Lord knows how
long, and I can tell just by looking at you wild horses
wouldn't drag you away."

"Jewish families like to be together when there's trouble," Sarah felt constrained to tell her.

"Catholic ones are no different. It puts me in mind of
me own family in Tipperary when my mother, God bless her,
had her first stroke. But the nuns were awful good and found
us a place to be. Even though we weren't like you, with a
doctor in the family."

Lou was listening with an expression of profound astonishment on his acne-scarred face. "I wouldn't have believed
it," he exclaimed when the Sister had swept away.

A few minutes later, they were installed in a two-bedded
side ward.

"Lucky for you it's a weekend, when most folk are too
busy enjoying themselves to take sick, or it wouldn't be vacant," Sister Reilly said when she had ushered them there.
She patted Sarah's shoulder. "I'll tell Dr. Sandberg where to
find you. And don't you be giving up hope now, my dear.
The little lad hasn't got any worse, even though he hasn't got
any better. Would you like me to light a candle for him when
I go off duty?"

Abraham almost swallowed his tonsils at the thought of his grandson's deliverance being prayed for in a church.

Sarah felt apprehensive about it, but wasn't there one God for everybody? So what did it matter if Jesus and the Holy Ghost heard the prayer, too? "I'd be much obliged, Sister," she said gratefully.

They were sipping strong, hospital tea when Nathan joined them.

"A nice little ward-maid brought it. Her name's Lucy," Sarah, who always got on personal terms with everyone, informed him. "Sister told her to look after us."

Nathan was as surprised as Lou had been. "We used to call Sister Reilly the Dragon when we were students," he recalled.

"To me she's an angel," Sarah declared. "And from her I heard hopeful words about Martin, which I haven't heard from anyone else. Miriam and Sammy are still sitting with him, Nat?"

Nathan nodded. "But he doesn't know they're there. He's not round from the anesthetic yet." He felt stifled in the small room and went to open the window.

"You want your father to get pneumonia?" his mother asked reproachfully.

Nathan exchanged a smile with Lou and closed it again. The older generation of Jewish immigrants were all the same, equating fresh air with disease, and they had brought up their children to have similar ideas. The two young physicians could usually tell whether a house was occupied by Christians of Jews by glancing to see if the windows were open or shut. They had no need to look for the *mezuzah* on the doorstep of Jewish houses, and it had become a joke between them.

Abraham chose that moment to cough up some phlegm and spit into his handkerchief. His family were accustomed to him doing this, but Sarah reacted as if the briefly open window had caused it.

"You see?" she exclaimed to Nathan.

Nathan sat down beside his partner on one of the high beds, with his legs dangling over the side. David was seated opposite him, on the other bed, his feet planted firmly on the floor. When I was a kid I thought I'd catch up with him one day, Nathan mused wryly. The difference in their height didn't matter any more; David was now thirty-eight and Nathan was twenty-five. They were both men now—not a man and a boy like it had been when Nathan was growing up. But there was no such thing as catching up with David, thought Nathan. David wouldn't let you; he made you feel small.

His brother's proximity was setting him on edge and he went to stare restlessly out of the window at the ward opposite. He could see the nurses pushing a surgical trolley in front of the beds. Was one of them Mary? The thought that he might encounter her had caused his throat to constrict when he entered the hospital with Miriam and his parents. What would he have done if they'd come face to face in the corridor? But it hadn't happened, and he'd been thankful she wasn't on duty in Martin's ward, either. He wanted to see her, but there was a part of him that did not. And she certainly wouldn't want to see him.

When he turned from the window he saw his mother eyeing him. Why did being here with his family in this small room make him feel trapped? Because he was trapped and always had been. Just being one of them made it so. It was as if the family were a huge web with the parent-spiders in the middle watching to make sure all the little ones stayed caught in it. With the elder-brother spider aiding and abetting them, Nathan thought with an acid glance at David.

"Who's watching the shop?" he heard Lou ask Ben, and went to sit beside him again, grateful for his friend's prosaic presence.

"The kids, who else?" Ben replied.

"Harry and Arnold and Marianne are in charge? Well how do you like that!" Sarah said approvingly.

"Our Arnold isn't too keen," Ben shrugged, then his saturnine face lit with pride. "But our Harry's a chip off the old block. This morning a lady came in to buy a pair of twopence-ha'penny socks for her husband and—"

"You sell socks for twopence-ha'penny? How can you make a profit?" Sarah interrupted.

"The profit's in the turnover, Ma," Ben explained. "They come from all over Salford for them, like they do for our tenpence-ha'penny Brylcreem that everyone else sells for a shilling. But let me tell you about Harry. He sold the lady a gabardine jacket for herself."

Only Jews could have a conversation like this sitting in a hospital waiting for one of their own to live or die, Nathan reflected. They did the same at *Shivah* houses, and the mourners they were there to visit sometimes joined in. But it was better than morbid conversation, or no conversation at all. It helped to take people's minds off what they were there for.

"Tell Harry *Mazeltov* from me," Sarah said to Esther and Ben. "For a boy not yet fourteen to have such a business head deserves congratulations. So you're selling raincoats also, now, eh? The last I heard you were stocking up with coveralls and corsets. You did the right thing calling the shop 'Ben's Bazaar'!"

"I made him up a cheap line to see how he'd do with them," David told her.

"And why not? It's all in the family, and business is business."

Esther got up to stretch her legs and wrapped her rust tweed coat closer around her full figure, then leaned against the wall thinking of Miriam who was unable to have any more children. And now this terrible thing had struck down the only one she had. "Who cares about business at such a time?" she said emotionally. "Saturday's our busiest day, but when David rang up, Ben got the car out right away, to come here."

The brief interlude of normality dissipated into silence.

"Oy," Abraham sighed fidgeting with his moustache.

"When something like this happens, it gives a person a sense of values," David mused.

Nathan looked at him coldly. "I've always had one."

Lou dug Nathan in the ribs to prevent him from saying more and changed the subject hastily. "D'you want me to bring Rebecca here, Nat? Though in her condition I wouldn't recommend it."

"Rebecca's at my house," David said before Nathan had time to reply.

"Thank you for mentioning it," Nathan said sarcastically.

"I'm sorry, but I forgot. I've had other things on my mind. She sounded so upset when she phoned me, I decided to go and fetch her."

"I wondered why Bessie hadn't come with you," Esther said. It wasn't like his wife to let him out of her sight.

David allowed them to assume this was the reason. But he would not have brought his wife to the hospital anyway. All Miriam needed just now was one of Bessie's spiteful outbursts. With what they were here for, Miriam must come first.

Lou got off the bed and smoothed down the snowy bed spread lest Sister Reilly's eagle eye should discover a crease in it. He couldn't stand the way David was cracking his knuckles, and the looks Nat kept shooting at his brother were enough to make anyone feel jumpy. The atmosphere was rippling with undercurrents and Lou didn't want to be there when they erupted. Every Jewish family had a touch of grand opera about it, but his partner's was worse than most.

"I'll push off home, Nat," he said awkwardly. "Cora'll still be keeping my *cholent* warm in the oven."

"She cooks butterbeans for *Shabbos*?" Sarah asked him conversationally, ignoring the tension around her. "Malka Berkowitz used to give us *cholent* when we stayed with her and I haven't tasted it since."

"Such a memory my wife's got!" Abraham exclaimed tetchily.

Lou edged his way to the door and tried to catch Nathan's eye, but he was glaring at his brother again. Was Nat going to take it out of David forever for stopping him from marrying a *shiksah*? It was time Nat grew up and accepted that he wouldn't have been happy in a marriage that had broken his parents' hearts. "I'll pop back tonight," he promised as he made his escape.

"I think we should have Martin moved to a private room. I don't like him being on a big ward with all those sick men," David said immediately after Lou had gone.

"Are you at it again?" Nathan barked.

"At what, exactly?" David inquired trying to keep his tone even.

"Dictating what should be done! And if I let you, it'll be a *fait accompli* in no time. You'll have it all arranged without even consulting Miriam and Sammy. But this time what you're interfering in happens to be my province."

"If I were you, I'd watch what you're saying, Nat! Doctor or no doctor, you're getting too big for your boots."

Sarah quelled them with a glance. "I want you both to watch what you're saying. Stop it, do you hear me?" Her voice was cool and calm, but her hands were trembling, "Thank goodness your wives aren't here listening to you shout at each other. Worry we can't avoid, but rows we can do without."

Fifteen minutes later, their wives arrived, wrapped in their fur coats.

"How could we sit at home listening to the wireless, when our nephew is so ill?" Bessie demanded. "We wanted to be with the family."

She means it, Sarah thought with surprise.

"If it was, God forbid, one of my kids, Miriam would be here," Bessie added feelingly.

David had forgotten his wife's emotions could occasionally function on that level. "Come and sit down, love," he said putting his arm around her.

Rebecca did not look at Nathan. "We got a taxi," was all she said.

"Make your wife comfortable on one of the beds, Nat," Sarah instructed, noting her pregnant daughter-in-law's exhausted appearance. "That nice Sister Reilly won't mind."

Rebecca sat down on a chair. "I'll be all right for the moment, thank you."

Then Sigmund Moritz entered with Carl and Helga.

"Mrs. Hardcastle had the decency to let Helga know," Sigmund said, implying that none of the Sandbergs had bothered to do so and stood shaking the raindrops off his Homburg hat in the uncomfortable silence.

Sarah had not noticed that it had begun to rain and now became aware of it lashing against the window. Sigmund was studiously not looking at her and she remembered how he had once let his pride cause a rift between the Moritzes and Sandbergs that had lasted for four years. But the joy of Martin's birth had brought them together again and destined them to share this anxiety.

"It was wrong of us not to think of telling you, Sigmund," she made herself say without offering excuses, though doing so was not in her own proud nature.

"I accept your apology," Sigmund replied graciously, then his expression crumpled. "The Sister wouldn't let me see Martin."

Sarah got up from her chair and embraced him. Martin was very precious to her, but he wasn't her only grandchild. "We haven't seen him, either," she said to let Sigmund know there had been no favoritism and patted his shoulder comfortingly while he shed a few tears.

Marianne stood on a stool behind the shop counter looking for the one-and-fourpence-ha'penny pure silk stockings.

"They're in a box wi' Prima Donna on it, luv," the customer told her. "I know, 'cause I cum in fer a pair every Sat'day."

"Excuse me a moment, madam," Harry said to the shawled matron whose vast waist he was measuring in order to sell her a corset. "We're out of that brand just now," he smiled to Marianne's customer. "But we've got some others and they must be good, my mother wears them herself."

He found a shiny purple box and put it on the counter for Marianne. "Put your hand inside the leg," he instructed her. "To show the lady how the shade'll look on."

"Where is yer mam terday, 'Arry?" the customer inquired after she had made her purchase and was waiting for her change. She wet her finger to fix a hennaed kiss-curl more securely to her forehead in front of a mirror, then picked up a bottle of "Californian Poppy" scent from the array of cut-price sundries on the counter. "I'd rather 'ave 'Evenin' In Paris' meself," she said after sniffing it. "Yer dad's not 'ere, neither, is 'e?"

Harry and Arnold exchanged a glance over their sister's head which was bent over the cash till.

Harry's customer looked up from the pink, whaleboned monstrosity she was examining. "Nowt's wrong, is it? Not a funeral in't family, I 'ope, or owt like that?"

Harry licked his lips as if they suddenly felt dry. "They just had to go out," he replied with a forced smile.

"Jews don't have funerals on Saturdays, or weddings either," Marianne told the lady, raising her head from the till. "What's one-and-fourpence-ha'penny from two shillings, Harry?" she asked desperately. Why couldn't she add up and subtract like her brothers could? The florin the lady had handed her felt hot and sticky from being clutched in her palm while she tried to do the sum. She felt funny inside, too, from what the lady in the shawl had just said.

Harry came to her rescue as he had been doing all afternoon. But not knowing where her parents were continued to make her feel uneasy. She had returned from the library at dinnertime and found them gone. "We've got to look after the shop instead of going to Bobbie Sarah's. Mom and Dad've had to go somewhere," Harry had told her and had said he didn't know where the somewhere was. But Marianne didn't believe him.

"Go and set the table for our tea," he instructed her at closing time. "Mom said we're to have it if they're not back."

She stood watching her brothers bring in the overalls and raincoats which were hung up in the doorway, then went to pick her way through the bundles and boxes on the stockroom floor, breathing in the special, draper's-shop smell of new clothing, cardboard and dust that she had already come to associate with home. But entering the living room was like stepping into a different world. Her mother had not allowed the business to overflow into her domestic domain. Here, the odors were those Marianne had always known. Mansion Polish and blacklead; damp pot-towels drying off by the fire; the lingering aromas of chicken fat rendered down with onions, and fish fried in oil. And, because today was the Sabbath, the tang of apples and oranges piled in a big glass fruitbowl beside the brass candlesticks on the table.

Marianne eyed the telephone on the sideboard. Her grandmother had no phone, so she couldn't ring her up and ask if she knew where Mom and Dad were. The square wooden clock on the mantelpiece said six-fifteen: why weren't they back yet? Perhaps Uncle David could tell her? His number was written on the front of the directory, with Uncle Nat's. But how did you make a phone call? She read the instructions and got through.

"Who's that speaking?" Shirley's voice inquired.

"It's me. Marianne."

"I thought it might be my mom 'n' dad ringing up from the hospital."

Marianne's heart missed a beat. "Has Zaidie Abraham been taken bad with his chest? Is that why there's no tea party?"

"It's Martin who's ill. He's very poorly."

"Who're you talking to, kid?" Harry said entering with Arnold.

But Marianne was unable to reply and he took the receiver from her. "We weren't supposed to tell Marianne," he said recognizing his cousin's high-pitched voice demanding to know what was the matter.

"Well I didn't know that, did I? Marianne phoned me up. Why weren't we supposed to tell her?"

Harry looked at his sister and saw the distress in her eyes. "Why do you think?" he snapped and rang off.

Arnold put a kind hand on Marianne's shoulder. "Mom 'n' Dad knew how upset you'd be. That's why they decided not to tell you."

"You'd miss Martin more than you would Arnold and me if we got ill and died," Harry said gruffly.

It's true, Marianne thought. They were her own brothers, but she loved Martin more. "Don't be daft," she said and avoided looking at them because she was ashamed of it.

"We'd better set the table, Arnold, seeing our kid hasn't done it," Harry said.

"I'm not hungry," Marianne told him.

Arnold got out the plates and cutlery and Harry went into the scullery and returned with bread and butter and a platter of *gefilte* fish. "You not eating won't help Martin," he said to Marianne in his down-to-earth way. "So sit down and have something."

She obeyed his instruction, but ate very little. The two boys sat silently munching their food and she could hear the clock ticking away the minutes.

"I wonder if our kid'll marry Martin when they grow up?" Harry said contemplatively, cutting himself another slice of *challah*. He spread butter on the soft, golden-crusted bread. "If he gets better."

"Of course he'll get better!" Marianne flashed fiercely because she could not imagine a world without Martin. "And you're being daft again, our Harry. People don't marry their cousins."

After tea, Arnold got out the pachisi board and they had a game, without the squabbles that usually resulted from the three of them playing together, in which Marianne always came off worst.

They're being nice to me because they know I'm upset, she realized with surprise, and had to admit that there was something to be said for having brothers.

Nathan went to the big ward to look at his nephew and found Sister Reilly beside the screened-off bed with Miriam and Sammy, taking Martin's blood pressure.

"Well, that's all right, Dr. Sandberg," she pronounced watching the mercury rise and fall.

Sammy was holding Miriam's hand, but she seemed unaware of it, her features as well as her body immobilized by fear as she gazed at her son's face.

"Does that mean he'll get better?" Sammy asked.

Sister Reilly felt the boy's steaming forehead, wishing, as she did every day of her life, that medical science would discover a drug to combat what ailed him. "It would if there were nothing else to worry about," she replied gravely, unwinding the restricting band from Martin's arm. "I'll be after having a word with Staff Nurse when she takes over from me, Dr. Sandberg," she said to Nathan as he left the bedside with her. "About the wee lad's family being here, as well as his parents."

Darkness had fallen outside the tall, narrow windows and the day nurses were tidying the patients' locker tops before going off duty. Nathan glanced at his watch and saw that it was almost seven o'clock. "Who's in charge tonight?" he made himself ask the Sister, though what he would do if she said it was Mary he didn't know.

Sister Reilly paused before a long table in the middle of the ward and studied him surreptitiously whilst moving a jar of chrysanthemums an inch to the right to balance the distance between it and those on either side of it. Nathan was standing beside her with his hands nonchalantly in his trouser pockets, as if the answer to his question was of no importance to him, and she could barely restrain a snort. Did these young people think her blind to what went on under her nose? She'd have to be deaf, too! His broken romance had been the talk of the hospital.

" 'Tis nobody ye know, Dr. Sandberg, so don't be after givin' it a thought," she replied to let him know she was not fooled and had the satisfaction of seeing him blush.

"By the way, Sister, I got married last year," he said as casually as he could and returned to the side ward wondering why he had told her.

Lucy, the ward-maid, was pouring more tea into the thick, hospital cups for the family, her freckled face registering her sympathy.

"I 'ope you all 'as a good night an' t'lickle lad's sittin' up 'avin' bacon'n egg when I get 'ere termorrer," she said warmly. "Miracles 'as 'appened in this place many a time," she added, before departing with a rustle of her starched uniform.

Nathan marveled at how the staff managed to bring to this clinical institution a human touch which had escaped his notice when he was a student on the wards. Perhaps you had to be on the receiving end of it to know it was there. Even the dreaded Dragon was being pleasant to him because he was a patient's relative.

"Doesn't that ward-maid know Jews don't eat bacon?" he heard Bessie say to David, but his brother did not reply. His mother was fingering her brooch pensively and his godfather Sigmund playing nervously with his watch chain. Rebecca was now lying on one of the beds and had taken off her shoes. He made a mental note to tell Lou her ankles were swollen. Doctors did not usually treat their own wives, so Nathan was supervising Cora's pregnancy and Lou was looking after Rebecca.

He could hear his father's phlegmy chest preparing for another bout of coughing and saw him take out his handkerchief in readiness. "You need some air, Father; it's too stuffy in here for you. Why not go for a little walk?" he said, loosening his tie and knowing the suggestion would be ignored. Hunger had begun gnawing at his stomach and the others must be feeling empty, too. "There's a café round the corner where they make sandwiches. Don't you think we should have a snack?" he said.

"Who could eat?" Esther exclaimed.

Ben patted her hand and gave Nathan a reproachful look. He received one from Helga, too, and Carl eyed him rebukingly over the top of the newspaper he was reading. Nobody else so much as glanced at him.

"You'd think a ward-maid would know we don't eat bacon, wouldn't you?" Bessie harped. "They must've had Jewish patients before and they'll have them again. Someone should tell her so she won't offend anyone else's relatives."

"Zelda Cohen put bacon on Yankel's throat when he had the quinsies," Sarah said. "But don't tell her son-in-law Dr. Smolensky; he thinks he cured them. Her Christian neighbor swears by it."

"I've got a patient who thinks wrapping a sweaty sock round his neck will cure tonsillitis," Nathan revealed. But nobody seemed interested.

"So long as he didn't eat it, what does it matter?" Abraham said impatiently as his phlegm rolled to a crescendo and was transferred to the square of linen.

"The sock or the bacon?" Nathan inquired facetiously and everyone immediately fell silent.

What good are we doing sitting here like this? he thought. But nobody would leave until Martin's medical crisis was over one way or the other, though their presence was serving no purpose. Why didn't he go home himself? His professional assistance wasn't required and his concern for his nephew would be no less if he were seated by the fire in his own house. Get up and go then, he ordered his body, but it refused to obey his brain. The inexplicable something, destructive and at the same time sustaining, which he had tried to exorcize from his soul and deny was in his blood, was holding him captive with his fellow-prisoners whose habits and stupidities would probably drive him up the wall before the morning.

Mary Dennis was drying her hair by the gas-fire when her friend entered. "Be a pet and draw the curtains for me," she requested, grimacing at the rain gushing down the long windowpanes. "I've been spending my weekend off doing all the chores I've let pile up since my last one."

"How thrilling!"

"As I've nothing better to do, I might add."

Ann Barker surveyed the lavender curtains with which she had just shut out the dismal night, and the patchwork quilt and cushions on the narrow bed. "You've been sprucing up your room, too. I'm surprised you could afford to on our lousy pay."

Mary smiled. "Well everyone knows nursing's a labor of love, don't they? If you're interested in money you don't go into it. Fortunately, I've got my Aunt Mabel who lets me rummage through the trunks in her attic and take what I want."

"It looks like a real home away from home now," Ann pronounced.

"It might as well be, as I'm likely to live here forever," Mary answered dryly.

Ann moved a pile of black stockings and a workbox from a chair and sat down. "What d'you mean, you're likely to live here forever?"

"I'll be my brother's kids' maiden aunt, like dear old Mabel's mine, that's what I mean," Mary declared with a grin. But her cornflower-blue eyes remained serious.

"For heaven's sake! You're only twenty-six."

Mary began brushing her tangled blonde curls. "So are you. But we've been at the Infirmary nine years. I feel like a fixture already. And you'll certainly be a maiden aunt, Ann, the way you're going on."

Ann shrugged her shoulders, but said nothing.

"We're a right pair, aren't we?" Mary said quietly. "I lose my heart to a Jew and you lose yours to a married man."

"Rob's going to get a divorce," Ann replied defensively.

"Is that why he's living with his wife?"

"Stop it!"

"When're you going to come to your senses?" Mary sighed. "He'll never leave her. He hasn't got the guts."

Ann sprang up from the chair and glared at her.

"He's been making a mug of you since we were probationers, Ann."

"Nat didn't make one of you, I suppose?"

"What happened with us was entirely different," Mary said, reflecting that everyone else called him Nat, but she had called him Nathan.

"The only difference was he was married to his religion," Ann retorted.

"That's one way of putting it." Nathan had told Mary he wasn't all that religious and in her view it was his family he was tied to. "But he didn't promise to marry me." She avoided Ann's eye. "He didn't sleep with me, either."

"Oh don't be such a prude!" Ann snapped; then her voice grew sympathetic. "You still care about him, don't you?"

Mary stared at the flickering gas-flames. She'd been out with several men since her affair with Nathan ended, but the thought of him had intruded between her and them. A young radiologist who had just joined the hospital staff was pursuing her at present, but she wasn't interested in him.

"Would you start seeing Nat again if he asked you to?" Ann asked her.

"Probably."

Ann sat twisting a lock of her long, dark hair around her forefinger edgily and Mary noted the anxiety lines beside her mouth and the hollowness of her cheeks. Her green wool dress hung loosely about her spare frame and the three-quarter-length sleeves revealed wrists thin enough to snap. Ann had been plump and pretty once, but her traumatic relationship with Rob had reduced her to this haggard state.

"Nathan didn't let me go on waiting forever," Mary said to her. "Spending all my off-duty time hoping he'd ring up."

"That was Rob on the phone before," Ann said, ignoring the inference. "He's had another bust-up with her and she's gone to sleep at her mother's."

"Well he's out of luck, isn't he?" Mary said brutally. "You're on nights, so you're not available."

Ann fiddled with her coral necklace. "I came to ask if you'd go on duty for me."

Mary picked some loose hairs from her shabby red dressing gown and did not reply.

"You know I'd do it for you."

Even if you knew it wasn't helping me? Mary wondered. But she couldn't dictate her friend's life. All she could do was advise—and support when the advice was ignored. They had been close since their training days, sharing their clothes and their troubles; had taken their SRN exam on the same day and been staff nurses in the same surgical unit, Mary on a male ward and Ann on a female one. Over the years, they had gone together to the weddings of girls who had trained and qualified with them and had each, more than once, caught the bridal bouquet when it was tossed from the going-away car. But this had not made either of them the next bride. Now they were Sisters and sometimes attended the weddings of young nurses who had worked under them. Ann still reached out hopefully for the magic posy of carnations and orange blossom, or whatever it might be, but Mary did not bother. The only man she wanted was forbidden to make her his wife.

"You don't like Rob, that's why you won't do it," Ann declared, though Mary had not said she would not.

Mary thought of the handsome laboratory technician who was responsible for her friend's plight. He worked at another hospital, but often came to the Infirmary staff dances, as a senior nurse had told them on the evening they met him at one—without his wife, she had added warningly, but Ann had not heeded the warning. "There's no harm in dancing with him," she had said and had been dancing to his tune ever since. How can I like a man I can't respect? Mary asked herself. But Ann's dejected appearance moved her to get up and kiss her pale cheek.

"All right. I'll go on duty for you," she sighed. "Though it's against my better judgment. And you can borrow the bath salts and talc Mom gave me for my birthday, if you like."

Ann watched her getting out her uniform. "Bless you, Mary."

"I don't knew who's the bigger fool, you or me."

Love, Mary thought wryly, as she left her quarters in Lorne Street and cut across the blustery forecourt of the Private Patient's Home which adjoined the hospital. And the things it does to people, came the bitter addendum as she entered the covered way. Once she'd been carefree and content in this big sprawling place, had walked these long, dismal stretches unaffected by the bleakness. But sharing a bench in Whitworth Park with a boy one autumn morning had changed her, heightening her perceptions and honing her sensations to a knife edge.

The echo of her shoes treading the concrete floor increased the loneliness that thinking of Nathan always evoked. Other nurses were going on and off duty, too, huddled into their navy-blue, red-lined capes. Some were walking along in groups, chatting to each other and several exchanged greetings with Mary. It was a familiar scene. The end of the bustling day-stint and the beginning of the long night's vigil on dimly lit, hushed wards where some patients would sleep peacefully, set on the road to recovery, and others would breathe their last before the morning.

Why can't I just take it in my stride, like I did before I knew Nathan? Mary asked herself. When they'd first met, she'd lectured him about his sensitivity and had helped him acquire the dispassionate approach his profession demanded. But he had never lost his deep concern for the human condition and the way that he felt had eventually rubbed off on her.

She hugged her cape closer around herself, but the comfort she needed was not to be found within its sensible folds. She hadn't found it in an increased dedication to her work, either, though she had sought it there. Work, however rewarding, was no substitute for the right man's arms. Why had she let herself fall in love with Nathan?

"All he thinks of is his stomach!" Esther expostulated after Nathan had been out and returned with a bagful of cheese and tomato sandwiches.

Everyone else took a sandwich to munch with their third cup of tea, which Staff Nurse Flaherty had just sent in.

"When Martin gets better, I'll bring a pound of Lyons to the hospital," Abraham promised.

"If" would be a better word, Nathan thought grimly. His nephew had been delirious and burning with fever when he looked in at the ward before going out to the café.

"A giver-away of tea leaves I'm married to!" Sarah exclaimed glancing at her husband. "Since 1905 he's been taking tea to the *Habimah Shul* every week, a present for Rabbi Lensky. And I've never known why. Sugar he takes also."

"So now I'll tell you why," Abraham smiled. "When I was out of work, every day he gave a hot drink to me and Shloime Lipkin and Yankel Cohen. And to plenty of others."

"That's what you've kept a secret from me all these years?" Sarah asked looking perplexed.

Abraham shrugged, but said no more. How could he explain the feeling that had existed between the unemployed immigrants who had gathered by the fire in a back room at the *shul*? The shame they had shared because they couldn't support their families. A shame that was so demeaning, they had not wanted their wives to know of the brief respite they allowed themselves from the day-long, fruitless search.

It was now nine o'clock and the nighttime hush that had descended upon the hospital had permeated the room. Every shuffle of a foot, Abraham's sporadic coughs, the replacing of a cup in a saucer and the sound of the tea being thirstily gulped down lent emphasis to the stillness.

"Sitting here makes a person feel cut off from everything," Ben said brushing some crumbs off his trousers.

"But no man is an island," Nathan quoted.

"What d'you mean?" his prosaic brother-in-law inquired.

"There's nothing that happens in one part of the world that doesn't affect the rest," Sigmund supplied.

"I'd say the interpretation was open to debate, Father," Carl said. "Ben was thinking about it on a personal level."

"Who, me? I wasn't thinking about islands at all."

"He's got better things to think about," Esther declared.

Bessie felt her wig to make sure she still had it on straight. "Some people've got worse."

Sigmund ignored the interpolations as he often did in order to pursue his own point. "While we're sitting here with our load of *tsorus*, our brethren are being persecuted in Germany."

"Oy," Abraham sighed.

"Listen, a person's own sorrow has to come first," Sarah told Sigmund.

"Am I arguing about it?" he retorted. "That's the trouble with this world. Everyone's got their own packet. They don't have time to think about other people's."

David stopped eating his sandwich. "Unless it arrives on their own doorstep."

"A clever boy you always were, David," Sigmund applauded. "And Nat also, but he's suddenly gone *shtum*."

"I wish I'd kept quiet in the first place. You daren't open your mouth in this family in case it builds up into something you never intended," Nathan said irritably. "This isn't the time or place to be worrying about what's going on in Germany."

"Didn't I just say that's the trouble?" Sigmund interrupted. "There's never a right time or place until it happens to you, like David said."

"The English aren't like the Germans," Esther chimed in.

"What about that Mr. Mosley?" Sarah demanded hotly.

Rebecca had a remote expression on her face, as if she had dissociated herself from the heated discussion taking place around her. There were times when Nathan agreed with her opinion of his family and this was one of them, though he would never admit it.

"I don't think Mrs. Evans and Mrs. Watson would be like the Germans," Sarah declared.

"The fact that it couldn't happen here is no reason to turn our backs on those it is happening to," David asserted.

"Who is turning their back?" Sarah said sharply. "But it can't be in the front of our minds all the time. We can only help those who manage to escape and in between we've got our own lives to live."

"That's not the right attitude, Mother," David persisted.

"You'd like me to get on a boat and go to Germany to fight with Hitler?"

"That's what it'll come to in the end," Sigmund declaimed. "Another war."

"You always were a warmonger!" Sarah accused him.

"It's true, Father," Helga endorsed.

"You'd prefer I should say what I don't think, just to please you?" Sigmund shouted.

"I'd prefer you shouldn't say anything!" Sarah retorted.

"I'm upset enough already . . ." Her voice petered out when the door opened. Then her fingers tightened on her brooch. The girl in the snapshot she had found in Nathan's pocket was standing in the doorway.

Oh God, Nathan and David thought simultaneously.

"What on earth's going on in here?" Mary inquired, surveying the littered room which momentarily distracted her attention from its occupants.

The pages of Carl's newspaper had found their way on to the floor, a pile of coats lay haphazardly on a bed, some discarded bits of sandwich were scattered on a table and there were cups and saucers everywhere.

"This is a hospital, not a station buffet," Mary said entering to gather up the disordered *Manchester Guardian.* "I could hear you shouting outside in the corridor. I'd be obliged if you'd remember there are patients here, trying to sleep."

Nathan had known she was now a Sister. The dark uniform suits her, he thought. Then she turned and saw him and the color drained from her face.

"Hallo, Mary," he made himself say. Only David knew who she was and the others wouldn't think it strange for him to be acquainted with others on the staff as well as Sister Reilly.

"Good evening," Mary said stiffly, aware of her heart fluttering wildly in her breast.

"I'm sorry about the mess," Nathan apologized. "We'll clear it up before we go."

"Sister Reilly left a message that she'd given permission for a patient's relatives to wait in here. But I've been doing my rounds; I haven't been on the ward yet. I'd no idea it was someone of yours."

"They don't have a Sister on every ward at night; it isn't necessary," Nathan explained to the others. "It's my brother's lad," he told Mary.

Mary's gaze moved to David and flickered with hostility. She had only seen him once before, but would remember the occasion always. He had found Nathan with her in the park one day and had treated her as if she didn't exist. He appeared not to recognize her, but she knew he had.

"My other brother," Nathan supplied.

Mary removed her gaze from the man she had come to think of as the representative of the enemy, who were all now collected in this room regarding her impassively, like a solid bloc united against an outsider. "I'm sorry your nephew is so ill," she said to Nathan.

Rebecca became aware of something in the atmosphere that had not been present a few minutes ago, and of her mother-in-law and David glancing at her uneasily. She looked up at Nathan and saw that his eyes were riveted to the Sister's. What she could feel was coming from the two of them! A wave of shock stirred the child in her womb. This young Gentile woman with the English-rose face was part of her husband's past and he was still in love with her. It was her shadow that hovered over their marriage.

Sarah saw the brief, unguarded glance of shared pain and longing, too, but hid her alarm. Everything is *bershert*, she told herself philosophically. She had always believed that Fate took a hand in people's lives. Her children scoffed at the notion, but it was Yiddish folklore that everything was fated, and over and over again she had found it to be true. It was fated for Martin to be a patient in this hospital so Nathan would re-encounter his *shiksah* sweetheart and his mother would have the opportunity to put paid to it once and for all. The knowledge that Mary ought not to have been on duty that night would have lent confirmation, but Sarah needed none.

"It's nice to meet people my son used to know," she said putting Mary firmly into the past tense. "Did you hear he'd got married, Sister?"

Mary's expression revealed she had not known, as Sarah had suspected.

"His wife Rebecca is resting on the bed," she added with a smile. "Her baby's due soon; we have to look after her."

Mary managed to return the smile. "Congratulations," she said to Nathan.

"Jewish people say *Mazeltov*," Sarah told her emphasizing the difference between Mary and the family.

"I know," Mary replied. You'd be surprised at the things I learned about Jews in the years I went out with your son, she thought bitterly. And the main one was the power of the blood-tie. She surveyed the silver-haired lady who had taken charge of the conversation; her birdlike proportions did not detract from her matriarchal bearing and behind her equable exterior was a hint of something that told you she would protect her family against whatever might threaten it.

"I must get on with my rounds," Mary said wanting to escape though she was no longer a threat.

Nathan took a step towards her and she saw David glance at him warningly.

"Shall I come to the ward with you, Mary?"

Mary let her eyes rest briefly on the beautiful young Jewess with the Old Testament name who was Nathan's wife and would soon bear his child, and accepted, as she had not really done until now, that a chapter of her life was irrevocably over. "It isn't necessary, thank you."

"A nice girl," Sigmund pronounced when the door had closed behind her.

And a sensible one, thank God, Sarah said to herself with relief.

Nathan went to stare out of the window so nobody would see his face. He would have been surprised to know that David wanted to comfort him and that his mother was similarly affected.

Later, Lou returned with a pile of smoked-salmon sandwiches wrapped in greaseproof paper.

"He thinks it's a wedding!" Esther snorted.

"Food is Jewish comfort," Sarah declared.

But nobody could bring themselves to eat.

"Let's have a peep at Martin, Nat," Lou said.

"Mary Dennis is on duty tonight. She'd rather we didn't."

"Is that so?" Lou replied putting two and two together and making five. "Well, she isn't going to frighten me off!"

It was Lou who went back and forth between Martin's bedside and the family, as the uneaten sandwiches dried up and the long night dragged on. At four in the morning, the boy's condition raged to a crisis and Lou brought Miriam and Sammy to the side-ward at Mary's request.

Another hour passed by and nobody spoke a word. But Sarah prayed silently and knew that Abraham and Sigmund were doing the same. Daylight was filtering into the room when a young doctor entered rubbing the morning stubble on his chin.

"The lad's going to be all right," he smiled and went to pat Miriam's shoulder when her pent-up emotion was released in a flood of tears.

There's never an ill wind, Sarah mused, traveling home

in David's Morris Cowley sedan through the wet, deserted streets.

"That Sister who ticked us off didn't seem to like Nat, did she?" Bessie remarked cutting into her thoughts.

David supposed it might have appeared that way to someone who didn't know what he did. "I wasn't in the mood to notice," he lied.

"When I see how those nurses boss doctors about, I'm glad I'm only a presser," Abraham declared.

Sarah said nothing. But she was thinking that the ill wind had done a power of good. Any ideas the *shiksah* might have had about Nat still being interested in her had been hit on the head now she knew he was married. She hadn't even let him go to the ward with her, which was as good as telling him his place was with his wife. Sarah couldn't help feeling sorry for her and hoped she would find a nice husband from among her own people.

A milk float was clanking its way to the local dairy as David stopped the car outside his parents' home. Tibby was asleep in the porch and Sarah carried her damp, furry pet into the kitchen, full of contrition that it had had to spend the night outside.

Abraham went immediately to the kitchen dresser to get his prayer shawl and the phylacteries he must put on to say the morning prayer. "This is the first time I've laid on my *tefillin* before going to bed!" he yawned putting on the *tallith* and rolling up his sleeve to strap one of the small leather-boxed, holy texts to his arm.

Sarah had just poured some milk for the cat and was eyeing the array of cakes on the table. She'd been putting them onto dishes for the tea party when Nathan came to fetch her. She watched her husband strap the second phylactery to his forehead before beginning the prayer.

"Today we've got plenty to thank God for," she smiled. Martin would get well. And Nathan would settle down now and be a happily married man.

She would have been less sanguine about the latter had she known how the night's events had affected his wife.

Chapter Nine

Though Martin remained in the hospital recuperating for several weeks, the family did not encounter Mary again. They took turns to sit with him during visiting hours, and at *Chanukah*, Sister Reilly allowed Miriam and Sammy to bring a *menorah* and light the little colored candles in it so he would not be deprived of his Festival celebration.

"I got a letter from Bobbie Sarah telling me to ignore Christmas," he told Marianne when she visited him on Christmas Day.

"She'd be here telling you in person, if she hadn't got flu. So would your mom and dad." Half the family had gone down with influenza and the other half were looking after them, or Marianne would not have been Martin's sole visitor.

"I'm rather enjoying Christmas, actually," he said glancing around the gaily decorated ward.

Marianne looked at the tree, resplendent with tinsel and colored glass baubles that tinkled in the draft each time the ward door opened. "I wish Jews were allowed to have holly and mistletoe and Christmas trees. My mom and dad won't even let us hang up our stockings," she added with a sigh.

"I hung mine up once, a long time ago," Martin said. "But it was empty the next morning."

"I suppose we can't expect Santa Claus to visit Jewish children."

Martin laughed and clutched his operation wound, which was still feeling sore. "There's no such person, you daftie! It's the parents who fill the kids' stockings."

Marianne eyed him accusingly. "You're always saying things like that to upset me! Remember how you told me there's no such place as Heaven? I kept thinking of it when everyone thought you might die and it made me feel terrible."

"Did they really think I was going to die?"

85

She nodded gravely.

"I wrote a poem about death, before I got ill," he said pensively.

Marianne studied his face which had lost its little-boy chubbiness and noticed he had been biting his fingernails again, a habit he had conquered a couple of years ago. "You used to write happy poems, Martin," she said in a troubled voice. "But the last few you've shown me haven't been."

"I wouldn't say your stories were, either," he countered. "When we were little, before you started writing them down, you used to scare me and all the other kids at school, telling them to us."

Marianne took off her red beret and flicked her fringe away from her eyes. "But my stories couldn't really happen, could they? I mean they wouldn't be likely to," she added confusedly, unable to explain more concisely that Martin's poetry related to real life, but her stories didn't and somehow that made the horrors she inflicted on her characters all right.

"You mean there aren't any tins of treacle big enough for people to sink into like they would into a swamp," Martin grinned, citing one of her tales to show he understood.

They were distracted by the arrival on the ward of a group of carol singers.

"D'you think we should put our fingers in our ears?" Marianne asked Martin anxiously. At school when carols were sung, the Jewish children were not expected to remain and left the room. Then the choir sang the first melodious notes of "Silent Night" and she forgot her misgivings and listened, spellbound.

"A person can enjoy something without believing in it," Martin said when the carol was over.

"But Bobbie Sarah'd say we shouldn't be enjoying you-know-who's birthday party," Marianne whispered, as the haunting refrain of "Away In A Manger" filled the ward.

"Sometimes being Jewish is very difficult," she said after the carol singers had gone.

The ward-maids were bringing round festive refreshments and Martin eyed the dainty sausage rolls and miniature meat pies on the trolleys. "Too true," he replied regretfully as a tray minus those non-kosher treats was brought to him.

"I wasn't thinking of food," Marianne told him, fishing a jam-jar of custard and peaches out of a carrier-bag. "Mom sent you this. I nearly forgot to give to you." She unscrewed the lid and passed him the spoon her mother had also sent in case there wasn't one handy. "I was thinking of all the other things Jews aren't supposed to do and how guilty it makes you feel when you do some of them."

Their Uncle Nat appeared at the foot of the bed in time to hear this. "The best thing is not to," he advised. Because you can't get away with it, he wanted to add.

Marianne turned around to face him. "I didn't know you were standing behind me."

Nathan smiled wryly. "There's always someone standing behind you when you're Jewish, love. Even if it's only in your mind."

"Do you mean God?" she asked thoughtfully.

"God's supposed to be watching and listening to everyone, whatever their religion," Martin informed her. "Isn't that so, Uncle Nat?"

"I'm not here for a theological discussion!" Nathan said. Every word led to a deeper one with these two kids. He deposited a pile of books on the bed. "I came to bring you these, Martin. And a piece of news. You like Miss Ritman, don't you?"

Martin nodded enthusiastically. "She's visited me six times. And she lets me call her Hannah."

"You'd better call her Auntie Hannah in future."

"Why?"

"If you'd seen her and Uncle Carl holding hands at the tea party last *Shabbos* you wouldn't need to ask," Marianne giggled. "Maybe they'll let me be their bridesmaid," she added hopefully.

On the bleak, January day when Martin returned home, the King was lying on his deathbed at Sandringham and Miriam cancelled the family celebration she had planned.

The impending national bereavement had cast its shadow on the Jewish community, prayers for the King's recovery were said in the synagogues and naturalized subjects like Abraham Sandberg and Sigmund Moritz, for whom England had been a haven from oppression, grieved for the beneficent monarch who had ascended the throne during their early immigrant days.

"Only a few months ago it was his Silver Jubilee," Abraham said sorrowfully after he and Sarah had listened to the bulletin on the wireless which told them George V was dead.

"A nice start to 1936 this is," he sighed. "But what can you do? Two kings we've seen go in the years we've been here. Royalty are only human."

"And thank God what they stand for in this country doesn't change from one to the next," Sarah declared fervently. "Everything goes on like it did before, not like it was with the Tsars."

"With those barbarians things always went from bad to worse!"

Sarah watched her husband put on a black tie to mourn for the King. "Edward VII died just before our Nat was born and now his son's passed away when Nat's child is due," she reflected. "Maybe it's *bershert* for Nat to call the baby after the King, like we gave him Edward for his second name."

Abraham swallowed down the strong dose of Glauber salts with which he always started the day and reached for the cup of tea Sarah had poured for him, to take the taste away. "Rebecca wants to call the baby Leon if it's a boy," he reminded her.

"And why not? It was her single name and she has no brothers to carry it on. So what's wrong with Leon George Sandberg? To me it sounds very nice."

Rebecca wondered if George V's namesake had decided to arrive a week early when a sharp twinge shot from her womb into the small of her back, while she waited for Carl and Hannah's marriage ceremony to begin. Her mother-in-law and Esther were seated beside her and Sarah had just voiced her disapproval of the synagogue being unadorned with flowers for a wedding.

"So Hannah doesn't believe in a big fuss," Esther shrugged.

"A register office she'd have got married in if she'd had her way!" Sarah said tartly.

Carl's prediction of the effect Hannah would have upon her had materialized at their first meeting.

"God she doesn't believe in, either!" Sarah went on. "When she told me, I nearly fainted."

"She's a very unusual woman, Ma," Rebecca said placatingly. "Perhaps it's because she went to university."

"So did your husband, but his Maker he hasn't yet abandoned," Sarah replied. "And such a short engagement as

Hannah and Carl's I never heard of. With my children I wouldn't allow it."

Esther shared a smile with Rebecca and adjusted the silver-fox tie Ben had given her for her birthday, enjoying the luxurious feel of it. She still didn't know how he had managed to pay for it, but it looked superb with her black coat and eye-veiled hat and for once she didn't care.

"You can know a person all your life, Mother, and still make a mistake," she said. "Like Carl and I nearly did. Thank God I had the sense to break our engagement and marry Ben. And in my opinion, Hannah's the right girl for Carl."

"She's got peculiar notions if that's what you mean. A navy blue costume to get married in?" Sarah gasped when Hannah entered on Sammy's arm. "With a green hat and blouse!"

She surveyed the rest of the bridal entourage with more pleasure. Having no family of her own, Hannah had asked Miriam and Sammy to accompany her under the marriage canopy and nobody could say Miriam did not look right for the occasion, Sarah thought eyeing her daughter-in-law's soft, cream dress and matching turban.

Helga was matron-of-honor in dusky-pink and had made her own outfit and her sister's, as she had been doing they were girls. She had offered to make a wedding-dress for Hannah, but the unconventional young woman had refused to wear one. Despite this, Helga and Miriam had decided to wear what was suitable for the occasion. Not for anything would they have let their dead mother down.

Sarah was thinking of their mother as she watched Sigmund take his place beside Carl, with his new wife. Life has to go on, she thought to herself with a sigh. But he was already showing signs of not being happy with her. "At least Hannah agreed to have bridesmaids," she said, admiring her granddaughters, who were positioning themselves self-consciously. "Even if their frocks don't match."

The little girls' dresses were the same style, but Marianne's was lavender and Shirley's lemon.

Esther laughed and wished she could get up and straighten the slippery satin bow in her daughter's hair. "Hannah didn't want them to match," she told Sarah.

"I'm not surprised."

The reception was held at Helga's.

"Smoked salmon they can't afford!" Gertie Moritz, whom the family still privately called Gertie Fish, sniffed, eyeing the refreshments Helga and Miriam had prepared. She sat down beside Sarah. "And if I'd known Carl's bride would not be wearing white, I wouldn't have stood under the *Chupah* with him."

"Seeing you are his father's wife, you had no choice," Sarah replied crisply. Her own disapproval of Hannah was no reason to ally herself with the monstrous Gertie.

Sarah helped herself to a chopped-herring sandwich and let her eye wander around the room. The brass candlesticks on the table, in which Carl and Hannah's wedding-day candles were burning brightly, had been brought from Vienna by Rachel Moritz, but had not lost their luster. Helga had preserved them as she had the homely atmosphere that had always pervaded this household and had no life outside it. What would she do now she was no longer needed here?

David was considering this, too, and hoped he knew the answer. He had just seen Moishe Lipkin follow Helga into the scullery. A few minutes later Moishe returned alone, looking gloomy, and David ushered him into the lobby for a private word.

"Helga said no to you again?" he said sympathetically.

Moishe straightened his gray silk tie in front of the hall-way mirror and nodded. "They want her to stay," he sighed thrusting his hands into his trouser pockets and leaning against the wall disconsolately.

"And what about what *she* wants?"

"You know Helga. When did she ever put herself number one? First it was her mother, then her father and next her brother. Now, she's thinking of Carl and Hannah's children, would you believe?"

"No, I wouldn't."

"Neither would I, but it's true. She said if she was going to marry anyone it'd be me. But Hannah told her she'll never have any kids if it means giving up her career to look after them. That was all Helga needed to hear."

"She's still young enough to have her own!" David ex-postulated.

"That's what I said to her, but it did no good."

"I'll have a talk with her if you like."

Moishe knew David's reputation as the family "fixer" and smiled gratefully. "This is something even you can't arrange, or believe me I'd let you. Helga's always been a mug for other people, and she wouldn't keep on being one unless she enjoyed it; some folk are like that. She's here for life. So I won't have a wife on my conscience when I'm away traveling," he shrugged with a wry grin. "Let's go back inside and have a *schnapps* on it."

Bessie drew David aside as he entered the crowded room. "Rebecca thinks her labor's started. But she's only told me; she hasn't told Nat."

David saw his young sister-in-law bite her lip and put down her tea cup. His mother would have recognized the signs immediately but she was seated with Esther on the other side of the table and a big vase of flowers in the center was shielding Rebecca from their view. Nathan was beside the window, talking to Lou and Cora.

"Perhaps you should tell him?" Bessie said playing with her pearls anxiously.

"I think we should keep out of it," David replied. Even in a matter like this his brother was capable of accusing him of interfering.

Rebecca said nothing to Nathan until they were driving home. "Everyone would have fussed around me," she said after she had told him. "I didn't want to spoil Hannah's wedding day," she added and the poignancy of her smile made Nathan think she was remembering her own.

How naïve I was then, Rebecca reflected. And how trusting.

"If you don't fancy him, you don't have to have him," her parents had said when the matchmaker arranged a meeting with Nathan. He'd been the first suitor she had agreed to meet and she had only done so because her father wanted her to marry a professional man and had finally worn her down. But she'd fallen for Nat the moment he walked into her home and appraised her with his soft, dark eyes. Not like her sister, who'd turned down two doctors and an accountant before settling for a good-looking solicitor.

I was happy at first, she thought, fingering the silky, brown ermine shrouding the rise of her abdomen in which lay the child she had believed was the proof of their love for each other.

"All right?" Nathan asked in the kind of voice she had heard him use addressing his patients.

Rebecca nodded and smiled to herself bitterly. Happy in

her ignorance, that's what she'd been. Thinking she'd kindled the same fire in him that he had in her. But now she knew he loved someone else—that all she had aroused in him was lust, which a man could feel for any woman, and the baby was proof of nothing more than that.

Nathan kept his eyes on the road, aware of his wife's unspoken reproach. She had plenty to reproach him for, but what could he do about it? Other than be completely honest with her, which wouldn't help. Instead he gave vent to jibes and innuendo whenever the pretense his marriage was became unbearable, hurting and confusing Rebecca in order to relieve his own feelings, then resuming their uneasy relationship until the next flare-up.

Re-encountering Mary in his family's presence had brought home to him how far they had moved apart and he'd thought of her less often since then. Perhaps because the warm, affectionate girl who had obsessed his thoughts no longer existed. In her place was a cool, abrasive woman who, except for a brief moment, had avoided looking at him. So why couldn't he love Rebecca and make her happy, like Lou had done with his wife? Cora was plain and dumpy, but her father Harry Rothberg owned property as well as a rainwear factory, and her dowry had enabled Lou to find something lovable in her. A few weeks ago she'd given Lou a son, which seemed to have enhanced his manufactured feelings for her. To hear him talk about his wife these days you'd think their marriage had been a love match!

I'm capable of manufacturing feelings, that's my trouble, Nathan said to himself dispassionately. Then he saw Rebecca blanch as another pain gripped her and he was beset by guilt because he had brought this upon her. He'd have to try to be, for the sake of his wife and child.

"Everything's going to be fine, love," he said determinedly when they arrived home. "After the baby's born we won't be on edge with each other like we've been lately." He took her coat to hang it in the cloakroom and did not see the look she gave him.

Bridie had just returned from her Sunday evening out and was hovering in the hall, eyeing her mistress speculatively. " 'Twon't be long now, Doctor-surr," she pronounced.

But Rebecca's labor continued for three days.

"My Cora, bless her, had more *mazel*, having our Philip

so quickly," Lou commiserated while he sat playing *pisha-paysha* with Nathan on the third evening.

"Luck's your middle name, Lou. For you everything's easy, but for me it's always the hard way," Nathan said abandoning the card game and getting up to pace the room. "If Rebecca was someone else's wife she'd probably be out of her misery by now."

"Come off it, Nat!"

"And she won't even let me sit with her, will she?" Nathan exclaimed.

His placid friend poured him a whiskey and made him drink it. "She will when it's over, and then I can have a drink, too," he declared crossing his fingers as Bridie summoned him upstairs.

Rebecca had refused to have a midwife attend her, and Nathan was thankful for the maid's reliable presence in the house. Bridie must think it strange that his family weren't rallying around him, but Rebecca liked her privacy and had asked him to tell everyone but Bessie not to come.

Why his disagreeable sister-in-law was the exception, he had no idea. His mother and Miriam would gladly have left their households, to be with his wife during her travail, but he had thought it best to humor her. David had brought Bessie each morning before going to work and collected her in the evening when Nathan returned from the surgery. Life was still conspiring to put him in his brother's debt!

The cry of a new-born infant cut into his thoughts, then he heard Bridie shout joyfully from the upstairs landing. " 'Tis a girl, Doctor-surr! An' as bonny as iver ye did see!"

Nathan sat numbly by the fire listening to the clock tick away fifteen minutes. Rebecca would not want him in the room yet. When he went upstairs, she was wearing an oyster-satin nightgown and Bridie was brushing her hair.

"You don't look as if you've just given birth," he smiled kissing her cheek.

Lou was rolling down his shirtsleeves. "What's that in the cradle, then?"

Nathan turned to look at his daughter. "She's got red hair," he said sounding surprised.

"It's in the family; you can't blame the milkman," Lou grinned. "Pick her up already!"

Nathan eyed the infant nervously.

"Anyone'd think he'd never held one before," his friend teased.

Handling babies is part of a doctor's routine, but it's different when it's your own, Nathan thought, lifting the tiny bundle and cradling it against him. It was not just a thought, but a sensation, too, that clutched at your entrails and turned you to jelly.

"How does it feel?" Lou inquired.

Nathan touched his daughter's fragile hand and felt it close around his thumb and it was as if she had taken hold of his heart. He surrendered himself to the primeval emotion, unknown to him until that moment. "Marvelous," he said swallowing hard.

"But we can't call a girl Leon George, can we?" he laughed to Rebecca. "She'll have to be Leona Georgina."

"Whatever you like, Nat."

"I was joking, love."

"It doesn't matter."

"Of course it matters."

"All right. We'll call her that."

"Are you sure you want to? We don't have to decide this minute," Nathan said.

"The name's all right; stop making such a fuss about it," Rebecca answered irritably.

"Put Leona back in the cradle, Nat," Lou interceded. "We'll go downstairs and let Rebecca rest. Bridie can bring her a nice glass of milk."

"I don't want any milk."

"It isn't for you," Lou smiled, "it's for the baby."

"I'm not going to feed the baby."

There was a moment of silence while Nathan and Lou avoided looking at each other and Bridie stood twisting a corner of her apron, with a shocked expression on her face.

Lou began packing his medical bag. "What do you mean you're not going to feed the baby?" he said to Rebecca.

"I don't want to," she replied studying her fingernails.

Nathan was aware of a new tenderness spilling over to his wife from his feeling for their child. "Every mother breastfeeds if she can, love," he said gently.

"And Rebecca won't have any trouble," Lou added, casting a professional glance at her full, blue-veined cleavage. "She'll change her mind," he told Nathan as they walked downstairs.

But Rebecca did not change her mind, and when Sarah called to see her new granddaughter, Bridie opened the front door with a full breastpump clutched in her hand.

" 'Tis a tirrible waste t'throw it away, ma'am," Bridie said grimly.

"So what can you do?" Sarah sighed. Nathan had called to see her whilst doing his rounds and told her about it. When she entered the bedroom, Bessie was giving Leona a bottle. Rebecca was lying reading.

"You don't want to feed her the bottle either, Rebecca?" Sarah said. "So what is a mother for?"

"I hope you haven't come to lecture me, Ma."

"Anyone can hold a bottle, it doesn't have to be the mother," Bessie declared. "You can give it to her if you like, Ma."

"No thanks."

Sarah's disapproval changed to disquiet. She stayed for an hour and noticed that Rebecca did not glance at the baby once.

"Who looks after Leona when Bessie's gone home and Bridie's asleep in bed?" she asked Nathan the next time she saw him alone.

"Who do you think? But I don't mind, Mother," Nathan smiled. His love for his child had deepened day by day and getting up during the night to attend to her was no trouble to him.

Early one morning, when he had fed the baby and was changing her diaper, he was called to a patient who had had a seizure. "You'll have to finish cleaning Leona up," he said to Rebecca, donning a pullover and trousers over his pajamas and hurrying away.

When he returned, the baby was lying exactly as he had left her, her thighs and bottom crusted with the stool he had not had time to clean away, and now blue with cold.

Rebecca was lying in bed with her back towards the cradle.

"How could you leave a young baby in a state like that? She wasn't even covered!" Nathan rebuked her and began rubbing Leona's legs to restore the circulation.

"It was you who left her like that."

"But I asked you to see to her, didn't I? What would happen to her if Bridie and Bessie weren't here during the day?"

"I don't know."

"What do you mean, you don't know?" Nathan asked angrily. "You'd have to do what they've been doing, look after your child, like every other mother does. You weren't lazy before Leona was born."

"I'm not lazy now. I baked a cake this morning."

"So why won't you do anything for the baby?"

Rebecca stared up at the ceiling impassively as she had done throughout the exchange. "I don't want to."

It was then that Nathan accepted what Lou had been saying to him for days. His wife was suffering from post-natal depression. They had similar cases among their patients. Women sometimes neglected their homes after childbirth, or their appearance. Some turned against their husbands, but it was rare for a woman to reject her child.

That evening, he called to see his parents on his way home from the surgery, letting himself in with the latch-key his mother had insisted he keep when he married.

Sarah and Abraham were sitting by the kitchen fire, the singing kettle on the hob lending an air of peace to the homely room.

Nathan shut the door and leaned against it. "I don't know what I'm going to do," he told them.

"First you'll sit down," Abraham said rising from the rocking chair.

Nathan lowered himself wearily into it and warmed his cold hands in front of the flames.

"And now you'll talk to us about it," Sarah said to him quietly. "What are parents for?"

Nathan could feel their love reaching out to him and regarded them gratefully. But there was nothing they could do to help him. "There's nothing to talk about. You know the position," he said.

Sarah smiled. "Positions of one kind and another there always are in a family, Nat. So everyone puts their heads together to see what can be done. And once or twice I've taken matters into my own hands."

"That, there's no need to tell us," Abraham put in. "We know you already. Remember when she got rid of Bessie's Auntie Rivka who was ruling the roost in David's house?" he reminded Nathan.

"For months Bessie lay in her bed after that stillborn child," Sarah reminisced. "With no reason to get up while that woman was there waiting on her hand and foot, encouraging her not to get better. So now Bessie's doing likewise to Rebecca and no good can come of it."

"Rebecca wants her there," Nathan replied. "I've never liked Bessie, but I have to admit she's being a brick."

"That doesn't mean what she's doing is right for your wife," Sarah insisted. "Ask her not to come any more and send Bridie home to Ireland for a holiday. Then Rebecca will look after the baby, you'll see."

"No she won't, Mother."

"Twenty pounds I'd bet you if I had it."

"You'd lose the bet. Because Rebecca doesn't love the baby."

Sarah and Abraham exchanged a shocked glance. How could a mother not love her own child?

Nathan got up to take an apple from the bowl of fruit on the dresser and bit into it. "My wife is mentally ill," he said flatly.

Sarah poked the fire and hid her alarm. "How did she get that way?"

"Childbirth brought it on. It sometimes does."

"Brought it on? Or brought it out?"

"What's the difference?" Nathan said impatiently.

"To bring something out it would first have to be there."

Nathan chewed the apple slowly and thought about it.

"You'd like my opinion?" his mother inquired. "I'll give it to you anyway. Rebecca stopped being herself before Leona was born. Anyone could see it. And if you ask me, she's bottling something up inside her which needs to be got rid of. Like a boil gets better after the pus is drawn from it."

Could his mother be right? Nathan pondered as he drove home. What she had said about Rebecca not being herself before the baby's birth was true. Was his treatment of her responsible for this trauma?

He brooded about it while he ate his lonely, evening meal. Rebecca had retired early, as she now did every night. She had not resumed her activities with the Refugee Committee, nor had she been to the *Shabbos* tea parties, and it struck him for the first time that his wife was escaping from something—that her rejection of Leona was not the only symptom of her condition. And why was it Bessie she wanted with her? Even her own mother's offer to stay for a while had been refused.

Why had he not attached any significance to all this before now? He'd allowed his personal involvement to blur his professional eye. Which proved it made sense that doctors shouldn't treat their own wives. When he went upstairs, Rebecca was buffing her nails at the dressing-table. And humming, as she nearly always was these days. Was that another symptom? He tried to recognize the tune, but it was just an unmusical buzz, flat and toneless.

How beautiful she is, he thought with a pang. Her hair, released from its daytime chignon, lay sleekly upon her shoulders and he could see the satiny gleam of her flesh through the coffee-lace négligé she had slipped on. It was the one she had worn on their wedding night, when her body had still been a mystery to him.

"It's been a long time since we made love," he said thickly. But she went on polishing her nails and continued humming, as though she had not heard him, her expression telling him nothing. What was she thinking? The intimacies he had shared with her did not enable him to read her mind.

Nathan got his pajamas from under his pillow and began to undress. "Remember how we used to go to bed on Sunday afternoons?" he said to Rebecca, but again she did not reply and he had to restrain himself from grabbing her beautiful shoulders and shaking her out of her apathy. There was no physical reason not to resume their sexual relationship; she had had the baby in February and it was now May. But her indifference to their child had dulled Nathan's libido. He had not felt the urge to make love to Rebecca until tonight. If he tried to, would he be rejected, too?

"Cora came round with Philip this afternoon," Rebecca said conversationally. "I never saw such an ugly baby."

But his mother adores him, so what does it matter? Nathan wanted to reply. His desire had fizzled out like a snuffed candle; but memories of the bodily pleasures he had known with Rebecca were all about him in the room, as the pungent aftermath of the candle would be. He brushed them aside and put on his dressing gown. Leona was in her cradle in the kitchen and he must bring her upstairs, so Bridie could go to bed.

"There was never such a pretty child as ours," he declared.

Rebecca's humming grew louder and he knew she was trying to shut out what she did not want to hear.

"You'd know if you bothered to look at her," he went on.

Rebecca got into bed and pulled the covers over her head.

The next morning, whilst they were eating breakfast, David rang up to tell them Bessie had a head cold and would not be coming.

"Bridie can see to the child," Rebecca said.

Her impersonal reference to their daughter chilled Nathan to the marrow. But the day-to-day problems of raising Leona were uppermost in his mind. Bessie couldn't be expected to do what she'd been doing indefinitely.

Rebecca was eating a boiled egg and had the *Daily Express* propped up against the teapot in front of her. "Mussolini's conquered Abyssinia," she said.

Nathan had not even glanced at his *Manchester Guardian* and at that moment could not have cared less about what was going on in the world. "We'll get a nurse to live in; then we won't have to trouble anyone," he said wearily.

Rebecca raised her eyes from the newspaper. "Any particular nurse?"

How long had she known about Mary? Nathan's throat constricted and his heart began to pound, so great was his shock in discovering that she did know. Then his mind detached itself from his emotions. Draw the pus from the boil, his mother had said and perhaps the truth was the best poultice. "So I was in love with a nurse once," he made himself say casually.

"You still are."

Rebecca's face was expressionless, but Nathan could feel her anger pulsating beneath the surface. "I was when I married you," he admitted unreservedly and paused to consider his next words. "I don't think I am any more."

Rebecca poured herself a cup of tea and stirred it carefully.

"David's marriage wasn't a love affair, either," he added. "But Bessie's happy with him."

"Is she? I know all about it, Nat. He was still in love with Miriam when he married Bessie, wasn't he? And he married her for money, like you did with me. She told me everything that day we went to the hospital together; she was upset because they'd had a row."

"Did she tell you about Mary?"

"No. I told her. It was written on your face that night. Bessie and I are in the same boat. She hates Miriam and I hate that Sister."

The reason for his wife's sudden affinity with Bessie was now clear to Nathan. But it was only a side effect of what ailed her. "Leona's the one you seem to hate," he said bitterly. "What's she done to deserve it?"

"It's what she represents," Rebecca replied staring at her egg. Then stabbed the spoon through it, violently, as though whatever she was containing within herself had broken free and caused her to do it. "The things I let you do to me in the name of love," she said quiveringly. "But it wasn't love. You were using me."

Nathan got up and went to stare out of the window at the heavy blossom on the flowering cherry tree, but feasting his eyes on it did nothing for the hunger in his heart. He could hear Rebecca weeping, but did not go to comfort her. She wouldn't want him to. What was it he was hungering for? He tried to analyze it, but could not attach the feeling to anything specific. It was just a general emptiness that had suddenly overwhelmed him.

He turned from the window and saw his wife rocking back and forth in her chair, her arms wrapped tightly about herself, tears gushing down her face and splashing unheeded on to her housecoat.

"I'd better go; I'll be late for surgery," he said heavily.

Then a shriek from Bridie sent them both fleeing to the kitchen.

" 'Twasn't my fault," the maid greeted them. She was standing by the hearth with her cap on askew, trying to soothe Leona who was crying piteously. "Bridie wouldn't let no harm cum t'her own wee darlin'. 'Twas a wicked bit o' coal spittin' out o' t'foire on her precious leg. There, me little sweet—" she began to croon, but stopped in mid-sentence.

Rebecca had snatched Leona from her.

"Will ye look at herself now!" Bridie beamed recovering from her surprise.

Nathan required a moment to recover, too. His wife was cradling the baby against her breast, kissing the small red welt on the child's plump thigh.

"I hope you've got something good for burns, Nat," she said. "We don't want her to grow up with a scar."

After he had attended to his daughter's leg, Nathan went to tell his mother what had happened. His patients could wait!

Sarah smiled sagely. "Cats have been known to devour their own kittens, but they'd scratch to death anyone else who tried to harm them."

"And nobody can say you're not an authority on cats," Nathan teased her.

"By now, I know a thing or two about people, as well. So everything is all right, thank God. And also I hope you've learned something, Nat."

"I have."

Sarah resumed polishing her brass, which his arrival had interrupted. "Including that when a marriage is arranged and not a love match the wife needs a bit of extra attention to make her forget it? In my day she didn't. But from what I've seen with two of my daughters-in-law, these days they do."

Nathan had learned a good deal more than that and began applying his new insight to his work, probing his patients with questions when they unloaded their personal problems in his surgery, instead of just listening with half an ear. He established that Mrs. Kaplan's wheeze only occurred when her sons lost money at the dog races, that the medicine he prescribed had no effect, but a win for her boys cleared her chest immediately. He had not yet fathomed why little Sidney Jacobs stuttered when his father brought him to the surgery in search of a cure, but chattered away impediment-free when he came with his mother. Or why so many married women complained of headaches from which they had not suffered when they were single. Now, these and similar mysteries began to obsess his thoughts.

"You're a doctor, not a detective," Lou said when they discussed it.

"All diagnosis is detection and patients have minds as well as bodies. One can play havoc with the other."

"Me, I've got enough to do seeing with my eyes and listening with my stethoscope!" Lou exclaimed impatiently. "But trust you to get involved with intangibles."

"How can one treat the whole person, otherwise?" Nathan replied, but it fell on deaf ears.

Despite his partner's skepticism, the interrelation of psyche and soma continued to intrigue and absorb him as medicine in the accepted sense had never done, providing an incentive his working life had hitherto lacked. Persistent symptoms for which there was no physical cause were no longer a nuisance, but a challenge to him, and even Lou was impressed when young Sidney Jacobs's stutter was traced to his father once having threatened to cut off his tongue because he talked too much. Nathan was now required to convince the boy that his father had not meant it, but this too was a challenge and he relished the therapy as much as he had the delving.

Mother'd say there's never an ill wind, he thought after relaying his findings to Lou. The traumatic aftermath of Leona's birth had put him through hell, but it had led him to an exciting new aspect of medicine.

Chapter Ten

After Rebecca's crisis was over Bessie could not adjust to her normal routine. "I don't know what I used to do with myself all day," she told David one morning while he dressed for work.

Nor do I, David thought. The household had functioned as usual during his wife's absence. With a maid like Lizzie Wilson, who could produce traditional Jewish dishes in addition to coping with all the other household tasks, the mistress was dispensable.

"You used to see your friends in the afternoons, didn't you?" he reminded his wife. "Why not ask someone round?"

"Maybe I will," Bessie said. But the prospect appeared to offer her no comfort.

"Or go and have tea in town."

"I can't do that every day. It's a waste of time," Bessie declared.

David eyed her with surprise. Had she suddenly realized what an empty life she'd lived? He had always been aware of it, but would not have dared voice his opinion. He watched her get out of bed and put on her dressing gown. "You've lost weight, love," he remarked.

"When I was looking after Leona I didn't sit eating toffees." Bessie sat down at the dressing-table to brush her hair, which had regrown in curling, silver tendrils, though it had been straight and mousey-brown before the disastrous perm. "Fancy going gray at my age," she said as she did every morning. "I look more like fifty than thirty-six."

David made his regular reply. "It looks nice. On you it isn't aging."

Bessie surveyed her appearance, which was softer and more natural than the self she remembered. She put down her brush and shrugged. "I don't care if it looks nice or not."

David stopped knotting his tie. This was not the Bessie he remembered either.

"I'm fed up with myself," she added disconsolately. "Nobody needs me."

"The kids and I need you. What're you talking about?"

"But they're at school and you're at work."

"You didn't do much for them before they were school age," David said. "Lizzie looked after them, didn't she?"

The defensive outburst he expected did not come.

"I wish I had, but it's too late now, isn't it?" Bessie answered quietly.

David could not believe his ears. "By the way, I'm definitely changing the firm's name," he said to distract her. She had protested angrily when he told her he was considering doing so, but again the reaction he anticipated did not materialize. "The Sanderstyle labels are already printed, but I'll need your signature to register the company," he added.

"Naturally you will," she replied disinterestedly. "As Dad left his half of the business to me, I'm your partner, aren't I?"

David was dumbfounded. What had happened to the petulant, difficult woman he'd married? The conversation had delayed him and when he arrived at the factory, Eli, the cutter, was pacing the workroom waiting to consult him about the design detail for a special order.

"Let me take off my coat before you start on me!" David expostulated.

Eli took his watch from his pocket and glanced at it censoriously. "Ten minutes late he is and he wants I should wait."

"You tell him, Eli," Abraham, who had entered with David, said with equal disapproval. "He kept me standing in the porch, wondering where he was. Maybe I'll come to work on the tram in future."

"Who would let us in if Eli didn't have a key to the place and you were late like this?" Issie, the senior machiner, rebuked David above the rumble of the sewing machines.

"That's why he has one. In case I am," David retorted and went into his office with Eli dogging his footsteps.

"What's with double flaps on the pockets all of a sudden?" Eli demanded, brandishing the sketch David had left for him. He slapped it down on the desk and took out a handkerchief to blow his bulbous, red nose.

"The customer wants it."

"We're selling to lunatics these days?"

David curbed his impatience. "You thought I was one, didn't you, Eli? The day you and Issie made our first fashion sample."

"So I was wrong about you. I apologize for thinking it."

"If you and Issie'd had your way, raincoats would still be shapeless slip-ons! But I don't want your apologies, what I want is your cooperation."

Eli tucked his thumbs into the armholes of his waistcoat and stared down at the permanent stains on the shiny serge, ruminatively. "So you'll get it, don't you always? Only thank God there won't be the name Salaman on the labels of those double-pocket-flap coats!"

He returned to his bench to prepare the pattern for the garments he did not want to make, indignation in his every move, David noted, watching him through the glass partition. Eli didn't approve of the firm's name being changed, either. Nor did Issie. But David had not expected them to. Even though his father-in-law was dead and had taken no active part in the business since the war, employees like Eli and Issie, who had spent all their working lives at Salaman's, retained their respect for him though his treatment of them had merited anything but.

But there was no question of the workers' loyalty to himself, either, David mused while he opened the mail. The way Eli and Issie had ticked him off wouldn't have been countenanced by many employers, but it was their personal interest in the business that made them feel entitled to speak their minds and he would not have had it otherwise.

During the mid-morning break, he took his tea and bagel into the workroom, as he often did, ever cognizant of having once been a worker himself and that his staff were human beings, who appreciated a friendly word from their boss.

"How're the children, David?" Millie Greenbaum, another longtime employee, greeted him from behind her machine.

"I've brought some new snaps to show you," David smiled, taking them from his pocket and passing them around.

"Let me see already!" Millie said, impatiently snatching them from Eli. "Shirley's getting to look like your sister Esther, David," she pronounced.

"And Ronald's the image of your Nat," Eli declared. "He should only have his brains, also."

David smiled stiffly. Once he'd been pleased his son resembled his handsome young brother, but not any more! "Did I tell you our Shirley's passed the scholarship for Central High School?" he said proudly.

"Half a dozen times," Issie chuckled through a mouthful of blackbread and butter.

"My lad's passed ter go there, an' all," a quiet, Gentile woman who had joined the staff a fortnight ago said from the second row of machines.

"That's marvelous, Emily," David congratulated her warmly. Thank goodness education wasn't only available to kids whose parents could afford to pay for it, he thought. If it were, he wouldn't have gone, however briefly, to that school himself.

"That's why I've gone back ter work," Emily added sipping her tea. "Ter mek up fer what our John won't earn till later on. 'E's got 'is eye on't university!" she laughed.

"Good luck to him," David applauded. In the Sandberg family, only Nat had been that lucky and everyone else, himself included, had slaved to bring it about. "I've got something else to show you," he smiled collecting himself and handing a piece of paper to Eli. "Remember how our Shirley used to draw pictures on your bench with chalk, when she was a tiny tot? She's still at it, but she uses a pencil these days."

Eli studied Shirley's sketch of Lizzie Wilson. "She's a better artist than you, David."

"Who wouldn't be?" David grinned. But he was proud

of his daughter's talent. The drawing he had shown to Eli had a three-dimensional quality which even after years of sketching designs he could not achieve.

Millie and Issie had a look at it, too.

"P'rhaps she'll take over the designing here when she grows up," Millie said.

"That somebody should, I'm looking forward to," Eli added snidely.

"And then you'll maybe be better tempered," Issie said to him. "After all these years of trying to make head or tail of David's designs."

David took the bantering and the laughter at his expense in good humor. "Who knows?" he shrugged. But the possibility excited him. What could be better than having both his children in the business, helping him reach the heights he intended to attain? Ronald he was sure of. His son's future was here waiting. Shirley could turn out to be an unexpected bonus.

It had occurred to him whilst driving to the factory that Bessie could learn to type and keep the books, now she had lost taste for frittering away her time. But her presence at the factory was not a pleasant prospect. The workers who remembered her as Isaac Salaman's spoiled daughter wouldn't be comfortable with her around; nor would Sammy for whom she had only contempt.

Sammy was not at work today. The specialist Nathan had sent him to see had not advocated surgery, but was seeing him regularly and had just ordered a week of bed rest. David made a note on his desk pad to remind him to deliver Sammy's wage envelope on Friday. As if I need reminding, he thought. The secret guilt he carried for his brother's plight would haunt him till the end of his days.

Hugo Frankl, who owned a store in Oldham, arrived to see the new line, and David brushed his family problems aside and escorted him to the room where samples were hung on rails.

"How's your father?" he inquired.

Hugo sighed. "A businessman he'll never be, but I let him think he is. What can you do?"

"And your mother?"

"The same as always," Hugo replied cryptically.

David gave him a sympathetic smile. The brittle, nagging Paula Frankl he'd known since his childhood would never change.

"Not that Father wants to be a businessman," Hugo shrugged. "He'd still be working for that glazier in Red Bank, who he got a job with when we first came to England, if it weren't for me."

And he'd probably be a damn sight happier, David thought. All Ludwig Frankl had ever wanted was to earn his bread as simply as possible and, like his friend Sigmund Moritz, be left alone with his books and music.

Hugo was examining the samples. "My cousin with three shops in London tells me some of his manufacturers have got showrooms now," he imparted.

"Does it make the garments any better?" David smiled.

Hugo licked his lips, a habit David remembered from their schooldays. "Any garment is improved with a good figure inside it," he winked. "They use girls instead of coathangers."

There's a lot I don't know about selling, David mused after Hugo had given him an order and gone. Sending Moishe out to see buyers in other towns was only part of it. He thought of asking one of his machinists to try on the coats next time a customer called, but it would mean letting a machine stand idle for however long it took. And none of his female employees had a really good shape. For fifteen bob a week he could take on a young girl to help in the office and make sure he chose one who had.

As always, when he made a snap decision he implemented it immediately and went out to arrange a suitable advertisement in the *Manchester Evening News*. Afterwards, instead of returning to the factory to eat his lunch, he drove home to see Bessie whose depressed countenance kept floating to the forefront of his mind.

"T'missis 'as gone out wi' 'er nex' door," Lizzie told him. "An' yer could o' knocked me down wi' a feather when she said as she were goin' ter."

David was amazed, too. Bessie had never liked their next-door neighbor.

"Terday were t'first time they'd spoke since Mrs. Levy ticked t'missis off fer only wearin' a *sheitel* 'cause she lost 'er 'air an' not fer religion's sake," Lizzie added.

David could think of nothing his wife and Mrs. Levy had in common now that Bessie no longer wore a wig.

"She's a marvelous person," Bessie said when he expressed his opinion that night. "I went with her to help at the Soup Kitchen today."

He was putting a cigarette in his mouth and paused with it in mid-air. Their neighbor's devotion to charitable work was well known, but Bessie had never shown the slightest inclination to participate in it. He lit the cigarette and gave her a perplexed glance.

"I'm going to help there again; I enjoyed it," she declared. "And I'm joining the other committees she belongs to. There's a lot of good work to be done in this town."

It won't last, David thought. She'll soon be gallivanting around town with her friends again, like she used to do. No woman could change to this extent permanently.

Time proved David wrong. Bessie's appetite for doing good seemed insatiable.

"I'm pleased she spends her time helping people, but I still don't understand it," David told his mother when he called to collect some rummage she was giving for a sale which one of Bessie's committees was organizing.

"What's to understand?" Sarah answered. "Helping others is a pleasure, once you find it out."

David picked up an old saucepan Sarah had not yet put into the carton and fingered the lid absently. "But it isn't like Bessie to be so selfless."

Sarah smiled. "That, she isn't entirely being."

"You mean she gets personal satisfaction from it?"

Sarah took the pan from him and polished the pitted aluminium with a cloth; whoever bought one of her discarded utensils, even if they only paid threepence for it, would find it in shining condition. "Which do-gooder could deny that and be honest? But also they relieve a lot of misery, and they're entitled to their satisfaction."

A few days later, Bessie rang up David at the factory. "You won't believe who was queueing for soup today," she said grimly.

"I'll be doing it myself if you keep interrupting me when I'm trying to earn a living!" he answered impatiently.

"Who else should I interrupt and ask to deliver things sometimes to poor people? All my friends' husbands do it."

"I know. They've told me." Bessie's friends these days were not the shallow women with whom she had mixed prior to her transformation, and he preferred their husbands to the last lot.

"It was Sigmund Moritz, David."

"What?"

"Queueing for soup."

For a moment David could not take it in.

"But he didn't have any," Bessie said, while he was recovering from his confusion. "He ran a mile when he saw me."

After Bessie had rung off, David tapped on the glass partition and beckoned his brother into the office.

"My father-in-law'd have to be starving before he'd queue for free food," Sammy declared when David had told him.

"Exactly." David looked thoughtful. "But since he married Gertie Fish, his income's come from her business, hasn't it?"

"I think she just gives him spending money."

"What a lovely situation for a man to be in! He'd never have given up tailoring if she hadn't insisted on it."

Sammy's face was puckered with distress. "When he moved out, Helga wanted to clear his workshop to use it as a parlor, but he wouldn't let her. He goes to sit there by himself sometimes, when he visits them. Do you think he's left Gertie?"

"Why else would he be wandering about hungry and penniless? He told Mother his marriage wasn't paradise, but his pride would never let him tell any of us a thing like this. We must try to find him, Sammy."

They went first to Gertie's shop to inquire if she knew where Sigmund was staying and found her behind the counter in a muddle of the haberdashery from which she made her lucrative living.

"You've come for his things, I suppose," she rasped the moment she saw them. "So take them and good riddance!" She flung aside a dusty, red velvet curtain, her pouter-pigeon chest heaving, and shouted up a flight of narrow stairs. "Mona!"

A pair of stick-like legs, clad in wrinkled black hose and with two odd shoes on the feet, appeared on the landing.

"Throw down the suitcase with that dogsbody's belongings in it," Gertie instructed vindictively. "Me, I wouldn't soil my hands packing it. It's enough my poor charlady had to," she told the cluster of customers.

Sammy had turned crimson, and David had to fight the urge to throttle her. They exchanged an embarrassed glance. Had the woman no sense of propriety?

Gertie resumed measuring some blue-sequin trimming. "I don't blame them looking ashamed, related to such a *ganef*," she told the fat lady she was serving.

"It's terrible," the lady agreed.

"I beg your pardon?" David interceded.

The customer looked nervous, but Gertie's eyes merely grew stonier.

"It's no secret round here what a life I've had with him," she informed the brothers.

"You called him a thief," David said icily.

"What else would you call someone you catch with their hand in the till?" Gertie spat as Sigmund's suitcase thumped down the stairs.

David strode to get it, sending a boxful of tiny, silver buglebeads scattering on to the floor in his haste to escape from her venom. He could hear his shoes crunching on them as he made his exit.

Sammy was already outside. "It'll take her hours to pick 'em all up," he said with satisfaction watching Gertie scrabbling on her hands and knees.

Then the fat lady slammed the door on them.

David put down the suitcase and tried to pull himself together. "I don't know how I stopped myself from hitting the lying bitch!"

Sammy was looking at the battered old valise. "He brought that with him from Vienna."

"I know," David said heavily. There was something pathetically lonely about it, dumped on the pavement in the July sunshine, with its owner heaven-knew-where. "Carl told me it was so full of books his father couldn't walk more than a few steps without putting it down." How had a man of Sigmund's intellectual stature come to this? The same way Ludwig Frankl had let himself in for the life he had with Paula. Intellect didn't always go hand in hand with good sense.

"I'm devoted to Sigmund, but there're times when I could give him a good shaking and this is one of them!" he fumed as they got into the car. "Why should I have to leave my business to look after itself and go looking for him? If he had any sense he'd be with the family now, instead of causing us all this trouble."

He lit a cigarette and sat tapping his fingers on the steering wheel when a bread van, making a delivery on a side street he was using as a short cut to Cheetham Hill, held them up.

Sammy sat rubbing his leg, which always seemed to ache more than usual when he was under stress. "You don't think he'll do anything daft, do you, David?"

David did not reply, but prickled with alarm. The old fool was capable of throwing himself under a tram, rather than face the family after he'd been seen queueing for soup. "It's no use trying to keep it from Miriam and Helga. We'd better go and tell them," he said brusquely.

The sisters were sitting together in Miriam's kitchen, winding some knitting yarn for a shawl Helga was making for the baby Hannah expected in December.

Miriam let the white skein on her wrists fall to the floor when David and Sammy entered. "What're you doing here at this time? What's the matter?"

After they had been told, she leapt to her feet and paced the rug like an angry tigress. "I feel like killing that woman!"

"Make David and me a cup of tea instead, love," Sammy said gently.

Miriam stood with her fists clenched for a moment, looking into her husband's eyes, then her body relaxed and she lifted the kettle from the hob onto the low fire that had to be kept burning even in summertime to heat the hot-water cistern.

David marveled, as he often did, at his brother's soothing influence upon Miriam. But he had always known Sammy was the right man for her. His own love for her, now just a distant remembrance, had had the opposite effect, fueling the flames of her tempestuous nature and causing more pain than pleasure for both of them.

He watched her brew the tea in a brown earthenware pot, the kind Bessie called "working-class," and get out some thick, willow-pattern cups and saucers which his wife would also consider beneath her. Only the best was still Bessie's maxim; her new interest in good works had not removed her personal pretensions to grandeur.

But he had similar ideas himself. The difference between

him and Bessie was that he didn't look down on those who
hadn't. And he never would. Not even when he moved to
Cheshire and had a home like the one his Christian schoolfriend Jim Forrest lived in. He'd only been inside it once, but
the experience had given him something to aim for. That
Miriam had derided and which she had said was beyond his
reach, he recalled, as she handed him his tea.

None of them had spoken whilst the tea was being
prepared and the thoughtful silence remained whilst they
drank it.

"What're we going to do about Father?" Helga said,
when David pushed his cup and saucer aside and got up to
stand with his back to the fire.

"Why are you asking David?" Miriam said to her. "It's
Sammy who is Father's son-in-law."

"We'll have to ask the police to look for him, and it
doesn't matter which of us makes the phone call," David put
in tactfully. Was Miriam trying to take him down, or build her
husband up? What did it matter. "I see Sammy's made you a
new fruitbowl, Miriam," he said, to ease the awkward moment.

Sammy eyed the leaf-shaped receptacle on the dresser
disparagingly. His beautiful wood-carvings were all over his
home and had places of honor in those of the rest of the
family, too, but he was always dismissive about them. "I have
to do something in my spare time," he shrugged.

"Who's interested in fruitbowls with Father missing?"
Miriam flashed. "You'd better go to the phone box and report it, Sammy."

"There's no need," David said. "I'm going back to the
factory to lock up for the night. I'll make the call the minute
I get there."

Helga followed him out. "You may as well drop Father's
case, on your way."

David got the valise from the car and carried it across
the street to the Moritzes' house. "I don't believe it!" he exclaimed stopping short on the pavement and pointing to the
front room window.

Sigmund was in his workshop, bending over the cutting
bench.

Helga smiled. "I do! We'd better not pass any remarks,
or ask him any questions, David."

"I wouldn't dare," David laughed. He felt like jumping

for joy, but managed to contain himself. "Who's he making a garment for, Helga? He hasn't got any customers."

Sigmund provided the answer when they opened his workroom door and smiled at him. "I'm cutting myself a new suit before I get too busy again," he said without preamble. "After what I've been through, I deserve to give myself a present."

This was all he said to them. He made no comment about his belongings being delivered by David, nor did he say where he had spent the nights since leaving his wife. But Helga saw grass-stains on his trousers and surmised he had slept in a park.

The next morning, Sarah called to see him.

"You've come to interfere?" he said gruffly when she put her shopping basket on the bench and made herself comfortable on the only chair.

"With what?" she smiled.

Sigmund eyed her suspiciously. "You haven't come to tell me to go back to my wife?"

"God forbid! Here is where you belong, Sigmund."

"I'm glad everyone still thinks so," he said sounding sheepish.

"You were the only one who didn't."

"So now I know better."

Sarah watched him thread a needle and was warmed by the familiar sight. "You haven't been back five minutes and already your waistcoat has a hundred pins jabbed into it," she laughed. "For Helga to pick up when they drop onto the kitchen rug."

"Once a tailor always a tailor," he replied.

"Did you have to marry Gertie Fish to find that out?"

Sigmund went to stare out of the window and toyed with the frayed tape-measure slung around his neck. "I could have lived without a needle in my hand, Sarah. But a man can't live without respect." He turned to face her. "A *ganef* my wife called me."

Sarah pretended she had not known this, though David had told her.

"And all I was doing was exchanging the lousy ten shilling-note spending money she allowed me, for silver! To give Martin half-a-crown for coming top in the exams." The words had poured out of him in an angry gust and he stood red-faced, his stocky finger trembling.

"Such an evil mind," Sarah said with revulsion.

Sigmund simmered down and began tacking a jacket sleeve with careful, even stitches. "God will forgive me for leaving her. To a person like that I owe no allegiance."

Sarah went to kiss his cheek, which she only did on special occasions. "I agree."

Chapter Eleven

On the second Saturday in December, two topics dominated the conversation at Sarah's tea party. The King's abdication with its accompanying scandal had shocked the family, and nobody could quite believe it had happened. They also found it hard to take in that Hannah and Carl would shortly be the parents of twins.

Carl had taken his wife to St. Mary's Hospital during the night and was still there, with Sammy for company.

"I'll be glad when *Shabbos* is out; then I can get on with knitting the second shawl," Helga said. A complete layette for one baby had been prepared some time ago, but the necessity for a second one had only been revealed the previous week.

"You won't have time to knit, when Hannah comes home with the babies," Sarah told her. "And goes back to work, while you take care of them," she added with disapproval.

"I'm looking forward to it," Helga smiled. Life had denied her the chance to be a mother, but now she would be the next best thing.

"I wonder what Edward will say when he broadcasts tonight," David mused returning to the other topic.

"Who's that walking down the street? Mrs. Simpson's dainty feet!" Ronald sang out.

"Don't be clever," Nathan chided him.

"All the kids at school are singing it," Ronald informed him. "She's pinched our King from us, hasn't she?"

"So we've got another one," Sarah said philosophically,

though she had not expected Edward's departure to occur in her lifetime.

"And after him we'll have to have a queen, because he's got no sons," young Arnold Klein declared as if this were a deprivation.

"Two of England's greatest monarchs were queens," Marianne reminded him in defense of her own sex. "But I'm glad I'm not Princess Elizabeth. I wouldn't like to be one."

Shirley eyed Marianne's simple, brown wool dress and glanced at her own elaborate, burgundy velvet one. "You wouldn't make a very good one," she said condescendingly.

"And I suppose you think you would?" Marianne retorted.

"She would if all it took was dressing up," Martin said snidely.

"Those two are always getting at me," Shirley protested.

"It's because they're jealous of you, darling," Bessie comforted her.

Marianne and Martin shared a smile and got up and left the room.

David was still musing about the abdication. "You'd think he'd have more responsibility than to put love before duty."

Nathan smiled sourly. "You're a great one for duty, aren't you, David?" His sympathies were with the love-torn Edward, but he said no more. Rebecca was looking at him over the rim of her tea cup and he had learned he must watch his words in her presence.

"Leona's hair is even redder than Shirley's," Sarah remarked to change the subject. Things had not been too bad between David and Nat since Bessie stood by Rebecca, and she wanted them to stay that way. She lifted her youngest granddaughter from the rug and stroked the soft little cheek. Leona was much prettier than Shirley, she thought, cuddling the baby close and hoping she would also have a sweeter nature.

Sigmund was toying restively with his watch chain. "Why aren't Carl and Sammy back from the hospital yet?" he exclaimed, getting up to pace the room.

Miriam was putting on her coat to go to a phone and telephone the hospital when her husband and brother arrived.

Carl had a dazed expression on his face. "I'm the father

of two boys and I can't believe it," he said lowering himself into a chair.

"*Mazeltov!*" the family cried in unison.

"I had to hold him up when they let us see them," Sammy grinned while Abraham was getting the whisky out of a cupboard.

"They're not a bit alike," Carl supplied. "One's like me and the other's the image of Hannah."

"When Tibby had her last lot of kittens, three were her color and the others were like Mrs. Evans's cat," Ronald said helpfully.

Abraham handed around drinks amid gales of laughter.

The whole afternoon hardly anyone had laughed, Sarah reflected. Oh, what a bit of good news could do for a family! But this was a double joy. "With two boys, you can call one after Edward and the other after George," she suggested to Carl. "As they were born on such a special day."

Carl was gulping his whisky as if he needed it. "Hannah's already named them Frank and Henry."

"After whom?" Sigmund asked. "Her own forebears, she doesn't know who they were. And there was never a Frank or a Henry among yours."

Carl smiled. "You know Hannah. Frank was a man who used to bring sweets to the orphanage she was in. And Henry was someone who gave the kids rides in his van."

"Two very nice names," Sarah pronounced decisively, busying herself with the tea things so nobody would notice how the explanation had affected her. For Hannah to have attached so much significance to such small kindnesses told its own story. What a sad childhood she must have had.

Sarah thought about Hannah again that night, after she and Abraham had listened to Edward's farewell to the nation, on the wireless.

"Carl's wife was born to nothing, yet such a strong character she's got. It makes you think, Abraham."

"You, you don't need anything to make you think! But tell me what anyway."

"That a man can be born to rule, but in the end it's his own nature that rules him. The wonderful upbringing Edward had, what good did it do? He's let down his family and his country, to marry Mrs. Simpson," she said dabbing her eyes with her apron.

"You're crying for Edward?"

Sarah thought of Queen Mary who didn't have a son made of iron, like David, to stop his brother from doing the wrong thing. "I'm crying for his poor mother."

Chapter Twelve

David had succeeded in persuading Esther and Ben to let Marianne complete her primary schooling in Cheetham Hill, but it would have been better for her if he had not. She passed the scholarship examination, along with Shirley, only to learn afterwards that the Kleins' move from Manchester prohibited her from attending a high school in the city.

By then, all the places at equivalent establishments in Salford were filled, and she had to accept one at a lower grade of school, where the emphasis was on commercial subjects to equip the girls for secretarial careers.

Marianne found shorthand and typewriting easy to learn. But taking down business letters and typing them with the required neatness bored her. Bookkeeping confounded her and she came to dread the lessons, when the sight of long rows of figures awaiting her attention would throw her into a panic and cause her mind to close up whilst the teacher's voice droned on about double entry.

Latin was not taught at the school, and Martin, who was emerging as a Classics scholar, declared this disgusting. He advised Marianne to work hard at French, because she would need a language in order to qualify for university and was even more appalled when she said none of her schoolmates had university in mind.

Martin's views increased Marianne's feeling that she had been deprived of the kind of education her ability merited, and her consequent resentment eroded her will to do well. Her work suffered accordingly, and the report she took home at the end of her first year bewildered her parents.

"It doesn't make sense," Ben said, re-reading the marks

and comments. "How can she come bottom of a class of girls who didn't qualify for a high school like she did?"

The shop bell tinkled, but he did not rush away to make sure Harry could manage, the way he usually did. "What've you got to say about it, Marianne?"

Marianne shrugged, and munched the buttered teacake her mother had just put on the table for her. "Nothing."

Ben looked at his wife and spread his hands perplexedly.

"So your daughter won't be a professor," Esther smiled. "Be happy our Arnold's turning out to be one. A girl doesn't need to do well at school; she'll end up cooking and cleaning anyway."

Marianne escaped to the small, back bedroom she thought of as her private sanctum and lay counting the roses on the wallpaper, which she always found helped her not to think.

"Sometimes I wish we'd never come to live here," Ben said to Esther breaking the silence their daughter's abrupt departure from the room had engendered.

"Me too; it isn't the same," Esther agreed. Then her eye roved to the carved walnut sideboard and chairs and the new carpet they had recently acquired. "But I change my mind when I think of the things we've got now that we didn't have before."

Ben's policy of working on turnover had paid off handsomely, but it was not this alone that had caused the business to thrive. Esther's full-time presence had made an immense difference. The local women liked her and would come in just for a chat, but rarely left without buying something. She dressed the shop window, too, with row upon row of articles arranged on stands, one behind the other, and the effect was of a mountain of cut-price bargains, which tempted the passing trade.

Ben stuffed Marianne's school report into his pocket and stared out of the window at the dismal backyard. "But like you said, Esther, it isn't the same. For you and me it doesn't matter, but where our kids live can affect them. Have you ever wondered why our Marianne never invites her schoolfriends home like she did in Cheetham?"

"I can't say I have," Esther answered impatiently. The shop bell had just rung twice, but suddenly Ben didn't seem to care! "What's that got to do with her getting a bad report?" she added.

"I didn't say it had," Ben retorted. Sometimes he wished his wife's interest in their daughter wasn't confined to just her physical well-being. "But she's the only Jewish girl in the school, isn't she? Perhaps she doesn't invite friends home because she hasn't got any."

That night, Ben went to sit on Marianne's bed before she fell asleep, as he had often done when she was younger. "You've got something on your mind, love, haven't you?" he said gently. "Why don't you tell your old dad about it? Two heads are better than one."

Marianne gazed into the kind, brown eyes that were filled with concern for her and the deep love she had for him felt like a lump in her throat. But it was his fault she wasn't at a high school. Dad and Mom hadn't known how removing to Salford would affect her, but she was sure they would have done it anyway. They thought a girl's education wasn't important! She swallowed the constricting emotion down and hardened her heart. "You're to blame for everything!" she told her father.

Ben's long face creased with distress. "Me? What have I done?"

"If you don't know, why should I bother to tell you?"

"Because we've always been good pals, haven't we?"

Marianne stared up at him enigmatically.

"Sometimes you remind me of our Joe!" he exclaimed frustratedly recalling his journalist brother's moodiness. "And look how he's ended up!" he added irrationally, unable to think of Joe without a stab of pain because he had married a Gentile.

"He's my favorite uncle," Marianne said, though she had only met him once. "When I grow up, I'm going to London to stay with him and get to know my cousin Christopher."

"Meanwhile you're only a stupid little girl!" Ben shouted.

Marianne turned her face to the wall and he went downstairs, trembling with angry confusion, wondering how his attempt to comfort the daughter he loved had turned into a row about something else.

Ben had flicked off the light switch and Marianne could not summon the energy to get out of bed and put it on again, so she could count the roses. She tried counting them in her imagination, but it didn't stop her from thinking. She lay listening to the trams and lorries rumbling by on the main road, which could be heard even at the back of the premises, then pulled the quilt over her head to shut out the sound, just as she did when she was making up a story.

Once, it had only been Mom who didn't understand her, but now it was Dad, too. Why couldn't she talk to him any more? Because it hurt that he couldn't see why she was unhappy, that she needed telling. And she couldn't forgive him for what moving had done to her. She blamed him more than Mom, who'd always been just a parent, never a pal.

The next day was Saturday and she tried to avoid going to the tea party, where everyone would be talking about the children's reports, as if they affected the whole family.

"You're going with Arnold, like always," her mother said while they ate their dinner. "Now that Harry works in the shop, he isn't expected at Bobbie's until later, with me and Dad. But you've got no excuse."

"My head's aching," Marianne answered, providing one, and felt her temples begin to throb as she said it.

Esther gave her a generous helping of prunes with her *lokshen* pudding. "So I'll give you an Aspro and tonight you'll take syrup of figs."

Marianne pushed her dessert away. "Why do you think a laxative's the answer to everything, Mom?"

Esther wanted to slap her, but knew it would do no good and wished she could think of something that would. She ate her own meal quickly so she could go into the shop and let Ben have his.

Harry was finishing his soup, having just been relieved behind the counter by Arnold who, despite his lack of interest in the business, gave a hand when necessary without being prompted.

"It'd do our sister good to have to work on Saturdays, like I have to," he said to his mother.

"I help when I'm asked to," Marianne declared.

"But you never think of offering to, do you?" Esther pointed out.

"It'd be nice if she sometimes did," Harry said.

The feeling that everything and everyone was against her increased when Marianne arrived at her grandmother's house.

"I heard you came bottom of the class," Shirley greeted her the minute she entered the parlor.

Mom must have rung up Uncle David and told him, like she did about everything! Marianne went to sit on the floor in a corner of the room and listened to her Auntie Bessie boasting about Shirley and Ronald's high marks. Her grandmother was reading Martin's report, and Arnold had just handed his to Uncle Nat.

I expect Dad threw mine on the fire, Marianne thought despondently, opening the book she had brought with her and hoping Martin would notice it was *Wuthering Heights* and not the childish stories she used to read.

Martin did not notice. He was squatting on the hearthrug with Shirley and Arnold, discussing the Latin essay he had written for the end of term examination.

"Why not go and sit with them instead of hiding yourself in a corner?" Hannah smiled to Marianne above the clamor of voices and the clinking of china.

"Our Marianne is getting like Greta Garbo," Abraham chuckled. "She wants to be alone."

"What if I do?" Marianne said defensively though she did not. But there was no point in her joining the group on the hearthrug; she wouldn't know what they were talking about.

Hannah sensed her unhappiness and wondered what had caused it. "What's wrong, love?"

Marianne managed to smile. "I'd rather not talk about it."

"Anything you'd rather not talk about it's best to get off your chest right away," Nathan, who was sitting beside them, counseled his niece.

"My husband, the psychologist!" Rebecca interceded caustically, watching her daughter toddle precariously across the room.

"You should put Leona in clogs; she seems a little bow-legged," Sarah advised.

"Because her mother feeds her too well. She's over-weight," Nathan said.

"How do you know I do, when you're hardly ever home at mealtimes?" Rebecca countered. The extra time Nathan now spent at his surgery probing patients' psyches was a constant bone of contention between them. "Don't let your uncle get at you, love. He's a nosey parker," she said to Marianne.

"I'm used to people getting at me," Marianne exclaimed tempestuously and rushed out of the room.

"Go and calm her down, Martin," Sarah instructed the

only one of her grandchildren whom she knew Marianne would welcome.

Martin shook his head. "It won't do any good. These days she isn't easy to talk to."

Hannah deposited baby Frank on top of the newspaper on Carl's lap, where his twin was already seated. "I'll go."

"But don't fill Marianne's head with your *meshuga* ideas!" Sarah called after her.

Sarah's admonition amused Hannah, though it would have had the opposite effect once. They had not got on well during their early acquaintance, but she had learned there was much to admire about Sarah and sensed that the forthright woman no longer disliked her. In some ways they were similar, prepared to battle for the things in which they believed, and the knowledge of this had earned a grudging respect for the other in each of them, though their values were at opposite ends of the pole.

Marianne was curled up on the window seat in the dining room, surveying the sprawling tangle of pinks and marigolds in the back garden. "There won't be room for the Michaelmas daisies to show their faces this year if Zaidie doesn't make some space for them," she remarked when Hannah entered. "He could make a fortune if he plucked all those flowers and sold them, couldn't he?"

Hannah laughed, but Marianne's expression remained pensive. "You're not very pleased with life at the moment, are you, love?"

"That's no secret."

"Well, you haven't tried to hide it."

"Why should I?"

"Is it because you got a bad report?"

"Not exactly."

"I didn't think it could be."

"You mean I've had a face like a fiddle for ages, don't you? It didn't start today."

Hannah went to sit beside her and noticed that her profile was a replica of Sarah's, the same determined chin and aquiline nose. But strength of character in a child was not always an asset; it could make a girl of Marianne's age unhappy because she couldn't have her own way. "I don't know you very well, yet, but you don't seem the same girl who was my bridesmaid," she said carefully.

"How can I be?" Marianne answered. She untucked her

legs from under her and smoothed down the skirt of her flowered cotton dress. "When five days a week my life is purgatory?"

Her tone was as melodramatic as her words, but Hannah sensed the very real feeling from which both had emanated and let a sympathetic silence develop.

"I hate my school," Marianne declared breaking it. "And it isn't right I should have to be there!" she added in a passionate outburst. "When I passed the same exam as Shirley."

Hannah played with her wedding ring for a moment, conscious of Marianne awaiting her comments. But she must be careful what she said in an irretrievable situation. "You're entitled to feel cheated, Marianne."

"I do!"

"But being resentful won't make any difference. Nothing can, so you must make the best of it."

Marianne's gaze dropped to her red sandals and her fists clenched into white-knuckled balls.

Hannah surveyed the bent, black head and the thin little figure, stiff with anger, and saw herself at the age of twelve; a tall, fair-haired girl with the same bitterness as this small dark one, wanting to make the whole world pay for what life had done to her.

"You're not punishing anyone but yourself by not making the best of it," she said to Marianne, thrusting her hands into the pockets of her sensible, serge skirt and contemplating the design on the carpet. "You know sometimes a person has to rise above the circumstances they find themselves in; let them be a spur instead of a handicap," she added quietly.

Something in Hannah's voice impelled Marianne to raise her head and look at her. Hannah didn't wear powder, like other women, and her blouse was a plain white, open-necked one, not trimmed with lace like Mom and Auntie Bessie wore with their best costumes on *Shabbos*. Hannah never wore beads or brooches either, and it struck Marianne that she was different from the other women in the family. But it wasn't just the way she dressed. It was something special that shone from her.

"Is that what you did?" she asked feeling instinctively that what Hannah had just said had been her own experience.

Hannah nodded, her eyes misty with memory. "I usually talk to people from my head, not my heart, but I'm talking to you from both, Marianne. And this is just between you and me. I decided to make something of myself in spite of being raised in an institution because my mother abandoned me."

"I don't know how anyone could do that to their child," Marianne said with distress.

"That's how I felt, once," Hannah told her. "Before I grew up and learned how religion and the society we live in exert pressure over people. My mother wasn't married to my father. And you're old enough to understand what that means. They told me she was Jewish, but my father wasn't. You know what that means, too."

"Her family wouldn't let her marry him."

"Right. And because they wouldn't, I was dumped in an orphanage, as if my parents were dead," Hannah said, with a brief resurgence of the anger that had once been her constant companion.

"Did you hate your mother for doing it to you?" Marianne asked quietly.

Hannah nodded. "But now I pity her. I hated everything Jewish, too, though I never knew her or her family. I told them at the orphanage I didn't want to belong to her religion, and I felt that way for a long time. Then a few years ago, I thought what am I doing? My mother's blood is in my veins, why should I despise and deny what I am?"

"Mom told me that in Jewish law a child is the same religion as its mother, no matter what the father's is," Marianne said.

"Yes. But I'm not talking about the religious laws. Jews are a race and I feel part of it. When I think about what's going on in Germany my heart bleeds as if it were happening to my kith and kin. That's what woke me up to what I'd done. I'd turned my back on my own heritage. But we've wandered from the subject, haven't we?" Hannah smiled. "Carl says I always do."

"Martin says that about me."

"That's something else we have in common then."

Marianne liked what this implied, and felt that she had acquired a new friend. Hannah hadn't talked down to her the way adults usually did, but had entrusted her with a secret. "I'll never tell anyone what you've told me," she promised.

"If I'd thought you would, I wouldn't have confided in you," Hannah replied in her matter-of-fact way. She rose from the window seat and wandered absently around the room, halting by the sideboard to glance at a portrait of Sarah and Abraham with their young family.

"Pictures like this used to make me jealous," she told Marianne. "I couldn't even see one in a book without feeling I'd been done out of something. I spent my whole childhood thinking life could never be the same for me as it was for luckier children, and if someone hadn't given me a talking-to, I'd probably have gone on believing it."

"Who was it?"

Hannah smiled reminiscently. "The man I named Henry after. One Sunday, when he was giving us kids a ride in the country and it was my turn to sit in the front with him, he asked me what I was going to be when I grew up. I told him I wouldn't mind being a teacher, but it was out of the question for a girl like me. 'Why don't you prove it isn't?' he said. 'Teachers are educated people, how can I ever be that?' I answered. 'The same way I became the owner of a haulage firm. By making "I'll show 'em" your motto,' he replied. I knew he'd been brought up in an orphanage, but until then I'd thought he was just employed by the company. It made me think."

"But how did you qualify for university?" Marianne asked. "Did the orphanage send you to high school?"

"I was too old for that by the time Henry got to me. And I doubt if it would've been possible anyway, the standard of teaching I'd had was minimal. I worked in a paper factory after I left there and lived in a hostel with other homeless girls. But instead of idling away my evenings like they did, I went to night school and eventually passed the matriculation exam. The rest you know."

"It makes me feel ashamed of myself," Marianne said quietly.

"I'd rather it made you buck your ideas up," Hannah declared. "Or I've wasted my breath telling you."

Chapter Thirteen

Sarah was outraged when she heard that Oswald Mosley was to address a public meeting at the Manchester Free Trade Hall.

"How can they let him?" she exclaimed incredulously to Mr. Greenberg, the fishmonger, when he told her.

Mr. Greenberg wiped his wet hands on his striped apron, shoved his dusty Homburg hat to the back of his head and scratched his bald pate with a fishy fingernail. "Neville Chamberlain you should ask, not me."

"All he cares about is having his picture in the papers!" Sarah snorted. "With his famous umbrella! Instead he should use it to drive those Blackshirts into the sea."

Gittel Lipkin, Moishe's mother, was prodding a haddock speculatively. "In England they believe in free speech," she said rejecting the haddock and examining another one.

"Like vonce sey did in my country," a neatly-dressed young woman said from beside a box of mackerel. "Nobody stamped on se acorn, so it grew into un oak tree und now only von voice is heard."

Her accent marked her as a refugee. Her bearing, too, Sarah thought, noting the erect carriage and proud tilt of the chin she had come to associate with the German Jews who had sought refuge in Manchester. "You're living round here?" she asked her pleasantly.

"Unfortunately yes."

Sarah exchanged a glance with Gittel and gave her attention to a tray of flounder. Gittel did the same with the haddock and they did not raise their heads until the young woman had left the shop.

"Who does she think she is?" Gittel exploded the moment the door had shut behind her.

"She works for someone with a lot of children, on

Cheetham Hill Road, helping in the house," Mr. Greenberg supplied.

"For my part, I don't care where such highty-tighty persons work. Or where they live!" Gittel said, slapping a huge fish on to the scales to be weighed. "Moishe's at home this week; he's only traveling in Lancashire," she explained its size to Sarah, then resumed her tirade. "When they first started coming here I was sorry for them. But the way some of them behave it's hard to be any more!"

"They're lucky they don't have to live in a district like Strangeways, the way we did when we first came, and not know where the next meal's coming from," Sarah agreed.

"So they're not like us," the elderly fishmonger shrugged. "But how can you expect them to be? They haven't come from little *shtetlach* with muddy streets and no running water in the house, like we did."

"In Dvinsk the streets were clean," Sarah informed him. "And if you don't include the Russians it was a very nice place."

"Us, we didn't even have windows to look through," Gittel declared as if Sarah hadn't heard this a hundred times before. "And a lavatory chain, excuse me for mentioning it, we'd never heard of. Me, I'm not too proud to remember."

Mr. Greenberg was removing the haddock's head.

"I'll take that for my cat," she told him.

"Don't you always?" He gazed into the bulging dead eyes absently. "Everyone has their own memories, and what a person has to compare things with is bound to affect how they feel. For us, Mrs. Lipkin, what we came to was a step up in the world. For that girl who was just in here, it's the other way round. A banker's daughter she is, no less. She talked to me about herself one day. From a beautiful apartment in the best part of Frankfurt, where she never had to put her hands in water. Now she's a maid for people her parents could have bought and sold. Such a comedown can't be easy."

"Is that a reason for her to be rude to us?" Gittel demanded. "It's our community she's come into, isn't it? And if she goes round saying to the *goyim* what she just said to us, it won't do the Jews any good."

"Oy," Mr. Greenberg sighed, wrapping the haddock in a week-old *Yiddish Gazette* from the pile of discarded newspapers his customers saved for him. "You remind me of my wife, Mrs. Lipkin. She won't let me have the wireless on loud, in case it disturbs our Christian neighbors. It wouldn't matter if we lived next door to *Yidden*, she always says." He smiled wryly. "All these years our people have been in England and we're still trying not to offend anyone."

Sarah flopped her selection of fish on to the counter. "That's all we need worry about here, so don't grumble." But what the young German woman had said about letting an acorn grow into an oak tree had lodged in her mind.

"Remember how years ago you told me not to worry about the Fascists because they weren't very strong in England?" she said to Nathan the next time he called at the house.

"How could I forget it?" he grinned. "We ended up with a fullblown family row."

"And also indigestion," Abraham recalled. "It was the day your mother served up a lecture about Hitler and Mosley along with our *Rosh Hashanah* dinner."

"A lot of effect my lecture had," Sarah said scathingly. "All it did was turn David into a Zionist, so now he raises funds to make Palestine a better place for Jews."

"You don't think that's important in times like these?" Abraham asked.

"Sure. But what is anyone doing to make certain English Jews will never need to run there? A handful of Blackshirts in London is nothing to get worked up about; you all told me that day we had the row. And a few years later, Mr. Mosely is coming to speak in Manchester, in a great big hall!"

"Calm down, Mother," Nathan said soothingly.

"Your bedside manner you can keep for your patients," Sarah retorted, putting the kettle on to the fire with a thud that sent sparks flying up the chimney. "What I want to know is are my family as blind now as they were then? And also what that Blackshirt is coming here to say to the *goyim* about us."

"So go to the meeting and you'll find out."

"You want your mother should get beaten up by thugs?" Abraham said hotly. "When the Jews marched against the Blackshirts in Cable Street, Eli's nephew, who lives in London, got his lip split open."

"And what did the Blackshirt who did it get in return?" Sarah said. "Tell Nat the whole story, like you told me."

"A broken nose."

"But a meeting is not a march," Sarah declared. "And in any case, I've made up my mind I'm going."

Abraham mopped the beads of perspiration his wife's announcement had caused to break out on his forehead. "What can we do with a woman like her?" he said helplessly to Nathan.

"What you can do is go with me. And my grandchildren who are old enough can go also. It's time they found out what being Jewish really means."

Sarah raised the matter at her next tea party and her daughter and daughters-in-law turned on her irately.

She had waited for Esther to arrive from the shop, so the furor she knew was in store for her would not have to be repeated. But Rebecca, whose own child was not involved, was the first to snarl.

"What kind of grandmother are you? Sending the lambs into the lions' den!"

"A Jewish face is like a red rag to a bull with those people!" Miriam said vehemently.

"When they get their anti-Semitic blood up, they're like mad dogs!" Bessie shrilled.

Esther had blanched at the mere thought of it. "We have to protect our children from those Fascist pigs," she declaimed.

Sarah surveyed their set faces and heaving, maternal bosoms from behind her teapot. She knew how they felt, but did not allow it to deter her. "If you've all finished shouting about animals, we'll talk about it," she told them calmly, handing Esther and Ben their tea.

"There's nothing to talk about," Esther said.

"Pass your mom and dad the strudel," Sarah smiled to Marianne whom the exchange had momentarily silenced as it had all the children.

Esther pushed the cake dish away. "We don't want anything to eat."

"Speak for yourself," Ben said, taking a couple of slices.

"How can you sit there stuffing yourself, with what your children's grandmother's got in mind for them?" she flashed irrationally.

"I don't have to lose my appetite over something that isn't going to happen," Ben declared.

"Listen, a father isn't a mother," Bessie shrugged to Esther when David helped himself to some cake, too.

"A grandma isn't, either," Miriam said pointedly.

Sarah was brushing some crumbs off the white lace cloth that graced her octagonal tea-table on *Shabbos*. "My life I'd give for the children in this room," she said quietly. "And everyone here knows it. So why do I want to take them into the lions' den, which Rebecca called it—and she isn't wrong? Because their elders can't protect them forever. And how will they recognize the beasts who want to gobble Jews up if they haven't seen and heard them?"

"Photos of Blackshirts they can see in the newspapers," Esther countered. "And the kind of things they say, I won't stop my kids reading about."

"It isn't the same," Sarah declared. "They see photos of film stars too, and read about them. But who thinks of film stars as real people?"

"Zaidie Abraham does," Ronald said emerging from his uncharacteristic solemnity and giving his grandfather a playful prod. "He goes to the pictures a lot."

"The Riviera and the Premier would have to close down without him!" Sarah agreed caustically, allowing the conversation to digress for a moment.

"Is it my fault you won't come with me?" Abraham asked her defensively. His obsession with the cinema was a family joke, but it had never amused his wife. "Fifteen years ago Charlie Chaplin didn't make her laugh and she hasn't been since."

"About Mr. Mosley," Sarah said, returning to her subject.

Miriam rose from the sofa and began stacking the tea cups, though Lizzie and Bridie were in the kitchen waiting to be summoned to do so. "The kids aren't going, Ma," she snapped. "So why don't you just forget the whole thing?"

"If I forget I've got a blister on my heel, will it stop it from getting inflamed, Miriam?"

Nathan smiled at Sarah's homespun analogy and saw his sister-in-law's expression flicker with uncertainty. His mother was a better lay psychologist than he!

"If you're telling me Fascism won't go away, all right, I accept it," Miriam said edgily. "But that's no reason for the children to go where they might get involved in a brawl."

Sigmund sat fiddling with his watch chain, pondering on whether or not Sarah was right. Attending a Fascist meeting would not be a pleasant experience for the youngsters. But it would instil in them an awareness that English-Jewish youth lacked. Teach them that anti-Semitism went deeper than the occasional jibes they received from Gentile children had led them to believe. Knowing their grandparents had fled from oppression was just a piece of history to them. The reality of the oppressors, even the present day one, was far removed from their own lives.

"In a public place, with their *Zaidies* and their fathers and uncles, nobody will harm them," he declaimed decisively, ranging himself on Sarah's side. "And it will do them good to go."

David exchanged a glance with Ben. Sarah's decisions could sometimes be dismissed as emotional, but for Sigmund arriving at a conclusion was always an intellectual exercise.

Hannah had been listening silently. "I agree," she said firmly and glanced at her boys and Leona who were playing with some toys on the hearthrug. "It's a pity those three aren't old enough to go."

"Not in my opinion!" Helga said sharply. Frank and Henry were the twin apples of her eye and protecting them from their mother's unconventional attitudes had begun to obsess her.

Carl, who as usual had been reading all afternoon and had not heard a word of the discussion until his wife spoke, looked up from his book. "Go where?"

"To hear Mosley speak. And there's safety in numbers; we'll all go together," David decided.

"Nat can bring his medical bag in case any of us gets a black eye," Ben joked making it clear he had been influenced by Sigmund, too.

"I don't believe in starting a fight, but if anyone touches me they'll get a thump back," Martin said quietly and looked at Marianne to see if she had remembered his philosophy about sticks and stones. The smile she gave him told him she had.

"You're not going, Martin," Miriam said flatly.

"Oh yes he is," Sammy declared. "I've let you baby him for long enough."

David saw the glance that passed between them and felt he was witnessing a turning point in their marriage. Then Bessie started shrilling at him that Shirley and Ronald were not going to the meeting. Esther and Miriam also began upbraiding their husbands and he gave himself up to the general mêlée.

"Only Jews could behave like this!" Nathan shouted disgustedly above the din, as he usually did when the family gave vent to their feelings.

"You're worse than the Blackshirts!" Rebecca exclaimed, and they began quarrelling, too.

"Troublemaker!" Abraham accused Sarah.

She picked up Leona who had started crying and shared a smile of rapport with Sigmund, over all the angry heads. Sometimes you had to make trouble to achieve a good purpose.

How the men finally persuaded their wives to let them bring the children, Sarah neither knew nor cared when she was seated in their midst at the Free Trade Hall, waiting for the meeting to begin. But of one thing she was certain. Her grandchildren would never forget this experience.

She averted her eyes from the black-shirted stewards patrolling the aisles. Just seeing them there gave her the shivers. One, with a mean mouth and a cauliflower ear, had eyed the family speculatively as they walked by him to their seats and the youngsters had been instantly subdued, though the man had not spoken to them, sensing something predatory behind the uniformed facade.

"Those men remind me of Hitler," she heard Arnold whisper to Harry nervously. But it was what she had wanted. After tonight, what Hitler stood for would be a flesh-and-blood thing to the children; not just a newspaper picture of someone far away who was persecuting other Jews, but could not harm them.

She glanced around the crowded hall to see what kind of people had come to hear Mosley speak, but they looked no different from the ordinary men and women she passed in the street every day, and somehow this was frightening. Were they here because their ideas were the same as his? Even if only the number of Mancunians that would fit into the Free Trade Hall agreed with him it was something to be reckoned with.

There were some Jewish faces, too. Not isolated, but in clumps, seated together as her family was, like small islands of protest in a hostile sea. Would any of them raise their voices? Abraham had warned her she must not raise hers. He was sitting on her left and Sigmund and David were on her right. Carl and Sammy had taken Hannah, Marianne and Martin to sit between them on the row behind. In front, Ben and Nathan flanked David's children and Ben's boys.

"My schoolfriend Edie Perkins is here somewhere, with her dad," Sarah heard Marianne tell Hannah, and was relieved that at least two Gentiles in the hall were not Jewhaters. Esther and Ben had met the Perkinses and said they were nice people.

"I was surprised when Edie said they were coming," Marianne added.

"You don't have to be Jewish to be anti-Fascist," Hannah declared spiritedly.

Abraham eyed the stewards apprehensively and turned round to whisper to her. "Be careful what you're saying in such a loud voice. They could hear you."

Hannah smiled contemptuously. "They know I'm not pro-Fascist. I've got a Jewish nose."

"Edie's uncle's a Communist; they've come with him," Marianne informed her.

"You don't have to be that to loathe Fascism, either; you just have to be a decent human being."

"Keep your wife quiet, Carl," Abraham implored. "Or we'll all finish up in the hospital."

Then the lights dimmed down and a pool of brilliance filled the center of the platform.

Sarah felt her blood freeze as Oswald Mosley walked into it. She had never experienced such tension as that dramatic entrance evoked. Not just in herself, but all around her. A pin from Sigmund's workday waistcoat could have been heard dropping in the silence that filled the great hall.

"Buggar off to Deutschland where you belong!" someone shouted.

The family saw two of the stewards pounce on the man who had dared to challenge their leader and drag him, kicking and cursing, up the aisle towards an exit.

"It's Mendel, Father!" David exclaimed as the scuffling group passed by.

"Whoever he is, I'm proud of him," Abraham whispered. "Mendel who?"

"He worked for me as a machiner when he was a lad and wanted to turn us into a union shop. Didn't you recognize him?"

The stewards were dragging him backwards and Abraham caught a glimpse of burning eyes in a hawklike face. "Now I do and guts he always had. Even if he did cause you trouble."

David silently agreed. Mendel had given in his notice after his bid to transform the factory into a union shop failed. David had not seen him since, but was not surprised at the manner of his reappearance. Mendel would never be far from the political fray.

Mosley had begun his speech and the briefly dispelled tension gathered again, heightened by the ejection of the first heckler. Others who raised their voices were dealt with in the same way and the efficiency with which this was executed, engendering no protest from the respectable-looking citizens who witnessed it, was not encouraging to Sarah. The Jews here had a special reason not to cause trouble, but why were the Gentiles letting the Blackshirts get away with it?

She listened to the insidious words plopping like pebbles into a pond, insisting the speaker was not anti-Semitic, then saying in the next breath that the Jews owned the press. What sort of ripples would the pebbles cause? So far as she knew, Jews only owned the *Jewish Chronicle* and the *Manchester Jewish Gazette*, which they were entitled to do. And those papers were owned by individuals, not by every Jew in the country. She opened her mouth to shout that Mosley was telling lies, but Abraham gripped her arm so hard she almost cried out in pain instead.

Sigmund let the poisonous oratory wash over him. He had not come here to listen to it and was only breathing the same air as the Blackshirts because of the children. His brother Kurt in Vienna had a grandson, too. Young Peter had been *Bar Mitzvahed* last year and his mother, Ilsa, had sent a photograph of him in *shul* with his father Rudy. Sigmund had never met Rudy and had not seen Ilsa, who was his only niece, since she was a little girl.

Why hadn't Kurt listened to him and left Vienna, instead of saying Sigmund was making a mountain of a molehill? The Jew-baiting in Austria which had impelled Sigmund to leave in 1904 had been insignificant compared with the Russian and Polish pogroms that caused families like the Sandbergs to flee. But now the molehill had become a mountain and his relatives in Vienna could end up behind barbed wire.

He watched two more men being dragged to an exit. But it would take more than heckling to stem the evil tide that had burst the dams elsewhere in Europe. "This is what the next war will be about," he said grimly to David.

David turned to look at him and did not want to believe the inevitability he saw in his eyes. He felt the tic in his cheek that had troubled him in the trenches in the last war flicker to life again. It had stayed with him after he returned home, then one day he'd noticed it wasn't there any more and had known his recovery was complete, that he'd learned to live with the things he remembered.

The memories too had receded; he had not thought of Flanders for a very long time. Even the poppy he bought and pinned to his lapel on Armistice Day, and the two-minutes' silence, had become token gestures and did not stir up painful recollections as they had once. But now the stench of blood and fear rose to haunt him again, and the voices of his dead comrades returned to his ears.

He had not wanted to be a soldier, put on a uniform which gave license to kill, and even in their darkest hours he and the other lads had not known what the war was about. He gazed with revulsion at the black-shirted figures on the platform. Their leader was standing in front of a Union Jack, his face sinister as a death's-head in the white light centered upon him, preaching the doctrines that contradicted everything the flag stood for.

I'd like to throttle him, so he can't say any more! David thought, and was shocked by his own violence. What had happened to his pacifist principles? Perhaps you had to espouse a cause in order to feel the way he felt now, and, if Sigmund's prediction was right, the next war would be a battle between good and evil, a cause worth fighting for.

Marianne was glad when the meeting was over and they were outside in Peter Street, away from the men she had sensed wanted to harm them, though this had not been said in actual words.

"I wish you hadn't made us go to it, Bobbie!" Shirley burst out as the family walked to Albert Square, where they had parked their cars.

Until then none of them had spoken. The tension was still with them.

Sarah looked at her granddaughter's tall figure in the lamplight and thought, absently, that she looked older than thirteen with her well-developed body in the grown-up brown costume Bessie allowed her to wear and her long, red hair drawn back from her face and fastened with a slide.

"A picnic I'm sure you didn't expect it to be," she said to her.

"But I didn't expect it to frighten me like it did." Shirley glanced at Marianne who was walking pensively beside Hannah. "Didn't it scare you?"

Marianne was staring down at the pavement, which was how she always walked when deep in thought. She raised her eyes to answer and felt, as she had since childhood, that it wasn't fair that her cousin who was three weeks her junior should be so much taller. "It made me wish I wasn't Jewish," she confessed.

"Me too."

The men had strode on ahead with the boys and Sarah linked arms with her granddaughters. "Show me the Jew who hasn't wished that at some time or other," she said to them.

The two girls turned to look at her, and Hannah seemed as surprised as they did.

"So you're shocked to hear that from me," Sarah shrugged. "But lies I'm not in the habit of telling. A Jew would have to be not human not to feel that way sometimes. It would be like our Sammy never wishing he wasn't handicapped with his leg."

They turned into the Square and Sarah thought how elegant it was, with its gracious old buildings mellowed by time and the imposing statue of Prince Albert on the paved center, with the Town Hall silhouetted in front of him against the sky. When had she last seen it? Not since Martin was in hospital on the south side of the city. And she could not recall the time before that. Her world was her home and Cheetham Hill. Occasionally she went to Broughton Park to Nat's house, but if she needed anything from town one of the family got it for her. It had taken Oswald Mosley to pry her out of her settled routine.

"So sometimes we wish we weren't Jewish. But we are, aren't we?" she reminded her granddaughters.

"German Jewry are much more assimilated than us," Hannah said. "They've been there a lot longer than we've been here and intermarriage has been going on for generations."

"P-p-p!" Sarah spat superstitiously to ensure such a curse would not fall upon her grandchildren.

Hannah was accustomed to Sarah's incongruous combination of intelligence and belief in Yiddish folklore, and ignored the interruption. "But the Nazis sniffed out even those with a drop of Jewish blood in their veins," she added.

Marianne recalled the menacing dark figures on the platform with Mosley and shuddered.

"They thought they were safe," Hannah went on. "But you know the fable about what Thought did, don't you, girls?"

"Followed a funeral and thought it was a wedding," Shirley supplied grimly.

"Exactly. It's dangerous for Jews to think they're safe."

"That's what I wanted the children to realize," Sarah said.

"Don't worry, Bobbie," Shirley declared. "We do now."

"Do you think we ever will be, Hannah?" Marianne asked.

Hannah's expression tightened. "Not while Society goes on producing men like Hitler and the Blackshirts, who foster anti-Semitism to achieve their political ends."

Sarah could see Abraham and David pacing up and down at the far end of the Square and quickened her step. "Politics I'm not interested in," she declaimed. "And neither are my granddaughters. Anti-Semitism is enough for them to worry about, Hannah, so don't bother their heads."

Hannah lengthened her stride to keep pace with Sarah's trot. "How can you tell me not to bother the girls' heads with politics when you fought tooth and nail to take them to a political meeting?" she expostulated.

"What?" Sarah stopped walking and looked taken aback. "Is that what it was?"

"Well it wasn't a *Shabbos* tea party!" Hannah stood tapping her foot impatiently. How could a woman as bright as Sarah be so uninformed? But she was less so than most of the Jewish women of Hannah's acquaintance, who closed their minds to everything but family and domesticity and had no desire to let in the light.

"Why are you standing there like lemons, keeping us waiting?" they heard Abraham call, but Sarah paid no attention.

"So maybe I've just found out something," she conceded

grudgingly. She had lived all her life believing anti-Semitism existed solely to persecute Jews, but she was not too old to learn. "I never thought of it as political," she said as they resumed walking.

Hannah put a friendly arm around her shoulders and smiled. Sarah looked what she was, a little Jewish grandmother. Her coat was charcoal gray, and a black felt hat sat primly upon her head. But in some ways she was extraordinary and behind her homely façade was a steely will that matched Hannah's own. "It's time you started to," she told her.

Chapter Fourteen

"Me mam said I can 'ave you an' Dot fer tea on Duck-apple Night," Edie Perkins told Marianne whilst they were changing into netball outfits.

No, you can't, we're not edible, Marianne almost replied as she removed her vest in the icy sports pavilion and slipped an ugly striped shirt over her head. When had she begun noticing the other girls' broad accents and poor grammar? It must have been when they'd started doing play-readings in class. They'd all voted for her to be Miranda in *The Tempest*, and it was then that she had become conscious that she didn't speak the way the others did.

Her mother had always corrected Marianne and her brothers if they dropped an "h" or didn't sound the last letter of a word, and now Marianne was glad she had. And she'd decided to try to speak the way her English teacher did. Miss Briggs had no accent at all.

Edie prodded her in the ribs. "I just invited yer fer tea, but yer've gone off in one o' yer daydreams again!" she grinned. Marianne's pensive silences were a joke among her classmates. "Are yer comin' on Duck-apple Night, or aren't yer? I shan't mind if yer'd rather 'ave it at 'ome wi' yer brothers."

"What on earth is Duck-apple Night?" Marianne asked emerging from her thoughts.

" 'Alloween, o' course! But we call it that 'cause it's when yer ducks fer apples."

Marianne looked perplexed. "I've never heard of it, Edie."

"I'm glad there's summat I know as Marianne Klein doesn't," Edie said with another impish grin that spread her wide mouth from one side of her freckled face to the other.

"Is it a Christian festival?" Marianne inquired, as they ran out on to the netball court with a high October wind raising their short gymsuits and freezing their thighs. Her Christian friends at primary school had never mentioned it. But they hadn't been Catholics like Edie was. Perhaps it was something Protestants didn't celebrate?

Edie appealed to the other one of their threesome, who had arrived on the court late, as usual. "Did yer ever 'ear such ignorance, Dot? Fancy anyone not knowin' 'Alloween's t'eve o' All Saints' Day."

Dot was the tallest girl in the school and as lean as she was long. " 'Ow can yer expect a Jewess ter know, yer daft?" she said looking down on Edie derisively.

"I'd love to come, thank you. But remember to tell your mother I can't eat meat in your house," Marianne said, though all the girls knew this. They saw her eating a sandwich lunch every day while they tucked into a hot school dinner.

"Don't worry, yer not likely ter get any."

The games mistress arrived with the ball and Marianne, who disliked physical exercise, stopped trying to puzzle out what Edie's reply had meant and submitted herself to her weekly torture.

The meaning became clear to her the moment she entered the Perkinses' house, and so did the true meaning of the word poverty. Her two friends had been to the Kleins' for tea several times, and Marianne and Edie had been to Dot's which was a flat above her parents' back-street grocery shop. But this was Marianne's first visit to the Perkinses'.

Edie lived on a back street, too, and the single room downstairs led directly from it. The house was crammed in the middle of a grimy terrace, where not all the doorsteps were as clean as Edie's mother kept hers. Marianne had lived in a street of small terraced houses in Cheetham Hill, but

every one of them had had sparkling window panes and immaculate front doors. There had not been any litter on the
pavements, or dog dirt. It had not been like this.

Marianne was depressed by the street before entering the
house. She did not find the room into which she stepped depressing, but was immediately affected by it in another way,
that clutched at her heart.

She had never been in a home that was uncarpeted and
was aware of a damp chill rising from the stone-flagged floor,
though a fire was burning brightly in the small, blackleaded
grate. Her eye fell on the table and she saw it was not a real
one, but a long board balanced upon trestles, like decorators
used when they spread paste on wallpaper. It was not covered
with a cloth and the fare laid upon it for tea reminded Marianne of illustrations in Martin's volume of *Oliver Twist*.

Three loaves of bread were flanked by a packet of margarine, which Marianne had never tasted, and a pot of the
cheap brand of jam her mother called rubbish and would
never buy. There was also a pudding basin, with something in
it that looked like the *shmaltz* Jewish women rendered down
from the *Shabbos* chicken, except that it was white instead of
yellow. And a number of mugs and plates, all of which were
enamel.

The room had only one ornament, a plaster figure of the
Virgin Mary, which Marianne recognized because Bridie had
once showed her hers. It was on the mantelpiece beneath a
picture of Jesus, which was also like the one Bridie had. But
the eyes looked sadder and Marianne wondered if she just
thought so because she felt sad in this room.

"I told yer Marianne was always miles away, din't I?"
she heard Edie laugh and felt her arm being shaken.

She looked up and saw Dot towering over a lot of little
girls. Edie was the eldest of eight, but not the firstborn, she
had told Marianne. Mrs. Perkins had given birth to eleven
children, but three had died.

" 'Er mam said as she were a bit o' a daydreamer," Mrs.
Perkins smiled.

Marianne knew Mrs. Perkins went into the shop occasionally to buy her husband a pair of twopence-halfpenny
socks. The darned sweater she had on gave the impression
she rarely bought anything for herself. Except for Edie, who
was wearing her school uniform, her children were shabbily
dressed, too.

"It was nice of you to invite me, Mrs. Perkins," she said, because she could think of nothing else to say.

"She's proper posh, is our Marianne!" Dot laughed.

"But we don't 'old it against 'er," Edie added.

"Aye'n yer could tek a lesson from 'er, our Edie!" Mr. Perkins declared, raising his head from the stone sink in the corner where he was rinsing some bright green apples under the solitary tap. "It's good manners ter. be polite ter yer elders," he added, smiling approvingly at Marianne. "Mash t'tea, luv," he instructed his wife, " 'n get this lot sat down at t'table, or it'll be time fer Marianne an' Dot ter go 'ome before we start t'ducking."

Marianne took off her gabardine jacket and her velour hat and hung them with Edie's and Dot's and the assortment of children's coats which were piled one on top of another on a couple of pegs on the whitewashed plaster wall.

"Dump yer satchel on't floor," Edie said.

Marianne was conscious of the solid package inside it as she did so. They had come directly from school and that morning her mother had put the package into her satchel, as she had when Marianne went to Dot's for tea. It contained a cup, saucer and plate, and some cutlery, so Marianne would not have to eat and drink from anything that had been in contact with non-kosher food. But she had left it in her satchel at Dot's home, as she was doing here. Surely God would forgive her for not wanting to offend people? Her mother would certainly be insulted if visitors arrived with their own crockery and cutlery.

"We'll 'ave ter squash up a bit," Mrs. Perkins said as she brought a huge, earthenware teapot to the table and they all sat down on the two backless benches that served her family in the absence of chairs.

Marianne was hungry and enjoyed the thick slabs of crusty bread Mrs. Perkins had cut and spread with margarine. The contents of the pudding basin turned out to be dripping. Saved from Sunday, Edie told her and Marianne guessed that her remark on the netball court meant that they never had meat on any other day, and that what was on the table was their usual evening meal.

What had Edie thought when she ate at the Kleins' and was given things like lamb chops and fried fish? But the teas they'd had at Dot's had been knife-and-fork meals, too. Tinned salmon, and sardines on toast, with cake afterwards, she reminded herself. So Edie wouldn't think it was only Jews who ate well.

She wondered if Dot felt the way she did—as if she ought not to be here eating the food of people who obviously could barely afford to feed themselves. No, it wasn't bothering Dot, or she wouldn't be putting great dollops of jam on her bread instead of just a thin layer as Marianne was carefully doing.

"I like yer ring, Marianne," one of Edie's sisters said admiringly.

"Don't pass remarks, Theresa!" Edie rebuked her.

All the little girls were named after saints, Marianne had noticed and wondered why Edie was not.

"All right, Aggie!" the jammy-faced child retorted.

Edie blushed. "Me secret's out. I'm really called Agnes," she told Marianne and Dot. "But I 'ate getting called Aggie fer short, so me mam lets me use me second name."

"'Ow'd yer like ter be a Dorothy what gets called Dot when she's five-foot-ten like me?" Dot said.

"Nobody's ever cut my name down," Marianne told them.

"Yer not t'kind folk does it ter, is she, Dot?" Edie said studying her.

"What do you mean?" Marianne asked.

"I don't know. It's just summat about yer."

"Edie's right," Dot pronounced.

Marianne looked down uncomfortably at the gold signet ring on her right hand. If only she hadn't worn it today, then they wouldn't be having this conversation that made her feel different from her friends. But she hadn't taken it off since Uncle David gave it to her. He'd given Shirley one, too, for their birthdays last year, because Jewish girls didn't get special presents when they were thirteen the way *Bar Mitzvah* boys did, and because Shirley had said it wasn't fair.

"You can try my ring on if you like, Theresa," she said impulsively to Edie's little sister and wished she could give it to her.

After tea, they played the Halloween game and Marianne forgot her troubled feeling amidst the carefree laughter as everyone tried to grab an apple with their mouth from the big washtub of water in which Mr. Perkins had set the fruit to float.

The feeling returned when she arrived home and thought

of the mean room that was home to her friend. Its scrupulous cleanliness and the cozy fire had somehow emphasized everything it lacked and that night she cried herself to sleep, wondering how Edie could be the cheerful person she was when life had been so unjust to her.

The next morning, when Esther went to awaken Marianne, she found her stuffing a parcel into her satchel. "What's that?" she asked. "I already packed your cookery overall."

Marianne hesitated before replying. "It's my best frock, Mom. I'm giving it to Edie."

Esther eyed her silently for a moment. She did not need to be told why; seeing Mrs. Perkins carefully counting out the coppers to buy her husband's cheap cotton socks had told her enough. And if it had not, Marianne's description of the Perkinses' home would have explained the gesture.

"I don't mind, but are you sure Edie won't be offended?" she said quietly. "You never liked wearing Shirley's things when I couldn't afford to buy you much."

"We weren't as poor as Edie's family are."

"There were times when we were. But you kids were too young to realize it."

A distant memory of her father's shoes drying in the hearth, with gaping holes in the soles, assailed Marianne.

"Some weeks your father only made enough to pay the rent and Uncle David used to settle my grocery bill."

"I didn't know."

"There's a lot you don't know, love. Bobbie and Zaidie arrived in England penniless, and when I was a child they didn't know where the next pan of *borsht* was coming from. I used to wear boots that were too small for me because there was no money to buy me new ones. I've got corns on my toes because of it to this day."

Esther sat down on the bed and played with the fringe of the bedspread absently. "I sometimes think it's the memory of poverty that makes Jews drive themselves to get on. Most of us started with nothing and we'll never forget what it was like. We want to make sure it'll never be that way for our children."

Marianne thought of Edie's mother on whom poverty seemed to have the opposite effect; there was something about her that told you she didn't expect her life to be any different. And most of the men and women who came into the shop were the same. "Christians aren't like that, are they, Mom?"

"It must be something we're born with that they're not," Esther replied as if she had arrived at this conclusion long ago. "Your dad's education was no different from Mr. Perkins's and the home he came from was just as poor, but he's ended up owning a business and your friend's father is a laborer."

Marianne was eyeing the parcel uncertainly. The last thing she wanted was to offend Edie. "I'll say the dress is a Christmas present," she decided.

Esther smiled. "On November first?"

"I want her to have it and I've got to say something, haven't I? It isn't right that some people're well off and others have got next to nothing," Marianne declared.

"I agree with you, love. But you giving Edie Perkins a frock isn't going to change the world."

Chapter Fifteen

"When you get a spare minute, be a good girl and type the invitation list for my Ronald's *Bar Mitzvah*," David said to his secretary.

"I should only get the chance not to be a good girl! And who has a spare second working for you?" Rita Sternshein replied.

"Any more of your lip and you won't be invited to the do," David grinned. When she first came to work for him, he had thought her banter disrespectful. That had been nearly two years ago, when she was only fifteen, and he'd soon learned that answering back was just part of her perky nature. "I'll need you to show some samples this afternoon," he said sitting down at his desk.

Rita looked up from her typewriter. "That's what I mean about never having a spare second. And it's lucky for you I don't put on weight, isn't it?"

"You dare!"

Rita had not been the best typist of the girls David had interviewed for the job, but her willowy figure was perfect for showing off the coats to customers. Facially, she was the ugliest girl David had ever seen, which was the only reason Bessie did not object to a female sharing his office.

"Am I really going to be invited to your Ronald's *Bar Mitzvah*?" Rita asked with her eyes on the statements she was copying and her fingers pounding the typewriter keys.

Nobody who worked for Sanderstyle would be left out, and David almost said this. Then he looked at Rita's buckteeth and sallow, acne-pitted complexion, about which she often joked when combing her dark hair in front of the office mirror. Her favorite joke was that she wasn't sure if God had really intended her to be a rabbit or a lemon. But David knew she made fun of herself to show she did not care, though she did. Sometimes he thought the perkiness was something behind which she hid, too, and had become second nature to her because she had been hiding her true feelings all her life.

"Sure you're being invited. You'll be the belle of the ball," he said to her.

"To those who see me from the back!" she quipped. "But thank you in anticipation. It's going to be a ball, is it?"

"At the Cheetham Assembly Rooms," David smiled, putting the guest list on her desk. So far as he was concerned it was complete, but his wife and his mother were still changing their minds back and forth about whom and whom not to invite. And Sigmund Moritz thought they ought not to be planning a big reception with the threat of war hanging over them.

The outcome of Chamberlain's trip to Munich had reassured many people, but had not allayed Sigmund's fears. He had been expecting further territorial claims since the *Anschluss* of Austria in March. "What is the word of such a man worth?" he had declared. "Only a fool and an ostrich would be surprised."

David, too, thought war was inevitable and had begun to think it a waste of time struggling to build Sanderstyle into a fashion-rainwear house of repute when before long he would probably be making uniforms, as the factory had done in the last war. But he was determined to give his son a memorable *Bar Mitvah*, Hitler or no Hitler.

It was a day every Jew looked back on as a major event in his life, and David recalled his own with mixed feelings. It was after the simple party, all his parents had been able to afford, that his mother had told him he must leave high school and become an earner. But nothing was going to mar Ronald's future and a lavish *Bar Mitzvah* celebration would be the start of it.

That evening, David stayed late at the factory to make up the wage packets. He always did this on Thursdays in winter because the early Sabbath Eve made Friday a short working-day. When he arrived home, Bessie was out at one of her committee meetings and Shirley had gone to *Chavurah,* the teenage group of the Zionist Youth Movement *Habonim.*

"You'll have to be satisfied with just my company, Dad," Ronald grinned as David sat down to eat the *gefilte* fish and salad Lizzie had put on the dining room table for him.

"I don't mind a bit," David answered. "If your mom was in, she'd be nagging me to move to Prestwich, wouldn't she?" he added with a smile.

"Like most of her friends've done," Ronald said. "And if I know Mom, we'll be living there before you can say Jack Robinson."

David had this feeling, too. Bessie usually got what she wanted. But why not when he was working hard to give it to her?

"So, Ronald," he said dismissing the subject. It was enough to have to discuss it with Bessie all the time. "What would you like from me for a *Bar Mitzvah* present?"

"It's only December and my birthday isn't until February," Ronald replied.

"But there's no harm in telling me now. I might have to save up for it!"

Ronald laughed, then he grew serious. "I can't think of a single thing I really want."

David watched him get up from his chair to take a pear from the big, crystal bowl on the sideboard and noticed how long his legs had suddenly grown. He still looked like Nathan, but was not small and slight like him.

"The only thing I lack is a brother," Ronald declared. biting into the pear.

"Trust you to want the only thing you can't have."

"You know it's nice, you'n me being by ourselves for a change, Dad," Ronald said. "I mean we hardly ever are."

"We'll be together all the time when you're grown up and in the business."

Ronald stopped eating his pear and looked uncomfortable. "I don't want to come in the business, Dad. I want to be a doctor, like Uncle Nat."

David hoped his shock and disappointment were not written on his face and told himself there was plenty of time for Ronald to change his mind. "That's a bit of a joke," he said managing to smile. "Because our Nat never wanted to be one."

"He told me he didn't."

"Oh, you've talked to him about it, have you?"

Ronald heard the stiffness in his father's voice. "Why shouldn't I discuss it with my own uncle?" he answered defensively.

"I think you might have mentioned it to me first," David said carefully. "As I'm your father."

"So I've done the wrong thing, shoot me!" Ronald exclaimed with one of his bursts of temperament that had always reminded David of Nathan when he was a child.

"If you want to study medicine when you're older, that's what you'll do," David told him. He had come to terms with disappointments all his life and would reconcile himself to this, too, if he had to.

Ronald's face lit with relief. "Thanks, Dad."

Then the doorbell rang and he went to open the door. He returned with Sigmund Moritz leaning heavily on his arm.

"What's wrong?" David asked Sigmund anxiously. "You look as if you've seen a ghost."

Sigmund was puffing and panting. "I hope I'm going to, David. And in the plural." He sank into an armchair and brushed some snowflakes off his overcoat. "The weather is terrible tonight, and I ran all the way here."

"Tell me why already!"

"Give me a moment to recover, David. I'm trying to collect my thoughts. You know I haven't heard a word from Vienna since the *Anschluss* and I'd begun to give up hope. So just now a man who arrived from there today comes to my house with a message from my brother." Sigmund paused to contain his emotion, but could not stop his voice from trembling when he resumed speaking. "I must meet a boat early tomorrow morning, in Dover, the man said. And, God willing, Kurt and his family will be on it."

"You want me to drive you there?"

"How else would I get there in time?"

David was already changing from his carpet slippers to his shoes, which he had left in the hearth. "Don't worry. We'll leave right away. But why didn't you send Martin to tell me, instead of running here yourself?"

"He's out tonight. At a musical evening in aid of refugees, with Carl and Hannah—and Miriam went, too. Sammy would take longer to get here than me and Helga's looking after the twins—you know they've got measles. I didn't think I could still run, but it only took me a few minutes," Sigmund conveyed without pausing for breath. "So let's go! Who are you making phone calls to, just now?" he demanded as David picked up the receiver.

"I'll have to ask Nat to come with his car, as well. There won't be room in mine to bring back four extra people."

Nathan had been called out to a house call.

"I'll ring Ben," David said.

"You know what I'm thinking right now?" Sigmund mused aloud whilst he was getting through. "When a person needs help, what a wonderful thing it is to have a big family."

David arranged to Meet Ben in Knutsford, so they could travel to Dover in convoy. "Fetch me your atlas," he instructed Ronald. It had suddenly occurred to him that they did not know the route. "And ask Lizzie to make a flask of tea and some sandwiches."

"A picnic he thinks he's going on!" Sigmund fumed impatiently.

"Can I come with you, Dad?" Ronald asked when he returned from the kitchen. "I might as well. I've never been to Dover and I'm on holiday from school."

David hesitated. Bessie would be furious if he took Ronald on a trip that would keep him up all night. But it would be an interesting experience for the boy. "All right. But wrap up warm and find a muffler for Zaidie Sigmund; he forgot to put one on."

"Who cares about mufflers?" Sigmund said exasperatedly. "Come on already!"

"Calm down," David said to him as they drove off. There's no certainty your relatives will be on the boat, he wanted to add, but did not have the heart to. Hugo Frankl had received a similar message from his uncle in Vienna, but had returned from Dover with an empty car.

Ben's Ford was parked at the rendezvous when they reached Knutsford. Marianne was curled up on the seat beside him.

"Harry couldn't come; he's got to be in the shop tomorrow with Dad away, so Arnold and I tossed up for it and I won," she smiled.

"Ronald might as well travel with us, then they'll both have company," Ben said.

Marianne wished it was Martin who had come, but if it had to be one of her other cousins, she was glad it wasn't Shirley. Her mother was always saying it wasn't right not to like someone you were related to, but Marianne didn't see why you had to just because of that.

"I've heard about the white cliffs of Dover, but I never thought I'd see them," Ronald smiled.

"First you'll see London," Ben said. "We have to go that way. It'll still be dark when we get there, but you'll see it on the way back."

"When we went there for Uncle Nat's wedding, all we saw was the *shul* and the reception hall," Marianne recalled.

"You won't see very much this time, either, love," her father answered. "But that's not what we're going down south for, is it?"

The children fell silent, affected by the gravity of his tone.

"Oy," Ben sighed eloquently. "Only for something like this would I be taking time off from the shop."

"It'll be terrible if Zaidie Sigmund's relatives don't turn up," Marianne reflected.

"More terrible for them than for him," Ben said quietly. "English Jews don't know how lucky they are," he added. "Going on a journey like this makes a person stop to think and realize it."

A sliver of moon had emerged from behind a cloud and lent a ghostly ambience to the Cheshire countryside through which they were driving.

"Everything looks different at night, doesn't it?" Marianne said, gazing at a dark clump of trees on a hillside. "And when everything is peaceful, like it is now, it hurts to imagine places where dreadful things are happening."

"So don't bother imagining," her father advised her.

"She can't help it, Uncle," Ronald said. "Marianne's an imaginative person."

Marianne looked at him with surprise. How did he know she was? They saw each other every week at the tea party, but rarely exchanged a word and she'd never bothered thinking about what sort of boy he was. To her, he was just Shirley's brother. "Are you looking forward to your *Bar Mitzvah*?" she asked him.

"If anyone else asks me that, I'll scream."

Marianne laughed. "Boys aren't supposed to scream."

"No, they have to do it silently, inside themselves. My *Bar Mitzvah* isn't for ages yet, but it's ruled my life for years, and for the last six months everyone in our house has talked about nothing else," Ronald said disgustedly.

"Now now, lad," Ben placated him.

But he was not to be placated. "All I hear is who's coming and who isn't. And what kind of frocks Mom and Shirley are going to wear for it. And what the menu's going to be. And how much it's going to cost my dad!"

"In my day nobody had those problems," Ben said dryly. "Sometimes I think it's when you get a bit in the bank your worries really start."

"How much is it going to cost?" Marianne asked Ronald.

"Hundreds of pounds, by the sound of it."

"How disgusting, when poor people are starving," Marianne declared.

"I'm glad somebody as well as me thinks that," her cousin said.

How could I have thought Ronald was the same as Shirley? Marianne asked herself. They were nothing like each other. She had another cousin who was nice and she hadn't known it. But there would never be anyone whose friendship mattered to her the way Martin's did.

They were nearing the Potteries and she could see the tall chimneys towering against the night sky with the fiery glow from the kilns diffused around them. "It looks like a painting," she breathed, enraptured.

Her father was staring through the windscreen and could see only a grim, industrial panorama. "Nobody but our Marianne could get excited about Stoke-on-Trent!"

"Sometimes there's beauty in ugliness," she informed him.

"Oy vay!"

"The way something that's sad can be funny, too," Marianne went on, undeterred by her father's prosaic reactions.

Ronald looked thoughtful. "But not to whoever the sad something is happening to."

"Why don't you kids have a snooze?" Ben suggested. He was beginning to feel out of his depth with them.

"I didn't come to snooze," Ronald replied.

"Me neither," Marianne agreed.

But before they reached London, both were sound asleep and did not awaken until Ben stopped the car at the docks in Dover.

David pulled up behind him. Sigmund's excitement had changed to tension and he had not spoken a word during the latter part of the journey, but had sat huddled in the blanket David had thrown around him, his hat dipped low on his forehead, shadowing his eyes. David could feel a tautness within himself, too. Uncertainty was affecting them both.

"Find out where the night ferry from Calais docks," he requested when Ben came to speak to him.

"Please God, let them be on it," Sigmund prayed, breaking his silence.

David gazed through the windscreen at the sunrise, assailed by hazy memories of his own arrival in England as a refugee. He'd been eight years old. A frightened kid in a long, baggy overcoat and a coarse wool cap with a shiny peak, getting off a stinking herring boat at Hull with his family and the Lipkins, Cohens and Lenskys. Now, he was nearly forty-two and had come to meet Jews who were seeking sanctuary for the same reason the Sandbergs had. How unreal it all seemed. But the reality was all too stark. Would the repetitive pattern of Jewish history never end?

The ferry had already docked when they walked on to the quay and the gangway was being fixed into place.

Sigmund's face was paper white, except for the gray morning stubble on his chin and he seemed unaware that Marianne and Ronald had linked their arms through his.

"It takes me back," Ben said to him.

"Which Jew who found refuge here would it not affect that way?"

"It's so long ago, I don't think I'd recognize Vienna," Ben reflected.

Sigmund sighed. "Me, I can shut my eyes and see the Ringstrasse, where I used to walk with Rachel and the children on Sunday afternoons," he said nostalgically. "Such a beautiful street, who could ever forget it? And the scent of the lilac in spring mingling with the aroma of freshly ground coffee when you strolled beneath the trees beside the cafés."

"My dad was only a little boy when he left there; that's why he doesn't remember," Marianne reminded Sigmund. "I'd like to go there when I grow up," she added. "And see where my ancestors lived."

"With a chain across the street to separate the ghetto from the rest of the city," Sigmund reminisced bitterly. "Even before the trouble with Hitler started, Kurt wrote me that the one at Eisenstadt, where our family used to live, was still there. Only if you were rich or famous did Viennese society accept you. In my time there the rest of us were second-class citizens, though not officially. We could go anywhere we pleased, the opera and the art galleries, everything was open to us; but the chain that cut us off was there to remind us of our status when we returned to our homes. So my brother got wealthy in recent years and moved away from Eisenstadt. A lot of good it did him!"

Sigmund controlled his emotion and gave his attention to the bustle of activity building up around them. Crates and boxes were being unloaded from the ferry and a crop of porters now waited expectantly with their trolleys at the foot of the gangway. There was mounting noise, too, as daytime sounds began filling the early morning stillness. Clanking and grunting from freight wagons; the thrum of the traffic that had begun entering the docks; a ship's siren hooting and the cry of some lonely gulls overhead.

I can't bear it, Marianne thought as the first passengers disembarked from the ferry. Supposing the people they were hoping to meet had not come? She felt Sigmund grip her hand tightly and saw Ronald cross his fingers.

David was studying everyone who walked down the gangplank. Most were Gentiles, or obviously French. But a few Jewish refugees had already disembarked and were being greeted by small groups of English relatives weeping for joy. It was easy to pick out the Jews, even before those waiting for them shrieked an emotional welcome. They were all dressed in garments that had seen better days and had faces that looked as if they had forgotten how to smile.

He could hear a middle-aged couple in a group behind him talking about their journey.

"My wedding ring they took from me at the border," the woman was saying distraughtly.

"I made her give it to them," the man said. "I was afraid to argue in case they sent us back."

Several Yiddish conversations were audible and the word "afraid" featured in all of them.

"It makes you go cold," Ben shuddered to David.

But Sigmund was oblivious to everything around him. "He's here! My great-nephew Peter Kohn!" he shouted suddenly and rushed forward, dragging Marianne and Ronald with him.

David recognized the stocky, fresh-complexioned youth from a photograph Sigmund had shown him. But he would have done so anyway. It was like looking at Carl when he was that age.

"Why is he hanging around at the top of the gangway?" Sigmund exclaimed excitedly.

"He must be waiting for his Zaidie and his parents," Ronald said.

They saw the boy turn around to take the arm of someone behind him and caught a glimpse of a dark shirt.

"Ilsa's here, too," Sigmund beamed. "Kurt and Rudy are probably waiting behind for the baggage," he added. Then the brightness dimmed from his face as he saw that Peter's companion was not Ilsa, but a young girl.

"Who is she?" Marianne inquired.

"I don't know," Sigmund replied waving to Peter.

Peter and the girl had the same stiff expressions on their faces that David had noted on those of the other refugees. As if some inner paralysis had rendered their features immobile, he thought.

"How do you do, Uncle Sigmund?" Peter said in perfect English when he joined them. "I knew you from your picture. And also you resemble my grandfather."

Sigmund kissed him on both cheeks and allowed a few tears to run down his own. "You'll have to excuse me for weeping. But I'm thanking God, inside me, because you're here. Where are your parents and my brother? They're attending to the bags? I can't wait to see them."

The boy looked at him mutely for a moment. "There are no bags, Uncle. And I do not know where my parents and grandfather are."

David saw Sigmund's knees buckle and caught hold of him to prevent him from falling. The silence that followed seemed endless, but Peter just wet his lips as if he was thirsty and made no attempt to break it.

Marianne was eyeing the girl and thought it was rude of them all to have ignored her. But she seemed not to mind and was standing like a statue beside Peter, clutching a brown paper parcel.

"I'm Marianne Klein, what's your name?" she smiled to her, but received just a scared glance in return.

"It is all right," Peter said to the girl gently. "These people are friends. There is nothing to be afraid of any more. In Vienna these days, there are even Jews whom one may not trust," he explained to the others. It was not a pretty lesson to learn—that some people would betray their own mother in order to save their skin."

"Your English is a lot better than my German," Ronald complimented him.

"At school, languages were my best subject. And hers also," he said looking at the girl. "This you will find out when you hear her speak."

But the girl maintained her frozen silence.

Sigmund managed to collect himself. One of his relatives safe from the Nazis was better than none. This was cold comfort, but he tried not to show it. "The two of you traveled together?" he asked his nephew.

Peter nodded. "She is Hildegard Blauer and has relations in Manchester. I hope we can take her to them."

"Why not? Are they called Frankl?" Sigmund turned to David and Ben. Blauer was Paula's maiden name."

"Mrs. Frankl is Hildegard's great-aunt," Peter supplied.

"My grandfather was her brother Otto," the girl said as if the mention of her family had removed a stopper inside her.

Sigmund took her hand. "I went to school and *cheder* with him," he smiled. But the smile hid the chill that had gripped him when she referred to his old friend in the past tense.

Hildegard stared down at her scuffed, brown brogues. "My mother was his only daughter."

Her relegation of her kin to the past affected David and

Ben, too. It was conceivable that her grandfather, who had been Sigmund's age, had died a natural death. But her mother had probably been the same age as their own wives and they did not let themselves think about what must have happened to her.

"Why're we standing here?" David said gruffly and led the way to where the cars were parked. "We might as well get going. Unfortunately, there's nothing to wait for."

The four young people walked along together and Sigmund positioned himself between them.

Ben fell into step with David, ahead of them. "I don't think I can drive back to Manchester without having a sleep," he said yawning and stroking his blue jowls.

"I feel the same way," David answered.

"So why don't we book in at a hotel and let everyone get some rest?" Ben suggested. "And drive home tonight."

"It would mean Ronald missing *shul* this evening and you know what rabbis are like when it's nearly a boy's *Bar Mitzvah*."

Ben recalled Ronald's complaints in the car. It was the same with me and my boys, he mused briefly. It dominated a lad's life and, he thought for the first time, somehow it wasn't right. "You'll get him there in time for the Service tomorrow morning," he said to David. "And if his rabbi isn't capable of understanding why he missed *shul* tonight and had to travel on *Shabbos*, then our religion's even narrower than I'm beginning to think it is!"

David was too fatigued to argue.

"Hildegard's only just dozed off and I don't think we should disturb her; she's been crying nearly all day," Marianne said tiptoeing from the hotel room the girls had shared and encountering David in the corridor that evening.

David had just peeped into Sigmund's room and had found him slumbering fitfully, fully clothed, as if he had thrown himself on to the bed in distress the moment he was alone. "We'll let Zaidie get some more sleep, too, Marianne. Meanwhile, the rest of us can have something to eat."

They collected Ben and the boys and went downstairs to the restaurant, where a young man in a tuxedo was tinkling a piano amid the potted palms.

"Peter and I had baths and spent the rest of the day talking," Ronald said while they were studying the menu.

"And can my son talk!" David quipped to Peter.

Peter smiled.

Thank goodness he still can, David thought.

"I am the same. Is it not so, Ronald?"

"I'd say you were worse."

"Possibly. I enjoyed our conversation immensely. It was just as it was at home, with my best friend."

"Peter's going to help me with my German, Dad," Ronald said.

"And Ronald will assist me with my English. He says I must learn to say 'won't' instead of 'will not'. Such items as that I need to practice."

David and Ben shared an amused glance.

"When we first got here, we couldn't speak English at all," David told Peter.

"And we still don't speak it as well as Peter does," Ben added wryly. "Not when it comes to grammar, anyway!"

"That's why he sounds foreign, Uncle," Ronald pointed out. "His speech is too perfect."

They gave their order to the waiter and ate some melba toast while they waited for the food to arrive.

"You don't keep kosher, I notice," Ben said to Peter.

"I hope I am not offending you by having roast beef? That you all ordered fish for that reason did not occur to me. At home we ate no differently from the Gentiles," Peter explained without embarrassment.

Marianne recalled what Hannah had said after the Mosley meeting, about the German Jews being more assimilated than the English. Apparently it was the same in Austria. Peter's home life didn't seem to have been very Jewish. But his family had been reminded of what they were, in the end, by Hitler.

"Nobody can blame you for doing what you were brought up to think was all right," David said to Peter. "But I imagine you'll be living in my brother's house. He's married to your cousin Miriam and they have a son who's almost your age. And it's a kosher household, like they all are in our family."

"Whoever gives me a home, they and their household I will respect, Mr. Sandberg," Peter replied sincerely.

"I'm sure you will," David smiled. "And you'd better start calling me Uncle David."

Peter looked perplexed. "But you are not my uncle."

"The Sandbergs and Moritzes are one big clan, Peter. Though the only official relationship is our Sammy being Miriam's husband. Sometimes friendship can be a tie as strong as blood," David reflected. "As you'll discover now that you're joining us."

Peter crumbled the toast on his side plate and stared down at the tablecloth, his face puckered with emotion. "Two weeks ago, I had a family," he said slowly. "Since then, I have felt I had nobody at all. Maybe I will never see my parents and grandfather again. I am not a child. I must face it."

The lad's got guts, David thought. And by God, he needed to have.

"I did not want to leave them behind and come here alone," Peter said, raising his head to look at David and Ben. "But I thank you and my Uncle Sigmund for allowing me into your family. Now, I do not feel alone any more."

The waiter served the main course and Peter helped himself to a crusty roll.

"Oy! Meat and milk he shouldn't be mixing!" Ben exclaimed, watching him plaster the bread with butter. "Even though the meat isn't kosher," he added irrationally. "And on Friday night no less he's doing it, when the *Shabbos* candles are lit everywhere."

"So he won't eat dairy foods at the same time as beef when he gets to Manchester," David said tolerantly. He had found the boy's words deeply moving and knew Ben had, too, and that Ben's remonstration had just been a cover for this.

Marianne watched David stub out the cigarette he had lit between courses, though smoking on *Shabbos* was forbidden. Sometimes she found the way her elders kept some of the laws and broke others confusing.

Sigmund and Hildegard were still sleeping after dinner and David agreed with Ben that they should not set off for home until the following morning.

The four youngsters elected to travel together.

"I'll let you have the pleasure of their company, Ben," David said. He wanted to talk to Sigmund alone. "What are we going to do with Peter," he asked his old friend thoughtfully when they had left Dover and were traversing an icy, country road.

Sigmund emerged from the impassive silence he had maintained since he got into the car. "What do you mean, what are we going to do with him?"

David had had second thoughts about the boy's living at Sammy's house. "I wouldn't mind having him," he said carefully.

"Whose nephew is he? Yours or mine?" Sigmund flashed.

"But with you, he'd have to share Martin's room. And it's only a small one."

To this Sigmund could say nothing. He was occupying the spare bedroom at Sammy and Miriam's himself. The arrival of his twin grandsons had made it necessary for him to vacate the room he had occupied in his old home after leaving his wife.

"You think Bessie would agree to it?" he asked uncertainly.

"My wife's got a lot of faults," David answered. "But being hard-hearted with children isn't one of them."

"If all of them had come, I was going to ask your mother to have them in her big house, until they got their own place," Sigmund said sounding choked. "My brother wrote me Rudy was a clever man. It wouldn't have taken him long to find work and provide for them."

"But when a boy comes by himself, it's different, isn't it? We have to make certain he'll feel part of something and not like a lost sheep."

"What are you talking about?" Sigmund exclaimed edgily. "He'll be part of the family."

"But we don't all live together, do we?" David pointed out. "And we must make sure Peter lives where it's right for him. You've seen how he already gets on with my Ronald."

"Why do we have to decide now?" Sigmund said. He felt drained, emotionally and physically and he did not want to make a quick decision he might afterwards regret, as had been the case with his marriage to Gertie Fish.

"For Peter's sake," David replied. "We're not going to shift him from one place to another, like a stray parcel. The uprooting he's had is enough. Wherever he sleeps tonight he should know will be his home."

Sigmund lapsed into a silence that lasted for most of the journey and David knew better than to press him for an immediate answer. When they stopped the cars to buy petrol and the children got out to stretch their legs, David saw him watching Peter and Ronald talking together and noted his thoughtful expression.

Marianne and Hildegard were strolling up and down the forecourt, ankle-deep in snow.

"I pity that kid, having to live with Paula Frankl," Ben said to David whilst they waited for their change.

"Hugo will take her," David replied. "She'll be company for his daughter, Eva, he said when I phoned him from Dover."

Ben snorted. "A nice reason!"

"I'm sure it isn't the only one." David lit a cigarette and watched the smoke mingle with his breath in the frigid air. "I've asked Sigmund to let me have Peter."

"Oh."

"And I'm not going to start examining my motives, in case you think I should. I know I want him and that's enough."

"It's the only reason that counts."

Sigmund did not return to the subject until they were nearing home and even then he did so indirectly. "You made a better job of Ronald than Sammy did with Martin," he opined.

David felt his hands tense on the steering wheel. Was Sigmund denigrating his brother? Or stating a fact based on something he knew that David didn't?

"I know what you're thinking; I can read you like a book," Sigmund said. "Listen, nobody loves Sammy better than me. A heart of gold he's got. And he's made my daughter Miriam happier than you would have done, though with you she would have been richer in the things that don't make happiness."

Sigmund had not passed judgment when David broke his engagement to Miriam. Nor had he referred to it since. Hearing him do so many years later was a shock, but what he had said was true, in every respect. "You seem to know me better than I do myself," David said wryly.

"As well as you know yourself. It was knowing yourself that stopped you from marrying Miriam."

"It was knowing her, too."

"That I'm prepared to admit. But I don't want to discuss what is over and done with. We were talking about Sammy."

"And the bad job he's made of raising his son, according to you!" David said hotly. "Personally, I think Martin is a fine boy."

"Would I think otherwise about my own grandson?"

Sigmund gazed pensively out of the window at the slushy pavement on Cheetham Hill Road as they sped along. "But there are things about him that worry me. And the way he writes poetry about death is the main one."

"Those rhymes he used to make up when he was younger weren't like that."

"So something's happened to change him, hasn't it? To make him morbid. And whatever it is, why has his father let it happen?"

"He's got a mother, too," David said in defense of Sammy. "And the way Miriam's always fussed over Martin could have something to do with it," he added. "She lives in fear of something happening to him."

"Don't I know it?" Sigmund sighed. "But all the same, Sammy shouldn't have let her be like she is with Martin. A strong father can make up for a weak mother. Though Miriam isn't weak in other ways."

The only occasion on which David had seen Sammy be firm with his wife about their son was during the family row about taking the children to hear Mosley speak. But by then it was probably too late; the damage had been done.

"Hannah told me about those morbid poems," Sigmund said. "She is worried also."

"So why doesn't she mention it to his parents?"

"And break the boy's confidence? She's the only one except Marianne he trusts enough to show them to. But me she could talk to about it. I'm only the old grandfather."

They were approaching the brightly lit Riviera Cinema and would soon be at Sarah's house, where the family were gathered at the tea party.

"Don't worry, Martin will grow out of it," David said stamping out his disquiet. "But you haven't given me an answer about Peter."

"He'll live with you. But not because I'm letting you tell me what to do, like everyone else lets you," Sigmund declared. "Because I've made up my mind it's right."

Thus Peter Kohn's future was decided, on a bleak December night in 1938 while David was turning his car into Heywood Street and he knew he would always remember that moment. He had just acquired a foster son. And Ronald would have the brother he wanted.

The children were standing beside Ben's car when David

pulled up behind it. He told Peter and Ronald immediately and the delight of both was plain to see.

"Never did I see so many people in a room this size," Peter said when they entered Sarah's parlor and he was introduced to the family.

"From now on you'll be seeing it every *Shabbos*," Ronald informed him.

David had ushered Bessie into the entrance hall for a private word.

"What kind of woman would I be, if I couldn't give a home to a boy in his position?" she said when he explained. "But he's Miriam's cousin, not ours," she added. "Won't she want him?"

"Our house is much bigger than hers," David replied. It was a reason with which nobody could argue and the one he gave Miriam and Sammy.

Hugo Frankl was in the parlor with his daughter.

"All afternoon they've been here waiting for Hildegard," Sarah said.

Hugo dabbed his eyes with a monogrammed handkerchief and returned it to his breast pocket. "I can't believe she's really here," he said emotionally. "When they weren't on the boat I went to meet, I thought all my relatives in Vienna were dead."

Hildegard and Peter exchanged a tortured glance and everyone fell silent.

"I think they would be better off dead than where they are now," Peter said quietly. "And my people also."

Hildegard shuddered. "They took them all away a fortnight ago."

Peter was struggling to contain his feelings and it was Ronald, who had learned the rest of the story when they shared a bedroom in the hotel, who told it to the family.

"They all lived in the same block of flats, you see. And it happened on a night when Peter and Hildegard were visiting a Christian friend who lived there too. This girl's parents hid them both in a big cupboard when they heard all the commotion and saw the vehicles parked outside in the street. They didn't let them out until the Nazis had gone and when Peter and Hildegard went home, their front doors were wide open and there was nobody there."

Sarah's flesh had prickled with horror as she listened. The implications were worse than the details Ronald had supplied, and she wanted to weep for the boy and girl whom Fate had deprived of their loved ones and destined would now be here in her parlor. It had to be Fate, she thought, fingering her brooch, because God was merciful, not cruel.

"Peter found the boat tickets in his father's desk," Ronald went on. "The Nazis had taken his mother's jewelry and furs and all the silver, but they hadn't looked in there."

"But how did Peter and Hildegard get to France, to get on the boat?" Arnold Klein asked. "Weren't you frightened of being caught?" he said to Peter.

"I realized I had not known the meaning of fear until recently," Peter replied finding his tongue. "We traveled with a party of Christian schoolchildren who were going to Paris to visit the art galleries and my heart was thudding like a hammer, all the way. The father of our friend, in whose apartment we were that night, was the teacher who was escorting the group."

"Such a wonderful man; I shall never forget him," Hildegard said with tears in her eyes. "He arranged for a boy and girl of our age to remain behind and pretended Peter and I were them. Somehow he managed for us to have their papers, to show when we crossed the border. He bought us railway tickets from Paris to Calais and put us on the train with a bag of food to eat."

"And before we left Vienna, he hid us in a cellar until it was time to go," Peter added. "We did not return to our own homes again after that night. That is why we have no baggage. To return for our clothing would not have been safe."

"But I have a nice blue dress, which was his daughter's who was my best friend," Hildegard said, displaying the paper parcel she was still clutching. "And now Marianne is my first English friend."

Hugo Frankl dabbed his eyes again and kissed her cheek. "You won't be short of dresses now you're with me, love. And Marianne will come and visit you."

"I'll ring you up, Marianne," his daughter Eva said as her father bore her and Hildegard away.

Bessie put a kindly arm around Peter's shoulder. "I'm glad you've arrived in time for our Ronald's *Bar Mitzvah*. We'll get Peter a nice new suit for it," she said to David.

"I'll make him one, like I'm making Ronald's," Sigmund told her.

"Will you have time to? You still haven't finished David's new evening suit."

"Dad won't need one," Ronald declared adamantly. "Because I'm not having that kind of *Bar Mitzvah* and nobody's going to make me."

David and Bessie looked taken aback.

"I won't have all that money spent on a lot of people who aren't short of food," their son informed them. He appealed to Nathan who was listening with evident approval. "You agree, don't you, Uncle Nat? I want Dad to give the money he was going to spend on a big reception to a Refugee Fund, instead."

Our Nat is Ronald's mentor and ally, like Sigmund was mine when I was a lad, David thought with a pang. But maybe every boy needed someone other than his father to turn to.

Nathan was sitting with Leona on his lap, turning over the pages of a picture book for her. "You've made it clear to your dad how you feel, Ronald," he said carefully, aware of David watching him. "And you've told him why. What matters now is what he thinks. It's his money, not mine."

"But I bet if you were my dad, you wouldn't need telling what was the right thing to do!" Ronald burst out.

"That's enough," Sarah intervened. The bad blood between David and Nat could be stirred up again because of this.

David felt as if he had been dealt a physical blow. He had always thought his relationship with his son an ideal one, but Ronald's behavior indicated otherwise. He was conscious of Ronald's gaze fixed on his face and of an air of waiting in the room. Peter seemed transfixed with embarrassment and scenes like this must be avoided in future for his sake.

"All right, Ronald. We'll just have a luncheon at home for the family and your friends, after *shul*," he said.

"And you will give the money to help refugees?"

David nodded. "But not because I'm letting you tell me what to do," he added borrowing the words Sigmund had said to him about Peter. "Because I think it's right."

Ronald's face was wreathed in smiles, but Bessie's was the picture of dejection.

"What's up, Mom?" Shirley asked her.

"Your father's just taken away my excuse for a new evening gown."

Bessie's reply made everyone laugh and lightened the atmosphere.

"So you'll have a new costume instead," Esther consoled her.

"I'd have had one for *shul* anyway." Bessie glanced at Peter, whose presence among them had temporarily changed her priorities. "But what does it matter?"

"It doesn't," Sarah declared. "The important thing is that we're all here together, safe and well. And we shouldn't underestimate our good fortune that we live in England."

Martin had been standing silently by the window. "Let's hope we stay safe and well," he said.

"Why shouldn't we, you silly boy?" Miriam chided him.

He studied his bitten-down fingernails pensively. "Most of this family seem to wear blinkers, but they're in for a shock. Some of the masters at our school are already taking ARP courses."

"What does he mean?" Sarah inquired.

"They're learning about Air Raid Precautions," Martin said roughly and watched his grandmother turn pale. "You took us to hear Mosley speak, to increase our awareness of the Fascist threat to Jews; but it isn't just Jews who are threatened any more."

"Hitler told Chamberlain the Sudetenland was his last territorial claim," Abraham intervened.

"And anyone who believes it deserves all they get," Martin declared.

"I agree," Sigmund said.

"Because you're a scaremonger and Martin takes after you," Sarah accused them both.

Martin gazed out of the window at the dark bulk of the Welsh Chapel across the street and the baker's shop on the corner where his mother sent him to buy bagels on Sunday mornings. He could hear the wind rustling the leaves of an evergreen in the garden and the distant hum of traffic on the main road that had lulled him to sleep at night when he was a small child. How peaceful it all seemed; but it was only an illusion.

He turned to look at the family. "There's going to be a war I tell you."

PART TWO

Sticks and Stones

Chapter One

"I haven't had such a miserable birthday since I woke up with chicken pox the day I was eight," Marianne complained to Shirley.

"It'll be mine soon, as well," Shirley reminded her. "Mom and Dad were going to take me and Peter and Ronald to the State Café, as it's on New Year's Eve. But I don't suppose they'll be going themselves now there's a war on."

The two girls were tramping along the deserted high street of the Welsh village to which they had been evacuated.

"It's like a dream, us being here, isn't it?" Marianne said.

"To me it's more like a nightmare."

They turned left by the gray stone chapel and walked down the now familiar lane that led to the beach, past the minister's long-johns ballooning on a clothes line in the blustery sea wind, behind a prickly hawthorn hedge.

Marianne thrust her hands into her coat pockets; even the thick woolen gloves Helga had knitted for her could not keep out the cold. "Martin was right," she mused.

"What about?"

"Don't you remember what he said to the family the day Peter and Hildegard arrived?"

"No."

"You were too busy making eyes at Peter."

"I was not!"

"You've had a crush on him right from the beginning."

"Leave me alone, Marianne! Try being funny with someone else."

Marianne gazed at the turgid ocean lashing the pebbles on the lonely stretch of shore at the bottom of the slope and smiled sourly. "Apart from Mrs. Ellis and the seagulls I never see anyone else."

"If they had to evacuate me, why did it have to be with you?" Shirley expostulated.

"Ditto," Marianne expressed succinctly. "I wonder who lives in that place?" she said glancing up at an old manor house that towered in solitary splendor atop a pine-clad hill.

"I shouldn't think anyone does. It looks as if it's crumbling to bits," Shirley said practically.

But Marianne was affected by the sense of romantic times past which seeing it always evoked in her. "If walls could speak, I bet it could tell some stories," she said thoughtfully. Then her shoes crunched on the pebbles as they reached the beach and the sight of the rusty barbed wire festooned along it to deter enemy invaders returned her to the gloomy present.

She would not have minded being here so much if they were able to attend school, but the one in the village would not take them; its pupils left when they were fourteen. Marianne had at first spent the days reading and scribbling, and Shirley had sat sketching. Now, they could only occupy themselves with these pursuits in the evenings. Even in bad weather, their landlady would not allow them to remain indoors during the day and they had to keep on the move.

Their fathers had rushed them to the village in David's car the day war was declared, though both girls had protested. Mrs. Ellis was the widowed sister-in-law of Sarah's Welsh neighbors and had agreed to take Marianne and Shirley if it became necessary. They could have been evacuated with their schools, but their parents had wanted them to be together and had considered this more important than the continuance of their schooling.

"They didn't do this to the boys, did they?" Marianne flared thinking about it. "Just because we're girls, they think our education doesn't matter! And that we've got to chaperone each other!"

"How much money have you got left from this week's allowance?" Shirley asked her. "I'm starving and mine's nearly all gone."

Marianne fished in her pocket and found two shillings. "You paid for the cakes we bought yesterday, that's why."

Their parents had refused to send food-parcels in case it offended Mrs. Ellis and supplied them with cash to buy fruit and buns to supplement the landlady's frugal fare.

"She's a stingy old thing as well as a fresh-air maniac,"

Shirley declared peevishly. "And in my opinion, the real reason she makes us stay out all day is she doesn't want us under her flat feet."

Marianne did not reply, just as Shirley had ignored her assertion that their parents treated them differently because they were girls. Their days were peppered with other outbursts and neither paid any attention when the other suddenly gave vent to her personal frustrations. Three months of each other's undiluted company had brought them no closer than they had ever been.

"Why don't we take off our coats and sweaters; then we'll get pneumonia and they'll have to come and take us home?" Marianne suggested desperately.

"Trust you to think of something so daft!"

"Your trouble is you've got no imagination."

"And yours is you've got no common sense."

"I'd rather be at home with pneumonia than stay here."

"I'm surprised we haven't got it already," Shirley snorted. "From Mrs. Ellis washing our hair under the yard pump. When we get home, I'll never want to set eyes on anyone Welsh again."

"You'll have a job not to, with Mrs. Evans living next door to Bobbie. And the Evanses are nice, aren't they?"

"Yes," Shirley admitted reluctantly.

They squatted uncomfortably side by side with their backs resting against a sandbank and contemplated the sea. "If you'd said you never wanted to see this place again, I'd agree with you," Marianne said dislodging an obtrusive pebble from under her behind. "But what you said about the Welsh—well, it's the way some Christians are about Jews, isn't it?"

"I'm not interested in having one of your boring discussions," Shirley snapped.

"What would you rather talk about? Which of the seven frocks you've brought with you you should wear for our landlady's bread-and-jam banquet tonight?"

Shirley leapt up and stormed off along the beach, her long red hair flying in the wind.

"I was just trying to make you realize something!" Marianne called after her, but Shirley continued walking and she scrambled to her feet and ran after her. "I'm going to tell you what it is, whether you're interested or not, Shirley. Generalizations like the one you just made are odious."

"Go and practice your big words on the seagulls!" Shirley flung at her.

"Not only odious, but absolutely disgusting," Marianne went on. "And Jewish people are the last ones who should make them."

"If they don't come and take us home, I'll drown myself in the sea. I've got to get away from you somehow!" Shirley shrieked. Then she tripped over a pebble and fell flat on her face.

Marianne tried to help her up, but was not allowed to. "You just took the words right out of my mouth," she said. "Except I was going to say escape, not get away."

Shirley lay sprawled on the pebbles, listening to the tide rushing in. If her parents really loved her, they wouldn't have abandoned her. And oh, how she loathed Marianne!

If we were Manchester Grammar boys, we'd be home by now, Marianne was thinking. Arnold and Martin's school had already returned from its evacuation to Blackpool. Ronald and Peter were MGS boys, too, and she and Shirley had pleaded to be sent to Blackpool so they could all have been together. But their parents had said the resort was full up. The boys are at home, but we're still here! Marianne raged inwardly. And what for, when not one German bomber had so much as appeared in the English skies?

Shirley raised her head. "I think I'm having a hallucination, Marianne. Can you hear singing?"

"No."

"Well, I can."

Then Marianne heard it, too. A chorus of youthful voices drifting on the wind.

Shirley heaved herself up and peered through the sea mist. "I'm definitely having one, if you can't see what I can. Look behind you. Over there."

Marianne turned around and gaped. A vast circle of boys and girls were singing and dancing the *Horah* at the far end of the beach. "They're real all right," she said to Shirley. "But what are they doing here?"

Shirley raced along the beach to find out. The *Horah* was danced and sung by Zionist Youth Movements and a familiar sight to a girl who was a member of *Habonim*.

By the time Marianne reached them, her cousin had broken into the circle and was singing and dancing with them.

"Who are you and what're you doing in this place?" a

sturdy, bespectacled man who was with them asked the two girls when the ring of exuberant youngsters broke apart from sheer exhaustion.

"We were going to ask you the same question," Shirley smiled and explained their presence.

Marianne was listening to the boys and girls talking together in German, but would have known they were foreign from their appearance. They had a certain look about them she had noted in Peter and Hildegard, though she could not have described it in words.

"Are they refugees?" she asked the man, who had said his name was Dov.

"What else?" he sighed and she experienced a surge of shame because she had been feeling sorry for herself.

"We're living in that manor house on the hill," Dov said. "It isn't the essence of comfort, to put it mildly. It's stood empty for ages, but beggars can't be choosers and we've done wonders with it, considering."

"Why haven't we seen you before?" Shirley inquired. "We come to the beach every day."

"This is the first time we've been down here. We only arrived last week and it's taken us till now to make the house habitable and settle ourselves in. But now we've met, why not come and see us?" Dov smiled. "We're having a *Chanukah* party tonight and you're welcome to join us."

They thanked him for the invitation and watched the boys and girls head back towards the manor.

"I wish he'd asked us to have dinner with them," Shirley said. The only time they had tasted meat since leaving home was on the three Sundays their parents had visited them and brought some brisket sandwiches.

"How do you know they keep kosher? Peter didn't used to, did he?"

"The boys wouldn't be wearing *yarmulkes* otherwise. Some of them were very good looking, weren't they?"

"I didn't notice."

"You never do."

Marianne thought Shirley was boy mad, but refrained from saying so. They had quarrelled enough for one morning and at least had something pleasant to look forward to tonight.

When they returned to Mrs. Ellis's cottage for dinner, their usual thin slice of cheese, two pickled onions and a half a tomato awaited them on the table, on two small blue plates that were part of a set on the Welsh dresser.

The two china dogs that sat one on either side of the slate hearth seemed to be scowling at them as always and Marianne wondered what they had to scowl about when they spent their days cozily by the fire.

Mrs. Ellis was dishing up a pork chop and some potatoes and leeks for herself, and put her laden plate to rest on the slab beside the sink whilst she filled the utensils with water from an enamel pail.

The girls waited for her to sit down at the table. They were not allowed to do so until she did.

"And where have you been till this time?" she inquired in the soft, lilting voice that did not match her nature. "Twelve o'clock sharp is dinnertime in this house."

They watched her lower her black-garbed bulk into a chair.

"Sit down then, indeed to goodness! What are you waiting for?"

They seated themselves opposite her, in their regular chairs, as they had been instructed to do on their first day here. Mrs. Ellis's regimentation knew no limits.

"It's only five past," Shirley said, glancing at the squat black clock with a white face that reminded her of Mrs. Ellis. She gazed down at her uninviting repast. "And our dinner won't get cold."

Mrs. Ellis had just folded her hands to say grace and Shirley's pointed remark washed over her. Her skin was as thick as her iron gray hair was sparse, but Shirley was determined to provoke her.

"Why can't you give us something hot to eat, in this weather?" she asked when the woman had thanked God for what they were about to receive. "A boiled potato, for instance? Like you're having with your chop."

"And what would I boil it in for you, tell me that? Your parents gave permission for you to eat from nothing but the plates that have only been used for cake and bread and butter. My saucepans have all been in contact with meat. Like my dinner plates have."

"You could buy another pan and a couple of plates for us," Shirley persisted.

"And what would I do with them after you girls have gone?"

Shirley exchanged an exasperated glance with Marianne. They had asked their parents to bring some saucepans and crockery, but David had thought it best not to do so. "Better the devil you know; if she gets touchy about it and asks you to leave another landlady could turn out worse," he had said.

"Eat up those pickled onions, Marianne bach. It's wasteful to leave them," Mrs. Ellis said, removing a blob of gravy from her whiskery moustache with a spotless handkerchief.

"It isn't wasteful. You always put them back in the jar if we don't eat them," Shirley reminded her.

"I'm a thrifty woman and always have been."

"You're telling me! But we won't be in to eat your thrifty tea tonight."

"And what does that mean?"

"We've been invited to a party," Marianne interceded hastily. If she left it to Shirley to explain, even Mrs. Ellis's skin wouldn't be thick enough to withstand the jibes and she wouldn't let them go. "At the manor house. It's a hostel for Jewish refugee children at present and tonight's our *Chanukah*, that's why the man in charge invited us."

"Indeed to goodness, did he?" Mrs. Ellis said.

Shirley glared at her. "Yes, indeed to goodness, he did."

Marianne could tell by the glint in the woman's eyes that her cousin had finally made Mrs. Ellis's hackles rise.

Their landlady's retort confirmed this. "Back to the bombs it is for you, Miss, if I hear another word from you."

"There haven't been any and I wish you would send me home."

Mrs. Ellis managed to contain herself. "There'll be no gallivanting for you girls tonight or any other night while you live under my roof, bach. I'm a God-fearing person and I promised your parents to watch over you like I did over my daughter Megan."

"No wonder she left home when she grew up," Shirley answered. "I wouldn't have waited that long if I'd been her." She sprang up from her chair and ran upstairs, bumping her head on the fumed-oak beam above the doorway, as she often did.

"Please let us go to the party, Mrs. Ellis," Marianne pleaded. "It's a Jewish Festival, where they light candles," she explained, appealing to the woman's religious zeal, but found she had said the wrong thing.

"Like the Catholics and the pagans do, is it?" Mrs. Ellis pronounced sanctimoniously.

Marianne stared down at the two soggy, pickled onions on her plate. The low ceiling, that made even someone of her height feel tall, seemed lower than usual and the tiny room was suddenly shutting her in. Even the mixed smell of cooking and carbolic soap seemed stronger than usual and the tick of the clock louder, as if all her senses has been sharpened.

She glanced around at the unadorned, whitewashed walls and the speckless stone floor that Mrs. Ellis scrubbed twice a day, like she did the table-top and the surface of her dresser.

The bedroom the girls shared had the same too-clean and tidy look about it. Mrs. Ellis went in there and stowed away anything they had left lying around. Even their hairbrushes and books had to be kept in a drawer, as though it were a sin to let God see them.

That it was for God that Mrs. Ellis adhered to her rigorous standards Marianne had decided some time ago. Nobody ever crossed her threshold to see her over-immaculate home. But Marianne did not think God wanted people to be that way, to have no joy in their lives and fear Him as Mrs. Ellis did.

She watched the woman's ill-fitting dentures masticating the last morsel of fat from her chop and wondered what Rabbi Lensky at the old *Hassidic shul* in Strangeways would make of her. The Sandbergs had been members of the *Hassidic* sect in Russia, and Zaidie Abraham still preferred to worship with the small congregation for whom religion was a pleasure and not a restriction. The rest of the family no longer went there, but Marianne remembered the joyous abandon with which the *Hassidim* celebrated the Harvest and Tabernacles Festivals. To a lesser degree, the more anglicized congregations did, too.

"Jews believe in thanking God with a smile on their faces," she told Mrs. Ellis and thought of the young refugees singing and dancing on the beach that morning, despite the horror they had experienced in Germany. "Life was meant to be enjoyed," she added recalling that Rabbi Lensky had once said this.

Mrs. Ellis was regarding her with pursed lips, but Marianne did not care, she had made up her mind. "We're going to the *Chanukah* party tonight whether you like it or not," she declared and went upstairs to join her cousin.

Shirley was sitting on the bed, sketching an unflattering portrait of Mrs. Ellis.

"Do you still want to go to art school?" Marianne asked her. Much as she disliked Shirley, she had to admit that her sketches were very good.

Shirley exaggerated the mole on Mrs. Ellis's nose with a vindictive jab of her pencil, then gazed through the tiny, latticed window at the cobblestone area behind the terraced cottages, where the water pumps and lavatories were situated.

"It depends on how long the war lasts. What's the use of making plans?" she said with the practicality Marianne had learned was part of her nature. "If it goes on long enough, I'll have to work in a munitions factory or something. And so will you."

Marianne lay down on the white-counterpaned, black-iron bedstead. The only decoration that relieved the room's austerity was an embroidered tapestry bearing the words "Home Sweet Home". And even that was black and white. Why did she have to be here? In this home that wasn't a home. Cut off not just from those she loved, but from the chance to study, to qualify for university.

She quelled her resentment and made herself think about Hannah's advice—that a person could rise above the circumstances in which they found themselves. Marianne had applied this to being at the wrong school and had begun to do well there. She must do the same in her new circumstances. Become a writer without going to college and getting an English degree.

The resolve stirred her from her lethargy. "Let's go out before Mrs. Ellis turfs us out," she said briskly to Shirley.

They returned to the beach, hoping to find the young refugees there again, but only a collarless dog with a sad look on its face was there to greet them.

"Who else but a homeless mongrel and us would be out in this weather?" Shirley shivered, eating her half of the sticky bun they had just bought. "So you'll wrap up warm and take an umbrella. And if you still catch a cold it's better than getting blown up," she added, mimicking her mother's reply when told the girls had to be out of doors all day.

"Our Marianne always did exaggerate," Marianne said mimicking hers.

"How many times a day can a person be expected to

walk up and down a beach and round and round a village?" Shirley burst out. "I'll go mad if I don't get away from here!"

"And I will if you keep on saying so."

Their misery was increased by a sudden hailstorm and they stood in silence for a moment, allowing the frozen white balls, which were almost the size of mint imperials, to bounce on and off them.

"I'm going back to the cottage," Shirley decided.

"She won't let us in."

"I wish her luck to keep me out."

To their surprise, Mrs. Ellis admitted them without a word and they went up to their bedroom without speaking to her.

"She didn't make us take our shoes off in the doorway, like she usually does," Shirley remarked as they mounted the dark, narrow staircase.

The reason for their landlady's unprecedented laxity became apparent when they entered their room and saw their suitcases standing side by side on the floor. The drawers were open and empty to emphasize that their belongings had been packed.

"We're being shown the door," Marianne smiled.

But Shirley was not amused by the manner in which they were being ejected. "Like a couple of housemaids who've been caught stealing!" She rushed downstairs to tell Mrs. Ellis what she thought of her.

Mrs. Ellis responded with a homily about Israelites who ignored the lesson of Sodom and Gomorrah and went to pagan orgies.

"Is she talking about us?" Shirley asked Marianne when it was over.

Marianne giggled because the woman's interpretation of Jews lighting *Chanukah* candles was so absurd. "We're the only Israelites here, aren't we?"

"I phoned Mr. Sandberg from Jones-the-grocer's and told him to come for you," Mrs. Ellis informed them.

"We're not staying here another minute," Shirley replied. "We'll ring him up ourselves and tell him to collect us at the pagan orgy."

They fetched their suitcases and left the house.

"I feel as if I've been let out of prison!" Shirley exclaimed ecstatically. "We're going home, Marianne!"

Marianne was all smiles, too. "Our parents'll probably half-kill us for getting thrown out, but I don't care."

"It's their fault for sending us to live with an anti-Semite."

"Mrs. Ellis is an anti-everything," Marianne declared halting to adjust the string of her gas-mask box, which she had slung hastily over one shoulder. Then she saw their reflections in the butcher's shop window and knew she would never forget the incongruous sight of her smooth, black head and Shirley's ruffled, red one, flanked by two dead pigs hanging from meathooks.

But this whole being-evacuated experience was memorable, she thought, as they lugged their heavy burdens along the high street in the swirl of snowflakes that had followed the hailstorm. Like a drab canvas spattered here and there with bright blobs of paint.

She wouldn't forget how the elms and oaks in the woods fringing the village had looked in autumn, either, with the sun lending them a last golden splendor before the wind came to sweep their leaves away. Or the fresh smell of pine needles mingling with the salty tang of the sea. And the little beach where every pebble had become like a familiar face to her and where she'd sat scribbling in the September warmth. She would remember Mrs. Ellis spouting about Sodom and Gomorrah, too.

They reached Jones-the-grocer's, which was also the post office, and Shirley dumped her case beside Marianne and went inside to telephone her father.

Marianne had halted when she did, but was not really aware of having done so, or of the layer of snow forming on her shoulders whilst she stood waiting. The stream of vivid recollections was still pouring forth. The minister in his tall, black hat and wing collar, standing sternly outside his chapel, like Mr. Barrett of Wimpole Street preparing to chastise his children. Herself and Shirley wriggling and shrieking, with their hair and eyes full of soup-suds under the water pump. The musical sound of the Welsh language which was the villagers' everyday tongue and Mrs. Ellis's larder stocked for the war with nothing but pickled onions.

Why has all this come into my head just now? she mused as Shirley emerged from the shop. And why was it tinged with regret?

"Dad was about to leave; I just caught him in time,"

Shirley said. "He wasn't a bit cross and I'm sure your dad will say what he did. They wouldn't leave us under an anti-Semitic roof for one more night."

One half of Marianne's mind was thinking it was wrong of her cousin to have used that as an excuse; it was too easy for Jews to jump to that conclusion. The other half was answering the question she had just asked herself. Those random thoughts had been because the experience was nearly over and it was time to store the memories away. But why she felt regretful, when she desperately wanted to go home, she could not understand.

They began climbing the steep path up the hillside, which was a shorter way to the top than the winding lane used by vehicles.

"Come on, will you!" Shirley shouted. "You're always stopping to stare at things."

Marianne had paused to look down at the white-capped breakers pitting their might against the shore, and the village nestling snugly within its fringe of trees, like a tiny island cut off from the rest of the world. Perhaps people who lived in such an isolated place couldn't help being like the folk were here, she reflected. They'd made their own little community and wanted to keep it that way and had closed their minds so that nothing would change them.

"People who don't stop to look never see anything," she retorted to Shirley, resuming the climb. She had just seen the village and its inhabitants from another point of view and was glad she had, because after today she would never see them again.

The path grew steeper as they neared the hilltop and would have been a hard climb even had the girls not been burdened with suitcases. They reached the manor puffing and panting, and barely had strength to push open the heavy gates.

Marianne peered up at a coat of arms on the rusting wrought iron and prickled with excitement as they set off along the broad, curving drive.

The spice of pine needles was very strong here and there was the rotting odor of the sodden, decomposed leaves that made the drive slithery as her shoes cut through the soft snow and of the woodsmoke she could see spiralling from a chimney.

"I said the place was crumbling to bits, didn't I?" Shirley

said critically as they drew nearer to the house. She plodded on, looking neither to her left or her right.

Where's her artistic eye? Marianne wondered. On either side of the drive, great tangles of holly bushes had spilled their scarlet fruit onto the white carpet and their spiky foliage, too slippery to hold the snow, gleamed in the wintry light as though it had been newly polished. Behind the bushes, tall conifers towered darkly against the sky and seemed oblivious to the whirling flakes around them. There was something dramatic about the ambience that made Marianne hold her breath.

"It's so beautiful here, it makes me want to cry," she said to Shirley when they reached the house.

"Now I know you're out of your mind," Shirley replied prosaically. She grimaced at the white-pillared portico that was chipped with age, then walked up the disintegrating stone steps and pulled a rusty contraption beside the door. "I'm glad I didn't live in the days when they had these things instead of doorbells," she declared.

"I don't think I would have minded," Marianne answered. Her cousin had no sense of history.

Dov opened the door and apologized for keeping them waiting. "I forgot to tell you to come round the back. It takes a long time to walk through to the front from the kitchen," he smiled. "You're early, but welcome," he added, taking their suitcases without asking why they had brought them.

Shirley told him and the way she put it made Marianne cringe with shame.

"We're refugees now, too."

"Don't be ridiculous, Shirley!" How could her cousin compare them with boys and girls who'd been persecuted by the Nazis?

"Well, we are in a way, aren't we? From a woman who doesn't like Jews."

Marianne was tempted to argue with her, but knew it would not change her opinion of Mrs. Ellis. Shirley would store up the Sodom and Gomorrah memory, just as Marianne would, but to her it would be an anti-Semitic experience.

Dov led them across a vast, oak-panelled expanse.

"This must have been a ballroom," Marianne remarked hurrying to keep pace with his long stride. The floor was parquet, roughened with age, but there was still a hint here and there of the original glossy surface.

"Maybe so," he answered distractedly and she sensed that he had other things to think about and fell silent.

"It's like a freezing-cold barn. How can you bear to live here?" Shirley said to him.

"We only use the kitchen and the bedrooms, except for a butler's pantry that I've made my office."

The kitchen was huge, but warm and cozy, redolent of the familiar cooking smells that to Marianne and Shirley epitomized home. Several huge saucepans of goulash were simmering on the hob beside the big open fire and a lady in a white overall was making strudel, sprinkling cinnamon onto the apples and raisins.

The young refugees were helping to prepare the festive meal and Shirley went to talk to a group who were peeling potatoes.

Marianne, who had not learned German at school as her cousin had, felt somewhat out of it.

Dov patted her shoulder comfortingly. "Evacuees're running back home all over the country. It's nothing unusual," he said mistaking her silence for anxiety.

His gray eyes were twinkling at her from behind his thick lenses. But his face wore the weary expression of a man whom nothing would surprise. "Mrs. Ellis isn't anti-Semitic, she's just a narrow-minded person," Marianne said to set the record straight. There was something about this man that demanded total honesty.

"Good. That makes one less," he answered. "Now forget about her and go and chat with the other kids. If you can't speak German, you'll get by with Yiddish; it's similar."

"I only know a few words and phrases of that."

Dov grinned wryly. "Whatever is the Jewish race coming to? I don't suppose the next generation will know any Yiddish at all. But I was only pulling your leg, dear. All these kids speak English. They're letting your cousin practice her German on them because they've very polite."

"I'd rather talk to you, if you don't mind," Marianne said. The reticence that always affected her among strangers made it difficult for her to do what Shirley was doing; her cousin was what Bobbie Sarah called a good mixer.

"You can help me peel some apples for the next lot of strudel then," Dov smiled.

"I've never spent *Chanukah* away from my family before," Marianne told him when they had begun the task.

Dov eyed his young charges. "So how do you think they feel?"

"A lot worse than me."

Dov split an apple in half and removed the core pensively. I can't get over how excited they get about *Yom Tov*. Especially as some of them come from families who'd forgotten Jewish Festivals existed."

"It might be because of the way they were reminded."

"You could be right."

Later, Marianne helped lay the supper table.

"My name is Hans Shlager, how do you do?" a boy beside her said, placing glasses beside the cutlery she was setting down.

"Did you help like this at home?" Marianne asked him, struck by the way the boys were sharing the domestic tasks with the girls. "My brothers don't."

"And nor did I," he smiled. "It was not expected of me. But on a kibbutz in Palestine it will be and here we are preparing ourselves for that. They have there the sex equality," he added.

Marianne wished they could have the sex equality in England, instead of Harry and Arnold sitting with their feet up whilst she helped her mother wash the dishes.

After supper, Dov lit the little colored candles in the brass *menorah*. They were about to begin singing the *Chanukah* hymn when David arrived.

"You're just in time to sing *Maoz Tsur* with us," Dov said, handing him a prayer book opened at the appropriate page.

David accepted the book, though he knew the words by heart. The long drive had wearied him; he was not looking forward to repeating it in the opposite direction and was filled with disquiet about taking Shirley and Marianne back to the city. He had toyed with the idea of spending tomorrow in Wales to try to find alternative accommodation for them, but the factory had begun turning out army greatcoats in addition to the fashion rainwear, and Eli, who would be in charge though Sammy was nominally so, might go to pieces under the strain.

He could not summon the energy to raise his voice in song with the others and stood gazing at the candles, beset by the unreality of being in a Welsh manor house listening to *Maoz Tsur*. Then the familiar melody moved him the way it always did and he ceased to think and stared down at the prayer book.

His eye fell on the translation on the left-hand side of the page and he saw it was not like the one in his own prayer book, but a hymn in its own right. This must be the kind of book used by Reform congregations, where much of the service was conducted in English.

He read the last verse, with the ancient Hebrew words resounding all around him, and its contemporary appositeness lingered in his mind after the final rousing notes had died away.

> *Children of the martyr-race,*
> *Whether free or fettered,*
> *Wake the echoes of the songs,*
> *Where ye may be scattered.*
> *Yours the message cheering,*
> *That the time is nearing,*
> *Which will see all men free,*
> *Tyrants disappearing.*

David was conscious of the youngsters milling around him, his daughter and niece among them. Whether a Jew was free or fettered was an accident of their birthplace and it was this alone that had saved Shirley and Marianne from the others' fate. Would the time ever come when winds of oppression would not scatter Jewish seed to take root where it may until the next storm? Was it too much to hope for that this war would put an end to it, that the children in this room, and their seed, would never be cruelly scattered again?"

He watched the refugee boys and girls help themselves to strudel from the big platter on the table, laughing and talking animatedly, and marveled at their resilience. But resilience was a built-in Jewish quality and thank God it was. Where would his people be without it?

The lady who did the cooking told him her name was Marta and handed him a plate of steaming goulash.

"It was the best meal we've had since we left home, Dad," Shirley called to him, then returned her attention to a group of admiring lads.

Marianne was deep in conversation with the girl who had sat beside her at supper.

"All this way I *shlep* for them at a minute's notice and

they're too busy to be bothered with me," David said dryly to Dov.

Dov sat down at the littered table and played with some discarded orange peel. "Some of the stories I could tell you about what the kids here have been through—well, it's made me believe in youngsters having a good time while they can." He eyed Shirley who was smiling up at the boys. "That daughter of yours is a knockout, isn't she?"

"I think so," David said proudly.

Dov glanced at Marianne. "But what your niece lacks in looks, she makes up for in the head. I still haven't got over something she said to me." He told David about Marianne's reply when she learned how much the religious Festivals meant to the refugee children from assimilated families. "I'm sure my nieces and nephews wouldn't have realized it's because Hitler reminded them they're Jews."

David smiled. "Your nieces and nephews haven't got Sarah Sandberg for their grandmother. Shirley would have understood why, too, and so would all the other kids in our family. They've got an unusual Bobbie, who keeps them on their toes."

"It's a pity there aren't more like her."

Chapter Two

By the time the "phoney war" became a real one, Marianne and Shirley were ensconced in their fathers' businesses and nobody suggested evacuating them again.

Harry had been conscripted early in 1940 and Marianne was called upon to replace him in the shop, where trade was booming due to the swollen pay-packets brought home by war workers. Arnold remained at school; Ben was determined that nothing must prevent his brilliant younger son from entering a profession.

Shirley's presence in the factory was not only a pleasure

to David, but lightened his load considerably. His assistant cutter, Ludwig Steiner, had never taken the trouble to become a naturalized British citizen and had consequently been interned in a camp in the Isle of Man. David had not found a satisfactory replacement and was filling the breach himself in addition to his other work. His daughter offered to help in the office and was now lending a hand wherever it was required.

The fashionwear production was overshadowed by military orders, and David gave most of his attention to the latter, insisting that servicewomen were as entitled to perfection in their garments as civilian ladies.

"You're quite right, Dad," Shirley said to him one day after he had reprimanded a machinist for botching the seams of an ATS greatcoat. "But I hope you're not going to let the fashion side of the business slide."

"With a war going on, she's bothering me about fashion garments!" David exclaimed irritably.

"I know you look on me as only a kid, Dad, but I'm nearly sixteen, and I'm not daft."

"Are you inferring I am?"

Shirley met his gaze steadily. "I think you would be if you neglected our real trade. One day the war will be over. We've got to bear that in mind and keep Sanderstyle's smart reputation in the public eye."

David had received a similar lecture from Moishe Lipkin and, had he been less harassed, he would have been proud of his daughter's astuteness, but all he registered was impatience. "So keep it in the public eye! Who's stopping you?"

"Women still buy coats to wear for best," Shirley answered calmly. "And smart rainwear, as I shouldn't have to tell you, Dad, serves a double purpose, so it isn't extravagant. But we haven't updated our line since the war began, have we? I'll design something."

"If you want to amuse yourself, who am I to say no?" David could see Eli beckoning him wildly and strode out of the office to see what the latest problem was, picking his way through the extra row of sewing machines he had installed in the workroom to cope with Government orders.

He returned an hour later and found his daughter seated at his desk sketching. His secretary was gazing admiringly over Shirley's shoulder. "Is that all the pair of you have got to do?" he snapped.

Rita eyed one of David's clumsy designs which was pinned on the wall. "I never saw a real artist at work before," she said pointedly. "Have a look at Shirley's drawing, Mr. Sandberg."

"I haven't got time to. And if my daughter wouldn't mind, I need my desk to sit and work at," David replied. But he could see the sketch from where he was standing and even upside down it looked impressive. He was impelled to move to Shirley's side and view it the right way up. "Who taught you to draw like that? It's just like the pictures in Zaidie Sigmund's pattern books."

"So you've been studying them, too, have you?" Shirley smiled, putting the finishing touches to the sleek garment on the leggy lady she had created.

"Naturally. He used to get them from Paris."

"That's why I asked him to let me borrow one."

"But now France has fallen, he won't be getting any more," David added grimly.

"Forget about the war for a minute, will you, Dad? I borrowed the pattern book to learn how to draw this way. But the garment is my own design."

"Why have the shoulders got epaulets?"

"To give it a touch of the times," Shirley answered shrewdly. "The leather buttons do, too."

"The fit's a big snug for a raincoat."

"Mom told me your first fashion garment was an exact copy of one of hers that wasn't a raincoat."

The reminder pitched David backwards in time to the dismal morning when he'd seen Bessie dashing out into the rain to buy pickled cucumbers and sour cream for her father's dinner, wearing her best coat. He had asked her why she had not put on a raincoat and her reply that she wouldn't be seen dead in one had been his incentive to produce rainwear that was smart as well as practical. At the time, Bessie had been nothing more to him than his empoyer's dumpy, bad-tempered daughter and neither of them had known that one day she would be his wife. Now, their daughter was following in his footsteps, eager to build the firm's future.

"You'll be Sanderstyle's designer from now on," he declared and watched Shirley beam with delight. "I always had a sneaking suspicion you'd do me out of the job sooner or later."

Shirley got up to hug him and he thought of Ronald, whose determination to be a doctor had not faltered. He would not have his son with him, but nobody could expect all their hopes to materialize. And maybe Peter Kohn, who had not yet decided what he wanted to be, would come into the business.

Rita wafted a sheaf of Government orders under his nose and peered through the window into the street, where a lorry was unloading some bales of khaki and airforce-blue cloth. "It's time to come down to earth again, Mr. Sandberg! We've still got a war to win and we can't let the Service girls go naked. I'd be one myself if I didn't have to look after you and my widowed mother."

David returned to the workroom, where Issie was chastising one of the young girls who had replaced the men who had been called up.

"Fifty times I've shown her what to do and she still doesn't know!" he exclaimed to David.

"I'm used ter mekking gloves," she said, fiddling with her curling pins.

"So what are you doing in a garment factory?" Issie inquired exasperatedly.

"I wanted t' 'elp war effort. An' sewing uniforms pays me better."

"Garment machinists get well-paid in peacetime, too," David told her. "Why not learn to make a good job of it and after the war you can stay in the trade."

Shirley was right, he mused. A person had to think of afterwards, when there'd be no more orders for uniforms and they still had their living to make. He decided to give more attention to the fashionwear and showed Shirley's sketch to Moishe the next day, during their Saturday morning discussion.

The little salesman's eyes gleamed with approval. "Get her to design a few more, David. And let's get them into production already."

"It'll mean sub-contracting some of the Government orders."

"With the orders I'll bring in for coats like this," Moishe said appraising the sketch, "you won't be out of pocket. It'll balance itself out."

David found Shirley awaiting him anxiously when he went home for *Shabbos* dinner.

"She's been on edge all morning," Bessie told him whilst they ate their chopped liver. "In case Moishe didn't like her design."

"Well, he's the one who'll have to sell it," Shirley said. "So his opinion's more important than Dad's."

"Please put her out of her misery, Uncle David," Peter requested watching Shirley sitting rigidly in her chair.

"How anyone can get so worked up over a coat!" Ronald exclaimed with his mouth full.

"Moishe liked it," David relayed. "And we're putting it into production."

Shirley sprang up from her chair to kiss him and knocked over his glass of shandy in the process.

"Look what you've made her do, David!" Bessie said as he had known she would.

David mopped the tablecloth with his napkin, but his wife snatched it from him. He had expected her to do that, too. He watched her place a dinner plate between the soaked linen and the polished surface. Her predictability was a joke, but the way she instinctively made him the butt of all her irritations was not. He quelled the desire to snap back at her and made light of it as he had learned to do. "So I'll pay the laundry bill, love."

The youngsters were smiling at him sympathetically. Like his mother had once said, children were a compensation for everything.

"Now our Shirley's working with Dad, all we ever hear at mealtimes is business talk," Ronald remarked.

Or were they?

Peter was admiring the coppery glints a wintry sunbeam had painted on Shirley's hair. "It is Uncle David's business that provides the food we eat," he reminded Ronald. "And therefore we should all be interested in it."

The contrast between the two boys' attitudes was heightened for David day by day. Ronald had no respect for him other than a filial one and this was hard to take.

"Uncle Nat's bringing his stethoscope to Bobbie's this afternoon to show me how to use it," Ronald said.

David brushed aside his jealousy of his brother, but could not hold back a sharp retort to his son. "You're a long way off the stethoscope stage, my lad!"

"He might end up in the army before then, if the war goes on long enough," Shirley said striking a chill in her parents' hearts.

"My turn will come first. And I am looking forward to it," Peter declared.

Lizzie had just served the chicken soup and David dropped his spoon into his with a plop that added a splash of yellow to the brownish shandy stain on the cloth. But for once Bessie made no comment. She too was shocked by what Peter had said.

Their foster son regarded them gravely. "You think it unnatural that I want to pay back the Nazis for what they have done to my parents and grandfather?"

"Martin can't wait to join up, either," Ronald revealed.

Nobody was talkative during the rest of the meal and David just picked at his main course and refused the dessert. What he had just heard had ruined his appetite. Peter's feelings were understandable. But Martin had no personal vendetta with the enemy and wanting to get to grips with them was contrary to his gentle nature. Being a conscientious-objector would have been more in keeping with it.

"Meanwhile, Peter and Martin aren't old enough, and Esther had a nice letter from Harry yesterday," Bessie said.

But this did not comfort David. Peace was a long way off and for the first time it struck him forcibly that the lads in the family who were still only schoolboys might be called upon to sacrifice their lives. One of Eli's nephews had died at Dunkirk and what was there to show for it? David thought, with the bitter sense of waste that had haunted him during and after the last war. But this time there'd have to be something to show for it, or it would be God help the human race.

Meanwhile, though London was being bombed mercilessly, in Manchester nothing had really changed and it was difficult not to feel remote from the war. This feeling remained with him at his mother's tea-party that afternoon. There was more apple than raisins in the strudel and saccharine instead of sugar in the tea, but apart from that and a reference to Harry's letters, which were still, thankfully, coming from "somewhere in England," everything was just as it had always been. Except that a new lot of young children were making their presence felt.

"I don't like you, Henry. I only like Frank," Leona, who

would soon be five, declared tempestuously pushing the handsome, fair twin away and hugging his mousey brother.

"You'll get your bottom smacked if you don't stop being naughty," her mother warned.

"And I like Daddy better than you," the spirited child retorted.

Nathan picked her up and stroked her fiery hair.

"That's why she behaves badly. Nat lets her get away with everything," Rebecca informed the family.

"So let's all have another cup of tea. These days we mustn't waste it when the pot's been filled up again with water," Sarah intervened diplomatically. She had learned to recognize the danger signs in her daughter-in-law and the sudden glint in those lovely eyes was one of them. It would only take a wrong word from Nat for one of their regular tiffs to blow up.

Abraham glanced at the clock and sighed. "It's blackout time again." On winter weekdays, his wife drew the curtains before he arrived home from work. But on Saturdays and Sundays the task fell to him and was a token reminder of what the night may bring.

It was to the others, too. And to Rebecca in particular. "When I think of my family in London, sleeping in air-raid shelters——" she shuddered. She watched Abraham swish the maroon chenille, which Sarah had lined with thick, black material, across the bay window. "We're so lucky living here. The war's hardly touched us."

"I've been thinking that all day," David said.

Sigmund added his usual note of down-to-earth doom. "Things have got to get worse before they get better. And the way Manchester is being left alone, with the docks and Trafford Park here, can't last."

Sigmund's prediction materialized the following night when the brief but devastating Manchester blitz began and brought the war into the forefront of their lives.

Sarah was putting the kettle onto the fire to boil when the air-raid siren sounded, and wondered if her neighbors the Evanses were back from Chapel yet and whether Bridie was safely home after her Sunday evening out.

"Get out the thermos flasks while I make some sandwiches," she instructed Abraham.

"Even sitting in the coal cellar she wants to give people

food to eat!" Abraham watched her pick up the telephone receiver. David had had a phone installed for them, in case of emergency. "Who are you ringing up just now?"

"Esther."

"You think she didn't hear the siren?"

Sarah replaced the receiver sheepishly.

"But you just wanted to make sure! Another mother like you I don't think there is in the world."

"Every mother is like me."

"But they don't act like you."

"So shoot me!"

Ten minutes later they were installed in the cellar. With them were Sigmund, Miriam and Martin, who had brought the twins wrapped in blankets. Carl and Sammy were air-raid wardens, and Hannah and Helga were on duty with a mobile canteen.

"Just tonight had to be their turn," Sarah said anxiously listening to the sound of aircraft and the ominous, distant thuds. "Sammy and Carl remembered to put on their tin hats, Miriam?"

"They're steel helmets, Ma. And if they'd didn't it's their own lookout," Miriam answered edgily. The rush through the streets with her young nephews had unnerved her, but the alternative was to crouch in the broom cupboard under the stairs where she would not have felt safe. The nearest public shelter was no nearer her home than Sarah's house.

"Sigmund must have a crystal ball inside his head, what he said yesterday," Abraham joked to calm everyone's nerves.

"A black one," Sarah said grimly.

"What I've got in my head is a brain. And rose-colored spectacles I don't wear, like some people," Sigmund declared.

"The ones to be angry with, Bobbie, are the swine who're bombing us," Martin said as a thud, louder than they had yet heard, reached their ears.

"You think I'm not?" Sarah demanded in an outraged voice. "I wish I could do something to stop them!"

"As soon as I'm old enough, I'm going to," Martin replied tensely.

Miriam had little Frank on her lap and stopped stroking his hand, abruptly. "You'll be at Oxford by that time," she made herself say evenly. But her heart was thudding with foreboding. "The war will be over and you'll be wearing a cap and gown and riding a bicycle with the other students, like you've always wanted to."

"Come out of your fool's paradise, for God's sake, Mom!" Martin exclaimed. "England's got to take the initiative to win the war. Drive the Germans out of France and take the battle into the enemy's territory. And it's going to take a long time."

"I agree," Sigmund said.

Miriam's eyes looked charcoal instead of their usual translucent green, in her deathly-white face. "Be quiet!" she rasped to her father.

"Zaidie keeping quiet won't change the facts," Martin declared. He pointed his fingers towards the ceiling and the shadow this cast on the whitewashed wall was that of a gun. "I'll be up in the sky shooting the bastards down before the war's over and any Jewish mother who doesn't want her son to fight the Nazis should be ashamed of herself."

Sarah handed little Henry to Abraham and went to put her arm around Miriam's quivering shoulders. "I think it's you, Martin, who should keep quiet."

Then a tremendous crash that sounded as if it was right beside them reverberated through the cellar.

"It must be the same for the Germans when we bomb them," Martin whispered. "But I'm not going to let myself think of them as human beings. If they were, they wouldn't have let Hitler do what's he's done to the Jews."

Nobody replied and he sat with his knees hunched up, sickened as much by the pangs of humane conscience which sometimes eroded his will to hit back, as by the fumes from the paraffin stove heating the cellar. Were the German lads who were now pounding Manchester with their doom-laden missiles thinking of the people down below? He doubted it. And he wouldn't allow his mind to dwell on that when the time came.

"All right, Martin?" his mother asked.

"Sure I am." But the horror which these days darkened his private thoughts was gripping him like a sudden cramp and words began spilling from his lips as if of their own accord:

> *"From out the night sky*
> *Fell a hideous rain.*
> *Below, the people left their games*

> *To shelter 'neath steel umbrellas.*
> *Some blew inside out,*
> *The shelters with them*
> *While the storm raged on,*
> *Puddling the city streets with blood.*
> *And the stench of death*
> *Rose thickly heavenward,*
> *Mingling with the breath*
> *Of brave young men in aeroplanes."*

"That boy needs his head examined, the things he comes out with!" Abraham exclaimed after a chilled silence.

"You don't know poetry when you hear it?" Sigmund inquired.

"Poetry shmoetry! It didn't even rhyme."

"My husband would like it to rhyme, as well as give us goose-flesh," Sarah shuddered.

Sigmund smiled at Martin. "It isn't good you should be so morbid," he said as lightly as he could.

Miriam said nothing, but Martin could see her eyeing him anxiously. Which was nothing new. "It just came into my head," he said with false nonchalance.

"You made it up yourself?" Sarah said with surprise.

Martin nodded pensively. "Except it doesn't happen that way any more. When I was younger, sometimes I'd see something and think I'd like to write a poem about it. But now—well they seem to happen by themselves."

"Whoever heard of a steel umbrella?" Abraham asked him derisively.

Martin smiled at his grandfather's lack of imagination and tapped the girders with which David had had the cellar reinforced.

"A nice cup of tea will make you better, Martin," Sarah said as if poetry were a sickness. Then the naked light bulb above their heads went out, leaving her floundering beside a pile of coal with the thermos flask in her hands.

"I bought some matches this morning, they should be in my handbag," Miriam said, fishing in its cluttered depths.

She found them and struck one, and Sarah got a candle from her secret hoard on the shelf above the wringing machine, about which she did not feel guilty. War or no war, they were essential for *Shabbos*.

When the candle had been lit, she poured the tea and

they sat in the flickering light, in the old deckchairs that before the war had only been used in the back garden on summer Sundays. The twins were sound asleep, undisturbed by
the noise of the aircraft overhead and the falling bombs, their
vulnerable innocence heightening the others' waiting tension.

"God is watching over us," Sarah whispered, fingering
her brooch.

"If He hasn't been blasted out of Heaven," Martin replied cynically.

David was on duty that night close to his home, but
apart from escorting people to the shelters and checking
blackout curtains, the local air-raid wardens had no tasks to
perform. The blitz was concentrated on the city center and
its perimeters.

After the all-clear siren had sounded he stood in the
street with his neighbor, Hershel Levy, gazing at the distant
roseate hue of the sky.

"How can something that looks so beautiful be the aftermath of destruction?" Hershel muttered taking off his steel
helmet to wipe the sweat from his bald head. "There must be
buildings in town still on fire."

The smoke had drifted northward and was hanging like
an acrid pall all around them.

"I wonder if they got the docks, as well?" Hershel said,
folding his arms and resting them on his paunch. "Your sister
lives near there, doesn't she?"

David hurried home to telephone Esther, but Bessie had
already done so.

"Everyone's all right," she reassured him. "I've rung up
the whole family."

Shirley and the boys were in the kitchen with Lizzie,
munching bread and jam, ravenously, as though waiting to be
blown up had given them an appetite. David was hungry, too,
and sat down to eat with them.

"Maybe the Germans'll leave Manchester alone again,
now they've given it a bashing," Bessie said.

David swallowed some scalding tea and smiled grimly.
"Only you could be such an optimist, love."

"Where will it get us to start being pessimists?"

"But we've got to face the facts, Mom," Ronald declared.

"An' one o' 'em's ye're filthy dirty, our Ronald, from

bein' in't coal cellar," Lizzie told him. "Peter an' all. Away yer go ter scrub yersels, this minute."

The boys had coal dust on their faces and clothing and went to clean up. Neither would dare to disobey Lizzie, though they loved her, too.

"I mus' get t'cellar spruced up'n a bit more comfortable afore t'Germans come back," Lizzie said.

"God forbid," Bessie shuddered.

"I wouldn't bank on 'im ferbiddin' it, Missis," Lizzie answered. "Wi' one thing'n another, it looks as if God's got fed up wi' sortin' out t'mess 'is children's made o' t'world."

David left the house and got into his car with Lizzie's words echoing desolately in his ears. In many ways he was not religious, but still clung to the principle of a Divine Being whose merciful goodness was mankind's one remaining hope. The Germans had largely eschewed this, had made Hitler their God and Nazism their creed. But the few who had not, the Lutheran pastors and Catholic priests who had refused to abandon their Christian beliefs and ethics, had not been rewarded with God's mercy. Instead, He had allowed them to be incarcerated in concentration camps along with His chosen people, the Jews.

And now, havoc was being wreaked upon Christian England, where the churches were filled with God-fearing people every Sunday. God had not lifted His hand to strike down the Nazi non-believers against whom His devout flock were fighting His battle against evil. David sat gazing through the car windscreen at the evidence of this which still lingered redly in the sullen December sky.

He tried to start the engine, but it was too cold and he got out to use the crank, cursing savagely because there was no immediate response. But the anger gripping him had nothing to do with the car. It was the searing resentment that had affected him in the trenches during the last war, directed against God for requiring people to suffer to prove their allegiance to Him. And according them no different treatment than He meted out to those who had cast Him aside!

"Where are you going, David?" Bessie called from the doorstep. She had put on her dressing gown, and set her hair in flat pincurls as she always did before retiring. "None of us has had a wink of sleep. Aren't you coming to bed?"

The engine had just sprung to life and David got back into the car. "First I'd better make sure the factory's still there." He roared off along the street with the picture of his wife's shocked expression still before his eyes. It had not occurred to her that Sanderstyle was near enough to town to have gone up in smoke, and their livelihood with it. But it had to him.

The pungent odor of burned-out buildings thickened as he drove down Cheetham Hill Road and drew nearer the city center and he steeled himself for what he might find. The factory was on a side street with many others, in the heart of the Manchester rainwear district where men who had started out as workers now had their thriving businesses. Years of sweat and toil accounted for their progress to affluence, and David's was not the only car parked on the street in the drab gray dawn.

"Everything's all right here, thank God," Harry Rothberg, who was Lou Benjamin's father-in-law, called to David in the kind of voice he would have used if his nearest and dearest had just been spared an untimely end.

David joined the group of middle-aged and elderly men whose faces wore the grateful expression he knew was on his own. The street was entirely intact, but the acrid clouds drifting from the near distance were ominous.

"In town it must be terrible," said Solly Butensky, whose factory was next door to Sanderstyle, with a shake of his head. "From what a policeman I spoke to told me, when I tried to drive round and take a look, it'll never be the same again. I couldn't get through for fire engines and the stink was something awful."

David thought of the old buildings he had known since he was a lad. The face of the city was not all beautiful, but age had mellowed it to a state of grace that was all its own, and which newly erected edifices could not attain. He looked up at the small, Sanderstyle building that was like a redbrick box, but infinitely precious to him. "Let's hope our *mazel* lasts, round here," he said gruffly to the others and strode back to his car. To go on being lucky was all a person could hope for in wartime.

The German bombers repeated the blitz that night, but David's luck had run out. The street of factories was a shambles the next morning and Sanderstyle had been razed to the ground.

David stood in the road and surveyed the heap of rubble that was all that was left of what he had worked for since boyhood. The toiling to acquire his own business had begun long before he married Bessie and received the half-share in the firm, which was her dowry. As a lad of fourteen he'd known he must labor hard if he was to make something of himself. By seventeen, he had become Salaman's right-hand man and had spared no effort to mount further up the ladder he was still climbing.

He could hear Harry Rothberg, whose place had also been completely destroyed, weeping beside him. Harry was not a well man and his usual liverish pallor was tinged with gray.

"What do we do now, David?" he asked pathetically, watching the civil-defense workers milling around in clouds of dust.

David put a hand on his frail shoulder and spoke with more confidence than he felt. "Whatever it takes, we'll do it. We'll get going again somehow."

"You're damn right we will!" Solly Butensky said vehemently behind him.

David turned around and saw that Solly's florid face was consumed by rage, his treble chin quivering and his fishy gray eyes steely in the early light.

"I'm not going to let the Nazis get the better of me!" he declared and strode off to survey his own pile of rubble.

Maybe anger is healthier than acceptance, David reflected. But all he himself felt was an all-pervading numbness, as if his emotions had been temporarily paralyzed. He shepherded Harry Rothberg to his car and got into his own to drive home and tell Bessie they no longer had a business.

Chapter Three

Marianne stood on the pavement across the road from the shop, gripping her mother's arm while they waited for her father to emerge through the doorway and join them. A time-bomb was ticking away in the building. Was he going to be blown to pieces?

"I never saw 'im go back in. I told 'im so when I turned me 'ead t'other way," the special constable beside them said for the umpteenth time. "Everyone 'eard me say it, din't they?" he demanded of the huddle of neighbors and customers standing with bated breath awaiting Ben's possible demise.

"You shouldn't have let him, Mom," Marianne said in an agonized voice.

"Could I stop him?" Esther had a mesmerized expression on her face and the tip of her nose looked pinched as though with fear. "You know how he values those candlesticks."

"Candlesticks?" the constable exclaimed. "Riskin' 'is life fer a per o' candelsticks? What're they made of, Missis? Solid gold?"

"No, brass. His dead mother brought them with her from Vienna in 1904 and they're all he's got to remember her by."

The policeman stared ominously at the dark bulk of Ben's Bazaar. "If 'e doesn't get a move on'n come out o' there, 'e could end up bein' reunited wi' 'er."

"It might not go off, our'n didn't," Mrs. Rilk, the local newsagent, said.

"I'm velly hopeful it won't or my laundly will explode with it," tubby Arthur Chang, whose place was next door, answered mournfully. "Your husband is a velly blave gentleman," he added to Esther.

"And if the bomb doesn't kill him, I will when he comes out!" she declared as her pent-up feelings got the better of her.

Marianne glanced at her watch, but it was too dark to see the numerals. How long had her father been in there? It seemed like hours. "Hurry up, Dad!" she shrilled in a voice that did not sound like her own when she saw him appear on the doorstep and fumble in his pocket. She hid her face against her mother's coat sleeve. "Why doesn't he come? What's he doing?"

"Locking the door, would you believe it!" Esther shrieked.

"You want me to leave it open? All right, I'll unlock it again," Ben shouted to her jokingly. Then he walked calmly across the road with his mother's candlesticks cradled in his arms and seemed surprised at the fuss everyone made of him when he reached them. "I thought I might as well bring you this, as well, Esther. If the bomb goes off, God knows when I'll be able to afford to buy you another one," he said giving her her fox fur, and one of the endearing crooked grins that she had feared she might never see again.

"What a case you are!" she exclaimed, kissing his cheek tenderly.

"Yer'd better come 'ome wi' me," Mrs. Rilk told them briskly. "Wi' me lads away in t'army yer can 'ave their bedroom, like I slep' in your 'Arry's when I 'ad a time-bomb. Your Marianne can curl up downstairs on't couch."

Old Mr. Higgins, who owned the hardware store next door to the newsagents, invited the Changs to stay with him. "If folk can't 'elp each other out in wartime, it's a poor lookout," he declared.

"Why are you crying, Mom, now Dad's safe?" Marianne whispered, seeing Esther dab her eyes.

Esther was listening to the warm cries of encouragement and hope the simple, working folk clustered on the pavement were calling to her own family and the Changs as they trailed off in the darkness behind their kind hosts. "Because the people round here are so wonderful, Marianne," she answered. "I told you they were, didn't I? Before we came to live here, when you didn't want to come."

The barber and his family who occupied the premises next door to Chang's Laundry were spending the night at the confectioner's opposite. All the other stores on the block were lock-up premises, but the houses on the back street running parallel with it had had to be evacuated, too, and the occupants had gone good-humoredly to a church hall to await the fate of their humble homes.

Esther had slung her fur carelessly over one shoulder, and one of the Changs' young children, whom she was carrying, was rubbing his snotty nose against it, but she did not care. She was reflecting on how the war had made everyone the same and wished it could be that way in peacetime as well—with nothing extraordinary about a Jewish woman cuddling a Chinese child on her way to be the guest of a Christian neighbor.

Marianne was holding seven-year-old Jimmy Chang's hand.

"We might 'ave no 'ome termorrer, Marianne," he said to her solemnly.

"Let's not think about it, Jimmy."

"But what if me new Meccano set gets blown up?"

"Your dad will buy you another." Marianne tightened her grip on the cardboard box in her other hand, which contained all the stories she had ever written. Like her Viennese grandmother's candlesticks, they were something no amount of money could replace and she always took them with her to the cellar when the air-raid siren sounded.

She looked down at the plump little boy trotting beside her. Even in the dark his hair and his round face had a sleek shine. She hadn't really noticed until tonight that Jimmy and his brothers spoke with the local accent and didn't pronounce the letter "r" as an "l," the way their parents did. Why had she always assumed that Chinese were born with a speech impediment? Mr. and Mrs. Chang only spoke the way they did because they'd been born in China, and Chinese was their native language; just as her grandparents had retained Yiddish speech mannerisms that marked them out as immigrants. The Chang children were as English as herself; yet she had always thought of them as foreign, because of their appearance, in the same way as some Christians thought her foreign because she looked Jewish.

"I'm glad we came to live round here," she said to her mother. "I've learned a lot from it."

Esther smiled at her as they reached their destination and waited in the wild March wind for Mrs. Rilk and Mr. Higgins to unlock their shop doors. "So have I, love."

Newsagents' shops had their own special smell, Marianne noted when they followed Mrs. Rilk inside and passed behind the cluttered counter to the living room. She had not been conscious of it when she came here to buy things and the front door stood ajar, but tonight the scent of newsprint, pipe tobacco and aniseed balls mingled pleasantly with the mustiness of old wood and damp plaster noticeable in most of the local shops.

"Mek yersels at 'ome," Mrs. Rilk invited, shooing her fat, black cat off the faded chintz couch and poking the fire into a cheerful blaze. "It's nice fer yer a widder woman like mesel' t'ave comp'ny though not fer t'reason I've got some ternight."

"This is a lovely room," Esther said glancing around,

and Marianne wondered if her mother was just being polite. This was certainly not Esther Klein's idea of lovely.

Old-fashioned was how Marianne would have described it as she eyed the dark, heavily-carved sideboard with its mirrored back and the many framed photographs on the mantelpiece, which had a maroon velvet cover with bobbles on it. One of the photographs was of the late Mr. Rilk in the sergeant's uniform he had worn in the last war. All the others were of the two Rilk lads and charted their progress from babyhood to the smart young soldiers they were now.

A couple of gilt-framed pastoral scenes adorned the brown lincrusta walls and the threadbare carpet still had traces of its original rose-pattern. China shepherdesses and thick, pottery Toby jugs completed the decor, occupying every inch of surface. But the room had a comforting coziness and in its own way was lovely, Marianne thought. Lovely and welcoming.

"I'll mek us some cocoa," Mrs. Rilk smiled, bustling into the adjoining scullery, where more mugs and cups than any family could ever need were visible hanging on hooks above the sink.

"We'd better ring up David," Esther said to Ben. "He must be worried stiff because he can't get through to us."

"He worries about all the family, doesn't he?" Marianne reflected whilst her father was in the shop, making the call.

"He always has," Esther answered. "But we all care about each other in our family, don't we?"

"I can't say I do about Shirley."

Esther sighed. "Maybe you think you don't. But I'll have a bet with you and I hope it never gets put to the test. You'd be there if she was in trouble and needed you, or if any of her children did in years to come. And she'd be there for you and yours. You'll never turn your backs on each other after the way you've been brought up."

"David said to phone him if I need him, even if it's in the middle of the night," Ben said when he returned to the living room.

The words had an ominous ring and they sat in silence until Mrs. Rilk brought the steaming mugs of cocoa.

After they had drunk it, she escorted Esther and Ben usptairs to her absent sons' bedroom, then fetched a blanket to tuck Marianne up on the couch.

"Yer'll nod off in no time, luv," the kindly woman said kissing her cheek.

But slumber did not come immediately and Marianne lay in the flickering firelight, listening to the night noises she had discovered all houses had. The whisper of the water in the pipes carrying it from the cistern. A creaking floorboard that made her think someone was walking about, though she knew nobody was. The whistle of the wind in the chimney and a rustling in the eaves by she knew not what. And in this room, tonight, the sputtering sound the coal made as the last little tongues of bluish flame licked away its oily, tar-smelling kernel.

A year ago, she'd slept beside Shirley in a Welsh cottage. Now she was somewhere else that wasn't her home. Where would she sleep tomorrow night? she thought with an ache in her throat. Would the room above the shop, that she'd made her very own with two planks resting on some bricks to hold her books and the washstand she'd turned into a desk to do her writing at, still be there in the morning?

She got off the couch and took the cat under the blanket with her for company and soon afterwards fell asleep.

The tremendous explosion that occurred a couple of hours later did not awaken her. Mrs. Rilk was drawing the curtains back to let in the gray daylight when she opened her eyes and saw that the cat had deserted her during the night and returned to its basket by the hearth.

"The bomb went off, didn't it?" Marianne said flatly. One look at the woman's distressed countenance was enough to tell her so.

Mrs. Rilk avoided her eye and fiddled with a button on her floured smock overall. "I'm afraid it did, luv. Woke up 'alf t'neighbor'ood, 'n fair catapulted me'n yer mam'n dad out o' bed. Pr'aps it were wi' bein' downstairs yer never 'eard it, Marianne. T'rest o' us was nearer t'sky. Want a cup o' tea, luv?"

"No thanks, Mrs. Rilk."

"I 'ad ter give yer dad a drop o' brandy."

Marianne put on her coat and followed Mrs. Rilk into the shop, where she resumed marking addresses on a pile of *Daily Sketches*. She had already dealt with the rest of the morning papers and the two gray-jerseyed schoolboys who delivered them for her were leaning on the counter with grimy, hessian bags slung around their necks, their cheeks bulging with the mints she always provided to sustain them whilst they waited for her to complete the task.

Marianne listened to the lads crunching their sweets, aware of them eyeing her pityingly. She could not recollect having seen either of them before, but most people in the district knew who she was, because they were regular customers in the shop and everyone probably knew about the bomb by now.

She scanned a *Daily Dispatch*, but only the date registered with her. March 12, 1941, the day the Kleins became homeless. Our Arnold will get the shock of his life when he gets back from school this afternoon, she thought detachedly. He had stayed overnight with a friend and had missed all the excitement.

She thought of Harry, too, who would find a hole in the ground when he came home on leave, instead of Ben's Bazaar that had meant as much to him as to Dad. But she was only thinking these things and not feeling upset or anything. What was the matter with her?

"Did South Manchester get it last night, as well?" she asked Mrs. Rilk. "The pal our Arnold stayed with lives in Withington."

"I think it were only us got it, luv. Withington 'ad its turn on New Year's Night, didn't it? What wi' Manchester Grammar gettin' badly damaged an't 'igh School fer Girls blown ter smithereens. I don't think yer need worry about yer brother."

But Marianne had not felt worried, nor did she now feel relieved. She was feeling nothing, as if a shutter had lowered itself between her mind and her emotions. "Thank you very much for everything, Mrs. Rilk," she said in a voice that sounded stiff and polite, though she had not meant it to. And she could not make her face smile when she said goodbye and departed with her precious box of stories.

The wind clutched at her tweed coat with its icy fingers and flapped her fringe up and down on her forehead as she set off along the main road. It occurred to her that now she had no clothes apart from the ones she was wearing and that she would not be able to change her undies like she did every day. But it was as though she were someone else thinking this about herself.

The same remoteness was there when she glanced at the cloth-capped men boarding a tram, on their way to work in

Trafford Park, and the lace-curtained windows in the council flats she passed, where the occupants were awakening to a new day. The clatter of empty barrels being rolled from the cellar door of the pub on the corner to a waiting lorry sounded distant, too. And the pub owner's voice cursing the lorry-driver for calling too early and getting him out of his bed seemed to have a hollow echo to it.

Even the malty reek of beer, that always hung strongly in the air hereabouts, was a once-removed sensation in Marianne's nostrils this morning as she drew near her own block and became aware she was now inhaling dust, with an unpleasant mildewy tang to it. Then she saw the yawning gap on the opposite side of the road, where Ben's Bazaar, Chang's Laundry and Larry's Barbershop had been last night and stopped in her tracks.

The emptiness was emphasized by the drab little houses behind, which previously had not been visible from the main road. How sad they looked, huddled closer together than Marianne remembered them being, as if they were seeking comfort from each other and suffering pain from their fractured chimney pots and splintered windows.

The staircases and upper floors of the lock-up premises on either side of the gap were still intact, though each had had a wall torn asunder. One was a grocery and the other a bookmaker's and Marianne could see a side of bacon still in the slicer on the grocer's blue-painted counter, with a mountain of spilled salt all around it and jagged chunks of glass embedded in some sticky red stuff that was probably jam, but reminded her of blood. Upstairs, where the grocer had his stockroom, the floor seemed to be thickly carpeted in black, then she realized it was tea from the overturned chests he must have begun hoarding before war was declared.

The bookmaker's was a tangle of telephones, upstairs and down, and the little wooden cubby holes, where her father had told her the bettors stood reading the *Sporting Chronicle* and making their bets, gave the place the appearance of a larger-than-life office-desk full of empty pigeon-holes.

Army vehicles and police cars were parked at the curb-side, and Marianne saw her parents and her Uncle David with Arthur Chang and the barber in the middle of a group of policemen and soldiers.

She walked across the road, oblivious of an approaching

tram, but they were too engrossed to notice her and she stood
looking down into the vast crater, from where the mildewy
smell was coming. Some of her father's stock was strewn
around in its muddy depths. Striped flannel pajamas and
once-white towels; a salmon-pink corset and several boots. A
baby shawl, only recognizable by its frill peeping from
beneath a zinc tub which Arthur Chang had used for soaking
shirts. And her mother's black silk dressing-gown, that was
patterned with huge golden chrysanthemums like a Japanese
kimono, had hooked itself on an upended girder and was billowing gaily in the wind.

"I'm that sorry, Marianne," a familiar voice said; then
an arm was placed around her shoulders and she raised her
head and saw Edie Perkins's freckled face regarding her sympathetically.

"I'm on me way ter work, or I'd stop'n see if there were
owt I could do fer yer," Edie said. "But me mam sez you'n
yer family's welcome at our 'ouse fer a cup o' tea if yer feel
like one."

Marianne managed to smile, but was momentarily unable to speak. She glanced around and saw that several pas-
sers-by had paused to view the debris and were consoling her
parents.

"I'd offer ter lend yer summat ter wear, but we're not
t'same size any more. I've grown upwards'n outwards'n you
'aven't," Edie said. "I 'aven't fergot yer once gave me a
frock, Marianne, 'n I never will," she added. "We don't see
much of each other nowadays, but I still think of yer as me
friend."

They had drifted apart after Marianne left school to go
to Wales, but she knew it would have happened in any event.
She sometimes saw Edie walking down the main road arm in
arm with Catholic boys and girls she knew from church, just
as her own friends were all Jewish. These days, she saw a lot
of Eva Frankl and Hildegard. They went to Hallé concerts
with Martin and some of his schoolmates and met in each
other's homes on Saturday nights to talk and listen to gramophone records.

Marianne had come to realize that these new friendships
were on a different level from the relationship she had had
with Edie and Dot, who were not interested in books and
music and politics. Their drifting apart was not only attribut-
able to their different religions. But even if Edie and Dot had

the same interests as herself, they would have gone their separate ways, like Christians and Jews always did, and Marianne regretted that it had to be that way.

"Did yer know I'd got a job in't Ship Canal Office'n I'm
courtin' Jack Renshaw?" Edie asked her. "'E's t'lad whose
mam'n dad's got that fish'n chip shop on't corner o' our
street. 'Im'n me's savin' up, so we can get wed an' open one
oursel's after t'war."

Edie wanting nothing more from life than to settle down
with Jack in a back-street chip shop makes us different, too,
Marianne reflected. But the thought was unaccompanied by
feeling, as had been the case with all her thoughts that morning. She became aware of a faint, musical sound and raised
her eyes to a pile of torn timber on the edge of the crater.
The inside of the barber's piano was teetering pathetically on
top of it like an abandoned harp, with the wind rippling its
strings.

The sight and sound moved her as nothing else had
succeeded in doing. "Oh Edie, I'm glad you're here," she
gulped, clutching her old friend's arm. Then she burst into
tears.

"There, there, luv," Edie comforted her.

Marianne would not have liked Eva or Hildegard to see
her weeping, but with Edie it was all right. And what a relief
it was to feel like herself again.

"I'd be wettin' me knickers, never mind jus' cryin', if I'd
'ad t'shock you 'ave," Edie declared, giving her a handkerchief.

"I'm lucky to be alive," Marianne whispered, as the
thing she had refused to let herself think about returned to
her mind and her vivid imagination transformed it into a
drama.

"Yer mean wi' it being a time-bomb?"

Marianne shook her head and tried not to visualize herself hurtling into the crater, split in half by the deadly missile.
"I went to bed right after tea last night, because I had a
headache," she said, concentrating on the facts. "When the
siren sounded I didn't want to get up and go down to the cellar. I had a row with my dad about it and in the end he told
me to please myself. About half an hour before the all-clear
sounded, I got up to go to the bathroom and while I was in
there, there was a tremendous thud that shook the walls and
threw me against the door. I thought a bomb had landed in

the next street. It often sounds right on top of you when it isn't, doesn't it?"

"You're trembling," Edie said.

"So would you! When I got back to my room, I nearly choked with dust and the light had gone off. So I ran to the cellar for my dad to bring a flashlight, and when he shone it, we couldn't believe our eyes. There was a great big hole in the ceiling and another in the floor, where my bed had been."

Edie remained silent for a moment, then she straightened Marianne's hair that looked as awry as it sometimes had on the netball pitch. "Didn't yer once tell me yer was born wi' t'cord twisted round yer neck, an' t'doctor said it were a miracle yer came inter t'world alive? Well, in a way, what 'appened last night's t'same thing. An' if I were you, I'd jus' say a silent prayer ter God fer savin' yer twice. I'll say one ter Jesus, fer good measure. I mus' go now, Marianne, I'm late fer work already."

Marianne watched her run across the road and leap aboard a tram, clutching the scarlet tam-o'-shanter that matched her high-heeled shoes but clashed with her mustard-colored coat. The cheap scent she wore lingered briefly in the air after she had gone and Marianne was assailed by the aching pity for Edie and her kind that had dogged her schooldays. But the way they accepted the drab niche in which life had placed them and had no aspirations to climb out of it affected her more.

She blew some dust off the box of writings she had, thankfully, remembered to grab before abandoning her room, last night, and went to find her parents in the crowd now assembled on the pavement. But she could only see her mother, talking to Mrs. Chang.

"So that's that, love," Esther said with determined cheerfulness when Marianne joined them. "We'll have to start from scratch again, only this time we'll be starting off with something in the bank."

Mrs. Chang went to speak to her husband, her five children trailing behind her, and Marianne drew Esther away from the crowd for a private word.

"Where will we live, Mam?"

"At Bobbie's, where else? Until we fix up another home. She never wanted that big house when Uncle David rented it for her, but now all those spare bedrooms will come in useful."

"Where are Dad and Uncle David?"

"At the undertakers."

Marianne paled with alarm. Was someone in the family dead?

"The Christian undertaker's, down the road," Esther said seeing her expression. "He passed away himself, last week, and your dad remembered his wife saying there was nobody to carry on the business, when she came in to buy black stockings for the funeral, and she was going to rent the place out." Esther sighed, then shrugged philosophically. "One person's misfortune can be someone else's *mazel*. Your Zaidie Abraham got his first job in England, when half the immigrants in Strangeways were unemployed, because Auntie Bessie's mother died and her father needed someone to replace her as his presser."

"I didn't know."

Esther's eyes misted with remembrance. "There's plenty you don't know about those days, Marianne. But why should you have to? They're over, thank God."

"But they're part of my family history, aren't they?"

"They're part of Jewish history," Esther answered with a bitter smile. "But let's get back to the present. You know your dad, he doesn't let the grass grow under his feet. He's already been on the phone to the undertaker's widow and he's looking the place over with Uncle David, now."

The undertaker's windows were varnished black and whenever Marianne walked past them she imagined the grisly secrets that lay behind their sinister gloss. "I'm not going to live there. It'd give me the creeps, Mam!"

"It's a lock-up, so you won't have to. But I wouldn't set up home again near the docks in wartime. Last night was enough. I'd rather *shlep* back and forth from North Manchester like I used to. And this time I won't grumble."

They could see Ben walking wearily towards them, rubbing his blue-jowled chin.

"You'll feel better when you've had a shave and a bath," Esther said when he reached them.

"First I'll have to buy a razor and borrow a bathroom," he reminded her dryly. "That shop's like a barn, Esther. Except for a little room at the back, all the walls have been knocked through to make it into two big floors."

Marianne shuddered. "I expect he stored the shrouds in

the little room and used all the other space for bodies and coffins."

"If imagination was marketable, our Marianne'd make a fortune!" Ben exclaimed witheringly. Then he studied her forlorn expression and thought of the lucky escape she had had last night. Troublesome she was, but, oh, how dear to him. He gathered her close for an emotional moment, then resumed the conversation with his wife. "David's gone off to the factory, but he thinks I should take the undertaker's place."

"And what do you think?"

Ben surveyed the wreckage of his years of labor and felt the way David had under the same circumstances; then he thought of his mother-in-law's favorite saying, that everything was *bershert*. "Sometimes Fate gets you where you intended to go sooner than you expected," he said with the wry grin his family had always found immensely reassuring. "Didn't I always say I wanted a walk-around store?"

Chapter Four

By 1943 the elder Sandbergs and the Moritzes were the only members of the clan still living in Cheetham Hill.

The North Manchester community's exodus to Prestwich and Broughton Park had begun some years previously, as families accrued sufficient capital to put down a cash deposit on their own homes, and pay off the mortgages instead of the weekly rent they had expended all their lives for houses which would never be theirs.

But living in a pleasant, residential suburb was also a status symbol, an indication that they had "got on," and, like Golders Green in London, both these districts had acquired a distinctively Jewish ambience.

In Prestwich where David and Sammy and the Kleins now lived, the stretch of Bury Old Road close to Heaton

Park, and the thickly populated, tree-lined avenues on either side of the main highway, bore witness to the influx. On the Sabbath and High Holy Days, bowler-hatted gentlemen and their smartly-clad wives walked decorously to worship at the imposing Holy Law Synagogue. On fine days they would stroll in the park, or on the broad pavements where kosher grocery and butchers' shops, bakeries and delicatessen had their blinds lowered as the stores in Strangeways had been respectfully shuttered on these occasions in the community's early immigrant days.

"The only thing about *Yom Tov* that's changed since I was a kid is the style of clothes," David remarked to Bessie while they were walking to synagogue on *Rosh Hashanah*, shortly after they had moved house and found themselves part of the elegant throng.

Bessie was using the shop windows as a mirror to admire her new hat. "What else would you like to change?" she replied, as insensitive to the way Jewish tradition moved her husband as she was to all his deepest feelings. "It's a lot nicer than Cheetham Hills, round here," she declaimed with satisfaction, enjoying the air of middle-class affluence as they crossed the road to the synagogue in company with other congregants.

"But Alderley Edge is even nicer," David answered.

"Alderley Edge he still wants to live in! With all those stuck-up *goyim*."

And one day I will, David said silently to his wife's receding back when she left him in the crowded, synagogue foyer to take her seat in the gallery with the ladies. Meanwhile, he was content with the home he had now. No, content was the wrong word. That, he would never be until he reached his final goal, and living in Cheshire epitomized it. But Prestwich would do for the time being.

The familiar, soporific atmosphere that all *shuls* seemed to have, with a hint of fresh-smelling fragrance as if a spray had been recently applied, greeted him in a warm wave when he entered and walked to his seat beside Sammy and Ben.

He donned his *tallith* and glanced up at Bessie, who was sitting with Esther and Miriam, next to a girl in ATS uniform. Shirley and Marianne waved to him from their seats at the back of the raked gallery, but he could hardly see their faces for the array of millinery on the heads in front of them.

"Robin Hood feathers seem to be all the rage for women this year," he said dryly to his brother and brother-in-law.

"And my wife's got the longest one," Ben grinned. "I think Bessie's trying to say something to you."

"Where's our Ronald?" Bessie was mouthing.

David shrugged and spread his hands. They had left their son eating the cold, fried flounder which was their traditional *Yom Tov* breakfast, singling it out from ordinary mornings when they only had tea and bagels. When they warned Ronald he would be late for the service, he had replied that his legs were younger and faster than theirs. Shirley, on the other hand, had gone on ahead of them, fearing her pace would be slowed down by her new four-inch-heel court shoes.

"Kids!" Ben said expressively, eyeing Ronald's empty seat and David's frown. "They can drive you *meshuga*."

Sammy glanced around and noted the sprinkling of servicemen who were home on leave for *Yom Tov*. In one row of seats, several airmen were sitting together and he surmised they were from the air-crew cadet base in Heaton Park. "I only wish mine was here; I wouldn't mind how mad he drove me," he said looking up at Miriam whose expression was haunted, as it had been ever since Martin volunteered for the RAF.

"That's how I feel about my boys," Ben sighed.

"So do I, about Peter," David said. "I worry about him all the time."

"We all worry about them all," Ben declared. "But Peter's only in the Pioneer Corps, isn't he?"

"Because he's a refugee. It reminds me of the last war when the sons of Austrian immigrants weren't allowed to carry weapons. They'd been here for years and years and were ready to give their lives for the country that took the Jews in, just like Peter's lot are, now. But tell that to the War Office!"

"Anyone'd think you want him to be in danger, driving a tank like Harry, or in the Navy like our Arnold," Ben said sounding shocked.

"Or being an RAF bombardier, like Martin," Sammy added grimly as the rabbi and cantor entered, imposingly robed, and everyone rose for the commencement of the service.

"Of course I don't want Peter to be in danger," David

said *sotto voce*, with one eye on his son who was sidling towards them crabwise in the hope that his late arrival would pass unnoticed by the silk-hatted elders of the congregation. "All I'm thinking of is the lad's pride. Imagine someone of his intelligence digging ditches for latrines!"

"Sorry I'm late, Dad," Ronald whispered from beside him.

David made his customary terse reply. "We had more respect when I was young." Then the cantor's voice and the mellifluousness of the choir soothed his ruffled feelings and the changeless pattern of age-old Jewish ritual, impervious to peace or war, poverty or affluence, washed over him like a gentle brook lapping the pitted contours of a pebble.

This was what he came to *shul* for. It was not just fear of the Almighty's punishment, or the hope that observing the High Holy Days would mitigate all his nonobservances, that drew him to God's house year after year when the Festivals came around. The fear was there, conditioned in him from the cradle; he felt defiant when he lit a cigarette on *Shabbos,* as if doing so was tempting Fate, and he would no doubt experience those pangs to the end of his days, even though his brain told him it was ridiculous, that being a person of integrity and charity meant more than adhering to laws dating back to the Wilderness. But David was drawn to *shul* by an emotion stronger than fear, one he could not label because there was no name for it. It was born of the necessity to identify with his own, to assert his oneness with them, though some had personal characteristics he could not respect.

That's probably why we're all here, he mused, glancing around the crowded synagogue. Even the ladies who want to show off their new outfits, whose eyes never read a word of the service because they're too busy examining the other women's attire. This could be any *shul* in the world on *Rosh Hashanah.* The prayers the men knew from memory being recited in unison whilst their minds toyed with other things. Business or family problems. Some were no doubt wondering what they would get for *Yom Tov* dessert, hot strudel or *lokshen* pudding. Was anyone thinking about God?

It doesn't matter, David reflected. The need to be here was all that counted and so long as that stayed as strong as it had until now, Judaism would remain invincible.

He watched the synagogue president, his tall hat gleaming in the light from windows endowed as memorials by congregants, rise from his seat in a small pew at the front of the *bimah* and step up to the Holy Ark to draw back the heavy, velvet curtain behind which the *Sefer Torah* were kept.

An elderly man was waiting there with a soldier and an airman who had also been called up for the *mitzvah* of lifting out the Scrolls for the Reading of the Law. Some self-conscious lads with a well-scrubbed look and Stand Grammar School caps on their heads, hovered beside them, weighed down by the responsibility of receiving an honor coveted by every other boy present. They had been called up to remove the richly embroidered covers from the *Torah* prior to their being unfurled.

"I thought I'd feel like a stranger here, after all those years at the Central *Shul*, but it's funny how you don't," Ben whispered.

David smiled. "If we went to *shul* in New York, we'd feel at home." Such was his conviction. "They call smoked salmon lox and eat doughnuts and Danish pastry for breakfast, but I bet you ten bob that in their orthodox *shuls* it's exactly like here."

"I expect it is in Timbuctu, if there are any Jews there," Ronald said thoughtfully and was ticked-off by his father for talking during the service.

After *shul* they all walked to Sarah's for midday dinner and did not make good time because of Sammy's disability. But none of them would have dreamed of riding on the High Holy Days.

"If we'd stayed in Cheetham, you wouldn't have had this long *shlep*," said Miriam—who had not wanted to move to Prestwich—to Sammy.

"We'll hire a bathchair and next time you can push me," he joked.

David's expression tightened as it always did when his brother's handicap was emphasized. These days, he rarely remembered that he was responsible for it. But occasionally, like now, guilt returned to taunt him. If he hadn't disobeyed his mother and taken Sammy to play by the River Dvina that day, the Cossack wouldn't have brutally cantered over Sammy's leg. He noted the bluish shadows under his brother's eyes. Were they caused by anxiety about Martin? Or was Sammy in pain? He could never make up to him for spoiling his life. But he would never stop trying to.

"Uncle Sammy should've got on a bus," Marianne declared whilst admiring her burgundy cuban-heeled shoes. They had cost sixteen shillings-eleven pence and were the most expensive she had ever had, but her mother had not minded because they looked so nice with the gray tweed coat she'd bought Marianne for *Yom Tov*.

Shirley was a rhapsody in blue teetering beside her, still head and shoulders taller. The soles of her feet were burning and she envied Marianne her low-heeled comfort, but had accepted that you sometimes had to suffer to look smart. Her cousin had no dress sense and wore no makeup, didn't seem to care if she looked drab. Marianne was always coming out with shocking things, too! "God would never forgive Uncle Sammy if he rode on *Rosh Hashanah*," she declaimed.

"Nobody can be expected to walk a long distance if they've got a bad leg," Marianne replied.

"Shut up, the pair of you!" David thundered.

But Marianne was not to be muzzled."Why do people bother to keep all the *Rosh Hashanah* laws, when they break the *Shabbos*, which is a much holier day?" she demanded.

"You're talking through your hat, as usual," Shirley said nastily. "If what you've just said was correct, everyone wouldn't be walking today, would they?" she added, eyeing their well-dressed brethren thronging the pavements.

Marianne gave her a withering look. "Perhaps they're as uninformed about their religion as you are. And I have to admit I thought *Rosh Hashanah* was more important than *Shabbos* myself, until Bobbie Sarah told me it isn't."

Shirley looked taken aback, but could not question her grandmother's knowledge of religious matters.

"It's a misconception that's become accepted over the years," David said. "And by now, most folk have probably forgotten it is one."

"Including you," Shirley accused him. "I mean fancy me not knowing!"

"Will it make any difference now you do? What're you going to do about it, Shirley? Stop breaking the *Shabbos*, or start riding on *Rosh Hashanah*?" David smiled.

Shirley did not reply.

"She'll go on doing the same as everyone else does," Marianne said contemptuously. "Sticking to the false standards Jews who aren't truly religious live by. All that seems to matter to most people is being seen to do what the majority do and it makes me sick! Bobbie Sarah says keeping *Shab-*

bos is inconvenient because it comes every week and plenty of folk would ignore *Rosh Hashanah*, too, if it came around more than once a year."

"She's probably right," David said dryly.

"But at least our family hasn't joined the Reform *Shul*," Ben said defensively.

"I probably will when I'm my own boss," Marianne informed him. "I'd rather keep revised laws that make sense to me than have to break old-fashioned ones that don't."

Her father slapped her bottom and she ran off to hug her grandmother as they neared Sarah's house and saw her peering impatiently over the garden gate.

"Why did you smack her, Ben?" Esther, who was walking some distance behind with Bessie and Ronald, called.

Ben pretended he had not heard and exchanged a glance with David. The thought of his eighteen-year-old daughter allying herself with the Reform Judaism Movement was anathema to him and to David also. If Esther knew Marianne had such tendencies she would throw a fit.

"It's a pity Marianne never joined *Habonim*, with our Shirley," David declared. "She'd do better to be wrapped up in Zionism than mixing with Eva Frankl's crowd." The Frankls had recently joined the Reform Synagogue and Hugo had consequently sunk to the depths in David's estimation.

"And what would you say if Shirley wanted to go to Palestine after the war, to live on a *kibbutz* and work on the land?" Ben inquired.

"I'd have to accept it," David answered. "But I'm sure she won't. She's too interested in clothes and the good things of life. I've met some of the girls she knows who do want to be *chalutzim* and they don't dress like she does."

Nor does Marianne, Ben thought, but it wasn't because she was the *chalutzim* kind. His troublesome daughter didn't fall into any category and how he wished she did!

"The *knedlach* are ruined," Sarah greeted them when they entered the house.

Shirley was in the lobby taking off her hat and coat. "Don't shout at us, Bobbie," she winced. "My feet are killing me."

"So try wearing shoes instead of stilts," Sarah said eyeing her footwear with disapproval. She surveyed the rest of the weary party. "And if nobody had removed to Prestwich, they wouldn't have to *shlep* miles for their *Yom Tov* dinner and it wouldn't be spoiled, either."

Esther took a comb from her handbag to rearrange her hair in front of the hallstand mirror. "But as we have removed there, Mother, why don't you do the same?"

"There's a house for sale opposite Sammy's; you've just got to say the word," David put in.

"Don't even mention it!" Sarah said hotly. "How many times must I tell you all, I like my own house? I get on with my neighbors, the tradespeople also. I've got a nice garden. Strangeways with the dirt and the jail Cheetham Hill isn't. So what's to move for, except people should think I'm highty-tighty, which I'm not."

"Who can argue with a woman like her?" Abraham shrugged. "Let's eat already, or the *knedlach* will get hard as cannon balls and she'll end up throwing them at us."

Sarah popped her head into the kitchen and instructed Lizzie and Bridie, who were attired in their best, to show their respect for the Jewish New Year, to drain the water from the *knedl* pan.

"I tried one, Bobbie, an' it were soft as butter," Lizzie said.

"And our Lizzie's an expert on *knedlach*," David soothed his mother as they went into the dining room.

"She's an expert on everything Jewish, and Bridie also," Sarah declared approvingly. "Rebecca told me she got home five minutes late for *Shabbos* last week and Bridie had already lit the candles," she smiled admiring her *Yom Tov* table to which a long beam of autumn sunlight had added a mellow glow.

The hors d'oeuvre awaited them on little white and gold plates David had bought for her when the family began to outnumber her stock of china. Lace-edged napkins matched the cloth and Bridie had arranged them like tulips in the water glasses, the way Rebecca had shown her. The silver-plated cutlery was a ruby-wedding gift from all the family and the three-tier fruit stand in the center, laden with russet apples and pears, had been lovingly carved by Sammy.

Nathan, whose dining table always resembled a miniature banquet, was conscious of a lump having risen in his throat. There was something to be said for living simply all the rest of the time and only bringing out your best things on these occasions. The special ambience of *Yom Tov* in his

mother's house was all around him and the warm feeling that
went with it, too, that reminded him of his childhood. Even
in hard times there had been this atmosphere and he sometimes thought it was one his wife, for whom every day had
been like *Yom Tov*, had not encountered before she became
a Sandberg.

Marianne and Shirley were imbibing the atmosphere,
too, and exchanged a smile. *Rosh Hashanah* in their grandparents' home was an institution and, despite their differences, the memories it conjured up for them would always be
something they shared.

"If the boys were here, everything would be perfect,"
Miriam said looking at the chair near the foot of the table
which Martin had always occupied.

"God willing, they'll soon be back with us," Sarah said,
breaking the moment of silence Miriam's words had evoked.

Carl got up from the window seat where he had been
seated reading when the others came into the room. "We
haven't even started the invasion yet," he pointed out joining
them at the table.

"You're getting worse than your father with your doom
and gloom!" Sarah exclaimed. "But today I forbid you to talk
about the war. Let's all be cheerful for the sake of the children."

"I won't be cheerful if I have to sit beside Henry," Leona piped up from her seat between the twins.

Henry tweaked one of her ginger plaits mischievously.

"There, what did I tell you?" she shrieked.

Frank got up and changed places with her.

"Good," Henry said in the bright, authoritative manner
that made him seem precocious. "Now I'll be more cheerful,
too."

"Can you believe these little ones are seven already?"
Sigmund sighed. "It seems like yesterday that the ones who
now think they're grownup were sitting at the foot of the
table wearing short socks," he added smiling at Marianne and
Shirley.

"Oy," Abraham said in eloquent agreement. But his
elder granddaughters were grownup, he thought, surveying them. His wife had already been a mother at their age.

"Eat your chopped liver," Sarah said, noticing that he
had put down his fork.

Abraham seemed not to hear her. "When you feel as old

as I do, you know that time has not stood still," he told Sigmund.

Something in his voice made Sarah stop eating, too. "I'm not getting any younger myself," she declared, fingering her brooch. "In two years it will be our golden wedding."

Abraham chuckled. "She's reminding me now, so I can start saving up to buy her a present!"

But the chuckle did not comfort her and she glanced at him frequently during the meal, appalled by his appearance. He had looked frail for years, but now his fragility struck her forcibly. Why hadn't she noticed that his shoulders were even more hunched than they had been and that his complexion looked bloodless? Perhaps when you lived with someone you didn't notice a gradual change in them. It was the sudden weariness of his tone when he talked about feeling old that had chilled her.

Was he working too hard at the factory? How could he not be when doing so was his nature? He was now sixty-six and David had been urging him to retire, but had been unable to persuade him to agree. He would not be put out to grass, he had told her, and the fire in his eyes had stopped her from broaching the subject again.

That night, she lay in the old brass bedstead Isaac Salaman had given them after his wife's death, letting her mind travel the years between then and now. Salaman had presented them with the bed in the days when they had no money to buy one and were sleeping on bare boards, rolled up in the big, down-filled *perineh* they had brought from Russia. Now, thanks to their children, they had every comfort. But Abraham did not have good health. She heard him gasping for breath and got up to open the window.

"You want me to catch pneumonia?" he snapped in the darkness.

"From warm September air you won't catch it."

"Our doctor son has converted you!"

Sarah switched on the light and stroked his brow. "Anything I'd try to make you better. I don't want you to leave me," she added emotionally and could have bitten off her tongue the moment the words were spoken.

"Such a grand life I've given you, eh?" Abraham said quizzically. "Without David, you'd still be living in Strangeways."

Sarah did not deny this. After what she had said and the

way Abraham had accepted its implications, there had to be honesty between them. But there was something her husband seemed to have forgotten. "Who gave me David?" she asked softly." My children and grandchildren I wouldn't have had without you."

Abraham stared at the drawstring-bag containing his *tefillin*, which he kept on the dressing table. These days, hurrying downstairs to say the weekday morning prayer was too much for him. "I'm tired, Sorrel," he whispered.

"Then why won't you stop going to the factory? David can afford to keep us and pay someone else to do your job, like he's told you a thousand times."

"By my own son she wants me to be pensioned off!" Abraham shouted irately.

The outburst brought on a violent spasm of coughing and Sarah poured some of the medicine Nathan had prescribed and fed it to him.

"Hasn't Nat said the steam in the pressing-room's killing you? Why won't you listen to him?" she implored.

Abraham lay back on his pillow, momentarily incapable of speech, and the sound his chest was making was like a grinder bruising Sarah's heart.

"To be idle is another kind of death, Sorrel," he said when he gathered sufficient strength to reply.

After Abraham had dozed off, Sarah lay sleepless in the warm darkness, listening to the strident ticking of the clock which she usually did not notice. Some men would wrap themselves in cottonwool and sit twiddling their thumbs in order to live longer. But to Abraham that would not be living. The quality of a life is more important than the length, she had said to Sigmund when Rachel was nearing the end of her days. Now, she must find comfort in that herself.

But Abraham was not nearing the end of his days, she thought the next morning and chided herself for being morbid. He arose looking much better and seemed light-hearted, as if the things they had said to each other had somehow revitalized him.

"Today I'll come to the Central *Shul* with you," he smiled.

"Instead of going to the *Chevrah Habimah* to pray with your *Hassidic* friends? A favor he's doing me!" Sarah joked.

It was the second day of *Rosh Hashanah*, and she noticed a slight spring in his step when they walked up Heywood Street to attend the service. There would be days when he felt well and others when he did not and the well days would grow fewer as time went by. But he had made his decision not to preserve himself in idleness and she would respect it.

Nathan and his wife and daughter were standing on the synagogue steps when they arrived.

"Why can't we join the Higher Broughton *Shul*, Daddy, so I can sit with Lila Benjamin?" Leona asked. Lou's little girl was her best friend.

"Because your daddy likes this one," Rebecca answered, smoothing the skirt of her beige suit and adjusting her mink tie. Nathan's allegiance to a synagogue in Cheetham Hill, when they lived close to another, which she considered more select, was a bone of contention between them and she shot him a glance which said more than words.

If she had her way, we wouldn't even have *Yom Tov* dinner at Mother's, Nathan thought with the sourness his wife's indifference to everyone in the family except Bessie engendered in him. His family weren't good enough for her! But he had always known she was a snob. He ignored her glance and gave his attention to Abraham. "You look well today, Father. You should take time off work more often, it agrees with you."

Sarah saw the smile fade from her husband's face and noticed that the first trace of silver had appeared above the temples in her youngest son's hair. "Put your hat on, Nat! Standing outside *shul* bareheaded!" she chided Nathan who had only removed his bowler to set it on his head more comfortably. "And don't let me hear you nagging your father any more."

Nathan eyed her with surprise. What was the matter with her? She usually backed him up when she said things like that.

He was further perplexed that afternoon, when Sarah said she wanted to consult him and David about a damp patch on the landing wall. As a rule, it was David alone whose advice she sought.

"Come into my bedroom. I want to talk to you both and not about the wallpaper," she said when they were upstairs.

"Did Father have a bad attack last night?" Nathan asked seeing the sticky medicine spoon on the bed table, which in her anxiety Sarah had forgotten to wash.

Sarah nodded and played with her brooch which today she had pinned to a new white-lace jabot on last year's high-necked black dress.

The effect, with her severe hairstyle, was aging and David noted more lines on her face than he had remembered being there. But when had he last looked at her properly? He was always preoccupied when he came here and didn't call to have private chats with her as he had once—there wasn't time. At night he had his air-raid warden duty. All day he was bogged down by business. Money he was making, though he had a conscience about much of it coming from military contracts; the idea of profiting from war, like his father-in-law had done, was abhorrent to him. But somebody had to make uniforms and because he had a clothing factory he was one of those who did. He did not carry money on *Rosh Hashanah* and was aware of a flatness in his pocket where his bulging wallet usually reposed. War-risk insurance had paid for his bomb damage, as it had for Ben's, and cash wasn't a problem to him nowadays. But it couldn't buy his father renewed health, or reduce his mother's anxiety.

"You don't look too good yourself, Mother," he said flatly. "Father's putting years on you."

Sarah emerged from her thoughts and glared at him. "How would you like it if your Ronald said such a thing about you, to Bessie?"

"If I behaved as foolishly as Father's doing, he'd be entitled to. But I wouldn't."

"And how do you know how you'll behave when you're getting old? A man in his forties can't put himself in the place of one like your father, with the will to work still strong in him, but the health to do so slipping away. Such a terrible predicament, nobody should have to know from it," Sarah said distressedly.

"But one that comes to most men sooner or later," Nathan told her. "It's the kind of thing I see in my work every day."

"And the ones to whom it comes sooner try to preserve themselves if they've got any sense!" David exclaimed. "Instead of giving their family the kind of worry Father's giving us."

"Maybe he'd rather die in the factory than prolong his life in the kitchen rocking chair," Sarah said quietly. "And if that's what he wants, it's up to him."

"Like hell it is!" Nathan exploded.

"I'll read the riot act to him when I get downstairs!" David declared.

Sarah drew herself up to her full four-foot-eleven and quelled them both with one of her Queen Victoria glances. "Neither of you will say one word to him about it. Do you hear me? That's what I wanted to tell you, but first I tried to make you see it from his point of view. So I haven't succeeded, it's too bad. Maybe afterwards, when you've thought about it, you'll understand. But even if you don't, you're to leave him alone and let him be happy. Nobody is going to mention retirement to him ever again."

Chapter Five

The telephone rang whilst Sarah was in the cellar pressing her laundry, filling her with foreboding as its strident summons always did these days. She left Abraham's woolen underpants dangling from the machine in a cascade of water and went to answer it, rebuking herself for always expecting the worst. But how could she not, with three of her grandsons fighting in the war?

She wiped her damp hands on her apron and heard the sound of sobbing the moment she lifted the receiver. Was it Esther or Miriam? She didn't need a crystal ball to tell her it was one of them. In the old days, when they'd lived close by and she hadn't had this ugly, black contraption on her kitchen wall, they'd have come running to her and she'd have taken them in her arms, but you couldn't comfort someone over a stretch of wire.

"What is it? For God's sake tell me," she said with her heart pounding. But the sobbing went on and on. Then she heard a gulp, as if whoever was weeping was trying to control it.

A convulsive, "Oh Mother—" told her it was her daughter. Miriam called her Ma.

"Is it Harry, or Arnold?" Sarah made herself ask.

Another bout of weeping preceded the reply. "Harry."

A picture of her eldest grandchild flashed before Sarah's eyes, not as he had looked in his uniform the last time she saw him, but the long ago memory of an eight-day-old infant, with Ben's face in miniature and tendrils of silky dark hair peeping from beneath the little white *yarmulke* he had worn when the *mohel* circumcised him. The cap, and his cambric gown, had been worn by his Sandberg uncles for their *Brith* and by every male child in the family since.

"The telegram says he's missing in Italy, Mother."

A great wave of relief engulfed Sarah, weakening her legs. She leaned heavily against the wall, thinking of the *Brith* garments carefully stored in tissue paper and lavender in readiness for her future great-grandsons. Missing was not necessarily dead; there was still a chance that a son of Harry's would one day wear them.

"Ben's shut the shop," Esther said. "He hasn't spoken a word since the boy handed him the envelope. David's here, sitting with him and he said I wasn't to tell you and Father. But I had to, didn't I? You will tell David I had to?"

For the first time, Sarah became conscious of an element of fear in her other children's regard for their elder brother. She'd heard the same apprehensive note in Sammy and Nat's voices when they had done something of which David might not approve.

"I don't know what to do," Esther said tremulously. "David made Ben get into bed and I feel so alone."

Sarah pulled herself together. "You'll do what my neighbor Mrs. Watson's daughter did. When she got the telegram about their Albert, who afterwards turned up as a prisoner-of-war. You'll carry on, Esther. Go and open the shop and put a smile on your face for the customers. Ben can't lie in bed forever and when he sees you being strong, he'll find strength also."

"That's what David said. But it's easy for him to give such advice! His son is safe at home because medical students don't get called up."

Sarah made no comment. She knew how shock could affect people. "This morning I got a letter from Marianne and one from our Nat, as well," she said, steering her daughter away from the subject.

But this brought forth a further spate of resentment.

"Don't even mention our Marianne to me! She could have volunteered for the Army Pay Corps, that's based in Manchester, when she joined the ATS. Like plenty of Jewish girls did. But no! She has to be different as usual. It wouldn't suit her to be billeted at home, the way Eva Frankl and Hildegard are. And where is she now, when she could be a comfort to her mother and father? Stationed near Salisbury Plain with all those American soldiers. I don't sleep a wink at night, worrying about her."

Sarah remained discreetly silent. Marianne's virtue was the last thing she herself was worried about; no granddaughter of Sarah Sandberg's would ever give cause for concern on that account.

"And our Nat's another fine one!" Esther continued her diatribe. "Volunteering instead of waiting to be called up, even though he's got a wife and child."

With this Sarah agreed. She had been unable to dissuade Nathan, and David had refused to try: these days he seemed reluctant to interfere in Nat's affairs. "So what can you do?" she sighed.

Esther laughed abruptly. "That must be the most overused question in the Jewish vocabulary and it only gets asked when there isn't any answer."

Chapter Six

The platoon of khaki-clad girls trudged laboriously up the steep, hillside road that led to their quarters, wearied not just by the climb, but by their day's work at a Royal Army Ordnance Depot.

"This is all I need every evening, after the way the Colonel keeps me pounding the typewriter," Marianne puffed to one of her roommates who was marching beside her. "They ought to provide us with transport, instead of making us walk, Birdie."

"An' I wonder wot them bleedin' cooks 'as ruined fer

our tea ternight?" Private Bird replied through the side of her lipstick-caked mouth.

Talking during a march was forbidden, but the girls, and Birdie especially, thought most of the ATS regulations were made to be broken.

Marianne shrugged, then straightened her shoulders as Corporal Davies, who was escorting them, cast a beady eye in her direction. "We'll never know, will we?" she whispered to Birdie. Their meals were largely unrecognizable, but telling the orderly officer so when she made the statutory visit to the cookhouse to receive complaints, had no effect.

"It won't be *lokshen* soup, that's fer sure!" Birdie, who had once been a waitress in an East End Jewish restaurant, said nostalgically. "More likely bubble'n squeak, made wiv the leftover bacon rind, 'n bleedin' caterpillars fried up wiv the flamin' cabbage like the larst time!"

Another glance from Corporal Davies put an end to the exchange and Birdie raised her voice in song with their comrades who were rendering one of the bawdy ballads included in their nightly repertoire.

Marianne usually sang with them, enjoying the camaraderie of Service life that compensated for its less pleasurable aspects, but this evening she was dispirited. Who could be cheerful when their brother might be lying dead, his body not yet accounted for? She was trying to look on the bright side, but it wasn't easy. Meanwhile, she had applied for compassionate leave so she could go home and comfort her parents.

"You're out of step, Klein!" the corporal barked.

Marianne executed the necessary staccato shuffle and almost tripped over a stone on the unpaved road. What was she doing here, in the middle of nowhere? Wearing a uniform and being ordered about by an ex-schoolmistress from Cardiff? Sharing a room with two cockney girls who were man-mad?

"You're out of step again, Klein!"

And getting called by her surname by women and girls to whom a stripe or two on their sleeve, or pips on their epaulets, had lent unquestionable authority? She'd joined up, that's what she was doing here! But sometimes she had to pinch herself to believe it. That she'd gone against her parents' wishes and was miles away from home. The family would faint from shock if they could hear what her comrades were singing.

"Roll me over,
In the clover,
Roll me over, lay me down
And do it again!"

Marianne had blushed the first few times she had heard
it, but you couldn't blush every time you heard something
like that in the Services, or you'd walk around with a permanently red face. What a sheltered upbringing she'd had.
Some of the other girls had, too, and now took everything in
their stride, as Marianne had learned to do. But there were
still some things that shocked her.

"Gerrartofit yer fuckin' bleeder!" Birdie yelled after a
passing jeep that had raised the dust in their faces.

And the language was one of them.

"Arseface!" Marianne's other roommate hollered when
an army truck repeated the offense.

"That's enough of that," Corporal Davies rasped as she
did regularly in the same circumstances. Her uniform and
hair were as dust-laden as everyone else's, but, unlike her
lessers, she marched along stoically, every inch the living
image of a woman who has found her true niche in the army.

When it was not dusty underfoot, it was muddy, and the
girls invariably arrived at their quarters coated with one or
bespattered with the other. Marianne had to change and
make herself look presentable before going to Platoon Office
to find out if she had been granted leave. There was an evening train to London which would get her there in time to
catch the midnight one to Manchester. Barring delays, she
thought restively when she was left cooling her heels until the
CO found time to see her.

The distress that had lowered her spirits since her
mother's letter arrived that morning increased whilst she
waited. And the news about Harry only accounted for half of
it. Was the recrimination she had read between the lines just
her imagination? The praise for Shirley, who kept dropping
in to cheer up Marianne's parents in her absence. The reference to Eva Frankl's always being there when her mother
and father needed her, because she was stationed in Manchester. Even the mention of people they hadn't seen for years
caring enough to ring up and console them seemed an ob-
lique rebuke. The tin of homemade strudel with which the
letter had been enclosed did, too. A reminder that Esther

Klein did not neglect her maternal duty to her daughter, despite her anxiety about her son. Duty! Marianne thought and was shocked by the sudden surge of resentment aroused in her. Possibly these thoughts were just the product of her guilty conscience because she had left home, but her feelings about duty were not. It was the first time she had seen family ties in that light.

She glanced around at the ugly, green filing cabinets and the gray-blanketed camp bed on which an NCO would sleep that night. Acrid fumes from a paraffin heater in the corner caught at her throat and a huge poster beside a notice board, displaying a plate of half-eaten sausage and egg, asked "If you didn't want it, why did you take it?"

Marianne averted her eyes from the poster. She had wanted what she'd taken. A taste of freedom. This was why she had not done what the family called "the right thing" and joined the Pay Corps—maintained her allegiance to them and served her country at one and the same time. She had taken the opportunity to spread her wings because it might never come again and she had no regrets about having done so. But her troubled conscience was another matter.

The day-sergeant emerged from the officer's sanctum with a sheaf of papers in her hand and a bored look on her baby face. "Miss Platt will see you now, Klein," she said sitting down behind her typewriter and tucking a stray strand of flaxen hair into the fat roll servicewomen who preferred not to cut their locks to the regulation length were obliged to choose as their coiffeur. "But you don't stand a dog's chance of getting leave," she added.

This was immediately endorsed by the commanding officer. "It isn't an adequate reason, Klein."

Marianne steeled herself to argue, which was not easy when confronted by Junior Commander Platt's impersonal gaze. "It is in my family, ma'am."

Miss Platt raised her carefully plucked eyebrows and allowed an uncomfortable silence to develop.

Behind her desk, another poster blazoned a warning about careless talk, which seemed particularly apt to Marianne at that moment, but she did not allow it to deter her. "What I mean, ma'am, is that Jewish people always cling together when there's trouble in the family. All my relations are rallying round my parents, and even if it were only for a day or two it'd comfort them to know I wanted to be with them, too."

"The last time you requested special leave, Klein, you wanted to be at your cousin's engagement party."

And next time it'll be for her wedding, Marianne thought.

"I would hardly call that trouble in the family," Miss Platt said crisply.

Marianne did not reply. Her request to go home for the celebration when Shirley became engaged to Peter had not been granted and she had been unable to explain to the CO why it mattered for her to be there. What would Miss Platt have thought if she'd known Marianne didn't even like Shirley, but had wanted to be present nevertheless? God, how complicated this family thing was! She couldn't even explain to herself the hold it had on her.

Miss Platt toyed with the contents of her in-tray. Did the girl think there was a special set of King's Regulations for Jews? "I'm sorry about your brother, Klein. But the same rules apply for you as for the rest of us." She left her in-tray alone and twirled the bright gold band on her wedding finger. "It might interest you to know I didn't ask for leave when my husband was shot down in the Battle of Britain. I would probably not have been given it because his remains were not recovered and there was no funeral."

How could you discuss family feeling with a woman whose upper lip was as stiff as that? Marianne thought, studying her CO's pale and perfect features across which no tremor of emotion had so much as flickered whilst she spoke of her personal loss. But Miss Platt had "boarding school" written all over her and probably they'd trained her to be like this. Not like Temple School in Cheetham Hill where the teachers made a fuss of you if you fell in the playground and grazed your knee.

"Your hair is too long, Klein."

"Yes, ma'am."

"You'd better get along now, or you'll miss tea."

Marianne saluted smartly and left the office feeling like a robot with a muzzle clamped over its mouth. But there was no provision in King's Regulations for debate. Everything was either black or white.

Most of the time, she revelled in her away-from-home freedom, but every so often something like this would happen to remind her she wasn't her own boss, any more than she'd been under her parents' roof. And in some ways she was less so.

Cut your hair, Klein! Polish your buttons, Klein! Yes, ma'am, no, ma'am! Yesterday, there'd been the regular medical inspection and her dignity was still smarting from having her hair scanned for lice, her hands for scabies and her nether regions for worse.

When she'd signed on at the recruiting center on Market Street, Manchester, unable to control a sudden, wild impulse to do so, the smiling khaki-clad girl who'd greeted her hadn't warned her it would be like this, she thought, treading the long winding path to the cookhouse in the March wind. But she would still have joined up if she'd known. What were niggardly restrictions compared with the danger Martin and her brothers had to face?

She looked up at the starry sky and shuddered. Would Martin be setting off on another air raid on Germany tonight? It was still hard to believe he was a bombardier, that the gentle cousin she'd grown up with was no more. In his place had arisen a tight-lipped RAF sergeant who wanted to wipe the Nazis off the face of the earth.

She recalled how timid he had been as a child, but now he was afraid of nothing. "Sticks and stones may break my bones, but words will never harm me" had been his schoolboy philosophy. He wouldn't hit anyone unless they hit him first, she remembered him saying and this still held good. Only it wasn't himself he was avenging now; it was the whole Jewish people.

She thought of her brothers, too. Arnold, sailing the treacherous seas in a minesweeper, as if he, too, like Martin, had deliberately sought the highest degree of danger. It made her feel she had not really known him. But how well did he know her? Perhaps it was always that way with brothers and sisters? The familiarity of family life deadened your perceptions. Maybe she hadn't valued her brothers, either, she reflected with a lump in her throat. And now she might never see Harry again.

The cookhouse loomed blackly ahead as she turned a bend in the tree-lined path. Inside, the girls would be eating their tea, laughing and joking in the brightly lit, steamy warmth. Spreading hunks of bread with the margarine deposited like yellow bricks in soup plates on the long tables and diving greedily for the jam before it was all gone. In summer, the jam was left uneaten, aswarm with captive bluebottles and wasps tempted to a sticky end in the sweet morass, and some girls, Marianne included, were too sickened by the sight to eat the main course and fled to the NAAFI canteen to fill themselves with starchy food.

Why bother going in? she asked herself when she reached the cookhouse door. The empty feeling inside her was not hunger. She retraced her footsteps and went to her billet to take a bath before the other girls returned and used all the hot water. At her last unit, she'd lived in a big nissen hut and had had to cross a field to the bathrooms. Here, she was one of a single platoon of ATS attached to the Ordnance Depot for special duties and enjoyed the comparative luxury of peacetime married-quarters.

These little redbrick houses were set back from the road behind a broad, grassy verge and flanked by "Off Limits" notices to keep out the soldiers quartered in the huge barracks complex at the foot of the hill. In peacetime the barracks was occupied by the British; but now housed vast numbers of American GIs, with only a sprinkling of Tommies left to scowl at their better-paid, gum-chewing allies whose illusory, Hollywood-inspired glamor worked like a charm with the English girls.

Most evenings, a line of army trucks was parked beside the "Off Limits" signs, waiting to carry off the "Ats" to USO concerts, and dances; and it was not uncommon for a skirmish to break out between the drivers as they vied for the girls' patronage.

Tonight was no different and Marianne had to run a gauntlet of devouring male eyes in order to reach her quarters. Many girls found this persistent attention flattering, but she found it irritating. And sometimes insulting.

"Hi there, Shorty!"

"Come on over for a pack of Camels, hon."

"I don't smoke, thank you," she replied haughtily.

"Have a Hershey bar instead."

"No thanks."

"Say, you eat candy don't you?"

"No, as a matter of fact. English people eat sweets."

Her retort brought a chorus of laughter from the GIs and one of them shone a flashlight on to her.

"Did you ever see such a cute little number?"

"Get your eyes off of her, bud! I saw her first."

Marianne ran into her billet and slammed the door, wolf whistles ringing in her ears. Why was she always rude to them, when all they wanted was to be friendly? She took off her cap and borrowed Birdie's scissors to snip an inch off her hair before she forgot the CO's warning, though it was practically an Eton crop already! It was the way the GIs went about it, approaching girls as if they could be bought, that made her hackles rise. English soldiers didn't treat the "Ats" that way and she was sure the Americans didn't employ those tactics with girls in the States. You couldn't go into a Service canteen without them wanting to pay for your food, or take you to their PX store to buy you cosmetics that weren't available in wartime in English shops. Why did they think they had to buy your friendship?

After she had cut her hair, she switched off the light and drew back the blackout curtains to gaze moodily out of the window at the rows and rows of tanks and jeeps that stretched like a metallic sea in the moonlight. Beyond them, a clump of woods hid the US firing range, but in daytime the rat-a-tat of rifle shots was a constant reminder of its presence.

How lovely the trees looked, lit with silver. Viewed from afar they appeared frothy with blossom; but it was just the chalky dust that had settled on the leaves. Everyone knew this was the marshalling area, that the Americans were here preparing for the Second Front, but nobody talked about it. Was it waiting to be thrown into battle, the desperate will to live while they could, that made the GIs behave as they did? Perhaps if she took the trouble to find out, she'd discover that beneath their brash and sometimes crude veneers they were nice boys, like her brothers and cousins? And maybe, once they found out she couldn't be bought, they would stop trying to buy her?

She blacked out the window and switched on the light before Birdie and Joyce returned from tea; if they found her standing in the dark they'd think she was pottier than they probably thought her already. They couldn't understand why she had stopped going to the dances with them, why the nightly excitement had palled for her when it hadn't for them. How could she tell them that their promiscuity dismayed her? That she was saving herself for the man she would one day marry, like Jewish girls always did? And did not want to tussle with determined Yanks in order to do so.

She had had several such encounters already and enough was enough.

When the other girls entered clutching their enamel mugs and army-issue cutlery, Marianne had bathed and was sitting on her bed doing *The Times* crossword puzzle; the colonel passed on his newspaper to her every day.

"If you ask me, Joycie, she haint normal," Birdie observed. "The way she don't make dates nor nuffin', I'm beginnin' ter fink she's one o' those."

"One of what?" Marianne inquired naïvely.

"It's not just blokes what can be 'omos, cock," Birdie informed her.

"I bet she don't even know what an 'omo is," Joyce giggled.

"I don't."

"Oh Gawd, who's goin' ter tell 'er, Birdie? You or me?"

"She can look it up in that flamin' dictionary of 'ers wot's taking up all that space on the chest of drawers." Birdie picked up Marianne's *Oxford Concise* and dropped it in her lap.

" 'omosexual's the word yer wants, cock. Yer'll find it wiv the haitches."

Birdie exchanged a wink with Joyce and watched Marianne's face turn crimson when she finally found the word in the Addenda.

" 'avin' a sexual propensity fer persons of one's hown sex," Joyce read aloud over her shoulder.

Marianne closed the dictionary with a thud. "How could such a thing be possible?"

Birdie chortled. "Keep well away from Lance Corporal 'attersley, cock, or yer liable ter find out!"

"Yer know that black eye she 'ad larst week, what she said she got from walkin' inter a lamp-post in the dark? Well she didn't," Joyce confided. "Private Lockett's 'er girl an' she told us it was 'er who kyboshed 'attersley fer bein' hunfaithful wiv a Yankee Red Cross girl."

"Sorry ter spoil yer innocence, Marianne," Birdie smiled. "But it 'ad ter 'appen sometime. Why d'you fink Service girls never gets billeted two in a room?"

" 'cause three's a crowd," Joyce supplied sagely.

Hattersley and Lockett were part of the threesome in the room next door and Marianne recalled having seen them go into the shower together, but had thought nothing of it be-

cause they were both female. Now this, and other incidents
which had not registered with her at the time, assumed a new
significance. She would find it difficult to look them in the
eye next time she saw them. But she liked them both and
what she'd just learned didn't make them into different
people, any more than finding out Birdie and Joyce were
promiscuous with men had made her stop liking them.

She glanced at the snapshot of her grandmother she had
pinned on the wall beside her bed and wondered if Sarah,
whom she'd always thought knew everything, knew people
could be homosexual. How could she know, with her clois-
tered existence? Marianne would probably never have made
the discovery if she hadn't joined up. In some ways being in
the Services was better than going to university. It taught you
about life.

"Oh, well, off wiv me passion-killers!" Birdie said, divest-
ing herself of her pink cotton brassiere and khaki knickers.

Marianne watched her rummage in her kitbag for the
saucy black lingerie she kept hidden there.

Joyce was getting her spare skirt from beneath her
mattress, where she had laid it to be pressed into four sharp
pleats, the way all the girls do. "I dunno why yer bovvers,"
she said to Birdie. "Nobody sees yer undies in the dark."

"I bought 'em on the black market fer me 'oneymoon
an' they could rot wiv age before my Bert gets annuver leave,
bless 'is lickle bell-bottom trousers. I might as well wear 'em
art." Birdie lit a Chesterfield and showered herself and the
room with the Chanel Number Five talc she had recently received from a U.S. sergeant. "Private Dent in the 'ouse next
door fell darn the stairs last night, did you 'ear abart it, Marianne?"

Marianne shook her head.

"Fell my arse!" Joyce snorted. "If yer ask me, she
jumped. But she still 'ad a face like a fiddle terday, so it
couldn't've brought on a miscarriage."

"Serve 'er right if she ends up discharged under Para
Eleven," Birdie declared, citing the dreaded King's Regulation that provided for pregnant girls to be released from the
Service. "Like Lance Corporal Donnelly was. She never took
my advice, neither. I even hoffered both of 'em a dollop o'
me own gin ter boil up wiv vinegar an' swaller, but they said
it'd make 'em spew up."

"Why didn't they make the men take precautions?" Marianne pondered.

" 'cause they're simply country girls what knows nothing," Birdie said loftily.

Like I was a simple city girl before I met you, Marianne mused wryly. She had thought the GI she'd heard ask his friend to lend him a rubber had meant an eraser until Birdie put her wise.

"But Dent's even greener than Donnelly," Joyce giggled, smoothing on a pair of forbidden, sheer silk stockings and kicking her hideous, thick khaki ones into a corner. "Whoever it was what knocked 'er up, told 'er fuckin' was safe so long as she peed right arterwards, an' she believed 'im!"

Marianne, who had once thought knocked up meant being roused from sleep in the mornings, averted her eyes. Had Joyce used language like that in civilian life? Probably not. She had told Marianne she was a virgin when she joined up and had sung in the church choir. And Birdie would probably not have been unfaithful to her husband if she'd married him in peacetime. Everyone said war brought out the best in people, made them unselfish and united them in a common cause; but it brought out the bad in them, too. It had transformed Martin into a killer and girls like Birdie and Joyce into the next-best-thing to whores. But she wouldn't let it change her.

The other two exchanged a glance. Marianne's thoughtful silences were apt to make them feel uncomfortable.

"What's up, cock?" Birdie asked. "Finkin' up anuvver story, are yer?"

She had told them she wanted to be a writer and they sometimes found her scribbling when they returned after a night out, which had inspired them with a grudging respect.

"She's finkin' of 'er bruvver what's missin' in haction, yer clot!" Joyce exclaimed.

Marianne felt ashamed because she hadn't thought of Harry for at least half an hour.

"Mopin' won't do 'er nor 'im an 'af-pennyworth o' good," Birdie declared and went to put a kindly hand on Marianne's shoulder. "Come art wiv us ternight, cock. We're on the loose as it 'appens, them blokes we was datin' moved art today. We'll go ter one o' the dances darn the barracks 'n if you don't meet a GI yer fancies, Joycie'n me won't let any-

one take us 'ome. We'll stick wiv yer 'n all walk back together."

For an "At" to return up the hill alone at night was
asking for trouble. Drunken soldiers could be waiting to way-
lay her and one girl who had braved it had had to hit one on
the head with the bottle of Coke she was carrying, to escape
being raped.

"We won't leave yer on yer hown, Marianne," Joyce
echoed. "We're yer mates."

"An' we can manage wivout our slap'n tickle fer one
night," Birdie smiled. "If we 'ave ter."

They were both painstakingly arrayed for their outing
and had no doubt intended to find a couple of replacements
for the boyfriends who had been shipped out. Marianne knew
their offer was a real sacrifice, but she didn't want to go with
them. She surveyed Birdie's bloodshot, blue eyes, the lashes
caked with mascara, and the tiny, gin-swiller's broken veins
on her small, florid face above which a towering bird's-nest
of peroxide-blonde hair was crowned by an ATS forage cap.

Joyce was tapping her foot impatiently, her hourglass
figure encased in a uniform she had altered to fit her like a
second skin.

" 'Ow abart it, Marianne?" she demanded, licking off
some of the purple lipstick that was too strident for her
mousey coloring and made her look as if she suffered from
heart disease. "Standin' abart like this is a waste of good Joycie'n Birdie if yer haint comin'.'"

" 'Course she's comin','" Birdie insisted. "But she'd better
do 'erself up, or we're not takin' 'er."

Marianne rose from her bed reluctantly and gave them
each a slice of strudel to eat whilst they waited for her to
dress. What would Esther Klein say if she knew her precious
daughter was about to go to an orgy with these girls? Her experiences of nights-out with Joyce and Birdie could not be
described any other way. But there was no point in her having left home if she was going to let the family control her by
proxy; it was time she got them out of her system. And
maybe she would meet a nice American Jewish boy at the
dance, whose morals had remained as intact as hers had, war
or no war.

Chapter Seven

"It isn't fair of you to deprive Shirley of a big wedding," Bessie said, clicking away with her knitting needles to add another pair of khaki mittens to the pile she was sending to the Red Cross. "And now you've made me drop a stitch," she added, glaring at David.

When she was not knitting, she was out helping at a Services canteen in the city center and David wished today was one of her duty stints. She had been nagging him about their daughter's wedding reception since he arrived home from the factory half-an-hour ago. And also about why it was necessary for him to work on Sunday afternoons when his employees didn't. But if it wasn't this, it would be something else; she had to have something to nag about! "Ostentation in wartime is unseemly," he said irritably.

"You didn't think that when you wanted our Ronald to have a big *Bar Mitzvah*," Shirley put in from the sofa, where she was sitting sketching.

"The war hadn't begun yet," he reminded her. "You're getting like me, love. Feeling as if it's been going on forever." He lit a cigarette and rested his head on the back of his armchair, wearily. "Apart from anything else, how can we have a great big celebration when we still don't know if Harry's alive or dead?"

The reference to Harry evoked a gloomy silence. Several weeks had passed since the War Office telegram arrived and the family were by now steeling themselves for the worst.

"Why did you have to remind us, Dad?" Shirley shuddered.

"You shouldn't have needed reminding." David got up and went to look out of the French window at his large rectangle of lawn, picking his way through the over-furnished room. He had wanted to discard the furniture and ornaments from their parlor in Bellott Street when they moved to Prestwich, but Bessie would not hear of it. A few elegant pieces with a Persian rug to set off the parquet floor would make this big room look cold and empty, she'd said when David had suggested it. And only paupers didn't put down a wall-to-wall carpet, she'd added.

But one day, when they moved to Cheshire, he would have his way. What was the good of moving up in the world if your possessions didn't illustrate you'd acquired the good taste to go with it? His detached house was situated in a prestigious road and everyone knew you had to have money in order to live there. Nobody could say David Sandberg hadn't done well.

Bessie was still smarting because her daughter's wedding reception was not going to be the talk of the town. "Lizzie got a splinter in her finger this morning, dusting your damn orangebox," she lashed out at David.

"Why don't you set fire to it, Mom?" Shirley smiled.

The orange-box bookcase David had kept from his childhood was a joke to his children, but not to his wife. "She once threatened to," he told his daughter. "Then you started crying; you were in your cot at the foot of our bed and we were so busy trying to quieten you we forgot what the argument was about."

"I wouldn't let Peter keep an eyesore like that in the corner of our bedroom."

"He wouldn't want to," Bessie said. "But at least your dad's stopped wanting mirrors all over the house and I suppose I must be thankful for that."

"If I were Dad, I'd want to forget I'd once earned an orange box sweeping the greengrocer's floor," Shirley answered.

David smiled. But the stink of rotting cabbage leaves and overripe fruit had drifted from the past to his nostrils and he saw himself as a scraggy little lad, clutching Mr. Radinsky's broom in the Strangeways store. "My parents couldn't afford to buy me a bookcase," he said gruffly.

"But now you've got three, Dad, haven't you? Two in here and another upstairs. So why do you need to keep that horrible old box?"

David lit a cigarette and turned back to the window. How did you tell your child, who had never known privation, how precious something is to you when you acquire it by your own labors? But the orange box was more to him than just that. The Sandbergs had only had one looking-glass in Strangeways, everyone had had to queue up in the kitchen to use it; and when he married Bessie he had insisted on a mirror in every room to prove he was on his way up. Now, his rise from the ghetto was self-evident and mirrors had lost their significance for him; but the orange box he would always keep. Everyone needed a reminder of from whence they came.

The first shadows of evening had begun to fall in the garden and he watched a bird swoop down on to a laburnum tree and disappear into the foliage where Lizzie had told him there was a nest. One day, he'd remember to go and look at it. If other matters ever stopped pushing such simple pleasures from his mind! When he looked back, it seemed as if he'd never had time to enjoy anything. When had he last spent a day in the country, or by the sea? He hadn't had a break since before the war and it was now 1944. Even then, he had not taken real holidays; just odd weekends at old Mrs. Litvak's boarding house in Blackpool, where he and Bessie had spent their honeymoon. Bessie had taken the children there for a fortnight every August before they grew up, but the factory had always held him chained.

"Come and look at Peter's portrait, Dad," Shirley commanded.

David drew the blackout curtains and went to admire the sketch she had made of her beloved. "Another one?" he teased her. "We soon won't be able to see your bedroom wallpaper for pictures of Peter."

"She's romantic," Bessie declared. "She takes after me."

"After you, love?" David said dryly. "When she was satisfied with that weeny little diamond on her finger?"

Shirley glanced at her ring, for which Peter had saved up all his army pay. "It's all he can afford at present."

"But you don't mind, do you?" David smiled.

"I know he'll buy me a great big diamond one day, when he gets rich from coming in the business."

His daughter's materialistic reply was a shock to David. She *was* like Bessie. Calculating and acquisitive. Why hadn't he realized it before? Maybe he hadn't wanted to. He, too, had those characteristics, but a man had to have them, or where would he be? And they had never impinged on his personal relationships. In some ways Shirley had a man's mind. She'd inherited his drive and efficiency, as well as being artistic, and she was invaluable in the business. So she wasn't the sweet little thing he'd kidded himself she was. You couldn't have it both ways.

It had been Shirley who had organized their improvised workroom after they were bombed out, and dealt with the Jewish employees' qualms about entering a church, even an unused one with the pews removed so it could be rented out as temporary premises. How she had managed this, he did not know—and hadn't had time to care, with all the tasks he'd had to undertake himself. But his daughter had soon had everything running smoothly and later had helped him install the factory in the highly suitable building they occupied now.

He surveyed her sleek new hairstyle and the sumptuous figure her childish curves had promised and for once could not find in her the little girl she had been. Your children sped away and suddenly you were confronted with unfamiliar adults, he thought with misty eyes. Ronald was on the way to being a doctor and Shirley a comely young woman who would soon be Peter Kohn's wife. But still my daughter, he told himself with a surge of possessiveness. That, she would always be.

As for his son, he hoped the boy would be stronger willed than Nathan had been, let loose among all those Gentile nurses. "I'm surprised our Nat hasn't asked Rebecca to join him in Scotland," he remarked to Bessie.

"I'm not," she replied. "And I don't think she would if he asked her to."

David prickled with apprehension. That his brother's married life was, to put it mildly, traumatic, was no secret to the family. So was his own, but Nat wasn't the kind to come to terms with it as David had done.

"What would Rebecca want to be stuck in some out-of-the-way army camp for? Without even a decent school for Leona to go to?" Bessie said.

But David could tell she had deliberately made her tone light because Shirley was present.

"Go and make a cup of tea, love," she instructed their daughter. "We forgot to have any, like we always do on Lizzie's half-day." She waited until Shirley had left the room before continuing the conversation. "Nat had no right to join up," she pronounced censoriously.

"A man has to do what his conscience dictates," David answered.

"What conscience? He just couldn't wait to get away from his wife."

Bessie was still Rebecca's confidante and most of the things David learned about his brother were gleaned from her. "That little minx, Leona, makes a lot of trouble in that household," he said in Nathan's defense. "Haven't you noticed how she plays one of them off against the other?" He ground out his cigarette thoughtfully. "You and I have rowed about a lot of things, but we've never quarrelled about our kids, have we?"

Bessie stopped knitting. "But the real cause of their trouble is that woman."

"What woman?" David asked avoiding her eye.

"You don't have to pretend with me, David. Rebecca told me all about her."

"And who told Rebecca?"

"She didn't need telling; she's got eyes. And a wife's intuition. It wasn't just Nat's face that gave the game away that night at the infirmary when Sister whoever-she-is walked into the room. It was yours, as well." Bessie busied herself with her knitting again. "But I think Rebecca's a fool for letting it eat her up. She's the one who's got Nat, not that nurse."

David could barely conceal his astonishment. Had his wife forgotten she'd once behaved exactly the same way with him about Miriam?

Her next words told him she had not. "I didn't always use my head myself when I was younger. But I wasn't daft enough to do what Rebecca has. She doesn't sleep with Nat any more."

"What?"

"I think that must be why he joined up."

"So would I, if you did that to me."

"You're too old," Bessie said comfortably. "And I'm not going to."

David was stunned by what she had imparted to him. How could Rebecca treat Nat that way? To the best of his knowledge, his brother had forgotten Mary and been a good and faithful husband. But there was no telling what went on in the female imagination.

He surveyed his own wife placidly knitting, plump and silver-haired with two large diamonds sparkling on her red-nailed fingers. This woman had made his life a hell in their early years together, but time had taught her not to go too far with him and he had learned how to humor her. She still lashed out at him when some inner ire sought release, but these outbursts had become part of the fabric of their marriage and these days his home life was far from intolerable. If she suddenly stopped nagging him he would probably miss it!

"What're you smiling about?" she inquired.

"You and me." How had they progressed from constant strife to this? Sitting companionably by the fire together, like Darby and Joan.

"Children can bring a couple closer together if you let them, like they've done with us," Bessie said, with her thoughts still on Rebecca and Nathan. "You probably wouldn't still be with me if they hadn't," she added with unprecedented honesty.

David got up and kissed her cheek. She was right. He had his children to thank for everything.

In her modest semi-detached villa on a narrow tree-lined avenue Miriam was seated by the fire alone. She had just come downstairs after one of her frequent visits to Martin's empty bedroom and stared into the flames, restively.

Sammy was busy at the table, carving a tray to give to Shirley and Peter for a wedding present. He had padded the table with an old blanket, to protect it, and kept raising it to make sure he was not making pressure marks on the polished oak surface.

"I wish you'd stop doing that," Miriam said. "I don't give a damn if you mark the table, but like I've told you before, if you're worried in case you do, go and do your carving somewhere else." She gave Sammy an irritated glance and picked up a copy of *John Bull*, to browse through it.

"The kitchenette's too small; there's no room for me to work in there," Sammy answered. "And the shed's got that big fanlight that you won't let me paint to black it out."

"Why should I have to switch on the light during the day when I go in there to iron the clothes?" Miriam bristled. "This house isn't right for us, that's the top and bottom of it! We were better off where we were, with a nice big kitchen to live in, instead of two entertaining rooms and that poky little scullery I haven't yet learned to call a kitchenette."

Sammy remained silent. The conversation was more or less identical to the one they had most evenings. And as heated on Miriam's side as usual. He knew what she would say next, though he hoped she wouldn't.

"It makes me sick the way you always do everything David tells you to!"

That she wouldn't bring her resentment of his brother into it was too much to hope for. "David wanted us all to live near each other," he said giving his usual defensive reply and thinking she must be tired of hearing it.

"But your parents're still in their old house. They didn't let David make their minds up for them."

"Nor did I," Sammy said quietly. "I'm here because I want to be."

"Which is another way of saying you're here because you want to please David," Miriam retorted. "When are you going to be your own boss, Sammy? And I'm not talking about your job, I resigned myself to David being your boss in that respect years ago. I'm talking about your life."

Sammy chipped away at the delicate tracery he was carving on the handles of the tray, then he put down his knife and looked into his wife's angry green eyes which these days were the only thing about her appearance that had retained the vitality of her youth. "When are you going to stop hating David because you couldn't be what he wanted you to be, so he gave you up?"

Miriam caught her breath and the magazine on her lap slid to the floor. Her old romance with his brother was something about which they never talked. This was the first time in twenty-one years of marriage that Sammy had mentioned it. Why had he done so now?

"That's what you've really got against him, isn't it?" Sammy added.

"No!"

"Are you sure?"

"How could I still be harping on that? I'm not a romantic girl any more, I'm forty-five." She retrieved the magazine and flung it on the sofa. "And I've been your wife all these years; we've got a son we both adore. What're you talking about?"

"About how you've never loved me, but I haven't let it matter," Sammy said with a tightness in his throat. "All I wanted was to make you happy."

"You have."

He scanned her face and she got up to pace the room restlessly, as if what they were discussing was of no consequence and more pressing matters were on her mind.

"You don't seem happy now."

"Who could be happy when their son could get shot out of the sky any minute?" Miriam said tremulously, pausing by the sideboard to gaze at a photograph of Martin in his RAF uniform. She put out her hand and touched the thin, unsmiling face regarding her from behind the glass, then her eye fell on the bombardier's badge above his breast pocket and she turned away and shuddered. Every time she saw it she was reminded of the night in her mother-in-law's cellar when the bombs had rained from the sky and Martin had recited his terrifyingly cynical poem about death.

The realization that her son was a stranger to her had come as a shock. How could it be? When she had carried him in her womb, fed him at her breast, loved and nurtured him from childhood to manhood? Where had the timid little boy gone to, whom she had comforted on her lap when he shed tears of sorrow over a dying sparrow in the backyard? And who had once called her cruel when she put her foot on a cockroach.

Why had he changed? And when? It was not possible that she hadn't known what was going on in his mind. He was the center of her life, her very heartbeat. And yet it had happened, she could not deny it. She'd had to accept, that night in the cellar, that she knew nothing about him and it was still so. The dear warmth of his presence, when he came home on leave, the look and feel of him, was all he allowed her. The essence of him, the person he was and had always been without her knowing it, he kept locked within himself.

"I can't sleep at night for thinking of him," she whispered breaking the heavy silence that had fallen.

Sammy wanted to take her in his arms, give her his shoulder to weep on, which summed up his function in her life, he reflected bitterly, but steeled himself as he had never done before. Her obsession about David, the burning resentment of his regard for his brother, had festered for too long. What a fool he'd been to hope the open sore of the past would heal as if it had never been.

"Worrying about our son is something we share," he said roughly. "But Martin isn't the only reason you're unhappy."

"The other is I can't bear to see the husband I respect

dancing to someone else's tune about everything!" Miriam flashed.

Sammy sighed and withdrew into his shell again. He had said more than he'd intended already. It was fruitless to prolong the discussion—like walking round and round a revolving door that always returned you to the same place. His wife had two loves in her life, his brother and their son. The first she had lost and God forbid that she should lose the other.

"I'll make you a nice cup of tea, chuck," he said with his customary smile, that had once come naturally, but which he now wore like a mask to hide the ache in his heart.

He went into the kitchenette to put the kettle on to boil and saw Miriam gaze at the big calendar she had pinned to the wall above the mantelpiece.

"It's April already," she said dully. "Martin will be twenty in September. He was only seventeen when he joined up; he's been away two-and-a-half years." She picked up a thick, black crayon and obliterated Sunday from the calendar though it was not yet over, wanting to speed another day on its way so the time would come more quickly when her son would be home again.

Esther was garbed in the long-sleeved blue and white overall she had taken from the shop because it matched her kitchenette decor, her hair swathed in a scarf to protect it from the pungent fumes drifting from the red hot oil in which she was frying *gefilte* fish. One of her new silvery locks had escaped on to her forehead, she noticed when she stepped into the adjoining living room to glance at her dozing husband and saw her reflection in the mirror. So let her hair get greasy and fishy, what did it matter? She had only covered her head from habit. How she looked and what she smelled of wasn't important any more.

Before the War Office telegram came, she'd gone to the hairdresser's every week and had the aging streaks colored to match the rest. Now, there was more gray hair than ginger and was it any wonder? There were new lines on her face, too, but they weren't important, either.

Only Harry was important. The thought of him had shut out her fears for Arnold, and the apprehension of a different kind that had plagued her about Marianne. She hadn't set foot in the beauty parlor since the day her world was turned upside down, or even bothered to look at herself properly in the mirrow when she washed and dressed.

Yesterday at the *Shabbos* gathering, her mother had told her she was losing weight and Bessie had said enviously that she wished she could, which had amused everyone because her mouth had been full of cake when she said it. It was the way people still laughed, even those who loved Harry, that made the waiting more unbearable. The way everyday life went on, with the rain still raining and the sun still shining as it would continue to do if Harry never came home again.

The telegram had not included the phrase "presumed dead," and everyone said that was hopeful. But how long could you go on hoping? And what would the enemy do to Harry if he was a prisoner of war? Albert Watson had also been captured in Italy, but was now in a POW camp in Germany. Harry had "Jew" engraved on the identity tag which servicemen and women wore in case the military had to bury them. He had showed it to her and joked about it when she turned pale after learning its purpose. But she wouldn't let herself dwell upon what the Germans might inflict upon a live Jewish soldier.

Ben awoke with a grunt and sniffed. "Something's burning on the cooker, Esther."

She left him fumbling in his cardigan pocket for his cigarettes and went to rescue their supper. Once, he would have been there ahead of her, but it would take more than a panful of singed fishballs to rouse him from the despondency he'd sunk into, Esther thought as she removed them from the oil and laid them to drain on brown paper.

"When do you want to eat?" she asked Ben through the doorway.

"Never."

"So you'll live on cigarettes instead! A lot of good it'll do you."

"Only one thing will do me any good."

"You're going to stop living if our Harry doesn't come back?" she asked flatly and watched his face crumple with pain. "We've still got two other children, remember."

"Oy," Ben groaned and avoided her eye as she returned to the living room and stood beside his chair.

"I was saying it to myself as well as to you," Esther told him. "Because so far we haven't said it to each other, have we?" She sat down in the other armchair and listened to the clock ticking away in the silence, waiting for her husband to speak. "And maybe we should've done," she added when he did not.

Ben stared down at the scaly red patches on his hands, which Lou Benjamin had said was eczema when he went to the surgery for some ointment to relieve the itching. "Twice before I've had this rash," he said pensively. "The first time, I was only a kid of fourteen. It was after my parents died in the flu epidemic. I woke up with my hands like this the morning of their funeral. And I got it again, years later, when my brother married a *shiksah*."

"So other people sit down and cry when they've got *tsorus* and you break out in a rash instead."

"The kind of man who can weep I've never been."

"I know."

"Even when I was a lad I couldn't." Ben scratched his left hand which troubled him most. "But the way I feel, it's a miracle I haven't got this itch all over my body."

Esther looked at his sagging shoulders and straightened her own. If she had to be the strong one just now, she'd be it. In the past, she had always leaned on him.

"Why not nip across the road and invite Miriam and Sammy to come and eat our burnt supper with us?" she suggested to take his mind off himself. "The way Miriam looks these days, I don't think she ever eats, and to have company would do us all good. I miss how it was in the old days, when we used to pop into each other's houses across the back entry. Round here, where you've got to ring the doorbell because everyone keeps their side door locked, it isn't the same."

"It's a different life we live now, Esther. For one thing, everyone's got their own troubles. I don't mean the family's stopped being close; that could never happen. Maybe it's the war. Or perhaps it's being in a snobbier district. But there's a separateness nowadays that there never used to be," Ben reflected.

"Even so, go across and invite them."

"Miriam's company I can do without! She knows her son's alive and well and stationed in Lincolnshire, but nobody would think so from the way she goes on."

"You're forgetting how we worried night and day about Arnold being on a minesweeper, before the telegram about Harry came," Esther said in fairness to her sister-in-law.

"But we didn't go round depressing everyone else, the way she does."

"Miriam only has one child, Ben. Which brings us back to what started this conversation." Esther had to force her next words out of her mouth. "If Harry's dead—"

"Don't say that!" Ben cut in. "I don't want to hear it."

"I've already said it. Because it's something we have to face up to and we may as well prepare ourselves now, instead of pretending it's impossible. But if he is, we'll still have our other son and our daughter, won't we?"

For a moment Ben could not speak and when he found his voice it sounded hoarse and cracked. "In some ways you're as strong as your mother, Esther. Only I never knew it until now. However black things seem, she always finds something to hang on to. But I'm not like that, I never have been. I'm a fighter, yes, or I'd never have dragged myself up from nothing with no family to help and encourage me until I became part of yours. But what we're going through now—you and me—it isn't a fight, and that's why I can't cope with it. There's nothing to do but wait and I can't bear the waiting, Esther."

"You'll have to," she replied.

Ben gave her a dazed glance, then averted his eyes and stared into the fire, over which he had sat huddled for most of the day. "It's always worse on Sundays, when I'm at home with nothing to keep me busy."

"I should be so lucky."

He turned to look at her. "You're a wonderful wife. And me, I should be ashamed of myself."

Esther managed to smile and got up to lay the table. "What for? Loving your son too much?"

Ben watched her take the cruet set out the sideboard cupboard and rub the silver-plated tops of the salt and pepper pots with a corner of her overall. "For loving him more than I love his brother. Does that shock you?"

"I've always known it," Esther replied. "And it used to bother me until I mentioned it to my mother."

"Ma you had to mention it to?" Ben said nervously. "What must she think of me?"

Esther set the cutlery in place and brought a bowl of apples to the table. Bananas had disappeared from the English diet since the war and the few precious oranges, which she obtained from her fruiterer in Salford in exchange for under-the-counter pure silk stockings for his wife, she always took to the *Shabbos* tea party to be shared between Leona and the twins.

"Mother once told me you were another David," she informed her husband. "And coming from her, there couldn't be a higher compliment, so set your mind at rest."

"But what did she say about me and the boys?" There had been mutual respect between Ben and his mother-in-law since Sarah took him as a lodger when he was a young man. Her opinion mattered.

"That you don't love one more than the other—you feel different things for each of them, like she does for me and my brothers."

"P'rhaps it's true," Ben mused. "Harry gets on my nerves sometimes, but him I can talk to and I can read him like a book. Arnold, I've never understood. But I admire him. That lad knows his own mind and it's sharp as a razor. He could end up a judge one day."

Esther smiled dryly. "And according to Hannah, our Marianne who gets on my nerves, though you make allowances for her, could end up an author."

"Oh God," Ben said passionately. "I'd die for all three of them. Let them only come back to us soon, Esther, then we can start living again."

Esther went to put the fishballs on her big blue platter. Why was she filled with disquiet? Something Rabbi Lensky had said in a sermon years ago was filtering back into her mind. Nobody could live their life through their children.

Chapter Eight

Martin awoke in the seedy room and lay staring at the red-fringed lampshade suspended from the ceiling. His head felt as if it was weighted down with stones and his mouth parched and sour. Hangovers were not unfamiliar to him. But usually he knew the details

of how he had acquired one. All he could recall about last
night was going for a drink with a couple of the crew.

"Good morning, sweetie," an upperclass voice cooed
from beside him.

He managed to turn his head and saw a silky, naked
shoulder. Then the girl raised herself on one elbow and he
caught a glimpse of round, creamy breasts before his eyes
traveled to her face.

"How did you sleep, pet?" she inquired.

"Like the dead."

He got out of bed and moved groggily to the washbasin
crammed into a corner beside a wardrobe. The room was so
small, there must have been nowhere else to put it.

"We certainly had ourselves a time, didn't we, Martin?"

Martin was sure they must have done, but could not
remember and put his head under the cold water tap which
usually helped to clear it. She knew his name, but he didn't
know hers. Who was she? Her sharp-featured, blue-eyed face
had struck no chord in his memory.

When he reached for a towel and turned around, she
was sitting up with her back resting against the dark oak bed-
head, combing her fluffy, fair hair, her lush, pink-tipped orbs
now fully revealed in the morning sunlight filtering through
the fly-blown window. She must have awakened before he had
and drawn back the blackout curtains he thought hazily and
wrapped the towel around himself self-consciously when she
glanced at his floppy penis and laughed.

He had never seen this room before. How had he got
here? He'd intended to drive home last night. Tomorrow was
Shirley and Peter's wedding day and he'd promised to be
there in time to attend the *Shabbos* service in *shul* this morning, when Peter would be called up before the holy Ark as
Jewish bridegrooms always were on the Sabbath preceding
their marriage. But now Martin wouldn't be there. He had let
the family down.

His eye fell on a notice pinned on the door, requesting
guests to vacate the room before noon. The place was a
cheap, bed-and-breakfast dive, not the girl's digs as he'd
thought it might be. What had he done in his drunken stu-
por? Brought her here and registered as Mr. and Mrs.?

A sunbeam settled on her left hand and he caught the
flash of gold on her wedding finger. He might even have mar-

ried her, for all he remembered! But a special license couldn't be obtained that quickly, he reassured himself.

"My husband was killed at Crete," she said, seeing him staring at the ring. "But I told you that, didn't I, sweetie? After you said you never fool around with married women."

She didn't seem to be suffering from amnesia, the way he was. Obviously she'd had less to drink, but girls generally did. You gave them a gin and lime and they were yours for the asking. Like bitches in heat. The distaste that always followed his amorous exploits had begun to set in. Disgust for himself, too—for the desperate dissipation that loneliness, and the feeling of living on borrowed time, had driven him to.

He had been plagued from childhood by an inexplicable sense of insecurity, but now there was a reason for it. A bomber crew's tour of duty was thirty operations. He had just completed his fifteenth and according to statistics you only had a one-in-three chance of surviving the whole tour.

When an aircraft in the squadron got shot down and chaps you'd attended the briefing with just a few hours ago were suddenly no more, relief that you were still alive took precedence over your grief for them and made you feel ashamed. But how long would it be before you bought it yourself was always at the back of your mind and you filled yourself with liquor to forget . . .

"Come back to bed, sweetie," the girl said invitingly.

. . . And you tried to cram a lifespan's screwing into the time you had left. There were plenty of willing popsies eager like this one to aid and abet you—anonymous faces and bodies even when you knew their names, their function purely erotic. Were they really the mindless creatures they seemed? The fleeting encounters you had with them didn't allow time to find out and you were usually smashed out of your mind yourself, the liquor oiling your still-creaking civilian inhibitions into quiescence—or how would a respectable Jewish boy bring himself to behave this way?

But he had never been as drunk as he must have got last night. What would his mother say if she saw him now? She'd probably be upset most by her son sleeping with a *shiksah*. They're the only kind of girl available, Mother dear, he said to Miriam mentally, and experienced a stab of pleasure that his private life would shock her. Her disapproval was the most persistent of his inhibitions and the one that for some reason, even when sober, he wanted to defy.

The thought of his cousin Marianne got in the way, too. She'd looked up to him since they were kids and occasionally, when he had his hand up a girl's skirt, he had to blot out a sudden vision of Marianne's quizzical dark eyes.

He glanced out of the window at the narrow street. There was a pub he did not recognize opposite and an unfamiliar block of shops not yet open for the day's trade. This wasn't Lincoln. He knew the cathedral city, with its ancient, cobbled by-ways and mellowed old buildings, as well as he knew Manchester.

"Where are we?" he asked the girl.

"Andover, pet."

"What the hell are we doing in Andover?" He'd intended to drive north, not south!

The girl turned to look at an empty Vat 69 bottle on the bed table, which Martin had not noticed, and giggled. "I'm not surprised you've forgotten."

He didn't usually travel with a personal supply of booze. But he hadn't got it for himself, he recalled eyeing it. He had paid a GI a fiver for it and had been taking it home because his grandmother had written that Uncle David couldn't get hold of enough whiskey for Shirley's wedding.

"I could do with a cup of tea," he muttered confusedly.

"The landlady'll be bringing our breakfast soon, sweetie. It's included in the price and we get it at eight o'clock."

Martin shuddered at the thought of the probably greasy repast and crawled back between the sheets, his temples throbbing.

"Want me to fill in the blanks for you, pet?" the girl smiled.

"I wish you would."

"You offered to drive me home."

"Where's home?"

"Bournemouth."

"Good God."

"But we didn't make it all the way."

"Obviously not. Did I know where you live when I offered?"

"I thought so."

"I couldn't have done. I'm expected at a wedding in Manchester."

"When?"

"Tomorrow."

"I got married on a Monday, too."

Martin sat up. "Isn't today Saturday?"

"No, sweetie. It's Sunday."

He groaned and lay down again.

The girl put a cool hand on his fevered brow. "We've been shacked up here since Friday night."

"The wedding's at three-thirty this afternoon," Martin said weakly.

"You couldn't possibly get there in time, pet."

Martin thought he might just manage to if he left immediately, but could not summon the strength to argue with her.

"Not in the state you're in," she smiled. "You wanted to stagger out of here yesterday, put me on a train and go wherever you were going, which you didn't seem clear about. But I persuaded you to stay," she added coyly leaving him in no doubt as to the kind of persuasion she had used. "And you drank the rest of the whisky instead of eating your breakfast."

A rap on the door heralded the arrival of two plates of sausage and scrambled dried-egg, swimming in grease as Martin had anticipated.

The angular, pinch-nosed landlady clanked the tin tray on to the dressing table. "I usually put it on the bed table, so my guests won't be inconvenienced," she said giving the whisky bottle a censorious glance. "But it's otherwise occupied."

"You said that yesterday morning," the girl replied haughtily and Martin got the impression she always addressed those whom she considered servants that way.

"And I'll say it again tomorrow," the woman retorted. "If you and your bottle are still here," she added before departing.

Martin rubbed the two-day stubble on his chin and watched his companion leap out of bed alive with energy, pondering on the opposite effects sexual activity had upon male and female, leaving a man completely drained, but a woman revitalized and, as his crew skipper had once put it, rarin' to go.

The girl had a dimpled bottom, he noted, and long, graceful legs, but he had no recollection of what she looked like clothed. She was standing by the dressing table gobbling her breakfast ravenously and ate Martin's, too, when he said he did not want it. Afterwards, she poured the tea and

brought him a cup, lighting a cigarette from a squashed
packet of Players Navycut she fished from under her pillow,
before getting in bed beside him to sip hers.

"Want a puff on my ciggie? It's the last one left."

"I don't smoke."

"That's right, you don't." She put down her cup and saucer and slipped a hand under the bedclothes.

Rarin' to go was right! Martin knew where her insidious
fingers would settle before he felt them there. The whole
thing was just a mechanical exercise, he thought with disgust
rising in him again. But this did not prevent his penis from
rising, too. Once, he had viewed lovemaking romantically;
but there was no vestige of tenderness in the gyrations he performed with his popsies. Just animal sensation and afterwards
nothing but emptiness.

Would it be like that for Peter when he made love to
Shirley tonight? Or was there another dimension to it when
you knew and respected each other and the girl was giving
herself to you because she was your wife? He thought of his
father's devotion to his mother and knew that there had to be.

The girl had thrown back the covers and was gazing at
his erection. "I never saw one like yours before," she remarked running a finger around the drawn-back foreskin.
"Why is it different from the other blokes', sweetie?"

"I was circumcised. I'm Jewish."

The change in her expression was a mere flicker. "Oh
really? Some of my pater's best friends are Jewish."

Martin prickled. Anti-Semitism in bed! A Yiddisher boy
never knew where he'd encounter it next. And the ones who
shot you the best friends line were always the worst.

"Daddy's in banking, you see," she added as if that explained his socializing with the chosen people. "But I never
thought I'd ever do it with a Jew. I mean you don't look it,
sweetie."

"If that's intended to be a compliment, it isn't one."
Martin reached for his drawers which were hanging on the
bedpost and pulled them on.

"Oh dear, I've offended you," the girl pouted. "But I
didn't mean to."

They never did.

She leaned over the side of the bed and took a silver
powder compact from her handbag which she had dumped

on the floor. "Honest injun, pet," she said studying her reflection in the compact mirror.

When she snapped the compact shut, Martin saw the name Penelope engraved upon it. So that was who he'd frittered away two precious nights and a day of his life with. A girl with an upper crust name that went with her attitudes. Who possibly didn't know she was an anti-Semite, but was one. He had put on his socks as well as his drawers, but the rest of his clothing was lying in a heap by the window and he got out of bed to finish dressing.

"Why are you people so touchy?" she inquired.

Because people like you have made us that way, he answered mentally.

The girl eyed him sulkily and he noted a few lines on her face which had escaped his attention until now. She was older than he'd taken her for and there was a hardness about her that made him think she could be bitchy when crossed.

"Hand me my undies, will you?" she rasped proving it.

Had she really expected him to make love to her after that nauseous conversation? But it hadn't been sickening for her, only for him. And his libido had been affected accordingly. He gathered up the scraps of satin and lace lying on the threadbare rug at her side of the bed and tossed them to her, then went downstairs to pay the bill.

The girl appeared at the head of the stairs while he was waiting for the landlady to do her mental arithmetic, clad in a Land Army uniform, her nipples pressing like marbles against her tight, green pullover. Under other circumstances, Martin would have paused to admire them, but he turned away and handed the landlady the money for which she had just asked. His companion had apparently consumed dinner and tea whilst he snored the hours away, which had raised the bill from a guinea to two pounds, 10 shillings.

His attention was diverted by the empty whisky bottle hurtling down the stairs and several choice epithets with it. The final one was "bloody Jew-boy," erasing any doubts he might have afterwards had about being oversensitive, and was still ringing in his ears when he picked his way over the broken glass and made his exit.

When he reached the doorstep he realized he had no idea where he had left the car he'd borrowed from the rear-gunner. He would have to ask the girl to fill in another blank for him. He retraced his footsteps down the long, narrow hallway that looked as if its dingy brown paint had not been freshened since before the war, past the empty umbrella stand and a desolate potted palm that seemed to be crying out for water. Or maybe it just felt queasy from the stale cooking smells? He would have had to be blind drunk to stay in such a place.

The landlady was sweeping up the evidence of the girl's wrath. "Can't remember where you're parked, I suppose? And no wonder! You were paralytic when she brought you in here, without swigging another lot on top of it."

Martin felt something metallic hit his cheek.

"I did the driving and it'll do you good to have to go and look for your broken-down jalopy!" the girl called nastily from upstairs. "Who the hell do you think you are, walking out on me? I wish I'd taken your eye out when I threw you the blasted keys!"

Martin retrieved them from the floor and escaped into the clear morning air. That *Hell hath no fury like a woman scorned* must have been penned in the light of experience. What a bizarre episode this whole thing was. But perhaps not the wasted time it seemed. What was it that Uncle David had once said about his experiences in the last war? Which wouldn't have included bedding the ladies! There was no such thing as wasted time, he'd said. Because everything a person did was part of living.

He found the ancient Austin Seven in a side street near the bus station and slid the tattered convertible top back. He'd been cooped up for long enough. The yellow Hants & Dorset buses had a cheerful look about them and the people strolling by did, too. Elderly couples attired in their Sunday best, on their way to church carrying prayer books. And young women with children, heading in the same direction, some with a soldier or an airman on leave, by their sides. The scene had the same decorous ambience present when Jewish families walked to *shul*, Martin thought. Only the places of worship were different.

He spotted Penelope's jodhpured bottom undulating past the White Hart Hotel as he drove by and could not resist the temptation to honk his horn as a final gesture of derision before heading out of the town. Then a signpost marked Salisbury caught his attention and he stopped the car. Marianne was stationed between Andover and Salisbury.

A handy telephone kiosk clinched his decision to ring up and tell the family a cock-and-bull story and drive off in the opposite direction to home. Marianne mattered more to him than anyone—more than his parents, even, he thought whilst he waited for the telephone operator to put through the call. Or how could he be hardening his heart with the sound of his mother's bitter disappointment in his ear, he asked himself listening to it a few moments later.

The chance to be with the cousin whom he sometimes thought of as his twin-soul came but rarely these days. She irritated him madly, as he did her, he reflected wryly on his way to wash and shave in the railway station men's room before visiting her. But we're honest with each other, that's why we're so critical, he mused whilst lathering his stubbly chin. Honest and caring. There had always been something special between them.

Driving through the Wiltshire countryside, past old thatched cottages and trees lacy with the first fragile May blossom, was a pleasure in itself. But he couldn't wait to see Marianne. He hadn't been this happy since he was a kid who still believed there was a Heaven with God seated on a golden throne watching over Mankind. It's a beautiful, wonderful day, a joyful voice sang within his breast as he waited for a farmer to prod a herd of cattle into a daisy-strewn meadow and let him pass. But what had brought this sudden metamorphosis about, dressing everything he looked upon in rainbow shades of brilliance, instead of all-pervading gray?

He was halfway up the hill that led to Marianne's quarters, with the car engine chugging like a slow train, when the answer struck him with an impact so strong he had to pull up and rest his head on the steering wheel.

"Hey, bud!" a Yankee twang hollered nasally from the line of trucks and jeeps that had halted behind him, unable to pass because others were speeding downhill. "It's okay for youse Limeys, but us guys don't got all day!"

The protest was followed by a chorus of blaring horns, but even this was not sufficient to bring Martin down from the clouds. He turned around and gave the irate GIs a beatific smile. Then he started the engine and coaxed the little Austin up the hill to where he would find his love.

Chapter Nine

"Hand me my fur, Nat," Rebecca requested, settling a small pillbox hat aslant on her head and leaving him dangling the mink wrap awkwardly by its tail until she had fiddled with her hair.

Nathan watched her rise from the dressing table stool and smooth the skirt of her clingy crêpe suit over her hips. She was elegance personified, clad in her favorite muted brown. But who was the army officer reflected in the mirror with her? It was still hard to believe the real Nathan Sandberg was hidden behind that uniformed façade.

Rebecca was checking her stocking seams and his gaze traveled along the two bold lines emphasizing her shapely calves before disappearing from view into the region of her anatomy he was no longer allowed to touch.

"Who are you making yourself so fetching for?" he said sourly.

She gave him an enigmatic look and went to spray some perfume behind her ears, as though she wanted to taunt him. "We'll be late for the wedding if we don't get a move on." She picked up her handbag and gloves and went downstairs, leaving the muskiness of sandalwood behind her.

Nathan glanced at the negligée she had left thrown carelessly on a chair, as he followed her out, then closed the door on the sensual recollections the froth of chiffon and the familiar scent had evoked. And on the twin divans his wife had substituted for their marital bed to let him know his connubial pleasures were over.

"I hope your daughter doesn't do anything to disgrace us during the ceremony," Rebecca said whilst they were getting into the car. "I've been worried about it ever since Shirley asked her to be a bridesmaid."

"She'll be fine," Nathan answered shortly.

"With the twins standing beside her? She's liable to pick

a row with Henry while the rabbi's preaching the marriage sermon."

The twins were to be pages, but Nathan could not envisage Leona causing trouble in a synagogue. He started the car, irritably. "What about?"

"Since when does your daughter need a reason?"

"She's your daughter as well."

"But she's a Sandberg through and through. From my family tree red hair doesn't sprout."

Nathan tried to contain himself. His family was full of red-heads, their coloring, rare among Jews, inherited from Abraham. But only Shirley and Leona displayed the temperament associated with it and he resented the inference that they were an ill-tempered lot. His wife wasn't the epitome of sweetness and light herself, though the girl he'd married had seemed to be. Which just went to show! "You should've examined my pedigree more carefully," he could not stop himself from remarking caustically.

"And a few other things about you, too," Rebecca retorted.

Once, their arranged marriage had been a sensitive subject to her, but her skin had thickened in that respect with the years.

"Matchmakers can't be trusted to tell their clients everything," she added with a barbed edge to her husky voice.

"And we're the proof of it," Nathan answered. "But who ever knows what a person is really like? Until they live with them?" He forced his hands to relax their tense grip on the steering wheel and glanced surreptitiously at the svelte beauty by his side. Where had the tender young girl gone to, whose adoration had once seared his conscience because he could not return it? Was she still there, beneath the mature, sophisticated veneer? Yearning for the perfect love she'd hoped her marriage would be, and indeed thought it was until she learned otherwise?

The traumas of their early relationship had emanated solely from him and might never have crystallized into an irreversible situation had Mary not been on duty on the occasion his memory had recorded for all time as "that night." Since then, their differences had sprung from Rebecca, though when the nightmare aftermath of Leona's birth was resolved he'd thought everything was all right.

That this was not so had seeped through to him gradually. Initially, he had been too relieved to see the signs. Then he'd noticed that their lovemaking held no interest for Rebecca, that she was a cool and passive partner. When had he first realized she was performing a marital duty, experiencing no pleasure? When Leona was a year old and he could no longer fool himself that his wife's indifference was post-natal exhaustion.

The way she used their daughter as a pawn in a game, to score over him, became noticeable also. But Leona had quickly learned to play it, too, and was still doing so, with both of them. The name of the piece the child wielded was Parental Love and there was none more powerful on Nathan's checkerboard of life, where stalemate had been his every outcome.

A limousine, strung with white ribbons, was turning into the synagogue gateway as they covered the last few yards up Bury Old Road.

"A fine thing!" Rebecca exclaimed. "We're going to arrive after the bride."

"She'll be primping in the ante-room for ages, so what does it matter?"

"Getting there late is bad manners."

"Sod manners!"

"Lovely expressions you're learning in the army. And I bet that isn't all. There must be plenty of *shiksahs* stationed with you to teach you other things," Rebecca said cuttingly. "Not that you need teaching."

"I'm surprised you remember if I do or not."

Rebecca stared through the windscreen. "Some things engrave themselves on a person's memory." Revulsion was the only emotion sex aroused in her, and it was written on her face now.

Nathan was well aware of this. Her passivity had graduated to steeling herself when he embraced her and the last time he'd tried to, which was about two years ago, she had told him in plain words to keep away. But it hadn't always been like that. Some kind of shame was at the root of it, nibbling away like a canker at her natural feelings. Why was he being so vague, when he knew the cause? His wife couldn't look herself in the eye because she'd had sex with a man who loved someone else. Nor could she forgive him for bringing it about, though she had briefly tried to. Pride was the real canker.

"I suppose that's why you were in such a hurry to join up, because you couldn't get what you want at home. But I don't care," she said in a voice that revealed she did.

She still loved him, but he'd never thought otherwise. The belt of thorns she had braided for him to wear was also wound around herself. If he told her the truth, that he'd hoped a period of separation would result in a reconciliation, that he hadn't touched another woman, though not for lack of opportunity, would she believe him?

"I made up my mind a long time ago not to let myself care about anything you do," she informed him whilst he was parking the car in an avenue off the main road.

She had built another wall around her emotions, but this time it was a conscious decision, not something she couldn't control as her rejection of her baby had been. It would be a waste of breath telling her anything.

Rebecca linked her arm through his when they walked to the synagogue and Nathan watched her smiling and nodding to the guests thronging the entrance. As if she's blooming with happiness because I'm home on leave! he thought bitterly. But he'd learned long ago that keeping up appearances mattered to her.

There were no unhappy skeletons in the Benjamin cupboard, he reflected enviously when Lou—whom rheumatic fever as a child had rendered unfit for military service—joined them with his dumpy little wife. The smile on Cora's plain face radiated an inner glow. It wasn't just an outward show of domestic felicity when none existed, like Rebecca presented to the world.

"*Mazeltov*, Nat," Paula Frankl, who had been pigeonholed in his mind from childhood as a woman nobody in the family liked, said to him as he and Rebecca mounted the synagogue steps.

Nathan returned the greeting and surveyed Paula's condescending expression, which had grown more so with the years. Whether or not you liked a person wasn't important when it came to a Jewish wedding, he thought dryly. You invited them nevertheless, in case they go around saying your bank balance was such that you'd had to cut down the guest list!

But he knew this was not the real explanation of the presence of Mrs. Frankl and others of her ilk. Marriages, *Bar Mitzvahs* too, ranked as milestones in the life of a Jewish

family and most were impelled by sentiment or duty to share
their joyous occasions with everyone with whom they had
traveled the road.

"If this is David's idea of a small gathering, he'll have to
hold the reception at Old Trafford if he ever has a big one!"
Lou said to him when they took their seats with the bride's
close male relatives and friends near the marriage canopy.
"That very fat man's here, who I see at every Sandberg
simchah, but I've never been introduced to," he added with a
smile.

"You know who he is, though."

"How could I not? He's a legend in our family."

Nathan glanced along the row of seats to where Chaim
Berkowitz's pot-belly, which seemed larger every time he saw
it, protruded massively. It was from the Berkowitzes' humble
home in Strangeways, where they had arrived from Russia
penniless, that the Sandbergs had set out on the path to comfortable, English respectability. The couple had moved to
Leeds before Nathan was born, but his parents still felt indebted to them.

On the other side of the synagogue, where the women
were seated, Nathan could see Chaim's wife Malka, rotund as
her spouse, a diamond brooch pinned to one of the pastel
satin frocks she always had on in his imagination, whenever
his mother's mentioning the Berkowitzes conjured her up.
The hat she was wearing sported a sweeping feather that was
there when he pictured her, too, and it struck him that he
visualized her thus because he had never seen her in everyday
garments, only on dressy occasions like today.

The first time he'd met the couple had been at David's
wedding and he couldn't recall Malka wearing a diamond
brooch at that *simchah*. But the Berkowitzes' fortunes had
risen since then, like almost everyone else's here. Shloime and
Gittel Lipkin, Moishe's parents, looked prosperous, too, but
Nathan's father often talked of how he and Shloime had
tramped the streets together seeking work when they were
newly arrived immigrants. The Cohens, who had also come
over on the herring boat with the Sandbergs, were another
example. Yankel Cohen had somehow turned himself into a
furrier and had managed to stake his youngest daughter
Ruby, with whom Nathan had gone to the Jews' School, to
her own hairdressing salon.

"How had they all done it? Nathan pondered while he

waited for David, who had just made a self-conscious exit, to return with Shirley on his arm and Leona trailing behind. The Jewish leap from poverty to affluence seemed an inexplicable phenomenon. He had been left in no doubt by David that the phrase "blood, sweat and tears" summed it up and he had even been brutally subjected by his brother to emotional blackmail on account of this, when he'd wanted to tread his own path instead of the one the family had laid down for him. But that didn't make the transposition from a crust of blackbread to the world of smoked salmon seem any the less miraculous. Perhaps the centuries of uprooting the Jews had suffered had bred in them a need for material security deeper than that of others? And made them work harder in order to achieve it.

The organist struck the first notes of the bridal music, cutting into his cogitations, and he rose with the rest of the congregation to receive Shirley and her entourage. Lou's little girl Lila was a bridesmaid, too, and they shared a glance, and then another across the synagogue with their wives.

Leona's all Rebecca and I have left to share, Nathan thought sourly. Then the gall gave way to the sweet taste of the paternal devotion that made his other, unassuaged, hunger bearable, as the child who had held him captive since her infant fingers clasped his thumb on the night she was born, approached carrying his cousin's bridal train. Her resemblance to Shirley had always been marked, and Nathan noted it now, though his niece's face was lightly veiled. But Leona had Rebecca's unusual tawny eyes.

She gave him an angelic smile as she rustled past him, resplendent in lilac taffeta. What was it about being a father that melted your heart when your child smiled at you that way?

Nathan noticed that Sammy and Ben, whose children weren't here, looked pensive. But they had loving wives with whom to share the wartime emptiness, when the sound of young voices had gone from their homes. Without Leona his own home would be an aching void. Seeing David's daughter already a bride emphasized this. But he would not let himself think of the day some time in the future when Leona would marry and leave him alone with Rebecca.

His mother and father were standing under the flower-bedecked *chupah*, as grandparents always did, and he saw

Abraham take out a handkerchief and dab his eyes when the
ceremony began. His mother looked calm, almost detached;
but her fingers were at the little Russian brooch pinned to her
silver-gray dress, which meant her placid expression belied
her feelings. For the elder Sandbergs, today marked a very
special milestone. Shirley was the first of their grandchildren
to marry.

Was Sarah remembering the day she had been the girl-
bride and Abraham the young bridegroom, under a *chupah*
in Dvinsk? Nathan smiled at the notion. Seeing them now, it
was difficult to imagine them that way. Probably, knowing his
mother, she was thinking of something quite different, antici-
pating the great-grandchildren Shirley and Peter would give
her. And filled with a sense of personal achievement because
none of her English descendants had disgraced the family by
marrying "out."

The unforgivable sin was not quite as rare as it had been
when he contemplated committing it. But the war was to
blame for that. Jewish boys and girls were finding themselves
in situations into which they wouldn't have got in peacetime,
were mixing with Gentiles they would not ordinarily have
met. Yesterday at the *Shabbos* gathering he'd mentioned a
Jewish corporal in his unit who had just married a Christian
WAAF and his mother had said confidently that none of her
grandchildren who were in the Forces would succumb to that
temptation.

Nathan's own experience was now distant enough for
him to consider it dispassionately. Was his mother's confident
assumption correct? How could it not be when her grandchildren had been conditioned the way he had? It was that conditioning which had finally tipped the balance the family's way
for him. Sometimes he despised himself for his weakness, but
would he have been any stronger if he had his time again,
without the benefit of hindsight?

He heard little Henry Moritz shriek from beside Leona,
where he and his twin were balancing a small, blue velvet
cushion on which Ronald, who was best man, had a minute
ago deposited the wedding ring.

Nathan saw his wife pale and she seemed to be signaling
to him with her eyes. What had Leona done? He glanced at
the young bridal attendants again. The ring had gone from
the cushion! But how could it have done when the twins had
not yet borne it to the bridegroom?

Then Frank raced across the synagogue to Hannah, which seemed to amuse her and Helga whispered something to him that sent him hastening back to Henry, who was now on his white-satined knees searching the carpet.

The rabbi waited patiently, as though the antics of little bridesmaids and page boys were nothing new to him. So patiently, that Nathan wondered if on this occasion the reverend gentleman was perhaps unaware of exactly what had happened.

Those under the *chupah* were all too aware. Shirley had glanced over her shoulder, distracted by Henry's shriek and Frank's thudding footsteps and had blanched at the sight of the ringless cushion lying where Henry had deposited it whilst he searched on the floor. David had a thunderous frown on his face and Bessie was choking herself with her pearls, twisting them nervously into a knot.

Peter was visibly trembling. Nathan could see his *tallith* flapping. And Sigmund, beside him with Miriam and Sammy, who were deputizing for his parents, looked tempted to hold him up in case he fainted.

The rabbi glanced at Ronald, who went to consult with the twins.

"We can't find it," Henry announced in his piping voice.

"It must have rolled somewhere," Frank added apologetically.

A moment of silence followed, then Sarah removed her own wedding ring and beckoned to Ronald to come and take it.

Why hadn't it occurred to Bessie or Miriam to do that? Nathan thought. Because they were the kind who went to pieces in a crisis. But his mother was not.

"It's all your Leona's fault," little Lila Benjamin hissed to him indignantly. "She pinched Henry's bum, I saw her do it."

"Tattle-tale! You're supposed to be my friend!" Leona shouted and there was a sharp intake of breath from the entire congregation. "Henry made a horrid face at me, or I wouldn't have done it." She lifted her long, frilly skirts and ran tempestuously towards the exit, oblivious to the gaping and head-shaking lining the route, her artificial-anemone circlet bobbing up and down on her fiery hair.

"Place the ring upon the forefinger of the bride's right hand," the rabbi said firmly to Peter, whose eyes were glued mesmerically to the doorway in company with everyone else's.

Leona was just disappearing through it.

Nathan and Rebecca emerged from their shock simultaneously and went after her.

After Shirley and Peter had gone home to change, so they could catch the train to Southport where they were to spend their honeymoon, the evening stretched emptily ahead for the family.

"That's the trouble with afternoon receptions," Bessie said restlessly when the guests had departed and the Sandbergs and Moritzes were left contemplating the remains of the lavish tea littering the tables. "But my husband wouldn't hear of an evening do. God forbid people should think we're being his favorite word, in wartime! So they won't think we're ostentatious, they'll think we're paupers instead."

"Nobody could think that with the jewelry you've got on," her mother-in-law told her.

"All right. So they'll remember we didn't spend much on our Ronald's *Bar Mitzvah*, either, and say we're mean," Bessie retorted. She gave David a resentful look, and a frustrated twitch to the belt of her fifty-guinea, ice-blue gown. "If there's one thing I can't stand, it's being all dressed up with nowhere to go."

"Me, I'm glad it's over," David declared brusquely. His daughter's eyes had brimmed with tears when she hugged him goodbye and the sight of them had brought home to him that even though she would continue to live under his roof until Peter was a civilian again, her marriage was a parting of the ways.

Added to this, the wedding in retrospect seemed like a chapter of accidents, a far cry from the perfect day he had wanted her to cherish in her memory. The ring had turned up while they were signing the register, someone had spotted it glistening beside the *bimah*. But it wasn't the one over which Peter had made his solemn vows and this Shirley would not forget. None of the women in the family had ever removed their wedding rings; his mother's finger had been indented with a deep groove when she took hers off and it must have upset her to do so after nearly half a century.

He shot a resentful glance at Nathan and Rebecca seated stiffly side by side, like strangers on a train. They hadn't only made a shambles of their marriage, they'd made one of bringing up their child and his own daughter's wedding ceremony had been marred because of it.

But Leona, who was presently cuddled on Bridie's broad lap sucking her thumb like an innocent babe, couldn't be blamed for the mishaps that had followed. His own foot had stepped on Shirley's train when he and Bessie led the bridal party across the *shul* foyer after the service and his clumsiness had wrenched her headdress, to which the train was attached, halfway off her head. It had been dangling over one ear when she stepped outside, where a cluster of wedding-watchers was waiting to gawk at her.

As if this was not enough, his poor darling daughter had singed the front of her hair on the top-table candles whilst leaning over to shake hands with old Rabbi Lensky, who had been officiating at a funeral and arrived late. Then, to cap everything, the knife had been too blunt to saw through the rock-hard icing on the wedding cake. Peter had eventually managed to stab the point into it, but his attempt to carry this through to a slicing action had sent the whole sugary confection toppling off its base to land in a crumbling, brown and white mess on the floor.

"What's up wi' yer, Mr Sandberg?" Lizzie inquired.

David lit a cigarette, conscious of the maid surveying him and of his cheeks having flamed with mortification as he catalogued the day's disastrous incidents.

"I expec' yer in't dumps, an' I am mesen," she declared when he did not reply. "Why don't we go 'ome? If we 'urry oursen, our Shirley might still be there."

He glanced at her bony figure, familiar as a piece of his household furniture, but today incongruously clad in a beaded, purple dress Bessie had loaned her for the occasion. It was miles too wide for her, which an improvised sash could not disguise; and her flat-crowned straw hat, wreathed with cambric pansies, reminded him of the ones horses wore in carnival processions, with its streamers flowing behind and the brim tilted slightly forward above her long face.

"It's best not to get home till they've gone, that's why we're hanging around like this," he said kindly and saw her features crumble with disappointment. Dear old Lizzie, he thought with a surge of affection for her. But she wasn't old, she only seemed it. She'd been fifteen, he recollected, when she came to them from the mining village which she now rarely visited. His children had become the center of her drab existence. She had practically brought them up and they'd probably be the nearest thing to kids of her own she'd ever have. There wasn't much likelihood of Lizzie marrying.

Sarah was eyeing the uneaten food, displeased at the waste of her son's money, and unhappily aware of the gloom around her. A wedding shouldn't end this way. There should be an air of rejoicing as there'd been when a couple were wed in her Russian girlhood, when the celebrations had lasted for three days and not until the third had elapsed were the bridal pair allowed to desert the guests to consummate their marriage. Joy should not be just for the bride and groom, but for their family who had nurtured and guided them to this pinnacle of their lives, too.

"Everyone must come back to my house," she commanded and the Queen Victoria look in her eyes forbade anyone to refuse.

She sent the twins scurrying to the kitchen to ask the caterers for a big box, into which she personally packed all the edibles remaining on the tables and told Nathan to put the box in his car. David's had already been crammed with the remains of the liquor.

An hour later, she was ensconced in her parlor, smiling with satisfaction. "So," she declared to the others. "What could be a nicer end to the day than this?"

Nobody replied, but their tacit assent did not mean they could not think of preferable alternatives, of which Sarah was quite aware. And her own satisfaction was superficial, only a show. In the quiet of her own home, with the twins half-asleep and Leona quiescent for once, she could no longer pretend that the undercurrent she had sensed before they left the reception was not there.

Who was it coming from? She tried to decide. It only required one person to be privately eaten up with something for the air in a room to ripple. It invariably did when the family got together; everyone had their personal worries and the general anxiety about Harry was ever-present. But what she could feel now was something extra, that hadn't been there at her tea party yesterday.

She glanced around surreptitiously. Nat and Rebecca's lack of accord seemed no worse than usual and David was holding Bessie's hand, as if he was seeking comfort from her, the way Abraham had from herself on Esther's wedding night; a daughter's marriage was emotionally more of a wrench to a man than a son's.

She watched Ben light a new cigarette from the stub of the one he'd just smoked, but he'd been doing that since the War Office telegram arrived.

"Mother looks as if she's ticking us all off on a list!" Sammy joked.

Sarah avoided his eye, because this was exactly what she had been doing. Once there'd only been Abraham and her young children to concern her, but now keeping track of everyone wasn't easy, with the size to which her family had grown. Abraham had dozed off, she noted continuing her check. And Sigmund appeared no more morose than he'd been since the war began. Her gaze moved to Miriam, whose beautiful face was drawn into an expression of tight composure. The tension was coming from her; the tortured look in her eyes gave her away.

"I feel like a breath of air, come and keep me company, Miriam," she said, taking her hand and leading her out of the room.

They went to lean over the garden gate in the gathering twilight and neither spoke for a moment or two. Then Miriam gazed up at the overhanging branches of Mrs. Evans's laburnum, which carpeted Sarah's concrete path with yellow every spring.

"How still it is tonight. There's no breeze to stir the leaves," she said with a poignant tremor in her voice.

Sarah scanned her face. "What's wrong, Miriam?"

"Ask me what's right, it'll take less time to tell you. You don't miss a thing, do you, Ma?"

"You'd prefer I should?"

Miriam managed to smile, but it was as brief as a firefly flitting across the surface of a stone. She turned away and gripped the gate, her knuckles gleaming white on her work-reddened hands. "I rang up Martin's billet from the call box in the reception hall."

"Why?"

"After he phoned to tell us his leave had been canceled, I had an uneasy feeling and I couldn't shake it off. A kind of intuition."

That all mothers have where their children are concerned, Sarah thought. Like a sixth sense God provides you with for the purpose.

"But I shouldn't have given in to it. I wish I hadn't rung up," Miriam went on. "Because he wasn't there."

Her expression was now so abject with misery, Sarah feared she had been told Martin had been sent on some terrible danger mission. Only it couldn't be anything like that; such information was kept secret.

"They told me he'd gone home for the weekend, Ma. So everything he said when he phoned was a lie."

Sarah's heart bled for her. What Miriam had learned about her son had nothing to do with danger, but in a different way was just as painful. Each time a mother found out her child had told her a serious falsehood her trust in him died a little. Would she herself ever believe in Nat the way she had before she discovered he had the *shiksah* girlfriend? It still hurt her to think of how many lies that deceit had entailed.

"The lying is hard enough to take," Miriam whispered. "But that he preferred to spend his leave somewhere else . . ."

Sarah sighed. There was that, too. "You've told Sammy?"

Miriam shook her head. "Sammy's had enough hurts in his time, without this." She leaned against the gate, fiddling with a button on her dress, pensively, as if she were recollecting the injuries life had inflicted on her husband.

Sarah was remembering them, too.

Miriam emerged from her reverie and rubbed her bare arms. "Let's go inside, Ma, it's getting chilly. I shan't tell Martin I found out. But how will I ever forgive him?"

Sarah regarded her with compassion. "To forget about it—maybe not. But to forgive, a mother always finds a way."

Chapter Ten

Marianne lay with her hands folded behind her head, watching the blackout curtains, which they always drew back after lights-out, flapping in the night breeze. Her bed was beside the window, but even in cold weather the draft was preferable to the liquor fumes her roommates brought in with them.

Tonight she was grateful for the breeze. The day had been warm and stifling and the tepid shower she'd taken when she got back from Salisbury Plain had not helped her to sleep. It would take more than a shower to cool the fever in her blood and settle the kaleidoscope of thoughts jiggling like varicolored fragments in her mind.

She could hear Birdie's porcine snores and see her bony shoulder moving up and down with the rhythm of her breath, in a shaft of moonlight. Joyce was sound asleep, too. How she envied them their casual approach to life; the easy come, easy go attitude that left them unscarred, which even in wartime could never be hers.

Joyce's arm was dangling over the side of her bed, a heavy, silver identity bracelet engraved with her latest GI's name weighing down her hand. Marianne was the only girl in the unit who didn't have at least one of these souvenirs d'amour, which some girls displayed like trophies, wearing their whole jangling collection triumphantly together. They stitched U.S. Army emblems to the khaki pullovers they wore over their shirts at dances, too; Birdie's and Joyce's by now had so many of these patches sewn on, they looked like collages in which every piece could tell a story.

Marianne had only one emblem, which she kept in her box of treasures. The GI who gave it to her had wanted her to have his identity bracelet, also, but she had refused to accept it. How could she walk around with his name attached to her wrist, as if he owned her? She hadn't been sure, then,

269

if she loved him. Was she sure now? When he declared his love for her, she had told him it wasn't possible after such a short acquaintance. Then he had taken her in his arms and kissed her and the fire that had raged in her veins had made her think perhaps it was.

She'd met him the night she went dancing with Birdie and Joyce and there had been no need for them to walk up the hill with her as they'd promised. She had been happy to let Michael drive her to her quarters in his jeep. A nice Jewish boy, she'd thought when he kissed her chastely on the cheek.

His kisses had become less chaste as time went by and they saw each other every night. But she'd wanted them to, she had to admit now, lying in the dark with her face burning with shame. And had not demurred when she felt his hands on her breasts. She allowed the deliriously sweet recollection to swamp her senses, then ruthlessly blotted it out.

She had intended writing to her parents about him, to prepare them for the possibility of their daughter being a GI bride, because he'd asked her to marry him if he survived the war. Not until today, when they were picnicking beside Stonehenge in the sunshine and he'd inquired if she wanted a church wedding, had she discovered that Americans could have surnames like Weiss, but not necessarily be Jewish.

When she told him she was, he'd said his parents wouldn't mind and had looked offended when she said hers would. Then there'd been an uncomfortable silence and it had struck her that you didn't have silences like that with someone you knew well.

The moonbeam had moved from Birdie's shoulder to a picture of Frank Sinatra on the wall and she surveyed the singer's smiling countenance absently. What had she and Michael talked about during the short time they'd known each other? Books and music. Occasionally about their families, in the superficial way you mentioned your folks to somebody who hadn't met them. But most of their conversations had centered on the war and everything that went with it—the artificial present they shared, with only brief references to their separate pasts.

She knew Michael was a law student and intended resuming his studies when the war ended. But the student life at Columbia University he'd briefly described was no more real to her than the America she had seen on the cinema screen. Michael himself wasn't real to her; she'd only seen a single dimension of him. The one clad temporarily in uniform whom she could now see in her imagination.

And it was the same for him, about her. She had tried to explain why she couldn't marry a Gentile, but had failed to make him see that it wasn't only a matter of adhering to the religious laws. Her reason had begun to question these long ago, but the family aspect continued to hold her fast. And a person from a non-Jewish background couldn't be expected to understand the powerful force that was inexplicable to Marianne herself.

If she married Michael and went to live in the States, with the Atlantic between herself and the family, would the blood tie loose its hold on her? she pondered just before she dozed off. Maybe Mom and Dad would forgive her if they didn't have to actually see her bringing up a family of only half-Jewish children? Then a mental image of her grandmother fingering the little gold brooch she always wore at *Shabbos* gatherings replaced the one of Michael and her last drowsy thought was that she couldn't do it.

"When's the weddin', cock?" Birdie inquired the next morning whilst they were throwing on their uniforms to get on parade in time for roll call.

"There isn't going to be one."

"Well, stone a crow!" Joyce exclaimed, fumbling with her tie. "We fought it was the love match of the century."

"Turned art ter be 'andin' yer a snow job, did 'e?" Birdie said, rolling her cigarette from one side of her dry lips to the other. "Them Yanks is very good at shootin' girls lines abart marryin' 'em arter the war."

"Hespecially them whose knickers they can't get darn any hother way," Joyce said coarsely.

Marianne blushed to the tip of her fringe. "It might interest you to know I've still got my virginity."

"Don't look so miserable abart it, cock," Birdie grinned. "The war haint over yet. An' there's that RAF bloke waitin' in the wings, haint there?" she added slyly.

"Which RAF bloke?"

"The one what turned up lookin' fer yer yesterday. What yer'd never said a word ter Joycie'n me abart, yer dark lickle 'orse! Left 'er a note, didn't 'e, Joycie?"

"We heven 'ad ter supply 'im wiv paper'n an envelope. Where did we put it, Birdie?"

"'On the chest of drawers, I fink. Hif we 'adn't been boozed up, we'd've remembered ter tell 'er abart it larst night."

Marianne delved into the clutter on top of the chest and found one of the scented pink envelopes in which Birdie sent weekly letters to her sailor husband. The handwriting on it was Martin's, as she had known it would be; he was the only airman she knew. But he'd written her he was going home for Shirley's wedding; what had he been doing here instead?

She stuffed the envelope into her tunic pocket as the whistle blew to summon them on parade and opened it afterwards, on the way to breakfast.

"What's up, cock?" Birdie asked when she stopped in her tracks.

"Yer look as if yer've bin 'it over the 'ead wiv a mallet," Joyce declared.

Marianne gave them a dazed glance. "Do I?" she muttered confusedly and went to lean on the cookhouse wall with the sheet of notepaper clutched in her hand.

The message was quite clear, but she could not take it in. Her relationship with Martin had always been solid ground, without the shifting sands she had recently learned could exist between a man and a woman; the mood had sometimes changed—they were temperamental people—but never the essence, the comfortable friendship they had shared all their lives. But now it was over. There could be no going back to it after what Martin had written.

Birdie and Joyce were hovering impatiently beside her, watching the rest of the platoon crowd noisily into the cookhouse.

"Hif we don't get a move on, there'll be no bleedin' bangers left!" Birdie exclaimed, prodding her in the ribs.

Marianne folded the sheet of paper and replaced it in the envelope, but the words inscribed upon it were imprinted on her still stunned mind.

> *When shall we twain*
> *Join hands again*
> *No more to part?*
> *Thou hast my heart.*

Chapter Eleven

Sarah had observed over the years—and the series of mishaps at Shirley's wedding confirmed it—that things rarely happened singly. If she broke a cup, more breakages usually followed within a short space of time and it was like that with family matters, too, though sometimes the crop of events was a mixture of bad and good. You would jog along quietly for a while, then suddenly things happened one after the other to jolt you out of your routine.

Saturday, June 3, 1944, was that kind of day.

"Answer the phone, Abraham," she said when it rang whilst she was preparing breakfast.

"Harry's alive!" she heard Esther's voice reverberate joyfully over the line before Abraham had time to say "Hello" and Sarah rushed to grab the receiver from his hand.

"*Mazeltov!*" she said to her daughter as if Harry had just been reborn.

Esther laughed exuberantly, as she had not done for a long time. "We just heard he's a prisoner in Stalag Eight B, Mother."

Sarah paled. "It's in Germany?"

"Don't worry. We phoned the Red Cross to ask if Jewish servicemen are victimized in German POW camps and they said no. Ben's already packing a parcel to send to him. And we're going to shut the shop this afternoon and celebrate with the family, instead of arriving at the tea party late like we usually do."

Abraham was staring up at the ceiling.

"Cobwebs you won't see in my house, so don't tell me you've found one," Sarah said to him after she had rung off.

Abraham smiled and blew his nose emotionally. "It's times like this that strengthen a person's faith, Sorrel, when you can feel the Almighty's presence watching over you and

273

yours. He's answered the special prayer I made in *shul* for
Harry's deliverance, so I've been telling Him thank you. It's
only polite."

Sarah kissed his cheek. Nearly forty years he'd been in
England, but he had not lost his *Hassidic* ways. Her husband
still talked about God as if He were a flesh and blood person,
held conversations with Him even, like their Russian forebears had done. But to Abraham's anglicized sons and grandsons, respect for the Almighty had nothing personal about it.
Perhaps that was why they found the Hebraic laws so easy to
break? For Abraham to break them would seem to him like
letting down a trusted friend. There was a lot to be said for
the old ways.

"Tell God thank you from me also, and I hope He'll
carry on the good work with all our boys," she smiled.

The *Shabbos* gathering that afternoon was indeed a
celebration. Sarah had not seen so many happy faces in her
parlor for years. Sammy was going through a bad spell with
the arthritic pain in his hip, but Miriam made light of it
when she arrived without him and did not allow her private
distress about Martin's deceit, from which she had not yet
recovered, to surface and mar the joyous atmosphere.

Sarah was handing round the *kuchen*, spread thickly
with beetroot-and-ginger preserve left over from Passover,
when she heard the garden gate clank. "Every day should
only be like this one!" she beamed, pointing through the window excitedly.

Her grandson, Arnold, was striding up the garden path
in his naval officer's uniform.

"He's grown a beard," Leona giggled.

"Let him grow two; I'd still be happy to see him!" Esther shrieked ecstatically, rushing to the front door to let him
in.

"He's got thin," Ben said when Esther finally stopped
kissing her son and allowed the others to take a look at him.

"I've only just stepped into the room and my father's already criticizing me," Arnold joked. "Any news about our
Harry?" he asked, taking off his cap and smoothing his ginger
hair. "Well, that's one of us safely out of the war," he said in
his down-to-earth manner after they had told him.

"Why didn't you ring up and tell us you'd got leave? I
would've bought an extra chicken," Esther said, regarding
him fondly.

Arnold hesitated, then straightened his shoulders and looked her in the eye. "My leave's nearly over, Mother. I'm due back at my ship tomorrow."

"What do you mean it's nearly over?" Ben demanded hotly. "Where did you spend the rest of it?"

Sarah was glad Leona and the twins had gone to play in the back garden. She could feel trouble brewing, the kind that was not for little ears.

"I spent it with my girl," she heard her grandson say.

"So you're courting. I'm very pleased," Esther smiled. "But couldn't you have brought her home with you?" she added, sounding hurt. "Who is she, by the way? Someone you've met in the Services?"

Arnold nodded. "Her name's Lyn Rogers."

Ben stroked his chin. "There was a chemist in Leeds called Rogers. He changed it from Roginsky. Maybe she's related to him; they're a very nice family."

"She isn't Jewish, Dad."

"What did you say?"

"She's a Protestant. And I'm going to marry her; but I won't do it in a church."

"A favor he's doing us, Esther!" Ben slumped forward in his chair and put his head in his hands.

Esther was standing behind him and clutched at the chair back for support, as if she feared she might faint.

How lonely they look, Sarah thought in the silence that followed. Their son had made them feel like outcasts—marked them with the brand of the sin he wanted to commit. But the taint would reach out to the rest of the family, as well. Her own descendants would have Gentile blood in their veins and the notion was so terrible she was momentarily unable to speak.

David had a stony expression on his face, which had been there throughout the discussion. He was thankful that Nathan was out of earshot in Scotland and tried not to look at Rebecca. Must this serpent rear its head in every generation? he thought wearily and was loathe to embroil himself in the pain it caused a second time. But he knew he must. The mantle of patriarchy had fallen upon his shoulders years ago, because his father's had never been strong enough to support it.

"Let's go into the dining room," he said sternly to Arnold.

"What for?"

"It's time I had a talk with you."

"You're wasting your time, Uncle David," Arnold said when they were alone with the mahogany table stretching like a long barrier between them.

David had stationed himself by the head, near the window, and was aware it was from choice that his nephew had remained at the foot, beside the door. "But you'll do me the courtesy of listening to what I have to say."

Arnold smiled. "It won't be anything I don't know already. I've had a Jewish upbringing, haven't I?"

"And why are you prepared to turn your back on it? For a girl you've only just met?"

"I've known Lyn for a couple of years, Uncle. She's a Wren. I met her when I was stationed at Portsmouth."

"But you've been away at sea most of the time, haven't you? The time you've actually spent together can't add up to very long." David took an apple from the bowl of wax fruit on the sideboard and polished it on his sleeve, with a sense of the *déjà vu* that often assailed him these days. Perhaps because when you were middle-aged there weren't many things you hadn't done before. But when had he stood in this room with a wax apple in his hand, delivering a lecture? The time Nat had wanted to study the Classics instead of medicine and he'd had to bring him down to earth.

"You're not going to tell me the story of Adam and Eve, are you?" Arnold asked wryly, looking at the apple. "Because it isn't just sex between me and Lyn. She's a wonderful girl in every possible way. The kind who'd make any chap happy."

"But not you."

"I'm on top of the world when I'm with her."

"It won't last, Arnold."

"Why shouldn't it?"

"Because sooner or later, when the novelty wears off like it does in even the best of marriages, you'll wake up one morning and realize it wasn't worth it."

"Worth what?"

"The anguish you marrying-out will put your parents through. And not just them, the whole family."

"Now we're coming to it, aren't we?" Arnold said sharply. "It's not me and my happiness anyone round here cares about! I can stay single and be lonely all my life, or marry a

Jewish girl I don't love and live in misery, like Uncle Nat, so long as I don't disgrace the family!"

"What makes you think Uncle Nat's marriage isn't a happy one?" David said, avoiding his eye.

"I'm not blind. Or deaf. And I think it's a damn shame he was forced to give up his Christian girlfriend."

Was there nothing the younger end of the family didn't know about their elders? David wondered.

"Fortunately for me, I'm made of stronger stuff," his nephew declared.

And stubborn as a mule, David added mentally. The boy was the image of Esther, but this was the first time he had revealed he also had her fighting spirit. Arnold had always been quiet and self-contained, so you never knew what he was thinking. Not the kind who made his presence felt, like Ronald did! He had gone away a gangling lad, but the Navy had turned him into a man to be reckoned with. Or was it the girl?

"Uncle Nat's met Lyn and he likes her," Arnold conveyed as if he had read David's final thought. "I took her to Scotland to meet him, last week."

"I see."

"Well he's more broadminded than the rest of the clan, isn't he?"

"So it seems."

"And I've always been able to talk to him. So has Ronald."

David permitted himself a sour smile. But Nat's influence over his son was another story.

"Where is Ronald, by the way? I was hoping he'd be here to back me up." Arnold surveyed his uncle's expression and noted the flicker of alarm. "I didn't mean that Ronald's got a Christian girl. He doesn't want to tie himself up to anyone until he qualifies."

"Thank you for telling me," David said shortly. Why did he always have to learn of his son's private plans secondhand?

"But I shouldn't think he's the kind to marry-out," Arnold went on. "He's too involved in Zionism."

"And other Jewish affairs," David added, thankful that this was so. "He's with some fellow students this afternoon, as a matter of fact. They're up in arms about the Government not letting in enough refugees."

"It's hardly relevant at the moment, is it?" Arnold said coolly.

"It will be when those who manage to live through it are released from the concentration camps," David retorted. "But I didn't bring you in here for a political debate."

"No. The digression was due to me asking where Ronald was and there'd have to be a good excuse for him to be granted a special dispensation to miss the *Shabbos* tea party," Arnold said dryly.

"What the hell do you mean by that?"

"Never mind."

"But I do mind," David flashed.

Arnold eyed him for a moment. "The way you look now is how I always think of you, Uncle. Filling me with guilt and trepidation, even when I've done nothing wrong. Did you know you have that effect on people?"

David was too shaken to reply. He had seen himself as a benevolent father-figure, there to aid and advise, and now he was being told he was looked upon as an ogre.

"But it doesn't matter any more," Arnold informed him. "Well, not to me, anyway."

"I'm concerned with your relationship with this girl, not with the way you feel about me," David said curtly.

Arnold's lips tightened. "I'd be obliged if you'd refer to her by her name. Though you obviously consider her an anonymous fly in the family ointment."

"How else can I think of her?"

"And that's what I'm up against, isn't it? Did you ever meet Uncle Nat's girlfriend?"

"Yes." Why was he letting Arnold interrogate him?

"But it made no difference, did it, Uncle?"

The mental snapshop of a pretty young girl David had carried away with him, after finding Nathan in Whitworth Park with her, returned to his memory. He had only encountered her once again and she'd been an acid-voiced woman with wary eyes, whom his ruthless interference had probably helped to make that way. But David hadn't considered her side of it. Only what she represented.

"That's why I didn't bring Lyn home," Arnold said. "It would do no good, so why put her through it? I don't want you to think it was because I didn't have the guts."

David would never think that about this nephew again. He'd learned more about Arnold in the last half hour than he had in all the lad's twenty-two years. And a thing or two about himself, as well.

"Uncle Nat came to have a meal at the pub Lyn and I stayed at, and he and I had a private chat after Lyn had gone to bed. That was when he told me about Mary. I think he only let me in on his past to stop me from marrying-out. He said he can think of Mary dispassionately now and it's taught him there's nothing you can't get over if you try," Arnold revealed.

"Then why don't you learn from his experience?"

"Because I'm not Uncle Nat. The difference between him and me is I don't want to get over it. I see no reason why I should."

David looked at him coldly. "You don't see the family as a reason?"

He watched Arnold walk to the hearth, which his grandmother had filled with laurel leaves from the garden, as she always did in summer, and finger the brass *menorah* Sarah had brought with her from Russia, that had stood on the mantelpiece since before Arnold was born. What was he thinking? Was he moved by the familiar sight? By the home life and heritage it epitomized?

His nephew's face when he turned around showed that he was. But his tone belied it. "The family doesn't own me, Uncle David. I made up my mind not to let it, because of what it had become to me. Something to fear, as well as to love, if you want the truth." Arnold smiled bitterly. "A two-headed giant ruling my life. The love's still there, it always will be; but I've stamped the fear out. It was the only way to belong to myself."

The telephone had shrilled in the kitchen a few minutes ago, but David had barely been aware of it, or that the ringing had stopped. Then a piercing scream sent him running, with Arnold at his heels. They found Miriam leaning on the wall, ashen-faced.

"Oh God," she whispered when David reached her and fell against him. "God help me."

David could hear sounds coming from the receiver, which was dangling on its cord beside her. He had never been so terror-stricken in his life, but made himself grab hold of it and put it to his ear. "Who's there? What is it?"

"I—can't talk—" he heard Sammy's voice croak piteously. Had Sammy had some kind of seizure? The receiver clicked down at the other end and he could not ask. "Is something wrong with Sammy?" he said to Miriam urgently.

Miriam shook her head.

David froze. It had to be Martin.

The rest of the family had rushed in from the parlor, demanding to know what had happened and David could not make himself heard above the din. "Be quiet!" he shouted.

What followed was like taking part in your own nightmare, he thought in a remote part of his mind. Miriam was no longer leaning against him. She had jerked away and was looking up at him as if surprised to see it was he who had been supporting her. Then she began beating his chest with her clenched fists, as though she blamed him for the agony tearing her apart, letting it rip out of her like a tortured animal and the sound filled the room until his mother slapped her face and put an end to it.

"I'm sorry, Ma," she said in a brittle voice. "But you see I haven't got a son any more."

David saw Esther and Ben, still bowed down by their own trouble, sag beneath the weight of this greater one.

Hannah and Carl caught Sigmund by the arms in time to lower him into a chair as his knees buckled. Helga went to comfort Miriam. Bessie and Rebecca stood huddled close together, their faces shadowed with distress, and Abraham glanced up at the ceiling, then slouched into the scullery; he had always been the kind who had to lick his wounds alone.

David's mind was recording these unimportant details, detachedly. Why was he letting them clutter a moment of tragedy? he thought, noting Arnold biting his lip and catching sight of his own bleak expression in the mirror above the dresser. But wasn't it always the surrounding trivia that lived on in a person's memory when heartache lost its edge? He could still recall Miriam wearing a little green and white hat and the water gushing down from it when they ended their affair—in a rainstorm. But he couldn't reproduce the way he'd felt when he walked away from her. You couldn't keep the moment alive.

His mother's hand had fluttered to her brooch, but apart from that she had not moved.

"Get Miriam a drop of brandy," she said to him.

"I don't want any brandy. And if I did I wouldn't let him get it for me."

Why had she chosen now to behave this way with him, after showing no animosity after all these years?

"All I want is my son. But I might as well cry for the moon."

"He was my grandson, too," Sigmund said pitifully.

"You've got two others and Ma's still got three."

"But who's counting?" Arnold quipped brutally.

"Keep your mouth shut!" his father flung at him. "You've caused enough *tsorus* in the family today."

"In that case I'd better leave before I cause any more," Arnold replied. "I can't help my sense of humor."

Ben gave him a withering glance. "Is that what you call it?"

Arnold's lips twisted into a smile that was more like a grimace. "If you were spending your life in the midst of death—forgive the pun, there I go again!—like Martin did and like I still am, your sense of humor might've got a bit warped, too." He went to Miriam and kissed her. "I didn't mean to upset you, Auntie."

"It's all right, Arnold. I understand." Miriam stared pensively into space. "I just wish I'd understood Martin better. Perhaps I didn't try to."

"Who can understand their own children?" Ben declaimed, glaring at Arnold. "Why they do the things they do. Why they want to do them. What does it matter who gets hurt? What do they care about the cost?"

"Even if it turns out to be their own life," Miriam whispered.

"What are they trying to prove and who to?" Ben continued the dialogue which, on his side, was recriminatory.

But Miriam's voice held only regret. "And my son didn't even die gloriously, the way he wanted to," she revealed. "I'd felt for a long time that Martin wanted to die. But he didn't go to his Maker in a winged chariot, fighting for the cause. Did I tell you that, yet?" she added vaguely. "I can't remember." A tremor rippled through her. "He roared to Heaven on a motorbike. Killed in a motorcycle accident, Sammy told me the telegram said. I didn't know Martin could ride one."

"You ought to go home, Miriam," David said gently.

"But you're not taking me," she retorted.

"I will," Arnold offered. "If someone will lend me a car."

David hid his embarrassment. "Take mine; the keys are

on the hall table. The rest of us will come later. You can leave me to make the necessary arrangements," he said to Miriam.

"Sammy and I leave our son's funeral arrangements to you?"

David felt as if a whiplash had stung his cheek.

"That's one thing you won't have the satisfaction of doing for us," Miriam declared stinging the other one.

"Nobody's more brokenhearted for you than I am, but I can't have you talking to David that way," Bessie told her indignantly.

"If he didn't make it necessary, I wouldn't have to."

Sarah was relieved when Abraham came in from the scullery and diverted their attention. There was no knowing what Miriam might come out with in her present mood.

"A fine friend you've turned out to be," she heard her husband tell the ceiling reproachfully.

"That's no way to talk to God," she rebuked him.

Abraham was still gazing upwards. "All right, so I apologize. But maybe we could make a bargain, You and me. I'll stop blaming You for taking Martin, if You'll stop our Arnold from marrying a *shiksah*."

"There's nobody up there to hear you, Pa," Miriam said wearily. "I began to doubt it when I saw how my mother suffered with that long illness and now I'm certain."

"So why did you talk about your son going to his Maker?" Sarah demanded.

"It's hard to get out of a lifetime's habits. But from now on, to me He's just a figure of speech." Miriam's lower lip trembled and she turned her luminous eyes on Esther and Ben. "And there's something I'd like to say to you two. If I could get Martin back, I wouldn't give a damn who he married, so long as he was alive and happy."

"It's all right for you to say that now!" Esther exclaimed passionately. Then she gazed at her own son, who was standing stiffly in the doorway and her voice grew cold and matter of fact. "I want to say something, too. While everyone's present to hear it. If Arnold marries that *shiksah*, to me he'll be just as dead as poor Martin is. I'll have one son instead of two. He'll never set foot in his parents' home again."

A chill of foreboding raised the gooseflesh on Sarah's arms. Why was Esther tempting Fate who rarely let you get away with it? Pushing Arnold to the point of no return? She saw him swallow hard before he spoke.

"I'll take Auntie Miriam home, then I'll push off." He glanced briefly at his father, but Ben's expression was for once implacable and he said nothing. "Goodbye, Mother."

He hustled Miriam out of the room and it was not until they heard the front door slam shut that the family emerged from their shock.

"You know what I'm thinking?" Esther said, staring through the window into the back garden, where Frank was trying to stop Henry from pulling Leona's hair. "When Arnold was still my son, he used to call me Mom. Today was the first time he ever called me Mother."

Ben leapt up from his chair. "She's casting him out before the event! He hasn't even done it yet!"

"But he will," Esther answered tonelessly. "You don't know him like I do, you said so yourself. He's like me; he means what he says. When your Joe married-out, you said you'd never forgive him, but you have. Even though you hardly ever see him."

"He's my brother."

"But you didn't bring him up, work your fingers to the bone for him, like you did for your son. A lot of thanks you've got for it! Arnold's throwing everything you taught him back in your face and mine, too. As if we just plucked him off a tree we happened to be passing, as though he doesn't belong to us."

What a dangerous thing our possessiveness is, David thought, recalling that this had been the aspect of Jewish family life Arnold resented most, and the one that had finally pushed him over the edge. His own generation had not dared to question it. Nathan, thirteen years younger, had dared, but hadn't had the nerve to carry it further. Today, it seemed the youngsters lacked neither daring nor nerve, though they still found it painful to defy the family. He did not allow his mind to dwell on what the next decade might bring. The young Jews and Jewesses of the 1950s would probably go their own way without experiencing a twinge.

He saw his mother pick up a photograph of Arnold and Martin in the Manchester Grammar School caps they had worn as boys. If Arnold married Lyn, would she, like Esther, behave in the ritual way of her forefathers, as if he, too, were dead?

"No matter what he does, I'll still love him," he heard her declare firmly.

"What has loving got to do with it?" Esther demanded. "It's a question of duty, isn't it?"

Sarah gave her an imperious look. "For me with my family, you can't have one without the other. And bridges I haven't yet come to, I don't try to cross." She replaced the photograph on the mantelpiece with the rest of the family gallery. "Why are we wasting time talking about what hasn't yet happened, when Miriam and Sammy need us?"

She picked up the telephone receiver. "I'll ring up for a taxi. There won't be room for all of us in Ben's car."

How competent and resourceful she was, David reflected whilst she made the call. Not many aging grandmothers would present the calm exterior Sarah Sandberg did after receiving two such terrible blows, one after the other. But she was blessed with an inner strength few possessed. And without putting it into words, had indicated that she would not cut Arnold off.

Had she mellowed with the years? Or moved with the times? More so than her daughter? Tolerance had never been his mother's way with her children. But she was a wise woman. And a wily old bird! Maybe she had realized that with her grandchildren it might have to be.

Chapter Twelve

Another envelope bearing Martin's handwriting was waiting for Marianne when she returned from a day out in Salisbury. Beside it on her bed, was a typed note requesting her presence at the Platoon Office.

She had not heard from him since he called at her quarters in her absence two weeks ago. Why hadn't he let her know he was coming? But he hadn't the last time, either. It wasn't like Martin to do things on an impulse, but he had changed in more ways than that.

Birdie came into the room from the shower, swathed in a towel. " 'E came on a motorbike this time," she said, eyeing the envelope. "Said 'e'd borrowed it from the flight mechanic. You'n 'im's like a couple o' ships what keeps passin' each other in the night, if yer asks me!"

Marianne read the note, which was just two lines of his verse transformed into a quizzical sentence: "When shall we twain join hands again?" With the "shall" underlined.

She gazed at it with the troubled feeling that had dogged her since she received his first one, superseding her confusion about Michael, who had been posted out of her life last week.

The night after Michael's departure, Birdie and Joyce had dragged her to a British airborne unit dance at Bulford. A change of scene would cheer her up, they'd said and it had. But it had increased her confusion, too, and made her feel guilty that she could be cheered up so easily. She had found herself eyeing the stag-line of paratroopers quaffing beer, their red berets tucked into their epaulets, and thinking it wouldn't be difficult to fall for one of them.

This had set her musing about what being in love meant and added to her state of emotional flux. Was the feeling Michael Weiss had aroused in her as transient as his presence had been? Capable of being transferred to any number of suitable successors? The thought that it might be dismayed her. She had always thought of love as an emotion you attached to one special person. Romantic love, that is, which was different from the way you loved your family. From the way she loved Martin, she thought now, gazing through the window across the fields full of army vehicles without seeing them. And she couldn't love him the other way, she accepted with sudden certainty. That was what her troubled feeling had been about; why she hadn't written to him though he had rarely left her thoughts since he'd declared his new kind of love for her.

Birdie was winding her damp locks around pipe-cleaners. " 'Adn't yer better go an' see wot the office wants wiv yer, Marianne? The request fer yer company arrived 'alf-an-'our ago, before I went fer me shower. Yer said yer was only goin' fer a lickle walk when yer went art this mornin', where've yer bin all day?"

"The bus to Salisbury pulled up when I got to the bottom of the hill, so I hopped on to it."

"Spent all that time on yer own? Pull the other one!"

"Sometimes a person needs to be alone to think. I spent most of the day in the Cathedral."

Birdie laughed raucously. "What, on a *Shabbos*?"

Marianne laughed, too. Birdie's neighbors at her home in Stepney were called Horowitz and there wasn't much she didn't know about Jews and their ways.

"I've been wanting to see inside it for a long time," Marianne told her. "And it isn't like going into a church to pray, is it? To me, the cathedral's just a beautiful building steeped in history."

"Tell that ter yer *Bubbah*," Birdie grinned.

"The Jews up north call their grandmothers 'Bobbie'," she informed Birdie and brushed the intrusive thought of Sarah away.

Browsing around in the cool serenity of the cathedral had had a calming effect upon her and afterwards she had stood for a while drinking in the beauty of the gracious greystone edifice towering against the sky. There were other people standing around on the broad green sward, too, but she had hardly been aware of them. It'd been like being alone in the quiet of the cathedral close, the first solitude she had experienced for a long time.

In her quarters, someone or something was always intruding on your thoughts. Even when Birdie and Joyce were out and Marianne had the room to herself there was the noise of other girls clattering up and down stairs. And the American Forces Network seemed to follow you wherever you went, you didn't even have to go anywhere to hear it. Frank Sinatra's voice was now drifting from the common room wireless down the corridor, singing "Long Ago And Far Away."

If it wasn't Sinatra, it was Count Basie's "The One O'Clock Jump," or Lily Ann Carroll telling you "Saturday Night Is The Loneliest Night Of The Week." Vera Lynn hadn't made her presence felt in this neck of the woods and Marianne sometimes felt like an extra in a Hollywood musical. Especially when she walked down the main street in the barracks. Frankie's dulcet tones were invariably issuing from the loudspeakers attached to every passing tree, urging you to "Come Out, Wherever You Are" and it would not have surprised her to see the gum-chewing GIs and WACs suddenly break into a jitterbug.

"What yer bleedin' daydreamin' abart now?" Birdie asked her scathingly.

Marianne sighed. "It'd take me too long to tell you." She had not had time to record her impressions on paper lately. But perhaps it was best to let the whole experience soak into her mind, then after the war she could shut herself away with a typewriter and write a book about it.

"Yer've still got yer forage cap on," Birdie said when she was leaving the room to go to the office. "I fought I was habsentminded till I met yer!"

Marianne changed into her flat cap, which was the correct uniform for official occasions.

"Hif yer wasn't so bleedin' straightlaced, yer'd never remember where yer'd left yer knickers!" Birdie called atfer her as she departed.

The office was situated beside a small parade ground, with the cookhouse and sick-bay, a short walk from the girls' quarters, and Marianne wondered why she had been summoned there, whilst she strode along the path. Had they found out that she always put her roommates' kitbags under their blankets when they didn't return before lights-out, so their beds would look occupied if the duty NCO came around flashing her flashlight? But in that case, why hadn't Birdie and Joyce been summoned, too? Perhaps she was to be posted to another unit and they wanted to give her her orders immediately?

Junior Commander Platt wasted no time in ending her conjecture. "I received a telephone call from a Mr. David Sandberg," she said when Marianne had given her the obligatory salute.

"He's my uncle, ma'am."

"So he said."

He was the one who always took charge in a family crisis, and Marianne's heart had begun to thud.

"I have some good news for you, Klein," the officer smiled. "Your brother is alive. A prisoner of war."

Marianne sagged with relief and gazed down at her shoes, so the CO would not see the tears that had sprung to her eyes. When she raised her head, Miss Platt's smile had gone and she was toying with her propeling pencil.

"Some bad news, too, I'm afraid, Klein. Your uncle

asked me to break it to you gently, but there's no way, is there? He said you and the young man were extremely close."

Uncle David didn't use words like "extremely." Which young man? She knew, but she didn't want to open her mind to it. What was the CO saying? Something about a motorbike. The picture of an aeroplane falling from the sky that had just risen before Marianne's eyes disintegrated. Martin had been killed in a road accident. This afternoon. It must have happened after he came to visit her.

"Sit down, Klein," Miss Platt said.

Marianne gave her a dazed glance and she rose from her desk and shepherded her to a chair.

"Thank you, ma'am." If he hadn't fallen in love with her, he'd be out with a WAAF, or one of the civilian girls he knew in Lincoln. Alive and well. Instead, he was lying in a mortuary, because of her.

Miss Platt poured some water from a flask and made her drink a little. "I wish I had something stronger to offer you, Klein. You look as if you need it."

There's a human being inside that impersonal shell, Marianne thought remotely. The girls wouldn't believe it when she told them.

The officer was eyeing her sympathetically. "Your uncle asked if I would let you have compassionate leave. But you know the regulations by now, don't you, Klein? I had to tell him a cousin's funeral isn't a reason."

Not go to Martin's funeral? She, who'd been closer to him than anyone else in the world? "Yes, ma'am." Marianne rose from the chair, set the glass of water on the desk, saluted with machine-like precision and left the office.

Half-an-hour later, she was in Joyce's current GI's jeep, being driven by him to Andover, with the bag of civilian clothing Birdie kept handy for her periodic absent-without-leave jaunts on her lap.

"What'll they do to you, hon, when you get back?" the snub-nosed private asked when he dropped her at the railway station.

"I don't care."

"Me, I'd end up in the stockade if I went over the hill."

"I'll probably get the ATS equivalent. Birdie only got confined to barracks for a week, last time she went AWOL. But that was before the twenty-five-mile limit was put on our traveling. They'll take going off without a pass more seriously now."

"You're darn tootin', sugar! Things're hottin' up for the invasion as of now, a guy can feel it in the air. Everyone's waitin' to go. Are you sure you oughta do what you're doin', hon?" Joyce's boyfriend asked with concern.

Marianne glanced at her wristwatch. The train to London was due in twelve minutes and a pulse in her throat was fluttering nervously. But her resolve had not faltered. "I only intend being away for a couple of days and the girls are going to try to cover for me," she answered. "But if I'm found out, so be it. However they punish me it won't last forever. But if I don't go I'll regret it for the rest of my life."

She entered the station with the crowd arriving to catch the train to town and darted into the ladies' waiting room whilst the military policewomen patrolling near the platform barriers were looking the other way, emerging a few minutes later as a civilian, over whom the red-capped Amazons had no jurisdiction, her uniform secreted in Birdie's suitcase.

Don't march, walk, she instructed herself when she had bought her ticket and had to pass by them. All she needed was the rigid gait that had been drilled into her to give her away! This must be how criminals felt when they were committing their crimes—as if the eye of the law was burning into the back of their neck, but afraid to turn and look. Only they didn't have her additional problems. Birdie's court shoes were too big for her and the paper she'd packed into the toes wasn't stopping her from stepping out of them every so often. And she was afraid the skirt of her borrowed suit would slip to her ankles any second; it was inches too wide and the safety-pin with which she had anchored it to her ATS corset didn't make it feel secure.

Her anxiety lessened on the train when a grim-looking ATS sergeant-major seated opposite did not so much as glance at her. And after she had walked through the barrier at Paddington without drawing the attention of the MPs, she ceased worrying about anything other than whether she would get lost in the labyrinth of underground passages through which she had to find her way in order to reach Euston by tube.

She had only traveled home on leave from her present unit once before. It had been early afternoon when she arrived in London and the same on her return journey. The underground had not looked the way it did now, crammed with people for whom it was a nightly air-raid shelter.

The sight of them sprawled on their improvised beds jolted Marianne back to the grim reality of the war and heightened the feeling she had had lately that the life she was living in Wiltshire, surrounded by Yanks and jeeps, was not real, that she would awaken one morning and find it had just been a dream.

Some of the people she passed were dozing beneath grubby-looking blankets. Others were eating and drinking and a girl of about her own age was suckling a baby and chatting perkily to her nocturnal neighbors, as if there were nothing untoward about baring your breast in the underground. But it was probably routine to her by now, as this nightly, molelike existence was for everyone down here. Some were no doubt homeless already and others might find the homes they had left intact no longer there tomorrow morning.

Yet looking at them, Marianne mused, nobody would guess they had anything on their minds. There was an air of good cheer about the whole exercise. Perhaps it was the togetherness she could feel all around her that helped them maintain it, she reflected and had to smile at the sight of two very fat ladies dancing the Lambeth Walk. An old man with a concertina was providing the music. They even had their entertainment.

The ambience remained with her when she left the underground behind, like a gauze curtain dimming her thoughts about Martin without having taken them away. But speeding northward on the night train to Manchester, the terrible thing that was taking her there shut everything else out.

All the compartments were full when she boarded and she passed the long journey seated on Birdie's suitcase in the unlit corridor, staring through the window into the darkness, only dimly aware of the ghostly shapes of the trees being replaced by factory chimneys, with the train wheels clanking: "When shall we twain join hands again?" on and on, until she thought the sound would explode inside her head.

She had telephoned her father from Euston to ask him to meet the train, but it was her Uncle David whom she found waiting for her at London Road Station. To her surprise, Shirley was with him. Looking as if she'd just stepped out of a handbox, as usual.

"Wherever did you get that dreadful outfit, Marianne?"

And as obsessed by clothes as ever.

Shirley was eyeing Birdie's strident red costume. Her appalled gaze took in the matching, Spanish-heel shoes and sheer, black stockings, and the saucy beret, also black, which with Marianne's thick bangs gave her a gamine appearance. "Fancy coming home for a funeral dressed like a French tart!"

"Can't you think about anything else, even at six o'clock in the morning?" Marianne retorted. The warm, family feeling that Shirley's coming to meet her had evoked fled away. Even though we don't like each other, she's here, because we're cousins and one of our own is dead, Marianne had thought. But now Shirley's presence at the station seemed the empty duty it was.

"Now, now, girls!" her uncle interceded.

But he, too, had looked askance at Marianne's attire. "These aren't my things. I couldn't get a pass, so I came without one and I'd never have got here if I'd been in uniform," she told him whilst they were walking to his car.

"I see."

"I suppose you think I've done the wrong thing, Uncle?"

He did not reply until they had driven down Market Street and were turning right, en route for Prestwich. "I've been asking myself if I'd have done what you have, Marianne," he said thoughtfully. "It was a big decision for you to have to make. But the answer is yes and I'm glad you did it, love. Shall I tell you why? Because nothing is more important than family; it's what we've tried to instill into all you kids and you've proved we've done a good job."

"With one exception," Shirley declared. "You haven't heard about your Arnold yet, have you, Marianne?"

David glanced at Marianne's stunned expression after he had told her. "Your dad's a bit under the weather, what with one thing and another. He didn't feel up to meeting the train."

Marianne was not surprised. But the news about Arnold seemed insignificant beside the tragedy of Martin's death. How could the two simultaneous events have failed to make her parents see things in their true perspective?

They were sitting in the living room when she walked into the house. Her uncle had dropped her at the garden gate and had said he would not bother coming in. Perhaps he hadn't wanted to get involved in what he knew awaited her.

She approached it with apprehension herself, but this changed to pity when she saw the two middle-aged figures hunched over the table sipping tea, and the overflowing ashtray at her father's elbow.

Where had his springy step gone to? she thought after he had risen to kiss her and slouched silently back to his chair. She noted him scratching his hands and saw the eczema from which he had suffered after Harry was reported missing looked red raw. And what a mess her mother was, with her hair all over the place and her housecoat unbuttoned over her nightdress. She had always taken a pride in her appearance, like an older version of Shirley, and made sure she looked immaculate whatever the hour or circumstances. Marianne could understand why she looked the way she did, but it was a shock because it wasn't like her.

"I want you to promise you'll never do to us what Arnold's doing," her mother said after a silence.

Hadn't it entered her parents' heads what they were doing to him? Two pairs of pathetic eyes were riveted to her face. No, and it never would.

"Promise us, Marianne," her father implored. "If you don't want to finish us both off."

Marianne replaced her tea cup in the saucer and cast Michael Weiss and his kind permanently out of her life. "Of course I won't do it, Dad." How could she?

The two days she spent in the midst of the family passed in a blur of sights and sounds, with the bleak grayness of sorrow shading everything around her and the women's weeping rising to a terrible crescendo when Martin's coffin was carried from her grandparents' house.

She was not clear as to why the cortège left from there, instead of from his parents' home, but it seemed right and she supposed that was the reason; the elder Sandbergs' home was the heart of the family and the week of mourning was to be held there, too.

The funeral did not take place until Monday afternoon. The body, a term Marianne could not apply to Martin and shuddered when others did, had had to be brought north. She had wanted to look at him, then had changed her mind. It was better to remember him as he had looked before the spirit that was the real him had left his flesh, than have her last memory of him reduced to a lifeless shell shrouded in the *tallith* in which Jewish males were buried.

Because she was female, she was not allowed to go to the cemetery and see him laid to rest, though he would have wanted her to be there, and when the men returned from the interment she raised the subject with a young rabbinical student who had been a schoolmate of Martin's.

"There's no law against it, Marianne," he replied.

Had she heard him correctly?

Harold Shneider sipped the whisky that was always provided after a funeral and surveyed Marianne's astonished expression. "You only think there is because in Manchester the women don't attend burials. But it's just a tradition that's grown up because men think it best for them not to witness such a harrowing thing. In some communities, Sheffield for instance, the women please themselves and some do go to the cemetery."

Good for them! Marianne thought hotly. Why should men always take things into their own hands and women let themselves be told what was best for them, as if they were incapable of judging for themselves? She glanced at her aunt, who was trying to swallow down the salt herring, hard-boiled eggs and bagels that next-of-kin mourners were obliged to eat, though they had no appetite for food. Auntie Miriam had been misled into thinking the tradition was a law, just as Marianne had, or she wouldn't have bade Martin goodbye a moment before she had to.

What she had just learned caused her to question the Jewish way of life even more than she had already begun doing. How many more misconceptions were dictating people's behavior? Even if this was the only one, it was hard to relate some of the archaic laws and customs to the life of today. And only possible to observe them without question if you remained within a closed community. The family considered themselves anglicized, but this was just an illusion. They had no desire to be integrated and how could they ever be when they put up barriers against it and taught their children these must never be torn down?

Uncle David, whom she considered highly intelligent, had once told her how he had battled his way out of the Strangeways ghetto and at the time she had admired him for it. Now, she felt sorry for him because the word "ghetto" didn't just apply to a district. It could apply to your mentality, too.

She and Martin had talked about this the last time they

were home on leave together, when they'd felt themselves stifled by the narrowness of the family ethos. And, oh, how she missed not having him here, she thought that evening. The house was packed with people who had flocked to offer condolence—women trying to comfort Auntie Miriam and men gripping Uncle Sammy's hand unable to find words to console a man who had just said the *Kaddish* prayer for his only son.

But Marianne could relate none of the religious ritual to Martin, who had stopped believing there was a God or an afterlife. If there was, which she wanted to believe, by now he would have found out—and also whether there were two separate Heavens for Jews and Gentiles as they'd supposed when they were kids, she recalled poignantly.

"Your Marianne never grows an inch," she heard Paula Frankl—whom she always associated with weddings, *Bar Mitzvahs* and funerals because those were the only occasions on which she ever saw her—say to her grandmother, and escaped to the upstairs landing where she and Martin had sat sharing their secrets as small children.

"I don't blame you," Hannah whispered following her. "I've told Carl that when I die, there's to be none of what's going on downstairs. Mourning's a luxury for the mourners and apart from one's nearest and dearest, what have they done to deserve it?"

Marianne smiled for the first time in two days. Hannah was like a breath of fresh air.

"When are you going back to camp, Marianne?"

"On the midnight train."

"We've got time for a little chat, then. What's been going on in your life since you were last home?"

"Things that'd make a lot of people's hair stand on end," Marianne said dryly.

"But not mine."

How good it was to have this trusted friend. Someone to whom she could confide the traumatic events of the past few weeks.

After she had done so, Hannah was silent for a moment, then took her hand and stroked it, the way she had years ago when she'd told Marianne to let her handicaps be a spur.

"Let's talk about Michael first, shall we?" she said gently. "Or what he represents."

Marianne eyed her uncertainly.

"Most girls go through a stage when they're in love with love, Marianne."

"I don't know what you mean."

"I mean with the state itself, the fantasy that's woven around it. And it's easy to attach that to any nice boy who happens to be around. I did it myself when I was your age. Over and over again. Then one day, when I'd grown disenchanted with my current sweetheart, I became aware I was actively looking for another. Surveying the field is one way to put it and I thought what the heck am I doing?"

This more or less summed up Marianne's experience at the British airborne unit dance. She felt her cheeks grow hot at the recollection.

"It's nothing to be ashamed of," Hannah declared, noticing. "In a way, it's tied up with the feminine expectations we're conditioned to from our cradle. The concept that being some man's darling, cooking his meals and bearing his kids in a cottage with roses round the door is what we're born for. The roses are the romantic sugar on the pill, of course. That's how we get lured into the trap!"

"But you didn't, did you? Well, not in the way most women are trapped. You've got a life outside your home, your career."

"I might not have had, if I'd married one of the lads I thought I was in love with, instead of Carl." Hannah smiled reminiscently. "There was one called Colin who wanted to get engaged to me, but I couldn't face spending my life with someone who bit his nails. And another called Pete, who was always saying how nice it'd be to come home and find me and his pipe and slippers waiting for him by the hearth."

"I don't see you fitting into that picture!"

"But it sounded lovely at the time. I wasn't the me I am now. Not marrying young allowed me to become her and I've got a husband who hasn't tried to grind her under his heel. That's the sort of man you need, Marianne, and there aren't many around."

"I'll bear it in mind."

"And when he comes along, you won't give him up whatever the reason if you really love him. That, my dear, is the acid test."

Hannah went to peer over the stair rail at the people standing chatting in the hallway because there was not room for them in the parlor. "Miriam and Sammy're going to have to put up with this for the rest of the week," she said, sounding distressed. "People are kind and come because it's expected, but personally I think the Reform *Shul's* way is more sensible. Just one day of *Shivah* for everyone to pay their respects, then allow the bereaved to grieve in privacy and peace."

She turned around and saw Marianne's desolate expression, which referring to the *Shivah* had caused. "As for you feeling responsible for Martin's death," she declared firmly. "You always did dramatize everything, but this time you've gone too far. If your grandmother knew, she'd say the same."

"Why?"

"She's a fatalist and so am I. My own experiences and other people's have made me one. Do you really believe it was a coincidence that you got up to go to the bathroom just before that bomb shot your bed through the floor? And to carry it further, why was it a time bomb, that allowed you and your parents to escape being blown up?"

"Because God didn't want us to die that night," Marianne said thoughtfully.

Hannah smiled. "That's what your grandmother said. She attributes the good things to God and the bad ones to Fate. To me, they're one and the same. I eschew the religious trappings, but acknowledge the hand of destiny. When your time's up, it's up, and Martin reached the end of his that afternoon. Perhaps he was also fated to die without knowing you couldn't return his feelings," Hannah added quietly.

"And that was why I was out when he came? Both times?"

"Exactly."

What Hannah had said eased Marianne's feeling of personal responsibility for her cousin's untimely death. But nothing could lessen her sense of irreparable loss.

There would never be another Martin in her life, she thought on the train carrying her south that night. Relative and friend, mentor and ally, champion and critic, all rolled into one. She had not realized quite what he meant to her when he was alive. But losing him was like saying farewell to her *alter ego*, to the twin soul who'd been born into the family the same year as herself.

These were her thoughts when exhaustion overtook her and she fell asleep. She was still slumbering when the train pulled into Euston and she had to be prodded awake by the lady seated beside her.

People were queueing for the early edition of the morning papers when she left the platform. Others were standing around reading them, with broad smiles on their faces.

"What's everyone so pleased about?" she asked a porter who was also grinning from ear to ear.

"It's D-Day, love."

Marianne stood stock still.

"Old 'itler'll get 'is come-uppance now all right! The Allies 'as invaded Normandy."

She hurried to the tube, her mind awhirl. There had probably been a pre-invasion flap on at the Ordnance Depot, with the colonel demanding she be brought from her bed, head-cold or not. The girls wouldn't have been able to cover up for her, even with the medical orderly's complicity. But she must carry on with her part of the plan. Get back into uniform and try to sneak into quarters the back way, just in case.

At Andover station there were no military policewomen about. They were waiting for her in the ladies' room, or so she felt when she opened the door and saw them there.

"Great news, isn't it?" one of the pair beamed to her.

Even the redcaps had got D-Day euphoria. She'd have it herself in different circumstances. "It's the day we've all been waiting for," she smiled and went to wash her hands, because it would seem odd if she just did an about-turn and left.

"You comin' or goin'?" the other MP inquired conversationally whilst powdering her bumpy nose.

"Going," Marianne replied, making her exit and trying to decide where. There was no point in loitering at the station. If she went back to the ladies' room to change, after they came out, they'd recognize her when she re-emerged in uniform.

Klein on the run! she thought melodramatically, eyeing her reflection in a shop window on the main street. She had to find somewhere to shed her disguise. What would Bogart do? Head for the nearest bar. English bars weren't open this early. But residential hotels were, she smiled spotting one.

A trio of businessmen watched the tarty-looking girl in red teeter across the foyer on her borrowed stilts and enter the cloakroom. But didn't even glance at the prim little "At" when she marched out, Marianne noted disgustedly. Then she tripped over someone's foot and every head in the vicinity turned to stare at her.

The soldier responsible lifted her from the doormat, where she had landed.

"I seem to've done something to my ankle," Marianne winced.

"It's my fault," he answered contritely. "My feet are too big."

She managed to smile. "They go with the rest of you."

He was built like a rugby player and she had to crane her neck to look at his face, which was anything but handsome. But he had the most magnetic eyes she had ever seen. Hazel, flecked with green and sharply defined against the whites as if they had been ringed with a black pencil.

"Thank you for hoisting me up," she said dragging her gaze away from them and hobbling through the doorway.

"I'll drive you wherever you're going," he offered, following and taking her arm. He supported her to where his vehicle was parked. "But I hope it isn't Land's End or John o' Groats! I'm due in Salisbury this afternoon."

"You're in luck. Where I'm stationed is on your way."

After they had set off, he glanced at her painful ankle, which was now twice the size of her other one. "You'd better go to the sick-bag and have that strapped when you get back."

"Yes, Sergeant," Marianne replied facetiously.

"My name's Ralph Dean."

"Mine's Marianne Klein."

"That's not English, is it?"

"Nor is your twang."

"Is it that noticeable?"

"Yes. But I can't place it."

"It's got a bit watered-down with the years. I'm Australian, but I've lived here since I was a kid. People always retain something of their roots, don't they?"

Some more than others, Marianne thought. Herself for instance. "I'm English in spite of my name," she said.

"But you don't look it."

"I'm Jewish, too."

He gave her a sidelong glance. "There's no need to sound so defensive about it, love."

"I wasn't aware I had," Marianne answered stiffly. Probably because it's second nature with me, she thought, staring through the windscreen at the convoy of army trucks ahead of them. Born of the subtle something she felt in Gentile company, that kept her subconsciously on her guard.

"I thought you might be French," Ralph smiled. "With that hairstyle and those big, dark eyes."

"What does it matter what people are?" she said, wishing it didn't and changing the subject. "You're not having a very busy D-Day are you?"

"My usefulness will begin when the war's over, or so they tell me. Meanwhile I'm deskbound, preparing for then."

He did not elaborate and Marianne did not question him.

"Or I might not have been there to trip you up this morning," he added with a grin. The grin faded. "I was waiting for my wife, but she didn't show up."

Again he did not elaborate, but Marianne sensed a deep hurt within him. He had not struck her as the vulnerable kind, his appearance belied it, she thought, eyeing his strong hands on the steering wheel and the ruggedness of his profile. There was a worldliness about him, too. that made the other soldiers she'd met seem callow youths by comparison.

They fell into a pensive silence that lasted for most of the journey and Marianne guessed he was thinking about his wife.

"Where now?" he said, emerging from his thoughts as they reached the place where she was stationed.

There were very few GIs around and hardly any traffic. Instead, an unprecedented hush seemed to have enveloped the whole barracks complex, giving it the air of a deserted city.

"Up the hill if you don't mind," Marianne requested.

"Are you sure you don't want me to drive you to your quarters?" Ralph asked when he set her down by the roadside and saw her bite her lip as her foot touched the ground.

"And involve yourself in my misdemeanor?" she answered dryly. "I've been AWOL, Sergeant."

"I wondered if you might be when I noticed your quick-change act at the hotel."

He was more perceptive than she'd given him credit for. Straightforward, too, or he wouldn't have remarked on her defensiveness about being Jewish. It was his direct manner that had impelled her to be honest with him.

Ralph held her gaze for a moment. "With you, there'd have to be a good reason for it. Take care, Marianne."

She watched him turn his vehicle and speed away down the hill. She would have liked to get to know him better, but he hadn't suggested seeing her again. And she'd have had to refuse if he had. The easiest way to keep her solemn promise to her parents was not to make dates with Christian men. And also Ralph was married.

She made her way gingerly to the back of the ATS quarters, conscious of her ankle throbbing and of a sadness that had nothing to do with Martin's death. Perhaps it was because she had been in the company of someone she felt instinctively was a good person and had sensed he was unhappy.

The sight that met her eyes, when she reached the top of the rise she had been painfully climbing, wiped everything but the war from her mind. All the U.S. army vehicles had gone. It was as if someone had taken a paintbrush and transformed the military scene into the peaceful, country landscape it had once been.

By now, the rows of tanks and jeeps that had blotted the view from her window would be rumbling across Normandy, with boys she had probably passed on the barracks street, or sat next to in a canteen, inside them. And many would not return. D-Day wasn't just a term, the way it had seemed until now. It was the end of the beginning and for some, the beginning of the end.

The sickening realization diminished her personal trepidation. Being punished for going AWOL seemed trival by comparison and how small she suddenly felt: a tiny cog in the wheel of war whose absence from duty for a couple of days mattered not one jot.

She eased herself through the gap in the hedge the "Ats" used when they returned after lights-out. It was 12:30 p.m. and there was nobody about. The girls were always eating dinner in the cookhouse at this time. She collected her mug and cutlery from her room and went to join them. If her absence had gone undetected it would look as if she had risen from her sick bed because she felt well enough. If it hadn't, she would soon find out.

"Yer supposed ter be bleedin' sneezin', not limpin'," Birdie mouthed caustically when Marianne hobbled in and sat down beside her.

" 'N I wouldn't like ter tell yer wot capers we 'ad ter get

up ter, ter cover fer you," Joyce whispered from across the table.

Marianne smiled her thanks. There would be no repercussions, but she couldn't tell them it suddenly didn't matter.

"I 'ope yer didn't leave my civvies on the train, Marianne," Birdie said to her. "Knowin' wot yer like, I've been worried stiff abart 'em'n where I'd git the coupons from ter replace 'em."

Marianne was trying to summon the appetite to eat the mess of minced beef and soggy cabbage on her plate. She put down her fork with a clatter.

"Yer flamin' did, didn't yer? I knew it!" Birdie exclaimed.

"Not on the train, Birdie." She had left the suitcase in Ralph Dean's vehicle. But why did she feel pleased as well as contrite? Because she knew he would return it. She would see him again.

Chapter Thirteen

"What a place to spend *Chanukah*," Nathan joked to the Jewish soldier he was examining.

The boy gave him a wan smile. "It doesn't seem long since someone mentioned it was *Rosh Hashanah*. But at the time I was too busy being frightened for my life to care."

They were in a military hospital in Belgium and Nathan had no idea if today was *Chanukah* or not. But it was December, which meant it could be and he wanted to cheer up the boy.

"Did you go to *Chanukah* parties at *shul* when you were a kid, Kinsky?"

Kinsky gazed pensively at the wintry sunbeam that was lending an illusory warmth to the green walls and white-counterpaned beds. "Who didn't, sir?"

"You'll be back with your family soon," Nathan said to

comfort him and saw his lips tighten to a grimace in his thin face.

"Being fed like a baby by my mother, because I've got no hands."

Bitterness was as strong in the air here as the stench of blood and the lads' depression more difficult to treat than their post-operative conditions. Nathan patted Kinsky's shoulder wordlessly. He had considered himself something of a psychiatrist in civilian life, but it would take more than the simple methods he had employed to heal the psychological wounds of war.

His next patient was minus a leg. All the soldiers on this ward were maimed. Some were casualties of Arnhem, not yet fit enough to be shipped home. The newer cases had been brought in from the battle now raging in the Ardennes. Nathan had heard the Americans were bearing the brunt of it and shuddered to think how heavy their casualties must be.

"When's me stitches comin' hout, sir?" the pudgy lad, whose stump he had just exposed to view, inquired with forced perkiness.

"Not yet, Barton."

"I fought as 'ow it might be terday, when Nurse nicked me barrel of oats."

Barrel of oats? Barton's conversation took some working out.

"Hit's me fer the theatre, I fought, sir. Hup the happles'n pears. Look sir, they've gone from the hend of me bed."

He was referring to his case notes. "Are those Barton's?" Nathan called to the gray-clad figure just entering with a sheaf of papers in her hand.

"I'm just returning them. There was something I wanted to check with Dispensary," she replied. "I wasn't expecting the ward round to begin until ten, or I'd have been here when you arrived," she added as she drew nearer.

Nathan stared uncertainly at her composed, fair-skinned face framed by the big, starched-white kerchief Queen Alexandra's Nursing Sisters wore on their heads. It couldn't be her. But it was and why not? She was a nurse and he a doctor and there was a war on. "I'm a little early this morning," he said stiffly.

Mary remained at this side whilst he scanned the notes and finished examining Barton, then accompanied him on the rest of his round. Apart from the necessary medical exchanges, they did not speak a word to each other.

"Why haven't I seen you around before?" Nathan asked, halting in the flagstoned corridor when they left the ward together.

"I've just been transferred here."

Nathan had heard in the Mess last night that the Sister in charge of this ward had been relieved of her duties and had not been surprised. The atmosphere was enough to make anyone crack up and she had seemed on the verge of a breakdown for some time. He had expected a replacement. But not Mary! "Do you wish you hadn't been?"

"Do you?" Mary countered.

Her expression told Nathan nothing. What did he feel for her all these years later? Something was churning inside him, but was it anything more than regret?

Mary turned away and went into the office. She was already seated at the desk writing when Nathan followed her.

"I have a lot to do," she said without glancing up.

The sound of the nib scratching on the paper was like a blunt knife scraping his nerves. "Does seeing me again mean nothing to you?"

Mary put down her pen. "We were young and foolish together, how could it not?"

"Is that how you think of it?"

"When I allow myself to think of it at all. Which isn't often. You were a fool to think what you felt for me could be stronger than your family. And I was one for hoping it would be. How's your wife, by the way?"

Nathan did not reply. The question wasn't a polite inquiry about Rebecca's health; it was a deliberate reminder of her existence. But he needed no reminding. All his adult life he had been torn between these two women.

Mary cut into his thoughts. "The child she was expecting when I saw her must be about eight now."

"She's nearly nine."

"And no doubt has brothers and sisters."

"She hasn't, as a matter of fact."

"I thought Jews always had big families."

"Did you?"

"To keep watch on each other, like your brother did with you. I remember you accused him of spying on you, when he found us together in Whitworth Park."

"Why are you raking that up?"

Mary rose from the desk and went to gaze through the window at some ambulances that had just pulled up in the courtyard. "Why the hell do you suppose?"

"I ruined your life, didn't I?" Nathan said after a silence.

"Let's not be melodramatic," she replied, turning to face him. "It isn't your fault I happen to be a one-guy gal, as our U.S. Allies would put it. Not that I haven't tried not to be, Nathan."

"You never did call me Nat, like everyone else does, did you?"

Mary shook her head mutely.

A moment later they were in each other's arms.

"Mind my cumbersome headgear doesn't hit you in the eye." Mary warned with a tremulous laugh. "That little cap I used to wear was more convenient!"

The allusion to her cap, and the fragrance of lavender rising from her skin as it always had, transported Nathan back to a linen room at Manchester Royal Infirmary, into which they had sometimes crept for a few precious minutes alone. Remembrance was so strong, he could even smell the freshly laundered sheets that had surrounded them on the shelves.

"I'll never forget the time we heard Sister Reilly talking to someone outside the door and thought she might open it and catch us," he said reminiscently. "Oh, Mary!"

He rested his cheek on hers, as he had then; she still aroused tenderness in him. Affectionate friendship had deepened their young desire. Desire that had never been consummated, he thought, feeling her firm breasts against his chest and her heart beating with his. How ironic it was that life had given him Rebecca to assuage his sexual hunger, but had denied him fulfillment with the only woman he had ever loved.

"That's enough of that," Mary said, breaking away from him.

Nathan averted his gaze, conscious of the hardening in his loins as she had no doubt been, too.

"Nothing like a bit of slap and tickle to take your mind off the war, is there?" she said coarsely.

He watched her adjust her headgear. "Was that what it was?"

"What else could it be?" she answered. "We might all be dead tomorrow. A nice little armful's what every soldier wants."

"I'm not a soldier, Mary. I'm just a doctor in uniform."

"Away from home like all the rest."

"Why are you saying this to me?"

"So you won't get the idea what happened just now was important to me."

"You mean you're not going to let it be?"

"Not likely! Where would it end? Remember my friend Ann Barker? You wouldn't recognize her if you saw her now. That affair she started with a married man when we were students is still going on and a right wreck it's made of her. Personally, I'd rather live like a nun. Not that I do."

Mary sat down at the desk and smiled at Nathan's shocked reaction. "You taught me I'd got hot blood in my veins. And I've since discovered you don't have to be in love to enjoy sex."

"I've never been in love with my wife," Nathan said stiffly.

Mary borrowed another American expression. A barrack-room one. "Well, that's tough shit, isn't it? For all three of us." She returned her attention to the notes she had been writing and did not raise her head when Nathan left the office.

That night, she was surrounded by officers in the Mess, as newly arrived nurses always were. Nathan stood with a noisy group on the other side of the smoky room, feeling limp and drained. He needed some sleep, a night never passed without his being roused to deal with emergencies. It was the same for his colleagues, but most seemed able to burn the candle at both ends, he reflected, surveying the throng around the bar. But it was an ambience of false merriment, as if everyone were determined to forget where they were and why and suddenly Nathan wanted to escape from it. Instead he leaned on the piano listening to Pettifer, the radiologist, tinkling a tune, unable to tear himself away from Mary's presence.

Each time he glanced in her direction she was glancing at him, and he wondered which of them would get a stiff neck first, from hastily jerking their heads the other way. A beefy, orthopedic surgeon had his arm around her, damn him! And Mary kept smiling up into the fellow's bleary eyes, but the smile was like a mask glued to her face.

"I shay, Shandberg ol' chap, get me a refill, there'sh a good bod," the radiologist requested whoozily.

When Nathan returned from the bar with Pettifer's drink, Mary had gone. But the orthopod was still here, he noted with relief. Perhaps she'd just gone to powder her nose, but if the surgeon had disappeared, too—Nathan tried to curb his jealousy. The knowledge that she slept around was like a thorn in his side, but he had no strings on her, he told himself firmly and left the Mess.

Mary was leaning on the wall outside the door, huddled in her cape.

Nathan stopped short when he saw her there.

"I couldn't bear the way you kept staring over at me," she said.

"Why?"

"You know bloody well why!"

Nathan could see their breath steaming in the frigid air and a coating of frost forming on the roof of the sergeants' mess, opposite. Of course he knew why; it had been a ridiculous question. Being in the same room with him was probably torture for her, without his making things worse.

"I'm going to bed," she said, striding away from him.

"Let me come with you," he answered, following her.

"Let go! You're hurting me!"

He had gripped her shoulder and halted her, without realizing it. But he hadn't meant to say what he'd just said, either. He could hear Pettifer's aimless tinkling on the piano drifting from inside. Apart from that, there was no sound and no light except for the moon silvering Mary's blonde curls.

"It might as well be me you go to bed with as anyone else," Nathan said thickly, unable to prevent himself from doing so.

"That's where you're wrong. With you it would involve my emotions."

"I think I still love you, Mary."

She laughed abruptly. "You're honest. You admit you're not sure."

"I've never been knowingly dishonest with you."

"No. You kidded yourself, too. That we could have a future together. And there's an added complication now. Two, to be precise."

His wife and child.

"So why are we standing here discussing the impossible?"

Was it impossible? Nathan felt on the brink of a now-or-never decision. He could see Mary's shadow elongated on the cobblestones, as it had been beside him since they parted years ago. Now he could choose between the shadow and the substance. And the chance to be happy would not come again.

"To be happy, a person must first be at peace with the Almighty, or what should taste sweet will always taste bitter," his mother's voice counseled him inside his head.

When had she said it to him? He couldn't recall the occasion, but her Jewish wisdom was always at the back of his mind. How could it not be when she had implanted it there? And a Jew who disgraced his family doubly, with a divorce and remarriage to a Gentile, would know no peace at all. It was this that was stopping him from taking Mary in his arms and saying he'd never give her up again. Keeping him chained and manacled, like he'd been since the day he was born a Sandberg.

"Poor Nathan," Mary said, studying his beaten expression. "We don't stand an earthly, do we? We never did and I'm as sorry for you as I am for me."

Nathan felt her lips brush his fleetingly, like the wings of a passing butterfly, and was filled with an aching sadness because it epitomized what she had represented in his life. A transient glimpse of happiness that had colored the grayness of his days.

"Let's just wish each other well," she said with tears in her eyes. "And stay friends."

He watched her walk away from him across the courtyard. God had not destined him to be happy and there was nothing he could do about it.

Chapter Fourteen

On VE Day, Sarah sat in the porch with Sigmund, watching Abraham weed the garden.

"Everyone is celebrating, people are dancing in the streets, but my husband has to make himself busy," she said with a tolerant smile. She could hear his chest wheezing, though he was working a yard or two away from her, and wanted to tell him to rest. But it would be contrary to her decision to allow him to do as he pleased. She had hidden her anxiety since then and must continue to do so.

"While a person's busy, they don't have time to brood," Sigmund declared with a heavy sigh. "To have peace again in Europe is God's blessing. But why did He let there be a war?"

Sarah knew he was thinking if there hadn't been one, the family would not have lost Martin. But because of the war she was to be a great-grandmother. To a child who would not be Jewish. Arnold wouldn't have met the girl who was now his wife if he hadn't left home to join the Navy.

She took his letter from her skirt pocket to show it to Sigmund whilst her husband's attention was occupied by some stubborn nettles beside the gate. Abraham had ordered her to burn it.

"You've told Esther?" Sigmund inquired after he had read it. Apart from a curt note to his father announcing his marriage, this was Arnold's first communication with his elders since his defection.

"To her I daren't even mention his name. Ben I told." Hurt though he was, Ben did not pretend his younger son was dead, the way Esther did. "Maybe Arnold chose me to tell this news to because I'm only his grandmother, so he thinks I'll be upset once removed," Sarah conjectured. "And it's right he should let us know," she added. "We're still his family."

Sigmund was studying the snapshot Arnold had enclosed with his letter. "He wants us to know what a good-looking wife he's got, also."

Sarah glanced at the patrician features and long, dark hair. But she had already committed her Christian granddaughter-in-law's face to memory. It had kept her awake the whole of last night.

"In a crowd, she could even pass for Jewish," Sigmund said. "And even if she couldn't, why not write and tell Arnold she should be *megyah*, before the child is born?"

"Conversion is just on the outside," Sarah answered. "It doesn't change the person's blood. And there wouldn't be time for her conversion between now and the baby's birth. You're forgetting how much a convert has to learn, Sigmund, and how long it takes to reach the standard required by the rabbis." Sarah replaced the envelope in her pocket just in time to avoid Abraham seeing it. It was probably to work off his feelings about Arnold's news that he had spent the day toiling in the garden.

"Even so, you should suggest the girl converts and the child also," Sigmund declared. "Then afterwards Esther will have no excuse to keep Arnold cut off from the family."

Sarah sighed. "You think I haven't thought of that? But I wouldn't dream of suggesting it, Sigmund. And for a very good reason. How would I like it if her grandmother asked Arnold to become a Christian?"

"With that I can't argue." Sigmund opened the copy of Proust's *Time Regained* he had on his lap and left Sarah to her thoughts.

She knew he could not see the print in the fading light and was using the book as an excuse to lose himself in his own. We're three old people already, Sigmund and Abraham and me, she mused, drawing her shawl closer around her. It had been a warm day, but in the evenings she always felt cold. But what else could a woman of sixty-six expect? Even one who in some ways still felt young. Though her bones sometimes ached with weariness when she lay in bed, she had not lost her zest for life, or forgotten the painful longings that went with youth. The way being in love could cancel everything else out.

As her husband must have done, or how could he be so hard about Arnold? She didn't expect Abraham to accept their grandson's *shiksah* wife, nor could she do so herself. But to behave as if the boy had never existed? And to forbid Sarah to keep in touch with him, even? The great-grandchild would be the seed of their seed. Nothing could change that, whether they accepted it or not.

"We don't have to draw the curtains any more," Abraham called, collecting his gardening tools together to return them to the shed at the back of the house.

Sarah emerged from her distressing cogitations. The blackout had been relaxed to a less stringent "dim-out" for some weeks, but now even that would not be necessary. "The Japs don't travel this far," she smiled. No matter what your worries were, there was always something to be thankful for. But those families whose boys were fighting the Japanese would not be rejoicing tonight, with the lives of their loved ones still in jeopardy. Nothing could prevent her own from coming back, now. Except for the two casualties the family had suffered—and Arnold was only a moral one—everything was as before.

Sigmund closed his book and gazed apprehensively at a pinpoint of light that was hurtling through the gathering dark, against the sky. "You think the Japs have maybe invented a long-distance, lit-up buzz-bomb? That doesn't buzz?"

Sarah laughed. "You've forgotten what a shooting star looks like?" Her expression grew pensive. "What a world we've been living in these past few years, that even a beautiful thing like a star we can now mistake for an instrument of destruction. It will take some getting used to that for us the war is over."

PART THREE

Cords and Discords

Chapter One

The family stood huddled together watching the *Britannic* sail away, oblivious to the cold March wind gusting around them. It was Sarah's first visit to Liverpool Docks, but she would remember it for more than that reason. She could feel David and Nathan gripping her arms. Esther was holding onto Abraham. Did they think their elderly parents would capsize under the strain of this painful parting? She glanced at her husband's set expression and knew her own was the same. The years had schooled them both to withstand anything.

In her mind's eye, she could still see Sammy waving goodbye from the deckrail, a tall and handsome figure with more red than gray in his hair, despite the knocks life had meted out to him. Looking up at him, she had been struck by his resemblance to his father when Abraham was in his late forties. Their characters were alike, also. Kind and gentle. Which went hand in hand with their lack of drive. Lacking the strength to be master of their own household, too.

Whilst Martin was alive, Miriam had been too wrapped up in him to divert her attention to Sammy. But Sarah had always known she was capable of ruling him and this had now been proved so.

Miriam had not waved farewell, but had stood erect and unsmiling beside her husband, gazing down at the family group. As if she wanted to imprint the picture on her mind. This had brought home to Sarah that they might never see each other again. She would not forget the moment, either. Her son clad in a brown overcoat, with a yellow scarf around his neck. Her daughter-in-law wearing the elegant, gray suit Sigmund had made for her. He had sewn every stitch with a heavy heart, he'd told Sarah, but had wanted his daughter to look as fashionable as the American ladies when she walked down Fifth Avenue.

"We may as well push off. They've gone now," Ronald said from behind her. His tone was gruff and had a note of finality that jolted the others from their thoughts.

The pier had lost its bustling excitement. Most of those who had come to see passengers off had already left and the porters were stacking empty luggage-trolleys near the entrance to the customs hall. But the family had lingered on in the lonely aftermath that hangs in the air when an ocean liner has departed, unable quite to believe what they were doing there.

Miriam and Sammy's emigration to the States had assumed a dreamlike quality from the time it was first mentioned at a Sabbath tea party. Possibly because it seemed to be happening for no reason. Sammy had a good job with David. They owned their home and everyone who meant anything to them was in England. Their only child's grave was in Manchester. To begin again in their middle years in a new country, when they did not have to, appeared inexplicable. And Miriam had made it more so by refusing to discuss it.

Even David, who had booked their one-way tickets, and telephoned Malka Berkowitz's cousin Chavah in New York to ask her to meet the ship at the other end, had not thought they would go through with it and was stunned by the fact that they had. You did not leave your whole family and your home country just to escape from everything that reminded you that you had once had a son. This was Sammy's private explanation to his brothers, but it did not satisfy David.

He thought about it again as they left the pier. And tried not to think about what Miriam had said after kissing everyone goodbye except himself, which had felt like a parting stab in the back.

"Why did they have to do it?" Helga demanded.

She had never gained weight, and her petite appearance and small round face and kept her looking youthful. Today she looked like a bewildered old woman and it seemed incongruous to see her trudging along holding her father's hand.

Sigmund eyed her anxiously. "All I need is for you to go to pieces on me." Helga had been his support along the craggy path his life had been since her dead mother became an invalid. She was not one to show her feelings and it was a shock to find her unable to contain them now.

"I'll never forgive Miriam for leaving us," Helga declared tremulously. Then she pulled herself together, as if the resolve had given her strength to do so. "Let's hurry up and get out of this wind," she said, quickening her pace. "I'll just have to get used to not having Miriam and Sammy around. But the whole thing will always be a mystery to me."

Ben shrugged his agreement as he shepherded Esther, weeping copiously, towards the car park.

Leona was walking between the Moritz twins, her emerald coat and hair strident as a bird of paradise in the drab, dockside surroundings. "Maybe they won't like America and then they'll come back, Auntie Helga," she said hopefully. "It's awful for me, too. Uncle Sammy was my favorite uncle."

David tried not to feel slighted. Leona had not realized he was in earshot, or she wouldn't have said it, but that didn't soothe away its effect. What was it about him that didn't endear him to the younger generation? Since his revealing talk with Arnold, he'd noticed that Leona and the twins seemed to be wary of him. Probably they always had been and the young adults in the family, too, but he had mistaken wariness for respect.

His two-year-old granddaughter was trying to leap from Peter's arms to his.

"Lawa want to go Gwandpa!" she piped. Shirley had not allowed her to call her grandparents Zaidie and Bobbie.

David stroked her ginger curls and was rewarded with a gurgling kiss. Here was one child who loved him!

"Grandpa'll come and help to bath you, pet," Shirley told her.

"Pwomise?"

"Don't I always on a Sunday, Laura darling?" David smiled. It was a treat to which he looked forward all week.

Shirley was trying to make her ocelot swagger coat meet across her pregnant stomach. "It's a date, Dad."

"That's how they talk in America," Leona said mournfully.

"Do stop behaving as if you're at a wake, Leona," Henry rebuked her.

"And what is a wake?" Abraham inquired in a tetchy voice. "I never heard of it."

"How could you, when you never learned to read English," Sigmund interceded. "Me, I found out what it means from James Joyce."

"In 1905, when we first met, he made me feel like an ig-

noramus," Abraham snorted. "And now in 1947 he's still trying to do it! So who is this Mr. Joyce? He's Jewish?"

"Oy vay," Sigmund groaned.

"The way people are changing their names, nowadays,
you can never tell."

"He's an Irish novelist," Henry, who had begun dipping
into his grandfather's library at the age when other children
read fairy tales, supplied.

Abraham coughed up some phlegm and transferred it to
his handkerchief. "I should know from Irish novelists, when I
don't even know from English ones!"

"And a wake is a gathering the Irish have after a funeral," Henry explained.

"Bridie's never mentioned it, but I suppose it's their way
of sitting *Shivah*," Leona surmised.

Henry smiled at her patronizingly. "Why do you put a
Jewish interpretation on everything?"

"Probably because I'm Jewish," Leona replied with a
withering glance.

"But you don't have to let it color all your thoughts.
And also there's no need to relegate our departed relatives to
the past tense as you've been doing."

"What is Henry talking about?" Sarah asked hoping he
was not speaking ill of the dead.

Henry had a vocabulary and assurance beyond his years
and the family had already marked him out as a future bar-
rister. He gave Sarah the special smile he reserved for his
elderly relations. "Ever since the ship sailed, Leona's been
using the word 'was' when she refers to Auntie Miriam or
Uncle Sammy. Unless it hits an iceberg crossing the Atlantic—and I don't see how it could in March—they're on their
way to New York harbor, not the gates of Heaven."

Leona retaliated with barbed sweetness. "If only it were
you who'd gone forever, Henry. Then I'd be jumping for joy
instead of dragging my feet in sorrow."

If the family's ideas for girls had included the profes-
sions, they would doubtless have cast her in the role of future
advocate, too. The fist-fights and hair-pulling that had once
characterized her relationship with Henry had been super-
seded by lengthy, verbal duels as they grew older and sometimes, at Sarah's tea parties, everyone would sit with bated
breath to see which of them would win.

Frank put himself between them to stop them from glaring at each other. "Pack it in, you two," he said with a long-suffering sigh. He seemed to have been saying it to them all his life.

"I'll ride with Sarah and Abraham, in David's car, like I did coming," Sigmund told his branch of the family when they reached their vehicles.

Henry winked at Hannah. "Zaidie doesn't approve of women drivers."

"Which man does? But if we waited for a male one, the Mortitzes'd go everywhere on foot," Hannah chuckled, settling herself behind the wheel of their secondhand Ford. "Until you and Frank are old enough to chauffeur us."

"We're the only lads in our class whose father doesn't drive," Frank grinned.

Henry chased after his Manchester Grammar School cap, which a gust of wind had carried off, and returned with his fair hair awry. "Won't is the correct word, isn't it, Dad?"

Carl smiled at them mildly. "It wouldn't be safe. I'm too absentminded."

"That's been your excuse for all things all the years I've known you," Hannah said, patting his cheek affectionately as he got in beside her.

Sarah had listened to their comfortable chatter whilst she waited for David to unlock his car doors. But her thoughts were still with Sammy and Miriam setting forth to a new life. Would they have uprooted themselves if they'd shared the kind of contentment Hannah and Carl did? Since Martin's death, Miriam had been beset by restlessness, lashing out at Sammy as she had never done previously. And Sarah had no reason to suppose a different environment would change this. What was ailing Miriam came from within and would go with her wherever she went.

"Tuck the car blanket around Mother and Father's knees," David said to Bessie as they set off for home.

"What about mine?"

"The blanket is big enough for all three of us," Abraham said. "And if it wasn't, you could have my share, Bessie."

She smiled sourly. "But David isn't worried about me being warm enough, is he?"

"I don't have to be. I bought you a mink coat."

Bessie wrapped it closer around herself and clutched at her hair as the breeze from David's window blew upon it.

"All the time we were out in that wind I wore a scarf on my head to keep my hairset nice and the minute I get in the car my husband gets it blown all over the place!"

"You should've kept the scarf on."

"Wind your window up and I won't have to."

David obeyed her command, but Sarah saw his shoulders tense and knew he had bitten back a sharp retort. Nathan didn't bother controlling his feelings, he said whatever came into his head when Rebecca angered him. Most of their conversation sounded like bickering. Sarah often felt like telling them to stop it, but had learned it was wiser to hold her tongue—that a mother could intercede in matters affecting the whole family, but not in her married children's personal squabbles. Why did they have to squabble? Even Esther and Ben, whom she had once considered an ideal couple, weren't above being sharp with each other these days.

David was leading the six-vehicle convoy and Sarah glanced through the rear window to make sure nobody had been left behind. Even her grandsons had their own cars, though Ronald was still a student. Harry's was a big, two-tone one and Ronald's a little red sports model, his twenty-first birthday present from David. David had bought Peter and Shirley their car for a wedding gift—their house near Heaton Park, too, when Peter was demobilized from the Services.

But would all the luxuries the young people had acquired help them to be happy? Sarah had begun to doubt it. Harry had worn a worried expression since he'd married Dr. Smolensky's daughter, Ann, who was also Yankel Cohen the furrier's grandchild. Probably because he had to keep her in the style her wealthy family had. And Shirley always seemed to be criticizing Peter, telling him to take a leaf out of his father-in-law's book, as if she expected him to acquire David's business acumen overnight. Perhaps she didn't know how her dad had struggled. That getting where he was now had taken years and years.

"What a nerve, overtaking our Jag in that old tin can!" Bessie exclaimed, cutting into Sarah's reflections.

Hannah had just honked her horn and shot past them in a cloud of foul-smelling smoke issuing from her vehicle's exhaust pipe.

Money the Moritzes didn't have, yet they were more carefree by far than her own brood, Sarah reflected.

Bessie launched into another spate of nagging that confirmed the thought.

"Must we go to that meeting tonight, David?"

"You don't mind enjoying yourself at the ladies' coffee mornings, do you?"

"We raise funds for Palestine by holding them, don't we? So don't try to make out I'm not doing my bit!"

"There's more to being a Zionist than just raising funds," David said vehemently. "We've got to raise our voices, too. Where it counts, with what's going on at present."

Abraham shuddered. "When I think of those poor refugees from the concentration camps not being allowed in there—as if they haven't suffered enough."

"Turning away their boats, even," Sigmund said with feeling. "Where does the British Government expect them to go?"

"They don't give a damn," David answered. "They're not keen on letting many into England, either."

"If England had had this Government forty-odd years ago, the Sandbergs would be pushing up Russian daisies now," Sarah said to Abraham.

"So go and argue with them, David," Bessie said sourly. "A big shot like you I'm sure they'll listen to!"

David ignored her sarcasm. "The Jewish Board of Deputies is doing so."

"In that case we don't need to ruin our evenings going to meetings," she snapped, returning to her original point.

"You don't have to come with me."

"Maybe you'd rather I didn't."

Sarah shut her mind to the words they were flinging at each other. Their quarrel had turned full circle and had now begun on a different tack, as her children's quarrels with their spouses invariably did. Usually, they were rowing about something completely different by the time they had finished. What was the matter with them all? She could no longer pretend to herself that any of them had harmonious marriages.

"All right, Mother?" David asked, catching sight of her expression in the mirror.

"Sure." How could she be all right? With one of her sons on his way to what seemed like another world. And the discord that had surrounded her the whole afternoon. When she and Abraham arrived in Manchester with their young family and journeyed to Strangeways by horse-and-cart, they had not known what was in store for them. The material comfort that was their children's today they couldn't have even dreamed of. But what had it brought with it?

Bessie stopped nagging David and noticed her mother-in-law's pensive silence. "A penny for your thoughts, Ma?"

Sarah kept them to herself and laced her fingers through Abraham's as she had that long-ago evening in the jogging cart. They had always been happy together. Even when a penny was all they'd had.

Chapter Two

David was the first to receive a letter from New York. It arrived on a Saturday morning, which allowed him to peruse it whilst eating a leisurely breakfast.

"If you're going to look like that every time you hear from Sammy, I hope he won't write often," Bessie said through a mouthful of toast and marmalade.

The letter was full of spelling errors and ink blots, penned in the same childish scrawl that had been the despair of his brother's schoolteachers and aroused the rueful tenderness in David that Sammy himself always had. "How do I look?" he replied.

"As if you're not sure whether to laugh or cry," Bessie told him disgustedly.

This summed up David's feelings and he smiled sheepishly. "I've never had a letter from Sammy before."

"He's never needed to write to you. All his life you've carried him on your back."

David ignored the jibe. "Want to read it?"

"What for? I can imagine what's in it. *Dear David, please send me some cash until I get on my feet.* Which he never will! But you'd be daft to send them a ha'penny after what that ungrateful bitch, Miriam, said to you before they left."

David sipped his tea and remained silent. The whole family had heard Miriam's parting words to him and he'd been aware of them trying to hide their shock. Nobody had mentioned it afterwards except his wife. But he would have been amazed if she hadn't.

"How dare she say Sammy'll be able to be himself, once he's away from you? Instead of what you've made him into?" Bessie demanded. "Without you he'd've been nothing," she declaimed.

David maintained his silence. To Bessie, Miriam's words had been a vindication for her own years of begging him to stop carrying his brother. She had said so at length the moment they were alone on the day Miriam and Sammy departed, but had not mentioned it again. Which was contrary to her harping nature.

"He'd have been nothing and she'd have had nothing," Bessie said adamantly.

He watched her pick up her tea cup, her little finger gracefully crooked as she gripped the fine, Minton china handle. This was one of the affectations she had acquired over the years. David didn't remember his Christian schoolpal Jim Forrest's mother doing that when she drank her tea; but when you were born to the social graces there was no need to show people you had acquired them, he thought wryly.

His wife was wearing a quilted-satin housecoat and he glanced down at his maroon silk dressing gown. Once, he hadn't owned a dressing gown, let alone one like this. Who had known from such inessentials in the Strangeways ghetto? You put on your overcoat if you needed to visit the lavatory in the backyard in the middle of the night—if you owned an overcoat, and there'd been times when he hadn't.

Lately, he had found himself comparing the lifestyle he had now with the nothing he'd had then. But when you'd come up in the world, how could you take things for granted? It was probably only those who'd always had them who did.

"Me, I'm glad to see the back of those two," Bessie said, glancing at Sammy's letter. "Miriam always was a trouble-maker," she added, avoiding David's eye.

And her old enemy was now safely out of the way, David thought. That was why she had not harped about Miriam's ingratitude, he realized with a flash of insight. She had not wanted to keep reminding him about her. Oh, the craftiness of women!

The last time Bessie had revealed her fear that he would one day desert her for his still-beautiful first love was when one of Lou Benjamin's brothers left his wife and children, to run away with a widow, during the war. For weeks afterwards, Bessie had watched David like a hawk whenever they were in Miriam's company. As if Mottie Benjamin's infidelity had made her realize that even among Jews such things could happen.

What a fool you are, Bessie, David wanted to tell her. But he knew from experience it was wiser to hold his tongue. Only once had she ever expressed her insecurity in words. It had been while she was pregnant with their first child and he had promised her then that he would never leave her. Their baby boy was born dead and David's home life had been hell for months. His mother had eventually set things right. Somehow, she'd lifted Bessie out of the trauma into which she had sunk and ejected the bossy aunt whose presence in his household had had the opposite effect. This had been the unhappiest period of David's marriage. And he'd known plenty of them! But it had never once occurred to him to walk out on Bessie. You got married for better or worse; and now, he had his children and grandchild to comfort him.

"Put the damn letter away!" Bessie exclaimed. "I can't bear the sight of it."

David smiled at the smear of marmalade on her chin. Why did he always care for her most when she seemed ridiculous and vulnerable? And how many times had he asked himself that question over the years?

"Be careful, you'll make me spill the tea," she said characteristically when he got up and went to kiss her.

Even the mishaps which had not yet occurred were his fault, not hers! "You're a real case, aren't you, love?" he laughed.

"Who wouldn't be? Married to you?" Bessie watched him return to his chair. "So what did the letter say?"

He'd wondered when curiosity would get the better of her. "Not what you imagined. Sammy's got a job."

"He won't have when they find out what he's like."

"Doing what he's always wanted to, he says," David conveyed, letting her cutting comment pass and trying to pretend to himself that his brother's revelation was not hurtful.

He had always thought Sammy would be lost without him. "Harold Bronley's taken him on at his furniture factory. In the antique reproduction department where they do hand-carving."

"Who's Harold Bronley?"

"Ivor Bronley's brother."

"I'm no wiser now," Bessie said impatiently.

David poured himself some more tea and carried it to the window seat. "They were Hymie and Isaiah Bronsky when I knew them," he said, surveying the shrubbery separating his side-garden from the one next door. "But that was a long time ago, when we were all kids. They were staying at the Berkowitzes' with their parents when we arrived from Russia. Chavah, who I rang up, is their mother." David smiled reminiscently. "They left for New York the next day and all I can remember about them is their clothes were even shabbier than mine. But it seems they've done very well for themselves."

"You haven't?"

"Sure. But I'm not in their league yet and I shouldn't think I ever will be. Sammy says Harold employs three hundred workers in his factory. And Ivor—you won't believe this—is a Hollywood film producer, no less! That scruffy little kid who sat on his mother's lap at the table that night, dipping his fingers in her soup."

"America's the place to get on," Bessie declared.

"A person can do all right here, too."

"If they've got what it takes. So don't expect your brother to ever be more than a worker."

"All our Sammy ever wanted was to be happy," David answered. "But I don't think he's even been that," he said pensively. "I hope to God he will be from now on."

"It's up to him, isn't it?"

No, David thought with a poignant smile. Happiness was a fragile, fleeting thing, whisked away and destroyed by other people. "What would you like to do this morning, love?" he asked, collecting himself.

"You can come and help me choose a new hat to wear for our grandson's *Brith*."

Shirley's second child was due shortly and Bessie was certain, from her daughter's shape, that she was carrying a boy.

"You women and your old wives' tales," David teased

her. But his mother and sister had made the same prediction and he hoped they were right.

"I think Harry's wife'll have a lad, as well," Bessie said. "Last week at the tea party, I noticed she was carrying all at the front, too."

David laughed. "In that case we might bump into Dr. Smolensky buying Naomi a hat for their grandson's *Brith*."

Kendal Milne's was crowded with Saturday morning shoppers, many of whom were Jewish.

"Once, we'd all have been in *shul*," David reflected to Bessie whilst she tried on a pair of lilac kid gloves to match her purchase from the model millinery department.

"So nobody's frightened of God punishing them any more," Bessie shrugged.

David felt a pang of conscience. "Most people are too busy to even think of Him."

Bessie handed the gloves to the trim saleswoman. "I'll take these, thank you."

"Yes, modom."

"And you should talk" she rebuked David when the girl went away to wrap the gloves. "This is the first Saturday I've ever known you have off work, except when one of the family's been called up for a *mitzvah* in *shul*. Tell me who's busier than you are?"

David had sent Moishe Lipkin to the continent to try to interest buyers in the new Sanderstyle line, or he would have been in his office this morning for their usual weekly sales conference. Despite her pregnancy, Shirley had insisted on designing a selection of garments she hoped would initiate export trade and had personally supervised the making of the samples.

"Your daughter isn't too pleased about Peter doing Moishe's English traveling while he's abroad," Bessie said, when they were walking along Deansgate, laden with parcels. She had been unable to resist buying two romper suits for the possible grandson and some dresses for little Laura.

David had bought his mother a cardigan and his father a tie. He rarely went shopping in town and his parents never did. "Shirley isn't alone in the house at night," he replied, juggling Bessie's hatbox from one hand to the other.

"I wouldn't call having Lizzie sleeping there the same as her husband's company," Bessie retorted.

"We have to do what's best for the business. And that includes Shirley and Peter, as they're part of it."

"Shirley cares about the business as much as you do, David."

"That, you don't have to tell me. But she must be prepared to make some personal sacrifices if necessary, too. If I hadn't been prepared to, there'd have been no Sanderstyle." David caught a glimpse of his reflection in a shop window and vowed not to eat any *knedlach* at dinner today. Where had his waistline gone to? "If things click abroad we'll take someone on to handle the foreign trade," he promised Bessie. "Then Peter won't need to travel any more. Moishe'll be back in his old job."

"But the while, you're not being fair to your pregnant daughter."

David controlled his irritation. He'd move heaven and earth for Shirley! But when it came to business, he had to be firm. Sanderstyle's progress was for her benefit as well as his. One day, she and Peter would own it.

He had to be firm with himself occasionally, too. When the sun was shining and he felt like being out in the fresh air, instead of cooped up in the factory. There were times when he felt that if he didn't get a break from work, he'd crack up, and on one occasion he had made up his mind to leave his office and play a round of golf. But his accountant had rung up, while he was putting on his coat, to remind him the audit was due. Golf in the middle of the afternoon, with all he had on his mind? he had thought. And that had been that.

But it was the same for every businessman, he reflected. And there were plenty who didn't survive the strain; lately his contemporaries seemed to have been going down like ninepins. Was it catching sight of his portly figure that had set his mind on this track? Only last week he had attended the funeral of a man his age, who'd dropped dead in his warehouse. Hugo Frankl had been at the graveside, too. "A lot of good his bank balance'll do him now," Hugo had sighed when they were getting into their cars to rush back to their businesses.

This was not the first such reminder David had had that he was a candidate for an early burial. Each time he was reminded, he resolved to take things easier, but putting the resolve into practice was not in his nature. The dynamo inside him, which his father said had always been there, would not let him slacken his pace on the treadmill he had created for himself.

In a way, he was a prisoner of his boyhood dreams, too. When weariness overtook him, he would hear an inner voice telling him he had come too far to stop now. How could he stop when he was well on the road to making his dreams into a reality?

"You're very quiet all of a sudden," Bessie remarked while they were picking their way through the vehicles in the car park.

"I was thinking about what it will be like when we move to Cheshire and live in a mansion."

"You're crackers, wanting to live there!" Bessie, who did not want to, exclaimed. "They don't even let Jews join the golf clubs."

"So let them not," David retorted, though the bar was hurtful and not peculiar to Cheshire. Barring Jews from golf clubs was the last bastion of anti-Semitism in England and he'd heard it was the same in the States. But it had not prevented him from playing golf, or limited him to the public course at Heaton Park, where he had learned to play. The Jews had their own club, in Whitefield. Like those in London and the rest of the provinces, it had a thriving membership and David had joined last year.

Sometimes he saw Gentiles playing there, invited by Jewish friends, and membership was open to them if they cared to apply for it. It was not the club's policy to practice against others the humiliation inflicted upon Jews.

A few of David's acquaintances had already migrated to Cheshire. Leo and Otto Rosenthal, with whom he had attended the Jews' School, were among them. Their wives had not wanted to move away from their own community, but the Rosenthal brothers had built up one of the biggest textile houses in the north and intended to live accordingly.

Me, too, when the time comes, David thought, speeding homeward along Bury Old Road, past those of his brethren still sufficiently devout to be walking home from *shul*. What was the use of success if you didn't show people you had achieved it? That you'd done so in spite of the hurdles that life had set you. And when he had his Cheshire mansion, he would drive to Whitefield for his Sunday morning golf, like the Rosenthals did. And thumb his nose—mentally—at the *goyim*, no wealthier than himself, who wouldn't let him join their club.

"Pass the chopped liver to Daddy, Leona," Rebecca said whilst removing her napkin from its silver ring.

Leona picked up the heavy crystal dish and placed it within her father's reach. He was seated with his back to the window, at the head of the refectory table. Her mother sat at the foot and in a minute Leona would have to repeat the passing process in the opposite direction, after which Mummy would return the dish to her. Their food was always served in that order. Her father first, to show respect for him. Then her mother and last, herself. It had been that way ever since she was old enough to join her parents in the dining room, so why did it suddenly seem ridiculous? Because her mother had no respect for her father.

The realization had dawned on Leona gradually, as a lot of other things about her parents had. When had she begun noticing they never seemed comfortable together, like married people usually did? Instead, there was always something she couldn't define crackling in the air between them. And since Daddy's return from the army it had gotten worse: they now no longer shared the same bedroom.

Mummy had said this was because she didn't want to be disturbed by the phone when Daddy was called out to patients during the night, which had seemed sensible to Leona at the time. But that was before she had begun having her periods and her father had a private chat with her.

He hadn't said what her mother had: that it was a pity she had to start being a woman when she was only eleven. Instead, he'd told her exactly what the changes in her body meant. And how babies were made, which had been a shock. You couldn't imagine your parents doing something so disgusting and yourself being born because of it. But her father had said that when she got married she wouldn't think it disgusting. That it was Nature's way of letting a man and a woman express their love for each other and children were the natural consequences of it.

The night Daddy told her, she'd lain awake turning over in her mind everything he had said. Thinking how lucky she was to be a doctor's daughter and have the mysterious Facts of Life explained to her. It wasn't until later that she stopped relating the information to herself and connected it with her parents not sharing a bedroom.

"Stop daydreaming and get on with your meal," her mother said to her.

Leona ate a little of her chopped liver, though she was not hungry, and slid the dish to her father, who usually had a second helping. Why had they bought such a long table when they got married if they were only going to have one child? Because they hadn't known then that they were going to fall out of love and stop doing what you had to do to make babies. How frightening it was to know you couldn't be certain that loving someone would last.

There was a Christian girl at school whose parents were divorced, but Leona had never met any Jewish children to whom this had happened. Was it going to happen to her? Lucy Jameson lived with her mother and only saw her father on a Sunday.

She looked at her own father. His hair was streaked with silver at the temple, though he wasn't yet forty. How handsome he was and how dear to her. Her mother was, too. Lila Benjamin envied her her good-looking parents, but she didn't have to live with them. With no brothers or sisters to share the ordeal. Be their monkey-in-the-middle, the one who passed them things at mealtimes and was the subject of their conversation at all times.

This was how Leona felt when the three of them were together. When had she last heard them say a word to each other that wasn't concerning herself? It was as if they'd run out of other things to talk about. And all too often their discussions ended in a blazing row.

Bridie brought in the soup, her bustling entrance cutting into Leona's thoughts.

"There's *kreplach* t'day, peteen, as well as *lokshen*," she said, giving Leona the special smile she always had for her. "Oi'm a dab-hand at 'em if Oi sez so meself."

Nathan laughed. "I'm thinking of entering you for a Jewish cookery competition, Bridie!"

"Compliments from himself Oi'm gettin'."

"You deserve them," Rebecca declared.

Bridie straightened her cap and beamed. "Whin it comes t'me *kreplach*, Oi do indeed, Mrs. Sandberg. Bobbie Sarah, whin she came fer dinner, did whisper in me ear moine're noicer than Lizzie Wilson's. But Oi've got t'admit Lizzie's comes a close second," she added, departing to her kitchen with a rustle of her starched apron.

A faint odor of carbolic soap, which Leona also associated with her, lingered in the room. Dear, lovely Bridie. She was as familiar as the silver tureen from which Mummy was ladling the chicken soup. And the mellow, oak-paneled walls that matched the furniture and gave the dining room an air of coziness, despite its largeness. Like everything in the house, Bridie had always been there. So had the special little touches Leona's mother gave to their home. Leona could not recall a single meal when there hadn't been some kind of table decoration. In spring and summer, the centerpiece was flowers from the garden—sometimes just a single rose, or a fat rhododendron spilling its leaves over the edge of the vase. When the garden was empty of flowers and blossom, her mother would arrange some laurel in a crystal witch-bowl that caught the light from the chandelier and sparkled in a host of iridescent colors.

But it was only the room that was cozy, not the people in it. None of Leona's aunts took the trouble to do everything beautifully, even when it wasn't *Yom Tov* or *Shabbos*, like Mummy did. Nor did her grandmother. But mealtimes in their houses were much more enjoyable than they were here.

"You're very quiet today, Leona," her mother remarked.

"It's because she finished all her homework last night, so she's got the weekend free, isn't it, darling?" her mother smiled to her.

Her father was smiling at her, too. Why couldn't they smile at each other? If Bridie and herself didn't live here, they'd forget how to. Damn them!

"Stop frowning, love," her mother said.

But Leona could not. It was terrible to think like this about your parents, but how could she help it? Separately, she adored them. Together, they sometimes made her feel she was about to explode.

"Don't tell Bobbie and Zaidie I let you do homework after the *Shabbos* candles were lit," her mother advised. "Or there'll be hell to pay."

"She had my permission, too," her father said.

Even when referring to things they had done jointly, they rarely used the word "we," Leona thought resentfully.

"And I don't agree that she shouldn't tell my mother and father, Rebecca," he added curtly.

"Is that so, Nat?"

Other people's parents called each other "dear," or "love," or "darling." Hers could barely manage to be civil to each other. No, it was worse than that. They were staring venomously along the length of the table. If looks could kill, they'd both be dead.

"I won't have my daughter brought up to tell lies," she heard her father say, but did not remove her gaze from the cruet set, which was where it had settled. "Or even to hide the truth," he added.

Her mother laughed, but it was not a pleasant sound. "What people don't know can't hurt them."

Something in her mother's voice compelled Leona to raise her head. She saw her father avert his eyes and crumble a bit of bread on his side-plate. Had he done something terrible that her mother had found out about? He must have done, or why couldn't he look Mummy in the eye?

"Nor do I want Leona to be a hypocrite," he said after a silence. "Pretending to accept one set of standards and living by another, whether it concerns religion or anything else. She's old enough to begin making choices and once she's made them she must have the courage of her convictions."

Leona saw her mother's shoulders quiver.

"If you'd had the courage of yours, Nat, there wouldn't have been a Leona," she said. "Now let's finish our soup, shall we?"

Finish our soup? Leona thought, gazing down at the little meat-filled oblongs of dough floating amid the *lokshen* in the golden liquid. Sit here munching *kreplach* as if what she'd just heard had not been said? "What did you mean by that, Mummy?"

"Nothing. Forget I said it."

"But you did, didn't you?"

"When you're old enough to understand, maybe I'll tell you," her father said quietly and received a contemptuous glance from her mother.

Leona noted his tight-lipped expression. When he'd had the private chat with her, he'd said that although babies were the natural result of lovemaking, there was something called birth control that prevented them from being conceived. "Children can sometimes be born by accident, can't they?" she challenged him. Her voice grew tremulous. "Did Mummy mean you didn't want me?"

He sprang up from his chair and came to kiss her, but she pushed him away.

"Did she, Daddy?"

"That's the most ridiculous question I ever heard," he said, sitting down again. "How could you think such a thing when you know I adore you? It's because I do that I don't want you to fall into the traps I did. And the most dangerous is bending your life to please other people. Once you fall into that trap, you're there for ever. Take it from me."

"I don't know what you're talking about, Daddy."

"But one day you will," he told her with a twisted smile. "And even if you end up happily toeing the line, I want you to be the kind of person who isn't intolerant of those who don't."

"She's my daughter, too," her mother said sharply. "And I don't happen to agree with the selfish philosophy you're preaching."

"Think what we'd both have been saved if I'd practiced it myself!"

They were glaring malevolently at each other again. Leona dropped her spoon into her soup with an angry plop.

"Why don't you stop doing this to me?"

"What are we doing to you, love?" her mother said, putting on her maternal smile.

Her father's face was now wearing his paternal one.

"Making me wish I was anyone's daughter but yours!" Leona exploded.

They both looked so surprised she had to laugh, because it seemed absurd that they should be. Then her laughter became tears, and she fled to the kitchen and Bridie's comforting arms.

David and Bessie were the first to arrive at the *Shabbos* gathering. They found Sarah's neighbor laying a fire in the parlor.

Sarah was hovering apologetically beside her. "It was so warm and sunny this morning, I didn't think we'd need one, Mrs. Evans. I'm sorry to make you dirty your hands when you've got on your nice afternoon frock."

"You know I don't mind obliging you, Mrs. Sandberg."

"It's very good of you."

Mrs. Evans was trying to coax the flames to stay alight when Nathan and Rebecca arrived.

"Leona's got a bit of a cold," Rebecca said, explaining their daughter's absence.

"No, she hasn't; she just didn't feel like coming," Nathan declared.

"What!" Sarah exclaimed.

"A person doesn't have to be ill to miss one of your tea parties, Mother."

"They don't?" Abraham said uncertainly.

"No, Father."

David eyed Nathan sharply. "You're in a funny mood today, aren't you?"

"Just an honest one." Nathan watched Mrs. Evans trying to draw the reluctant flames with a newspaper, wondering what he was doing here himself if what he had just asserted was so. There were plenty of things he'd rather be doing. And reading, for which he never had time, was one of them. Yet he turned up at his mother's, Saturday after Saturday, as if drawn here by a magnet. "Let me hold the paper in front of the grate," he said to Mrs. Evans. "Why should you have to do it?"

Mrs. Evans's expression had tightened when he spoke bluntly to his parents and now did so again. "Because this is your mother's house, Nat. And she's like me—she doesn't want any sins committed in it."

She eyed Nathan through her owlish spectacles and he noticed that her shoulders were snowed with dandruff as they had always been, though there was never any sign of it on her stringy, gray hair.

"Indeed to goodness, I don't know what my children do in their own homes. They could be knocking back the beer, God-fearing though I brought them up to be. But in my home, bach, they wouldn't dare," she told him.

Nathan blushed. Mrs. Evans was still capable of making him feel like a criminal, the way she had when he and Lou had sometimes sent a ball soaring over her back-garden fence, in their youth.

"You tell him!" Sarah applauded. But what good will it do? she asked herself, glancing through the window to where her two *Shabbos*-breaking sons had parked their cars.

When they'd first begun riding to her tea parties instead of walking, they had shown respect for her, if not for God. Made sure their vehicles were not outside her door. Now, they didn't even do that. They were becoming less Jewish all the time and the sins they committed were like second nature to them. Perhaps it was because the family was becoming more and more English. And the two different influences pointed in opposite ways.

Sarah had begun realizing this a long time ago and accepted that it had to be. Well, about some things, anyway. Once, all God's laws had been on one level to her, none more important than another. And this still applied to the way she lived her own life. But for her children and grandchildren she now had a set of priorities. Some sins she was prepared to turn a blind eye to, thankful that, apart from Arnold, her brood was not committing the ones at the top of her list.

"You're the only woman I know, Ma, who still has a *Shabbos-goy* to see to the fire," Rebecca remarked after Mrs. Evans had gone.

"I could tell you the names of plenty who still do," Sarah retorted.

Rebecca smiled. "And I bet they're all great-grandmothers."

Among Sarah's acquaintances this was largely so and she did not try to deny it. Nor could she hide her contempt as her gaze took in her sons and their wives. Accepting the fact that they ignored many of God's laws did not mean she must pretend that she liked it. "So when my generation is all dead and gone, you and your children can forget there ever was such a thing as *Shabbos-goys* to help Jews respect the Almighty," she flashed. "And your children's children won't have to forget what they've never known."

"Calm down, Mother," Nathan said, placatingly.

Sarah tried to do so, aware that her outburst was contrary to her turning-a-blind-eye policy. But sometimes the things you'd decided in your mind could not quell what you felt in your heart.

"You can't expect people living in the twentieth century to obey rules laid down for wanderers in the Wilderness," Nathan told her. "The way you do, Mother," he added.

"Oy," Abraham sighed. "Today, they call them displaced persons, but it's just a different name. Wanderers in the wilderness is what some of our people still are."

David sat cracking his knuckles, longing for a cigarette, but he still would not dare to smoke here on *Shabbos*. "Father's got a point."

"But it doesn't relate to the one I was making," Nathan replied. "And I intend to join the Reform *Shul* because of it."

"What?" his parents and brother shouted in unison. Then they eyed his wife questioningly.

"Who am I to argue with him?" she shrugged.

"Trust Rebecca to make sure it's on my head, not hers," Nathan said cynically. "Even though the Reform way fits in with her lifestyle."

"Why not change your name to an English one, while you're at it, Nat?" David said coldly. "I'm thinking of doing so myself," he announced. "But not for religious reasons," he added scathingly.

His final sentence was drowned out by a three-cornered outcry.

"On *Shabbos* my sons come here and drop bombshells!" Abraham yelled and was overtaken by a fit of coughing.

"In our old age they want to give us heart attacks!" Sarah joined in. She picked up the Kendal Milne bags David had handed her when he arrived and flung them at him. "Take back the cardigan and the tie! Who wants them?"

"It's absolutely disgusting to even think of changing your name, David!" Nathan declared witheringly.

"Why?" David asked coolly. "The Sandbergs have been in England since the beginning of the century and we're here to stay. So why go on being lumbered with a foreign name, which hasn't exactly been an advantage? English people are suspicious of foreigners."

"It's even more disgusting coming from someone who sees himself as the head of the Sandberg family," Nathan said as if his brother's reasons were of no account.

Sarah saw her husband blanch. Her daughters-in-law were trying not to look at him and her sons busy glowering at each other. David was the head of the family and Nat knew it. But she hadn't known Nat had resented it. He of all people, who wouldn't be Dr. Sandberg if it weren't for David. Her husband had not known it and was sitting with a stricken look in his eyes.

"Apologize to your father and your brother," she ordered Nathan.

"To my father there's no need. I said David sees himself that way, not that I think he is."

Who wouldn't when it's thrust upon them? And they can't remember the time when they weren't burdened with it?

David thought. His brother was riveting him with a frigid stare.

"The head of a family's someone to look up to, David. And lashing out money right, left and center can't buy that."

"Thank you for telling me, Nat."

"I should've had the guts to tell you years ago."

Their old enmity was out in the open again, stalking the room like a living thing. Brothers shouldn't be this way with each other, Sarah wanted to tell them. But they were, and there was nothing she could do about it. She tried to speak, but her tongue seemed momentarily paralyzed.

"I never tried to buy respect in my life," David said tersely.

"And in my case you haven't got it," Nathan replied. "You had once. Until it hit me that what you were after was power. What Miriam said to you before they left was true. You take hold of people's lives and mold them to your own design. With me, you used blackmail to get away with it. With Sammy, you didn't have to, he was yours for the asking."

Sarah stepped forward and slapped Nathan's face, then was consumed by horror at what she had done. Even when he was a child she hadn't raised a finger to him. Not to any of her children and nor had Abraham. It hadn't been necessary. She fingered her brooch agitatedly. "If you don't say you're sorry to David, I'll never forgive you, Nat." How could a mother have any peace of mind with this terrible feeling between two of her sons?

Nathan was stroking his stinging cheek. "There's plenty I'll never forgive, either, Mother."

"Listen, who doesn't feel like that in a family sometimes?" Abraham interceded. He was panting after his coughing spell, his face crumpled with distress. He tried to smile. "But we get over it."

"Do we, Father? Or do we just pretend to? Because of the cords that bind us?" Nathan sat down by the hearth and watched the flames roaring up the chimney, the way he had liked to do when he was a small child and the Sandbergs gathered around the fire in Moreton Street, on winter evenings. How secure he'd felt then—as if nothing outside could harm him. But when he thought back, all the hurts he had suffered had been inflicted from within that cozy circle.

"There comes a time when the cords begin to get a bit frayed," he declared.

"And what causes them to?" David flashed. "Straining against them, that's what. The way you've been doing since you were a lad. Thinking you're entitlted to go your own way and to hell with the rest of us!"

"But you didn't let me, did you, David? Which is what I've been talking about. This to-hell-with-the-rest-of-us stuff you just spouted was what I meant when I said you'd used blackmail." Nathan glanced at Rebecca, to whom his brother and mother had conspired to chain him. "It's too late for some things," he said flatly. "But not for others." He was done with being a Jew who lived by double standards. "From now on, I'll please myself what I do. And that includes joining the Reform *Shul*."

"Oy," Abraham groaned.

"You'll just have to resign yourself to it, Father."

"And to me being called Sanderton instead of Sandberg," David said.

Abraham shared a sorrowful glance with Sarah. "What the years only do to a family."

"Especially a Jewish one," she answered.

"Christians don't need to adapt their religion," Nathan said.

"Or change their name so it won't sound foreign," Bessie put in on David's behalf.

"Plenty of Jews have anglicized their names and it hasn't made them any less Jewish," David declared. "But what Nat's going to do is something else. Me, I'd rather ask God to forgive me for breaking His laws than kid myself I'm not sinning by observing an adapted-for-convenience version of them."

"But you break them for convenience, don't you?" Nathan countered acidly.

Abraham treated them both to a withering glance. "So I'll have one son, a Mr. Sanderton, praying to the Almighty in an orthodox *shul*. And another, who is still called Sandberg, reading in English to whoever it is they pray to at that Reform place! Which of you is disgracing me most, I can't make up my mind."

"What can you do?" Sarah sighed. The answer, as always, was nothing. Two new bones of contention had been flung into the family arena that afternoon. How many more would land there in the name of changing times, before she had lived out her allotted span?

"In Russia this couldn't have happened," she heard her husband declaim.

But worse things could and did, she thought, as she always did when it was necessary to bend with the wind of change. What else but remembrance of past oppression could help her come to terms with the price of freedom? Which was how she had come to think of such painful aspects of the present.

Chapter Three

Marianne sat hunched over her typewriter, awaiting the mental spark that would set her work alight. It had been kindling in her mind when she awoke that morning, but hearing from home had extinguished it. If only Mom's letter hadn't arrived on Saturday, when she had two free days to work on her play. On the other five, she had to earn her bread by writing advertising copy and switching over to her stage characters in the evenings wasn't easy.

She cast a resentful glance at the blue envelope lying on her desk beside the synopsis she had written for Act Two. Her mother's epistles evoked the same guilt as the ones she'd sent when Marianne was in the ATS always had. Only the content was different. Come home, Marianne, we need you. All your old friends are engaged, or married with kids already. Giving their parents *nachas* and how must it look to everyone that you're not?

The Yiddish word, for which there was no English equivalent, embraced the special brand of pride and pleasure combined that Jewish parents hoped to reap from their children and increased Marianne's feeling that she was letting hers down. The "everyone" to whom her mother referred was the closed-in community from which she had fled to London, a month after her release from the Services. She had no regrets about having done so. Only a troubled conscience.

"How's it going?" the man in her life inquired from the scuffed leatherette armchair by the hearth.

And not just about that! Marianne tore the sheet of paper from the typewriter and tossed it into the waste basket. "It isn't."

"You shouldn't have opened that letter until Monday."

"But I did, didn't I, Ralph?"

He got up and came to stand beside her. "In some ways you're like a puppet on a string," he said, stroking her hair absently.

Marianne jerked away from him. "If I was, I wouldn't be here!"

"But they're still able to make you jump and flounder. From all those miles away."

"Who's floundering?" she retorted. "I'm my own boss."

"Then why won't you marry me?"

She watched him return to the chair and fold himself into it. "There's a hole in your pullover sleeve; remind me to sew it up for you. And you know perfectly well why."

Ralph sucked his empty briar pipe for a moment. "But I'll never accept it."

"Why did I have to run into you again?" Marianne exclaimed venting her feelings on him. "If Uncle Joe hadn't been abroad on an assignment when I went to see if he could get me a job on his paper, it wouldn't have happened. And out of all the firms that employment bureau could have sent me to, it had to be the one you work for!"

"Who can argue with Fate?" Ralph shrugged in the Jewish way he had acquired from her. Her moodiness never ruffled him.

Marianne transferred herself restlessly from her chair to the window seat, which was also a storage chest for her towels and linens. "That's what Hannah said when I told her. She blames Fate for everything. I don't, it's too easy. So we crossed each other's path three times, what of it? The second time was entirely due to my carelessness. If I hadn't left Birdie's civvies in your vehicle that day—"

"How *is* Birdie?" Ralph interrupted. "When's her baby due?"

Marianne smiled. "Any minute. She was knitting bootees the last time I phoned her, waiting for Bert to come home for his tea. I can't imagine Birdie living such a staid existence, but perhaps it was the war that made her behave as she did."

"It changed a lot of people," Ralph said pensively.

"Me, for instance. I'd probably have a nice Jewish husband and be living in the avenue next to my parents, just like my cousin Shirley, if being away in the Forces hadn't unsettled me."

"I was thinking of my ex-wife," Ralph said. "A sweeter girl than the one I married would be hard to find. But she got a job at the Stage Door Canteen; the attention showered on her there went to her head. And now she's a GI bride."

Marianne scanned his face. "Does it still hurt when you think about her?"

Ralph laughed abruptly. "Only my pride. That was all that was hurting by the time I met you, sweetheart. The night I returned Birdie's suitcase, I wanted to ask if I could see you again, but I wasn't divorced then. And I had scruples."

"Where are they now?"

Ralph reached for his tobacco pouch, which was on the floor beside his chair. "That was a bit below the belt, wasn't it?" he said, stuffing some of the dark tobacco into his pipe and applying a match to it.

"I didn't mean to say it," Marianne replied after a silence. She fanned away the cloud of aromatic smoke that drifted towards her. "It's my fault we're living in sin, not yours."

Ralph's expression, which had momentarily tightened, relaxed into a grin. "What've you been reading? *Peg's Paper*?"

"Not since I was a kid and my Auntie Bessie's maid, Lizzie, used to bring it with her to my grandmother's on a Saturday. I remember asking her what living in sin meant, but she wouldn't tell me."

"Officially, we're not even doing that. I'm paying rent for a place I hardly use."

"All I need is for my Auntie Rebecca to drop in when she's in London visiting her sister and find your socks hanging up to dry over my sink!"

"That's what I meant about your family pulling strings across the miles, sweetheart. Not just your parents, but all those aunts, uncles and cousins who keep cropping up in your conversation, with your sainted grandmother. To me, they're like those offstage characters who influence the action of a drama more than the ones you see. Like Edward in that play we saw a few weeks ago."

Marianne smiled reminiscently. Seeing *Edward My Son* had been a catalytic occasion for her. Halfway through the evening, she had known she wanted to try writing for the theatre, that the dramatic impact had triggered something off in her creative mind. It had made her set aside the novel on which she had been working and give her attention to learning, through trial and error, the playwright's craft.

But it wasn't easy, she thought now as her eye fell on her mother's letter. How could her imagination be given full rein when she was always being brought down to earth with a bump? And how Ralph put up with the things she sometimes said to relieve her feelings was nothing short of a miracle.

"You'll have to forgive me, love," she said to him impulsively. "When I hear from home, everything comes flooding over me and I start thinking I had no right to get involved with you. That I should have got another job instead of staying where I'd see you every day, then it wouldn't have happened. Instead of which—well, here we are."

Ralph balanced on his lap a rough layout he had brought home from the ad agency studio, and Marianne glanced at his big, capable hands. When she had seen them on the steering wheel the day he drove her to camp from Andover, she wouldn't have thought he was an artist.

"There was something between us at our first encounter, sweetheart," he said as though he had been reading her mind.

Marianne watched him accentuate a corset-clad lady's billowing curves with a swirl of his pencil. "Your enormous boot, which I tripped over," she smiled.

"I mean when I lifted you from the doormat. And even before that, when you were lying there, gazing up at me like an injured sparrow. I was scared you'd break if I touched you."

"But you're not any more."

They shared an intimate glance.

"Let's go for a walk; you look a bit peaky today," Ralph said. "You don't get enough fresh air."

"I'd like to. But I must make myself work or I'll never get anything written," Marianne answered resolutely, inserting more paper into her typewriter.

Ralph was still eyeing her with concern. "You don't eat enough, either. It's no wonder you're thin."

"Stop worrying about me, love."

"If I don't, who will?"

She watched him resume work and tried to concentrate on her own. But the inspiration she sought would not come and she allowed her mind to dwell upon the wonderful thing that had happened to her, which even Ralph's being Gentile could not mar. How lucky she was to have him care for her. Hannah had prophesied that when the right man came along, Marianne would not give him up for any reason. And she'd known Ralph was that man at their third meeting.

Her heart had leapt at the sight of him. It had been in a corridor at the agency, and they'd both stopped in their tracks. Even across the few yards that separated them, Marianne had been unable to fight the magnetism of his eyes. Then they'd walked towards each other and the feeling his nearness aroused in her had been like a physical ache sapping her strength.

The gruffness of his voice when he greeted her had told her the feeling was a two-way thing, and it had not taken long for the first, tentative stage of their relationship to become the sure and comfortable bond of love and friendship that was theirs now. They had been lovers for three months, yet there were still times when Marianne awoke in the morning and was assailed by unreality when she saw him lying beside her. Times when the whole of her life in London assumed the quality of a dream.

There'd been snow on the ground when her father, against his better judgment, drove her here. With a trunk full of the new clothes her mother had insisted on buying her when she was demobilized, and the curtains, cushions and other paraphernalia from home that brightened this shabby room and made her feel it was hers. Now, spring sunshine was mellowing the seedy frontages of the Edwardian houses across the street, transforming their brass letterboxes into a string of dazzling gold nuggets that stretched from one end of the long terrace to the other.

Like the house in which Marianne lived, most had been converted into furnished flatlets. This wasn't the best part of Kensington, her Aunt Rebecca had told her. Nor was it a Jewish district, she'd added when Marianne turned down the offer to live with a widowed relative of hers in Golders Green. Marianne had felt like telling her there was no such thing as a Jewish bedsitter-land. But they were at a *Shabbos* gathering and it would have reopened the family inquest about her leaving home.

Only Hannah and Carl had taken her side. Uncle Nat had remained neutral, but Marianne had felt he sympathized with her. She had not expected the others to understand. Their horizon began and ended within walking distance of a *shul*; they eschewed the world outside that embraced all peoples. Centuries of oppression had bred in them the need to cling together; but it wasn't necessary any more, Marianne thought, running her fingers absently over the keys of her battered Remington.

The last time she went home for a weekend, she'd spoken her mind about this. And antagonized the family, she recalled ruefully. Her cousins especially. "How can we be any other way? Look how we've been let down in Palestine," Shirley, who saw everything through Zionist eyes, had said angrily. "But we're English, too," Marianne had answered. "As English as they'll let us be," Ronald had declared with feeling.

Marianne had been surprised to hear him say this. He was more intelligent than his sister and not given to making emotional statements. Perhaps it wasn't possible for any Jew to divorce emotion from intellect regarding Jewish matters, she'd admitted to herself later. She had never become actively embroiled in the Zionist cause, but she had the same feeling for the Promised Land all her brethren had. "Next year in Jerusalem" was the age-old hope read from the *Haggadah* every Passover, when you were seated at the *Seder* table, with the bitter herbs before your eyes recalling your people's history. Lest your secure British citizenship made you forget it. In some ways, being Jewish was like being a split personality. Your nationality was that of the country in which your forebears had found refuge, but you were lumbered with congenital racial loyalties that confused you about where you belonged.

The escalating trouble in Palestine had caused her to think about this a good deal, lately. The children being born there now would be a new breed of Jew, unburdened by Marianne's handicap. But she had been born and raised in England and the knowledge that British soldiers and Jewish guerrillas were presently spilling each other's blood made her feel that she personally was being torn apart. The Union Jack was her flag, but Judaism was her heritage.

Six million had died in the holocaust because this heritage was theirs, Zaidie Sigmund had reminded her before she left home—as if he thought removing herself from the family ethos meant she needed reminding. To the family, Marianne had turned her back on her upbringing. They could not comprehend that it was possible to be Jewish without the Star of David being the sole illumination in your sky.

And here she was, letting them come between her and the play she was trying to write! A line of dialogue entered her mind and she began typing. The next line followed and her fingers flew feverishly on the keys, keeping pace with her racing brain.

When she looked up it was twilight and she sat in a daze, mental and physical energy spent, utterly drained as she always was after a lengthy creative stint. But with an inner satisfaction, too. She had stared at blank paper for most of the day, but in the end her work had gone well.

Ralph switched on a lamp, suffusing the room with an amber glow that softened the harsh lines of the cheap furniture and his own craggy profile. "Ready for a cuppa?" he inquired.

Marianne nodded limply and watched him pull back the curtain that hid the miniature kitchen and put the kettle on the gas ring to boil. "Don't you have enough of doing layouts at the studio?" she said, glancing at his work.

Ralph unhooked two yellow beakers from above the sink and took the teapot out of a cupboard. "I may as well earn myself some overtime while you're busy writing."

"Why not get cracking on a painting, instead?"

Ralph puffed his pipe, pensively. "I'm not like you, sweetheart."

Marianne surveyed him silently. What did he mean? There were depths to him she had not yet fathomed, despite their closeness. Her mind began groping to comprehend. Because he spent all his free time at her place, he had brought his easel and paints here. They had remained in a corner, untouched, with some blank canvases eyeing him accusingly beside them. Until one memorable afternoon.

Her gaze traveled to the still life hanging, unframed, above the hearth. It was then that he'd begun painting that. The sequence of events that led to him doing so flashed before her eyes like a series of slides beamed from a projector. Ralph returning from the barber's with a handful of oranges he'd bought from a barrow. Herself at the sink, drying the teapot lid with a crumpled pot-towel and laughing at his shorn-lamb appearance. Him swinging her off her feet to carry her to the bed. And the oranges landing on the table where she had dropped the things in her hands.

After they had made love, he had moved the table to the window, set up his easel and begun painting. He had not rearranged the composition of his subject, as though he wanted to record a treasured memory on canvas. Marianne had sat watching him and every stroke of his brush had seemed to her like a lover's caress.

She rose from her chair and went to study the picture more closely. It was real, as a still life should be. But with an extra something that wasn't just the way Ralph had captured the dewy sweat of oranges brought from the cold street into a warm room; or her own greasy thumbmark on the pot-towel upon which they lay; or the few grains of tea she hadn't rinsed off the teapot lid. He had seen them with a tender eye and when that eye was also an artist's, something magic happened.

"You were happy when you painted this, weren't you?" she said to him.

The kettle began whistling and Ralph removed it from the gas ring without replying.

Marianne went to stand beside him.

"Let's have coffee for a change," he said.

"What the hell does it matter?" she answered impatiently. All that mattered was the realization that had just hit her. He wasn't happy now.

Ralph took a tin of Nescafé from the shelf on which she kept her frugal supply of groceries, opened it and found it was empty. "It's a good thing I got another when I went shopping this morning. If I left it to you, you'd bloody starve."

"Stop digressing. Why don't you paint anymore?"

"Because I wasn't born with your tenacity, sweetheart. Your dogged dedication. Things have to be right with my life before I'm stirred by the creative urge."

"And what was especially right the day you began the still life?"

Ralph fished in a carrier bag that was dumped on the floor and brought out the bar of chocolate he always got for her with his sweet-ration coupons. "Are you kidding?" He found the instant coffee at the bottom of the bag underneath some carrots and onions and pried off the lid. "Do you really need to be told what was special about that day, Marianne?"

"I doubt if any girl ever forgets the day she lost her virginity," Marianne said after a silence. "But I'd never associated our lovemaking with your brief resurgence of artistic fervor. I mean we didn't stop making love after you finished that picture, did we? But you haven't painted anything since then."

Ralph made the coffee, then discovered Marianne had forgotten to order her usual bottle of milk and yesterday's dregs had turned sour. "When we're married, the first thing I'll do is give the milkman, the butcher and the grocer weekly orders. And I'll buy us a refrigerator, so the food you forget is there will last longer," he said wryly.

He carried his beaker to the armchair and sat down.

Marianne plonked hers on the draining board. "Returning to the subject, what you implied doesn't make sense. If us making love's all it takes to get you to your easel, you should be painting masterpieces one after the other."

"It takes peace of mind, too," Ralph said quietly.

She went to sit on the arm of his chair, her impatience replaced by a sense of her own inadequacy. She had given him her love, but it wasn't enough. She rested her hand on his shoulder and thought how tiny it looked there. But he was a big man and she a very small woman. Just like her grandparents, she mused irrelevantly. Why did she always end up thinking of the family? Because she was keeping Ralph a secret from them. She didn't like doing so and Ralph liked it still less. He wasn't happy in the circumstances in which she had placed him, aiding and abetting the duplicity she herself had settled for.

"You didn't go to bed with me without thinking about it, did you?" he said, looking up at her. "It was a considered decision that wouldn't hurt your folks. You said so when I came for breakfast that morning."

Marianne smiled reminiscently. "Over the pork sausage and bacon you brought. I'd been thinking it over for some time, but that clinched it. I thought, if I'm eating this without a qualm, I might as well have Ralph. The only way I can."

"It's as well you didn't communicate that unflattering logic to me."

She played with a lock of his shaggy, dark hair which

had not been reshorn since that day. "Would it have made any difference?"

"No."

"You're damn right it wouldn't! If I hadn't insisted on taking a bath and showering myself with talc first, like brides do on their wedding night, you wouldn't have gone out for a haircut. I'd have been deflowered there and then," she said bawdily.

Ralph laughed and pulled her on to his lap.

Once, sex had seemed a serious matter to her and perhaps it was with other people, Marianne reflected. But with herself and Ralph it was lighthearted as well as thrilling. Not at all the darkly mysterious business she'd imagined it to be; just part of their loving relationship.

They sat in contemplative silence, their arms around each other, gazing into the hissing blue flames of the gas fire, which Ralph had lit whilst Marianne worked on her play. The sunshine never entered this north-facing room and even on a warm evening it soon grew chilly.

"To you, what we've got now is an alternative to us being husband and wife," Ralph said against her cheek. "But I'll never be content with it." He straightened her fringe tenderly. "Everything looked so rosy to me that day. I felt like shouting from the rooftops."

"What did you feel like shouting?"

"We belong to each other now and that means she'll marry me. It seemed a great leap towards it, I thought."

Marianne sprang off his lap. "Well, you were wrong, weren't you?"

Ralph regarded her across the space she had put between them. "Why must you be so brutal about it? As if you enjoy taking the last shreds of hope away from me?"

"Enjoy it? It's as painful for me as it is for you. What you call brutality, love, I call facing the facts. I made a sacred promise to my parents and I intend to honor it."

"They had no right to exact it from you. Christians wouldn't dream of doing such a thing."

"They don't have Jewish reasons to," Marianne retorted. "Nobody's hounded them from place to place. There's nothing like suffering shared to make people stick together, uphold the laws that no amount of persecution has succeeded in breaking down. There are aspects of the Jewish way of life that I resent, Ralph; especially the one that's currently affecting me, that's turned my brother and my Uncle Joe into the next best thing to lepers. But that doesn't mean I don't understand the reasons for them, for the struggle that goes on in families between the elders and the more enlightened younger generation, to preserve the old ways. It takes the form of over-protectiveness, but it stems from something deeper. Even I, in my cool and collected moments—and this is one of them—have to admit that."

"Thanks for the lecture," Ralph said brusquely.

"I was wasting my breath, wasn't I?" Marianne replied with a weary smile. "It was stupid of me to expect a Gentile to understand." She went to the kitchen cubicle and drank some of her coffee. "Uggh, it's gone stone cold," she grimaced, pouring it away. "And so have I."

"What's that supposed to mean?"

Marianne turned to look at him. "That I don't feel close to you any more. The conversation we've just had makes me feel we're fish and fowl."

"I've never heard of a haddock and a rooster copulating, but you could be right."

"It was you who put the thought into my head."

"Some thoughts are best left unspoken, Marianne. They lead to others."

"Like this one. Maybe we should call it a day."

Ralph got up and enfolded her in his arms. "Never, sweetheart."

"I'd have died if you'd agreed," she said tremulously. "Why can't you be like me and make the best of things?"

"I'll try."

The buzzer that meant Marianne had a caller downstairs at the front door pierced the air and they sprang apart.

"Oh God! It might be Auntie Rebecca!" Marianne said.

Ralph eyed her nervous expression. "Shall I hide in the clothes closet, or under the bed?"

"You'd better lock yourself in the bathroom."

"I was joking," he informed her.

"Well, I wasn't."

He watched her rush around the room removing the evidence of his presence. "Aren't nice Jewish girls allowed male visitors?"

"Nice Jewish girls aren't supposed to be human." Marianne thrust his pipe and tobacco pouch into his hands and his artwork into a cupboard. She dragged the armchair into the corner where his canvases were stacked and placed it where it would screen them from view. "Or that's what it amounts to! Years ago, they had to let their husbands be chosen for them by their parents. And cut off all their hair when they got married, so no man but a devoted spouse would find them attractive."

"I don't believe it."

"It's true. They covered their heads, of course, but scarves and wigs'd be bound to slip off in bed, wouldn't they? Can you imagine going to such lengths to ensure fidelity?"

"Frankly, no."

"Ultra-orthodox women still do it," Marianne said as the buzzer sounded again. She hustled Ralph on to the landing, oblivious to his protestations and watched him reluctantly enter the bathroom. "You promised you'd try to make the best of things," she reminded him.

He stood in the doorway watching her clatter down the uncarpeted stairs. "I didn't think it'd involve anything like this!"

The caller was Marianne's Uncle Joe Klein.

"I'd have gone away if I hadn't seen a light on in your room," he said, kissing her cheek. "What took you so long, chick?"

"Hiding Ralph and his things."

He sighed commiseratingly.

"If I'd known it was you, I wouldn't have had to. Come on up."

"I can't, chick. I just got back from the Middle East and I'm off there again on Monday. I've promised Auntie Sally I'll take her out this evening. Though all I feel fit for is a good *shluff*," he added, stifling a yawn.

Marianne smiled. "You still come out with Yiddish words, Uncle. Though you haven't lived among Jews for years."

"What's bred in childhood is there forever, Marianne. I just came over to invite you and Ralph to tea tomorrow. It's a nuisance you living in a place where there's no phone."

"The landlord keeps talking about putting one in, but that's as far as he gets. The same goes for replacing the chipped bath."

"Are you sorry you left the comfort and convenience of your parent's home?"

"No, Uncle. Some things make up for the lack of others."

Joe Klein patted her cheek affectionately. "You've learned to see things in perspective at an early age, chick. I'm proud of you. I found a letter from your Arnold when I got home, by the way. I can't tell you how pleased I am that he keeps in touch with me. And that I see something of you now you're in London. It's nice to feel I've got some relations again." He sighed and gave her a poignant smile. "Your dad's not out of friends with me any more. I think he forgave me that night I came to your house in Cheetham Hill when you were a little kid. But it isn't the same, Marianne. How can it be when he's never accepted my wife? Or suggested meeting her and my son."

Marianne leaned against the flaking, distempered wall, studying him. His face was criss-crossed with lines, and browned by the sun from his frequent assignments in hot countries. But it wasn't just that which made him appear older than his fifty-odd years. He seemed to be carrying an inner burden.

"Is it Palestine you've just been to?" she asked, feeling instinctively that it was.

He nodded, then groped in his coat pocket for his cigarettes and tapped one absently on the squashed packet. "And I'll tell you something I wouldn't admit to anyone else, Marianne." He fumbled in his pocket again and found his lighter. "God knows why I'm telling you. I'm ashamed of it, but a person has to get things off his chest," he said, lighting the cigarette. "When it came to writing my report for the paper, I had to work hard to be the objective journalist I've always been."

He blew out some smoke and watched it rise to the high, ornate ceiling and Marianne felt he was avoiding her eye.

"It might have been better if they'd sent a non-Jewish reporter there," she said quietly.

Her uncle smiled. "One or two I could think of would have had the same struggle as me, only the other way round. And some don't bother struggling, or if they do they're letting their pro-British bias win. Don't tell me you haven't been reading the papers lately?"

"Of course I have, Uncle. But when you haven't seen things for yourself, you're inclined to believe what you read."

"In your morning bible," Joe Klein said cynically. "How

many times have I heard people say, 'It's got to be true, I read it in the papers?'"

"And what's true in this case?" Marianne asked.

Joe stared reflectively at the stained-glass fanlight above the front door. "There's an old Jewish saying that the truth is like an onion. Many layered. I've had reason to remember it more times than I could count, in the years I've been a journalist. I've also learned truth's never black and white, it's somewhere in the shades of gray that lie between."

"But how does that apply to the Palestine situation?" Marianne persisted.

"Maybe you should think again about not wanting to be a reporter any more," her uncle said. "With your inquiring mind, you'd make a good one."

"No I wouldn't," she smiled. "My overactive imagination'd lead me astray from the facts."

"I could use a rest from nothing but facts myself," Joe replied. "Especially the kind I'm confronted with in Palestine," he added grimly.

"Which you still haven't told me about. You've implied that the real picture's being shown to the outside world through a distorted lens, Uncle; but the Irgun Zvai Leumi are terrorists, that's a fact, isn't it? Even the Jewish establishment condemns what they're doing. How will there ever be peace there, while they're blowing up railway lines and government offices? And that terrible incident last year, with all those casualties, at the King David Hotel—" Marianne said with a shudder.

"Sure it was terrible. Loss of life and limb always is," Joe answered. "But nobody appeared to think so when Hitler first began persecuting Jews. The whole world is outraged by what the freedom fighters are doing in Palestine, but where was the great outcry then? One theory I've heard expounded is that everyone's accustomed to Jews being a scapegoat; it's always been taken for granted. I think it's true, that it's been the case for so long, we take it for granted ourselves."

Marianne regarded him silently for a moment. "But that doesn't excuse the terrorists, Uncle."

"Nothing excuses violence. But you and I can't put ourselves in the position of men like the Irgun. Most of them were in concentration camps. And now their dream of a Jewish homeland is being snatched away from them. You'd think, in the name of common humanity, all the survivors of the camps would be allowed to settle there. But no. The British Government has always restricted entry and now Mr. Bevin is waving a conveniently written White Paper to restrict it still more."

Joe deadened the stub of his cigarette between a nicotine-stained finger and thumb and tossed it into the metal umbrella stand. "What does a White Paper mean to a boatland of half-starved people turned back from the shores of salvation?" he said bitterly. "I've seen it happening, Marianne. And I'll never forget it. The bewilderment and disbelief on their faces. The hope in their eyes flickering out. And the silence when they know they must accept it. That there's no tomorrow for them—just an endlessly hopeless today."

He saw Marianne's distressed expression. "But my job is to report the facts, not load them with my own feelings," he said, pulling himself together. "That's what I meant about remaining objective and now you can understand how difficult it is. I felt like punching the soldiers who were stopping the refugees from landing. I almost did get into a scuffle with one of them."

"What stopped you?"

"Another journalist held me back, 'Forget you're a Jew, or ask to be taken off this assignment,' he said. I asked him where his heart was and he said it was bleeding, but not just for the refugees. Then I looked at the soldiers' faces, which I hadn't even noticed, and saw it was hell for them, too."

"I don't know how they can do it," Marianne declared hotly.

"Troops have to obey orders. They're just pawns in the political game that's being played out right now. Like the refugees are. And it's turned into one with no holds barred. Between Menachem Begin's Irgun guerrillas, who, like you said, at present don't even have the support of the Jewish establishment, and the British Government. Who've reached the stage where they'll do anything to save face—even make use of the gallows to prove to the world who's boss in Palestine."

"I read the United Nations might be going to intercede."

Joe buttoned his coat and pulled his shapeless trilby hat down on his forehead before opening the door to leave. "Someone'd better. Before any more men whose only sin is to fight for their cause get hung, like those poor devils it happened to last month."

He stepped outside into the cool night air and gazed

pensively at the sliver of moon emerging from behind a
cloud. "I talked with some of their comrades, off the record,
and it struck me they were the same caliber of man as their
counterparts in Spain, when I was covering the Civil War.
Wherever there's injustice, there'll always be freedom fighters,
Marianne. The kind of people who won't knuckle under,
who'd rather die than lose their vision. I can't condone Begin's tactics, but posterity will be the judge and I have the
feeling he'll be remembered as one of them."

Marianne walked with him to where he had parked his
car. "You've made me think, Uncle."

"So it'll take your mind off your personal problem.
Hadn't you better go and tell him it's all right to come out of
hiding," Joe said with a smile.

Marianne glanced up at the bathroom window and saw
her lover's burly silhouette against the frosted glass. "I forgot
he was there!"

Joe laughed. "Auntie Sally's bought us some strudel to
have for tea tomorrow, to remind us we're Jewish," he said as
she fled back to the house.

"Who needs reminding?" she called over her shoulder.

"That was supposed to be a joke, chick."

Some joke! she thought, tearing up the stairs two at a
time. But maybe when you'd exiled yourself irrevocably to
the no-man's-land that people who married-out lived in, a
sense of humor about it helped to ease the loneliness. That
her uncle sometimes got lonely for his own people she didn't
doubt, and she was sure her brother did, too. Each of them
had a family of his own, but it was an isolated unit, part of
nothing.

What a day this had been! First the letter from home to
prod her conscience anew. Then Ralph's revelation that he
couldn't paint because she wouldn't marry him. And, finally,
the things Uncle Joe had told her about the trouble in Palestine.

She arrived on the top landing puffing and panting and
banged on the bathroom door. If there was one person who
didn't need reminding what they were, it was Marianne
Klein. What with one thing and another, she had never felt
more Jewish in her life.

Chapter Four

Shirley's second child was overdue and Sarah was concerned to hear from Bessie that the baby was lying the wrong way round.

"You're only her grandmother, so how do you think I feel?" Bessie moaned before ending their telephone conversation. She had rung up to tell Sarah that Peter had taken his wife to the nursing home and had imparted the information about labor pains and a probable breach delivery in the same breath.

Only her grandmother indeed! Sarah thought. She could already feel an ache in her own back.

It was Sunday and Abraham was there to keep her company. "Sit down; you dusted the room this morning," he said to her.

But Sarah had to keep herself busy. It helped to pass the time. By mid-afternoon, she had washed all the laundry she usually tackled on Monday. It was a hot June day and the kitchen seemed airless. She began her ironing in front of the open window, and could see Abraham sunning himself in the back garden.

"If men had to give birth to children, instead of women, it would be the end of the human race," she told her pregnant cat. "And the same would go for pussies," she added, espying Mrs. Evans's lusty tom sprawled beside her husband. "If they just got one labor pain, they'd stop taking what females have to suffer for granted."

The telephone rang and she hastened to pick up the receiver. Abraham heard it and came in to hover at her side.

"So what has Shirley had? A boy or a girl?" he demanded, listening to Sarah's enigmatic hums and hahs into the mouthpiece.

"It isn't Peter; it's Harry. He's just taken Ann into the nursing home."

"Three weeks early?"

But Sarah was not surprised. She had said all along that Shirley looked too small and Ann too big, but nobody had heeded her. In her day, babies were born when they were expected. It had been the old wives, who'd had many children themselves, who worked out the dates and attended the deliveries. Nowadays, everything was done by the book and despite their education, doctors, when it came to this most natural of functions, were often wrong.

"Didn't I say Ann looked pinched around the nostrils yesterday at the tea party," she said to Harry when he allowed her to get a word in. "According to old Mrs. Katz, who delivered your mother and two of your uncles, in Dvinsk, that's always a sure sign."

"I thought of it when Ann's waters suddenly broke all over the lounge carpet, Bobbie," Harry replied.

"If you'd taken notice of your grandmother, you'd have had a towel handy. So her wealthy father will buy her a new carpet. Meanwhile, how is she?"

"Uncle Nat's with Shirley. I had to fetch Uncle Lou and he said it won't be long. Get the whisky out! I'll bring you the news in person."

After Harry had rung off, Sarah sat down in the rocking chair.

Abraham glanced at the ironing board. It was not like his wife to desert her chores. "You're feeling all right, Sorrel?"

"Sure," she smiled. "But two great-grandchildren you don't expect every day." It made you think of the years you'd put behind you, she thought. Which when you looked back on them seemed like a dream. Good times and bad viewed through a mist over your shoulder as you journeyed along life's road.

But that was how God arranged things, she thought, returning herself to the present. And who could fathom His ways? That He had seen fit to put two young women in her family in labor at the same time and given her a double dose of worry was just one of His small perversities. But why had He arranged for her first great-grandson to be born to Arnold's wife? To be a *goy*.

She brushed the final painful thought aside and got up to make some tea. Whilst they were drinking it, Harry arrived to tell them he had a son and had named him Howard, after one of Ann's cousins who had died in the war.

Shirley's son was born that evening.

"You're calling him Rudolph, after your poor father?" Sarah asked when Peter telephoned to give them the news.

"Shirley isn't keen on the name, so he can have it for his second one. She wants to call him Mark," Peter replied.

And her own way Shirley always gets, Sarah thought with a sigh. But one day her husband, who was no weakling, might emerge from the spell she'd cast over him and the sparks would fly in that household.

Abraham was beaming with satisfaction. "So now we've got two great-grandsons, Sorrel," he declared rapturously.

"You can't count any more?" she demanded. It was wrong to keep pushing away the thought of Arnold's Matthew. "Three we've got. You know it and God knows it. And you and Esther make me sick!"

"Is that so?" Abraham said stiffly.

"Ben would welcome Arnold back with open arms if he wasn't scared of what Esther would say. And so would I. I have to tell you the truth. What is the use of this game of Let's Pretend you and your daughter are playing?"

Abraham did not reply.

"Arnold hasn't been wiped off the face of the earth," Sarah informed him caustically. "He's living in Didsbury with his wife and child. And cutting him off doesn't stop him from still being ours. Marianne went to see her nephew when she was home for *Pesach* and took Arnold a pot of my homemade ginger jam to put on his *matzo*."

"Are you telling me he still keeps the Passover, even though he's married-out?"

"He keeps everything. Marianne said one of his wife's Jewish friends explained kosher housekeeping to her."

Abraham sat down. "They've got Jewish friends?" he muttered doubtfully.

"Why not? It's only Arnold's family who have ostracized him."

"I don't know what that word means. I don't read books like you do."

"It means what we've done to our grandson," Sarah said scathingly. "As if he's not fit for us any more, just because he's made a mistake. Well, me, I don't believe in that attitude. If you love someone, you love them whatever they do.

And I'm not going to kid myself I've only got two great-grandsons when I've got three," she added with a smile. "Even though it hurts that one of them isn't Jewish. I want my family to get bigger, not smaller."

Marianne went home for the double *Brith* and found herself envying the two young mothers their uncomplicated lives, which contrasted so sharply with her own. How lovely it must be to have your husband at your side, your union blessed by the family. Instead of having to pretend there was no man in your life.

The babies were circumcised in Sarah's dining room. Howard first, because he was the elder, and then Mark, attired in the family gown and hat that had just been worn by his second cousin.

"A very special bond this pair will have," the *mohel* said to Shirley and Ann when he congratulated them at the celebration in the parlor, afterwards.

As if the kids in this clan don't have enough bonds to contend with, Marianne thought. Her cousin and sister-in-law were seated side by side with their babies in their arms, on the new beige leather sofa Uncle David had bought for Bobbie after Mark was born. Did he think the old, figured-velvet one wasn't good enough for people to sit on at his grandson's *Brith*?

The velvet sofa had been there since Marianne's childhood, its multi-colored pile that had reminded her of a cascade of jewels when she was little, faded and threadbare in recent years. She missed its cozy presence and her grandmother had confided that she did, too, but had not wanted to deprive Uncle David of the joy of giving on such an important occasion in his life.

His wife and daughter were wearing the presents he had given to them. Shirley's was the string of cultured pearls gleaming against her blue silk dress. Competing with the heavy gold necklet around Auntie Bessie's fat neck. What a cat I am! Marianne chastised herself. But it wasn't really cattiness. Just the way things struck her and set up questions in her mind. Why, for instance, did Uncle David always try to please or comfort people with material things? She recalled the many occasions when she was a child and had looked miserable, or he'd thought she did, when he'd handed her a sixpence instead of inquiring what was wrong. As though, it seemed to her now, he thought money was the cure for all ills. And the things it could buy—status symbols, she reflected, glancing through the window to where his Jaguar was parked.

But Uncle David wasn't the only one with that attitude. Marianne's gaze fanned around the room, with the cool, observing eye she'd recently become aware she possessed, and which Ralph said was the eye of a writer.

Paula Frankl's fur coat was a status symbol; Auntie Rebecca's double mink wrap, too, or they wouldn't be wearing them indoors, on a summer day. The diamond rings most of the women had on were winking in the sunlight and Marianne's mother was wearing two. Even her brother Harry was parading the evidence of affluence, sporting a ruby tie-pin. What were they all trying to prove? And why didn't Christians need to prove it?

A Christian walking into this room would have every right to think that Jews were ostentatious! Marianne thought with chagrin, allowing her eye to lose its mere observer's viewpoint. Then it fell on her grandmother, and on Hannah and Helga. Three less showy ladies it would be difficult to find. All Jews were not alike, it was only Christians who thought so. They thought so because the gaily-hued birds in an aviary stood out more than the others. It was those with the bright plumage people remembered.

"So when is your granddaughter Marianne going to give you some *nachas*, Mrs. Sandberg?" Paula Frankl said to Sarah as if Marianne were not there. "It's time you had some pleasure from her also."

Marianne managed not to glare at her. Mrs. Frankl and Bobbie aren't even on first-name terms, though they've known each other all those years, she reflected, and wondered, as she had many times, why this hard, unpleasant woman, the whole clan's *bête noir*, had to be present on all their joyous and sorrowful occasions.

"A girl can give pleasure to her family in other ways, as well as by getting married and having babies, Mrs. Frankl," Sarah declared.

Marianne gave her a grateful glance, which she appeared not to see. Perhaps she was too busy avoiding her daughter's rebuking one?

"What, for instance?" Esther snapped. "If our Marianne writes a book, will I be able to cuddle it in my arms?" She snatched baby Howard from Ann and kissed his fuzz of red hair, to emphasize her point.

"When our Marianne's book is on the shelf at Central Library, nobody will be prouder than me," Sarah answered.

"What I'm hoping for at the moment is to have a play I'm writing on at a theatre," Marianne put in. "But my mother would rather I had something in a cradle," she could not stop herself from adding acidly.

"You could have both," Shirley said to her. "A husband and children, and a career. Like Hannah and me."

"For you it's different," Paula Frankl declaimed. "You're helping your daddy in his business. Otherwise you'd be at home instead of leaving little Laura, the poor child, all day with your mama's maid. Like now you'll be doing unfortunately with your baby boy, too." She cast her cold blue eyes upon Hannah. "As for someone letting her sister-in-law bring up her children, taking advantage of her good nature—well, say no more."

"You've said too much already," Hannah retorted.

"Everyone should be taken advantage of in such a way," Helga smiled. "I enjoy it, Mrs. Frankl."

"But your poor mama, whose dear friend I was from our girlhood, would turn in her grave to know how you've sacrificed your life."

Marianne saw Sarah exchange a glance with Sigmund. With dear friends like Paula, who needed enemies? it said. But her dead husband had been a real friend. A kind and gentle man with whom Sigmund had grown up in Vienna. Perhaps it was respect for Ludwig Frankl's memory that allowed the family to tolerate his widow?

Moishe Lipkin was beside Helga, as he always was when invited to gatherings of the clan. Still her faithful suitor, though he and everyone else knew he would never be more.

"Poor Moishe, also," Paula commiserated with him tactlessly.

His sallow complexion tinged with red as he tried to hide his embarrassment.

Paula's son Hugo was with her and hastily changed the subject. "Why not visit our Eva while you're in Manchester?" he said to Marianne. "What with her little boy and another baby on the way, she doesn't get out much. She'd be glad to see you; you used to be so thick with each other."

The last time Marianne had met Eva, she had wondered

what they'd ever had in common. Marriage had made Eva
into a different person; obsessed by recipes and nappy-rash
and how a nightly massage with olive oil prevented you from
getting pregnancy stretch marks on your stomach. "I'm going
back to London tonight," she told Hugo.

"A pity. Her husband's still got a few single friends. If
you were staying on for a few days, she could have invited
them round to meet you."

Marianne blushed and had to bite her lip to stop herself
from delivering a sarcastic retort. I'm only twenty-two! she
wanted to say caustically. And being a wife and mother isn't
the be-all and end-all. It would be useless to say this to
people who thought it was. To whom you were on the shelf if
you hadn't got an engagement ring on your finger by the time
you were her age. Ralph's being a Christian was the only
thing stopping her from getting married, but she could not
tell them that, either. Or that with him she would have the
kind of marriage Hannah had, in which the wife's personality
wasn't subjugated to her marital state.

"You knew Hildegard'd gone to Palestine?" Hugo said
to her.

"England, where she came to as a refugee, wasn't good
enough for her," his mother sniffed.

Marianne ignored the unkind interruption. "No, I didn't
know."

Hugo sighed. "We tried to talk her out of it. But there
was no chance once she went to the David Eder farm."

"What's that?" Marianne asked.

"How could anyone be so ignorant?" Shirley exclaimed.

"Not everyone is as well informed about such matters as
you are, dear," Peter said to her. "You've been steeped in
Zionism all your life. Marianne hasn't. The farm is where the
Habonim Youth Movement trains people to be *chalutzim*, to
work on a *kibbutz*," he enlightened Marianne. "It's in Kent,"
he added and a distant expression entered his smoky-gray
eyes. "I once thought I might go there myself. But things
didn't work out that way."

"Are you sorry?" Shirley challenged him.

He turned to look at her and at their baby son. "How
could I be?" he smiled.

But Marianne had detected a note of regret in his voice
when he spoke of what might have been. Possibly it had been
unconscious but it had made her recall the boy he had been

when he arrived in England. Before he became part of Uncle David's family. Got soaked up by it was more accurate, she thought, surveying him. The sharp edge of individuality she remembered was no longer there. It had already been blunted by the time he married Shirley, but there was now no trace of it at all; he was just a mild-mannered young man, enhanced by his continental charm. Perhaps it wasn't just wives whom marriage metamorphosed into a role of domestic conformity?

Her thoughts turned to Hildegard, the frail young girl who'd escaped from Vienna with Peter and been given a home by her relatives the Frankls. But she hadn't fallen into the conventional trap Peter had. She had gone her own way. And to do so demanded strength, especially to go the way Hildegard had. It was difficult to imagine her behind a plough, or tilling the fields. In a land torn by conflict, which required more than physical strength. You needed guts to make up your mind to go there.

"A place for nice Yiddisher girls right now Palestine isn't," Hugh sighed.

"So let's hope it'll be safe one day," Bessie said. "My husband's certainly written enough checks for it."

Marianne excused herself and left the room. Money again! But without the cash raised for the Jewish National Fund by Jews in the Diaspora, Palestine would be in dire straits, she reflected, passing the blue-and-white collecting box which had lived on her grandparents' hall table as long as she could remember.

There was one in her parents' house and in every Jewish home she had ever entered, even of those who were not active Zionists. A constant reminder of the hoped-for homeland and the necessity to help support the cause. Many, like her Uncle David, sent large sums every year. But the way her aunt had mentioned this in the same breath as a reference to the present strife, in which freedom fighters were paying with their lives, had seemed to Marianne immensely distasteful. Like Joe Klein, she could not condone the violence they were perpetrating, but what Joe had said about them preferring to die rather than lose their vision had affected her deeply.

She went into the dining room, wanting to be alone with her thoughts, but found her Uncle Nat there with his partner, discussing someone's spleen. "Don't doctors ever talk about anything but their work?" she smiled.

"What do writers talk about?" Nathan countered.

"She'll tell us when she is one," Lou grinned. "So far as I know, she's only dreaming up ads, so far."

Marianne bristled. "You mean so far that's all I'm getting paid for."

Nathan slipped his arm around her, affectionately. "Lou's teasing you, love."

"No, he isn't. He's like everyone else around here. He thinks nothing's important unless it spells money."

Lou remained unperturbed by the accusation, but Nathan's expression clouded.

"So that's how you see us, is it?"

"With one or two exceptions."

Nathan smiled wryly. "I gather I'm not one of them."

Marianne avoided his eye. Did she see him that way? She wasn't sure. On the surface, he was. With his big car and a wife like an expensive fashion plate. He wasn't just a GP any more, but was also specializing in psychoanalysis. Her parents had told her he'd taken a course on it and in addition to his work as a physician was treating patients with psychological problems privately. Many people had begun having nervous trouble during the war and, it seemed, Uncle Nat was cashing in on it. The outward signs of a materialistic attitude were all there. But he hadn't always been like that, Marianne recalled.

Lou did, too, and smiled reminiscently. "This reminds me of a conversation we once had when we were students, Nat. And you were talking just like Marianne is. I used to have to keep your uncle's feet on the ground in those days, love," he chuckled to her. "But people change, Marianne."

"I know," she replied, studying Nathan's face. He was still a handsome man, the best-looking one in the family. But there were lines of discontent around his sensitive lips and a film of disillusion dulling his eyes. "One day, I might write a book about why people change," she said thoughtfully.

"You'll have to do a lot more living before that day comes," her uncle answered with a wan smile. "To equip you to write it."

Marianne left the room and went to soothe her troubled thoughts in the cozy comfort of the kitchen. Lizzie and Bridie were not money-mad, nor would they be discussing spleens! She found them seated on the sofa, waiting, as always on such occasions, to help with the clearing-up after non-family guests had left. Her grandmother had so far successfully fought off suggestions that it was time she employed someone to help her in the house.

"Got fed up wi' t'cumpny, Marianne?" Lizzie asked.

"What do you think?" Marianne sighed. "It was bad enough having all my grandparents' old neighbors from Strangeways looking at Shirley and Ann's babies and saying, 'Please God by you, Marianne,' before they went home! But Mrs. Frankl's still here."

"If our Shirley can put up wi' 'er, you can," Lizzie declaimed. "None on us likes 'er, we only grin an' bear it fer ol' times' sake. But Marianne never was one ter put up wi' nowt," she informed Bridie, asserting her longer length of service with the family.

"I've known Marianne since her tenth birthday. 'Twas on me way from Liverpool in himself's car we did meet. After Doctor had fetched me from t'boat," Bridie recalled.

Marianne could remember her Uncle Nat coming to visit her father, who had tonsillitis. He'd left Bridie in his car, away from possible infection, and Marianne had gone to sit with her. Life was like a book of memories, but this was the first time she had turned back to that page. Perhaps you only did so with events that were important to you. As Bridie's arrival among strangers had been to her.

The matronly Irishwoman bulging out of her drab gray dress had been a comely girl then. Lizzie had not put on weight with the years, but her freckled forehead was corrugated as a washboard; probably all her employers' worries had been hers, too.

Marianne surveyed them fondly. If they left us, there'd be a great big hole in our lives, she thought. But they never would. The family was their *raison d'être*.

Bridie was knitting a cardigan for Abraham. "Yer Bobbie's a wonderful wuman, Marianne, bless her darlin' heart. But she never knits."

"When'd she 'ave time, wi' all t'troubles o' t'clan on 'er 'ead?" Lizzie demanded loyally.

"Is it accusin' me o' runnin' herself down, ye are now, Lizzie Wilson?" Bridie flashed. "An' who but ye were it said t'me Bobbie Sarah's gittin' past caterin' fer so many visitors? She'll be doin' what's t'be done till her dyin' day, I answered ye!"

"Stop it, you two," Marianne laughed. "We all know you both love my grandmother."

Lizzie gave her attention to the rabbit-wool hat she was crocheting for Shirley's little girl, who was snoozing on her lap. "Remember t'pretty frocks I used ter crochet fer you an' our Shirley, Marianne?" she smiled. "Yer were both t'same age as Laura is now, when I came ter work fer yer uncle an' auntie. An' I were a lass."

"Have you ever regretted coming, Lizzie?"

"Where'd I've ended up if I 'adn't? Four o' mi sisters 'as been widdered by pit accidents. Now, their sons is down t'pit. Wed ter t'lasses they went ter school wi', who'll be thankful if they're not left wi' 'ouseful o' bairns ter fetch up by thirsen." A faraway look had entered Lizzie's faded blue eyes. "Best t'lasses round there can 'ope fer is ter share their old age wi' an' 'usband coughin' up blood from t'chest disease miners ends up wi' if they live long enough." She retied the bow of yellow ribbon in Laura's hair and planted a loving kiss on the child's plump cheek. "I've not gone short o' kids ter warm mi 'eart, 'ave I, Marianne? An' I've got a gud 'ome. I reckon I'm one o' t'lucky 'uns."

Lucky by comparison with something worse, Marianne reflected poignantly. Lizzie's work-roughened hands and aging appearance had not been acquired on her own account, but by dedication to others. The same applied to Bridie, and Marianne experienced a pang of shame. They were human beings, not just pillars of the family; but she hadn't seen them in that light, had always taken them for granted. Uncle Nat was right; she did have a lot to learn before she was equipped to write a book about why people became what they were.

Leona was seated at the table, watching the twins play chess, their three heads bent over the board. None of them had uttered a word since Marianne entered the room. As if they had mentally obliterated everything outside themselves in order to concentrate on their game. That's how I used to be, she mused. But kids always are. Isolated by choice in the world of childhood. And privately contemptuous of the adults who didn't understand them.

The three youngsters at the table would soon enter their teens, and time would begin to fly more quickly, carrying them with it. Through the painful confusion of adolescence, when nobody's anxieties were the equal of your own, Marianne recalled wryly. Until dawning maturity began to open

your eyes and mind, ending your total self-absorption. Of
how total her own had been, she had only a moment ago become aware. It was as though she had been asleep and had
suddenly realized on wakening that there was more to the
familiar figures of her childhood than their relation to herself.
That they existed in their own right.

The re-alignment that had begun with Lizzie and Bridie
continued to function when she returned to the parlor. Her
parents weren't just the stumbling blocks between herself and
Ralph, motivated by nothing more than Jewish orthodoxy,
she thought, looking at them. They were a disappointed
middle-aged couple, who'd once been young and hopeful,
who'd lived for their children and been let down.

The way to avoid disappointment from your kids is not
to have expectations, she reflected, eyeing her father's bowed
shoulders and the downward curve of her mother's mouth.
But perhaps it wasn't possible to be a parent and avoid that
pitfall? To reconcile yourself to your children's ideas being
poles apart from your own. And for Jewish parents, religious
expectations came into it, as well as personal ones.

She was still musing about this when they saw her off at
the railway station that night. And found that her eyes had
misted over when the time came to say goodbye to them. "I
love you both very dearly," she told them.

Her mother gave her a searching glance. "What's
brought this on?"

Marianne smiled away her tears. "Nothing special," she
answered though it was not the truth. A few hours ago, she
would have resented her mother's suspicious tone. Now, all it
aroused in her was tolerant amusement.

"Me, I didn't mind hearing it," her father declared, hugging her.

Her mother sighed. "Dad means we're not sure you do."

"Because I've left home?"

They nodded.

"Hundreds of girls do it. I could introduce you to at
least half a dozen at my office."

"They're Jewish?" her mother inquired.

"No, as it happens."

"So there you are, then," her father declaimed.

They measured everything by that yardstick, Marianne
thought wryly as the train departed and she stood at the window waving goodbye. It was the length and breadth of their

vision. And a reason for pity rather than contempt, because it was the only one they had.

Ralph was waiting for her on the platform at Euston.

"I asked you not to come," she said as he kissed her. "Supposing someone who knows me traveled on this train?" she added, glancing nervously at the passengers still alighting. She did not relax until they had entered the underground. Visiting Mancunians wouldn't be likely to risk getting lost traveling by tube; they'd make for the taxi rank.

"I can't bear it when you go home," Ralph said on the train to Kensington. "I'm always terrified they'll chain you to the bedpost to keep you there. Are you happy to be back?"

"Of course," Marianne replied unhesitatingly, her fingers answering the pressure of his. But the minute I get here, I'm back to the old two-and-nine, all of a jitter because I'm scared of being found out, she added mentally. And the knowledge that this would always be so was depressing—like standing at the beginning of a long road down which two Marianne Kleins would tread the path of their double life. Not until she was in her coffin would she have any peace, be relieved of the burden of her deceit. And if she died before Ralph, he would probably give the game away by turning up at her funeral and the deception would all have been for nothing!

If he stayed with her that long, she thought, eyeing their side-by-side reflections in the train window. Would they still be together when they were her grandparents' age? With nothing more binding to tie them than shared memory of a long-ago passion?

"What're you thinking about, sweetheart?" Ralph asked, sensing her pensive mood.

"The children we'll never have," she said, carrying her last thought to its logical conclusion. "Not that I think I'm the maternal type," she smiled. "Heaven help any kid who had me for its mother!"

"Not if it had me for its father. But what're we talking about this for?"

"It just came into my head."

A week later, Marianne wondered if God had put it there to pave the way. Her menstrual periods had always been regular, but the one due the day after her return to London had not appeared. Ralph had once told her there was no such thing as a static situation. When she couldn't find a way to get the action of her play moving. And what was a play but a mirror of life? But a dramatist had to search for the catalysts life provided naturally. And what a catalyst this was—the major-disaster kind. Why wasn't she panicking? Instead of floating downstream on what felt like a river of inevitability? she asked herself as a fortnight slipped by.

It did not so much as occur to her to ring up Birdie, now a nursing-mother herself, and obtain the recipe for the gin-and-vinegar brew guaranteed to bring on her period. Or to leap down the stairs as one of her erstwhile comrades had. She thought about these things, but had no desire to try them herself. Desperation was not part of how she felt and she allowed another week to pass before opening her mind to the question of what she would do. A further week elapsed before she told Ralph.

He eyed her diminutive figure anxiously. "The first thing to do is see a doctor. You don't look big enough to have a baby."

"I'm the same size as my grandmother and she had four. Before there was such a thing as modern medicine," Marianne assured him.

Their conversation continued on these lines for several minutes, centering on the unborn child's welfare, before they got around to the crucial fact that its parents were not married.

To Ralph, only one course was possible and he seemed to think Marianne's family would agree.

"You're wrong," she informed him.

"Are you telling me they'd rather your child was born the wrong side of the blanket?" he said incredulously. "That they'd prefer that to it having its father's name, just because I'm not Jewish?"

Marianne nodded.

"I thought I'd learned all there was to know about the Jewish mentality," he declared, sitting down beside her on the divan bed. "But it seems there're still some surprises that make a person wonder what kind of people Jews are."

"This is a fine time for you to start being anti-Semitic!"

"I'm not anti-anything, sweetheart. It's your people who are bigoted, not me."

"It only seems that way to you because you're an outsider!" Marianne flashed. "And even if they are as you say, they didn't get like that by accident. It's a pity those who pass judgment, like you've just done, don't stop to think there must be a reason for it."

"All right, so I said something off the top of my scone," he placated her. "You're too bloody thin-skinned, sweetheart."

"There's a reason for that, too, that you wouldn't understand, because you've never needed to be."

"Don't get your blood pressure up. It's bad for the baby." Ralph straightened her bangs, which always went awry when her temper asserted itself. "How often d'you reckon I'll have to say that in the next nine months?"

"Eight," Marianne corrected him. "Possibly less."

"Which returns us to square one. Tomorrow you'll see a doctor."

Marianne rested her head against the pile of cushions that converted her bed into a daytime sofa, beset by a sudden weariness. "And what's square two?"

"You know what it is so far as I'm concerned, sweetheart. You can lie there and make your mind up while I get us a bit of supper."

They had been home from the agency for an hour, but neither of them had done anything about preparing a meal. Marianne watched Ralph take some eggs from the bag of groceries they had bought in their lunch hour and prepare to whip up an omelet. Make her mind up about what? Facing up to telling the family they were going to be married? That she had let a Gentile make her pregnant, and had no intention of abandoning her child to an orphanage? Like Hannah's mother had been coerced into doing under the same circumstances.

Ralph brought the omelet to the divan and made Marianne eat some of it. "Well?" he asked when she had done so.

"Nothing else could have made me do what I'm going to do to my parents," she said decisively. "But the baby has to come first. And I don't see how they can expect it not to," she added without conviction. "When their children have always come first with them."

In her heart she did not have the slightest hope that her parents would understand, and that night her sleep was troubled by dreams of the terrible things they and the rest of the family would say to her. All except Hannah and Carl. And Uncle Nat. She awoke to the sound of Ralph's voice telling someone to stop screaming. Who was he saying it to?

"For God's sake, sweetheart," she heard him implore, and became aware that the screams she could hear were her own.

Her lips clamped shut and the screams stopped. But she could not control the violent tremors that were rippling through her.

Ralph got out of bed and brewed some strong tea. He said nothing until Marianne had drunk it and her trembling had subsided.

"Tell me something, will you, sweetheart? What exactly is it you're so bloody petrified of?"

Marianne avoided his eye. "Petrified's the wrong word. I just don't want to hurt anyone. And I'm going to have to."

"I don't think you've really thought about this," he replied after a silence. "By which I mean, Marianne, you haven't seen this emotion that's tearing you to bits for what it is. Nor had I until it came to a head, tonight."

"It's guilt, Ralph, that's all. With a capital G."

"Guilt doesn't give a person the screaming meemies." Ralph sat down beside her and stroked her hand. "I've never witnessed anything so—well, primeval's the only way I can describe it. The way you were while you were screaming—and those rigors—the bloody bed was shaking from them. As if you were literally being consumed by fear."

Marianne tried to smile. "So would you be, if you had to face what I've got to."

"I'll be facing it with you."

"Oh no, Ralph."

"Oh yes."

Marianne removed her hand from his. "Just because I had an attack of the shakes, it doesn't mean I'm a coward. I've never been one. I'll go to Manchester today and get it over with," she said resolutely. "But I'm going alone."

Ralph eyed her anxiously. "You're not fit to travel. You look like a ghost."

"Do I?"

He passed her a hand mirror and watched her study her wan countenance.

"Well, I never look what you'd call rosy, do I?" she said with false nonchalance. Was that chalky face really hers? It looked as if someone had coated her olive skin, that usually had a sheen to it, with whitewash, and daubed purple paint beneath her eyes to make them look bruised. "If this is what pregnancy does to me, I'll have to wear a mask," she said to Ralph in the same jocular tone.

He took the mirror from her. "It isn't the pregnancy," he declared vehemently. "It's that bloody battle you were having in your sleep. And I'd like to throttle whoever, or whatever, you were having it with."

Marianne smiled wearily. "Nobody's ever succeeded in doing that to the Jewish religion, Ralph, though plenty have tried. And I wouldn't want them to."

"I said it was like watching something primeval, didn't I?" he said after a silence. "It isn't just your family you're scared of. It's God."

"Aren't we all?"

"Not like the Jews are, sweetheart. Still subjugating their reason to laws that don't make sense in the twentieth century."

"You sound like my Uncle Nat. But things can make sense if you believe in them, my grandmother says."

"And who am I to argue with your grandmother?"

An alarm clock ringing in the flat next door interrupted their conversation.

Ralph glanced at his watch. "It's seven o'clock."

"On a *Shabbos* morning," Marianne said wryly. "I'll be able to announce my forthcoming marriage and motherhood to everyone at one fell swoop, this afternoon. At the weekly gathering of the clan."

"The state you're in, you might feel ill on the train," Ralph said, watching her stagger to the window to revive herself with some fresh air.

"I'm stronger than you think," she answered, then found that her legs would not carry her back across the room.

Ralph caught her as they buckled. "That settles it, sweetheart. You're staying in bed until I say you can get up," he said, carrying her there.

"You're not my lord and master yet," she protested weakly.

"But I soon will be."

"On paper," Marianne countered. "But in reality, that'll be the day!"

Ralph tucked the bedclothes around her, then knelt down and cupped her face in his hands. "Why did I have to fall madly in love with a bloody-minded little creature like you?"

"Because I'm so beautiful," she said self-deprecatingly.

He kissed her dry lips. "You're the loveliest thing that ever happened to me. I'd go through fire and water for you."

"You might have to after I've told the family. Especially when my Uncle David gets at you."

"I can't wait to make his acquaintance," Ralph said grimly. "He's the head of the clan, isn't he?"

"How did you know? I mean I suppose he is. But I hadn't realized it until you said it."

"I knew from the way you talk about him."

Marianne felt constrained to say something complimentary about her uncle. "He's very nice under ordinary circumstances," she declared. It was true.

"It's how folk behave under extraordinary ones that matters, sweetheart," Ralph said, putting on his dressing gown.

"Everyone has his own code, love."

" But they don't have the right to apply it to others."

"Uncle David doesn't just apply it," Marianne said pensively. "He forces it down your throat. If I'd listened to him, I'd still be in Manchester. And our Arnold wouldn't have married Lyn. There'd have been no Matthew."

Ralph picked up his toilet bag and towel to go to the bathroom. "What you're saying is he changes the course of people's lives."

"If they let him. He did it to my Uncle Nat."

"How?"

"He made him be a doctor when he didn't want to be one. And stopped him from marrying a Christian girl."

"Your Uncle Nat sounds like a weakling."

"You didn't have to be one in those days to succumb to the pressure put on you. Knowing you had to was a state of mind."

"And the last bit hasn't changed," Ralph declared. "All that has, it strikes me, is that some of your generation have begun putting up a fight."

Marianne fell asleep whilst he was taking his bath. When she awoke, he had been shopping and was unpacking a carrier bag.

"I hope your Uncle Nat likes salad," he said, putting a lettuce and some tomatoes on the table. "I forgot to inquire when I rang him up. He'll be here for supper, sweetheart."

Marianne eyed him speechlessly.

"I got his phone number from your address book."

"You've been rifling my handbag, have you?" was all she could manage to say. She watched Ralph take the lettuce to the window and shake some soil off it, before dumping it in the sink. "Why did you choose him to ring up?"

Ralph ran some cold water on to the lettuce. "For one thing, he's a doctor and your state of health is causing me concern. For another, we could use an ally in your family and he seemed the likely one."

Marianne stared up at a crack in the ceiling. "You've set the ball rolling, haven't you?" she said resignedly. But oh what a relief it was just to lie back and let things happen. To know it was out of her hands.

Chapter Five

Nathan was stunned by Ralph's telephone call. But who wouldn't be? he thought after he had replaced the receiver. To learn their young niece had a private life of the kind respectable people wouldn't expect to encounter outside the pages of a novel? Girls in trouble were routine in Nathan's work. But they weren't Jewish girls and came from the kind of background where pregnant brides were nothing unusual and families took it in their stride. Marianne's plight would have constituted a disgrace to the family even if her young man was a Jew. As things were, it was a right kettle of fish!

Leona came into the hall from the breakfast room, munching a bit of toast. "Your boiled egg's going cold, Daddy."

"I shan't have time to eat it. I've been called away for a day or two and I must leave immediately."

"Where're you going to? Has one of your patients been taken ill in another town?"

"A doctor's daughter should know better than to ask questions like that." Nathan dragged his troubled gaze away from the vase of full-blown roses he had been absently admiring. Why did he feel like a conspirator? Because the young man had asked him not to tell the rest of the family about the phone call. He glanced at his watch, edgily. "Is your mother still asleep, Leona?"

"How would I know? I don't share a bedroom with her, either."

Nathan avoided his daughter's eye. This wasn't the first time she had made that kind of pointed remark. But he had told her the facts of life himself and ought not to be surprised that she'd applied them to her parents *modus vivendi*. And no doubt supplied her own reasons. One day, he would explain everything to her, but it must wait until she was mature enough to understand.

"You've changed your hairstyle," he remarked, noticing that she looked different. Her fiery locks had been shorn to ear lobe length and the front combed into a bang. The style enhanced her piquant features, which had looked a bit pinched with her hair dragged back from her face, as she'd worn it before. "It looks nice," he pronounced.

"I got up early and cut it before Mummy was around to stop me," she confided. "I was fed up with having a ponytail for that beast Henry to pull." She popped into the cloakroom to admire her reflection in the mirror. "I look more grownup, now, don't I, Daddy?"

She would be grownup all too soon, Nathan reflected, surveying her ripening body. But God forbid she should ever have the problem facing her cousin Marianne. "Do me a favor, love," he requested. "Ring up Uncle Lou at lunchtime, when he gets home from *shul*. Just say I've gone out of town and will he get a substitute to help out until I get back. Tell him I'll explain when I see him."

"And what shall I tell Mummy?" Leona asked as he went upstairs to pack a bag.

Nathan paused with his hand gripping the banister. To her I owe no explanations, he wanted to answer. "Tell her the same," he said, thinking how farcical it was to maintain the pretense of marital felicity, when his daughter, for whom it was being maintained, knew perfectly well that it was one.

The deadpan expression with which Leona received his reply set him on edge still more and he sat tapping his fingers restlessly in the taxi that took him to the railway station.

En route, they passed some men and boys from the

ultra-orthodox community who were walking to synagogue
for the Sabbath morning service.

"You'd think they'd just stepped off the herring boat!"
the taxi driver remarked. "Not that they were born here, like
you and me." He grinned at Nathan through his mirror. "I
heard you'd joined the Reform *Shul,* Doctor. Now that far I
wouldn't go. But those people we just passed, they're the opposite extreme."

"I agree," Nathan answered. "But maybe there's something to be said for it."

"What? Wearing long floppy coats instead of jackets?
And sidelocks dangling next to their ears like my Zaidie did
in Russia? It's no wonder they get laughed at."

"They don't get laughed at by me," Nathan said crisply.
"Everyone's entitled to his own way of respecting God."
And good luck to them if that's how they want to be, he
added mentally. One had to admire a faith strong enough to
ward off all outside influences. Only to ply their trades did
the members of that community venture outside the spiritual
wall they had erected around their lives. They even eschewed
the society of Jews less devout than themselves. God was
their sole influence and, in some ways, Nathan envied them
their uncomplicated existence. Who could fall by the way if
they never stepped on to a temptation-strewn path? Or be
ruffled by the wind of change when they kept their doors and
windows firmly closed against it? Such insularity would not
suit Nathan; in his view you'd have to be born without curiosity in order to be content with it. But, he thought dryly,
wasn't it curiosity that killed the cat?

No daughter of theirs would ever find herself in Marianne's predicament, he reflected on the train. Or her uncle
with the problem she now presented to him. Her young man
had seemed to take it for granted that Nathan would come,
as if they'd been together long enough for him to know a lot
about her family background. His manner on the phone had
been brief and to the point. Almost abrupt. What kind of
chap was he, to have got Marianne into this situation?

The train halted at Crewe and Nathan gazed unseeingly
at the passengers rushing on to the platform to buy tea and
buns from the station buffet before the journey was resumed.
His niece had always been headstrong. But never foolish. Her
affaire would not have been entered into lightly. She would
have weighed up the pros and cons. As he had done himself,

before he gave Mary up. And Arnold had when he decided
to marry Lyn. Like every Jew or Jewess must surely do before taking one painful step or the other. Because in the end
you only had two alternatives. But Marianne had tried to
compromise, to find fulfillment in the shady no-man's-land
between. He could have told her that compromise wasn't possible. But she had hoped it would be and was now faced with
a worse dilemma.

It should be David, not himself, making this journey, he
thought wryly. The one everyone in the family took their
troubles to. Who imposed his advice even when they didn't, in
the heavy-handed manner that told people not to bother arguing with him because he was never wrong. But the youngsters
of today weren't prepared to put up with that kind of treatment. Was that why Nathan had been summoned to London
instead of his brother? There was no shortage of medical prac-
titioners in the capital, but Marianne needed support, too. As
Arnold had when he brought Lyn to Scotland. Even David's
own son had chosen Nathan as his confidante. Because David
aroused trepidation, as well as commanding respect, Nathan
reflected, rolling up his *British Medical Journal* as the train
approached Euston. He had been too busy ruminating to read
it.

On the way to Kensington, he thought of Esther and
Ben. How could their attitude to intermarriage possibly be
reconciled with their daughter's situation? What would Ben
have done if he had received the young man's call? Col-
lapsed, probably. Esther too. Another marriage-out among
their children would be like catastrophe following in the wake
of calamity, to a couple who allowed emotion to override
reason as they did.

Briefly, Nathan wished he had his elder brother's cut-
and-dried standards, whereby everything was subservient to
the family. Avoiding disgrace at all costs would be David's
way of dealing with this. He would have Marianne secreted
in the back of beyond during her pregnancy and the child
passed to an adoption society the minute it was born. There
was no doubt whatsoever in Nathan's mind about this. But
David wasn't dealing with it, he was. And he was glad the
younger generation were by-passing David and turning to
him—that one by one they were deciding the archaic world
David's kind inhabited was not for them.

"I'm pleased you could come, Dr. Sandberg," Ralph said when he opened the door and they shook hands.

"Belonging to a big family like ours has its advantages," Nathan smiled. "There's always someone you can call on when you need help."

"But it has to be the right one, doesn't it? And I gather from Marianne belonging is the operative word."

They surveyed each other silently. Like boxers in opposite corners of the ring, Nathan thought. To him I'm from the enemy camp. I represent the family.

"You'll have to excuse me for giving you the once over," Ralph said, leading the way upstairs. "But apart from Marianne's Uncle Joe, you're the first of her relations I've met."

"I understand," Nathan replied, recalling Mary's hostility the night she walked into the side ward at the infirmary and found the whole clan gathered there. To a Gentile in love with a Jew, what could the family seem but a threat? "I was looking you over, too," he said dryly. "It's only natural."

"Under the circumstances," Ralph added as they reached the top landing.

Under the circumstances was right! And how ironic it was that Nathan, the one-time rebel, now represented the other side.

But one-time rebels retained their sympathies, he thought when he saw his niece. And what her plight had reduced her to. The poor kid looked like a wraith.

Marianne got out of bed and ran to his arms. "It makes me feel better just to see you, Uncle Nat," she said tremulously. "You don't know how grateful I am to you for coming."

"Gratitude has no need to enter into it." Nathan patted her shoulder comfortingly. How painfully thin she was, he could feel her ribs jutting out as she rested against him. Like a small boat that's found a haven in a storm, he reflected grimly. When you'd tossed on that same sea yourself, you knew how it felt! The deceit alone was damaging, without the extra burden which had accrued to Marianne because of it. Had God really intended the Laws of Judaism to cause such anguish? Why had He decreed that those whose only sin was love must be alienated from the tribe for ever? What had been gained from this perpetuation of the Jews' difference from others? A difference which had made them the rest of mankind's scapegoat throughout their long history. Rivers of blood had run because of it. God was supposed to be merciful, but there were times when He seemed otherwise to Nathan and this was one of them.

Ralph stood beside the hearth watching the long embrace between uncle and niece. "Everything's going to be all right, Marianne," he declared as if Nathan's presence had given him confidence. "I rang up the right person, didn't I?" he added with a shaky laugh.

Nathan met his gaze and noted its directness. He was a nice young man. "Yes, Ralph," he answered. "You did. And between us we'll sort things out. But first things first. We'll talk when I've examined Marianne."

After he had done so, he was able to reassure her anxious lover. "Everything's fine, but she must have a few days' rest after all that emotional upheaval. She can start by having a sleep while you and I go out for a pint and a chat."

Marianne watched him repack his medical bag. "I've shamed the family, haven't I?" she said quietly.

Nathan snapped the bag shut. "In my view, it's the family that's shamed you. And if, when it comes to it, they're not prepared to accept the part they've played in bringing this about, I'll be the one to tell them."

He had not been into a pub since his army days, he reflected when he and Ralph were seated opposite each other in the lounge bar of the Bell and Anchor on Hammersmith Road.

"How do you like our local?" Ralph inquired.

Nathan glanced around the well-kept establishment. "It's very pleasant."

"We think so, too."

Nathan could not prevent himself from raising his eyebrows. "Marianne's taken to drinking?"

Ralph laughed. "Good God, no! She does me a favor and sits here sipping lemonade, occasionally. Jews don't go in for pubbing, do they?"

"I've never known any for whom a bar was their second home," Nathan smiled.

Ralph quaffed some of his light ale and set down the glass in a pool of froth. "I keep telling my beloved an evening at your local is part of the British way of life, but she doesn't want to know," he grinned.

"I'd be surprised if she did. It's far and away from the

Jewish way of life and she's unlikely to forget her upbringing."

Ralph's momentary levity deserted him. "If it weren't for her upbringing, we wouldn't be sitting here. What're the chances of acceptance by the family? That's how I think of them, by the way. Captain T, capital F—"

"That doesn't surprise me, either. And there's no chance of your receiving their blessing, if that's what you were about to ask. So what we need, Ralph, is a plan of action. Marianne must face the music sooner or later. And when she does, I think if you were already married she'd be in a stronger position. It would cut out all the arguing and persuasion she'd be subjected to if she told them in advance."

"Which suits me," Ralph said vehemently. "Because I don't want her to have to go through what she's already endured in her imagination." He told Nathan about Marianne's harrowing nightmare. "Facing the music will probably bring on another one," he added.

"But you, as her husband, will be with her. When she's shown the door."

Ralph gazed pensively at two elderly ladies who were seated in a corner sipping port and lemon. "That's the only part of the whole shebang I'm not sure Marianne could live with." He took his pipe from his jacket pocket and stuffed some tobacco into the ash-stained bowl, his face shadowed with distress on Marianne's behalf. "Being cast out of the clan."

Nathan thought of his nephew Arnold, content with his wife and child, but still not a happy man. "I'm not a magician, Ralph," he said gently. "All I can do is advise you how to handle the present situation. Marianne knew what she was risking when she let things go this far. And she knows as well as I do that when it comes to Jewish attitudes, there are some things that will never change."

"Would it help if I became Jewish?" Ralph said after a silence.

Nathan hesitated before replying. Conversion was not a remedy for which he would instinctively reach, though it wasn't uncommon for Jewish families to do so when all else failed. Like his mother, he felt the outsider's religion must be respected, too. "How would your folks feel about it?" he asked Ralph and was surprised to learn he had none.

"I was an only child and so were both my parents,"

Ralph explained. "They died in a car crash when I was thirteen." His lips tightened. "Driving back to Melbourne from a weekend jaunt they'd been on. I was always being left with handy friends and neighbors on Saturdays and Sundays. It's something that won't happen to my kid." He drank some beer and lit his pipe. "My only other relative—the poor old dear's passed on now—was a maiden aunt of my mother's. She sent me a boat ticket and gave me a home here."

Nathan surveyed his faraway expression. "Ever fancied going back?"

"No. Australia's a beaut of a place, but I've no desire to return there." Ralph fanned away some smoke and fiddled with a beer mat. "What draws a person back—or keeps them away—is what they associate with it. The things they remember. There's too much about my childhood I prefer not to remember."

Nathan, the psychoanalyst, pricked up his ears. "Locking memories away in your subconscious isn't healthy, Ralph."

Ralph managed to smile. "All right, Doctor. I'll take 'em out and dust 'em off, if you think I should! But it's just one big memory, really. Made up of a lot of little things. Mum and Dad were too bloody wrapped up in each other to have time for me. I don't mean they were cruel; except in an unintentional way. I was fed, clothed and kissed goodnight. But I always had the feeling I was a nuisance. That they couldn't wait to be on their own together and wished I wasn't there. Have you ever met a couple like that?"

"I can't say I have." But who knows what goes on behind other people's closed doors? Nathan reflected, thinking of Leona, whose parents cared nothing for each other. Cruelty, the emotional kind, could be inflicted on a child unwittingly—he glanced at Ralph, compassionately—and scar the adult that child would one day become.

"My great-aunt Zena left me her house in Watford," Ralph conveyed. "And her seven cats," he smiled. "I had a helluva time finding homes for them when I sold the property. The cash is invested, by the way. It'll buy Marianne and me a nice flat."

Well, she won't be getting a dowry from her father, Nathan thought. That was for sure. Though Ben would have bought and furnished a home for her if she had married in the faith.

"But we were talking about me becoming a Jew," Ralph

said, as though picking up what Nathan had been thinking. "How did we digress this far?"

"You'd do it for Marianne?"

"I'd do anything for Marianne."

Nathan remained silent for a moment, then spoke his mind. "If you want my honest opinion, that isn't a reason to abandon your own faith."

"Officially, I haven't got one. I wasn't christened."

"You know what our equivalent to christening is? For a male?"

"Doesn't everyone? There was a Jewish boy at art school with me and when we all lined up for a pee the rest of us couldn't help noticing the difference between his and ours."

Nathan smiled. "I recall being the subject of that kind of interest in my grammar school days. 'Look, it isn't just their noses,' someone said once."

Ralph eyed his profile. "You haven't got a Jewish nose."

"But the lad who said it seemed pleased to find something different about me," Nathan laughed. His tone grew serious. "If you were to convert, you'd have to be circumcised."

"What!"

"With a grown man, it's done under anesthetic," Nathan assured him. "Like any other operation. Usually, by a Jewish surgeon."

Ralph shrugged philosophically. "Fine. When we get back, I'll tell Marianne I'm going to be a Jew. It'll cheer her up."

Nathan watched him take their empty glasses to the bar to be refilled. What a way to make such a momentous decision, he thought. As airily as if he'd decided to buy Marianne a bunch of flowers to raise her spirits. The mechanics of conversion to Judaism took time, but were not difficult. Just a set of requirements to be fulfilled to rabbinical satisfaction and Nathan had no doubt that Ralph would be a successful candidate. But coping with his new status in a world where hostility to Jews was a fact of life was something else.

"You've got a disapproving look on your face," Ralph said when he returned to the table.

"Because you're thinking of converting for expediency's sake."

"For Marianne's sake," Ralph corrected him.

"That's the same thing," Nathan drank some of his ale

and took out a pristine white handkerchief to wipe the foamy moustache from his upper lip. "I wouldn't call myself a religious man, but there's more to Judaism than its formalities."

"What, for instance?"

Nathan smiled. "I don't blame you for asking. The only aspect you've experienced is the pain one of our laws causes those whose hearts come into conflict with it. And nobody knows better than me how that can cloud a young person's judgment and make the whole thing seem nothing but strictures. I was affected that way myself once. Everything but that one aspect was blocked out of my mind." Nathan studied his fingernails reflectively. "For two pins I'd have rejected Judaism. But I'm older and wiser now. I've learned it can't be done. No matter how your brain tells you you're not chained to it, there's something that holds you fast."

"Nobody could be as close as I am to Marianne without being aware of that," Ralph said. "Only I'm damned if I know what it is. Maybe you can tell me?"

"I'll try." But how do you explain the intangible? Nathan mused. The indefinable feeling that encompassed your life. His thoughts roved to his childhood. Was that where it began? How did he know? It wasn't something you were consciously aware of, but when you looked back as he was doing now, you knew it had always been there. Like an invisible blanket warming you. As a child, he'd felt it all around him and been comforted by it. Not until he grew older had it begun to stifle him. The indefinable something had a claustrophobic quality, too. But that didn't stop you from gathering the blanket close around you in your bleak moments. How often had Nathan feasted his memory on its multi-patterned folds? His mother's home with the *Shabbos* candles alight on her white-clothed table, come what may, every Friday night. His father blessing the wine with the *Kiddush* prayer. All the timeless traditions they had passed down to their children to be respected in their family life, as their own parents had done with them. The Passover, with young and old gathered around the *Seder* table reading the story of the Exodus from Egypt, though centuries had passed since then. *Rosh Hashanah*, when Jews the world over celebrated their New Year. *Yom Kippur*, when they went without food or drink to atone for their sins and returned home from *shul* cleansed in spirit to break the Fast with their loved ones. And the colorful Harvest and Tabernacles Festivals, celebrated amid fruit and flowers in synagogues alive with rejoicing.

"I'm waiting to be enlightened," Ralph said, prodding him out of his thoughts.

Nathan felt as if he had been making a mental inventory of Jewish traditions. But reeling off the list to Ralph would not explain the feeling they evoked, or the special sense of belonging of which they were a part. "It can't be put into words," he said wryly. "You have to be Jewish to understand. But believe me, it has its compensations."

"In that case I've got something to look forward to," Ralph answered.

They got up to leave and Nathan put a friendly hand on his arm. "There's the other side of the coin, too, Ralph. So don't go rushing into conversion. Make sure the strange garment you're thinking of donning is one you're prepared to be seen in before you decide to wear it."

Nathan remained in London long enough to see his niece married by special license.

"Thank you for standing by me, Uncle Nat," Marianne said when they emerged from Kensington Register Office into the July sunlight.

He kissed her affectionately. Less like a bride she couldn't have looked, he thought, contrasting her simple navy-blue crêpe frock with the froth of lace Shirley had worn under the *Chupah*. But for Marianne there had been no marriage canopy. And no loving relatives around her to wish her well. Her Uncle Joe Klein was away on an assignment and her brother Arnold on holiday in the depths of Cornwall, where she was unable to get in touch with him. They would certainly have stood by her, but were family pariahs as she now was herself. It was the blessing of those who would not give it that her heart sought and Nathan's own hardened against them.

He watched her tilt her little red beret defiantly forward as they waited for a taxi to take him to Euston.

"Trust me to get married in a register office that's in the grounds of a hospital!" she said dryly, glancing up at the windows of St. Mary Abbot's. "We should have waited till the spring, Ralph. Then you could've dropped me off to give birth after you'd put the ring on my finger." The gamine grin that had briefly lit her face disappeared and she stared down at the gardenias Ralph had given her, twisting the stems with trembling fingers.

Ralph put his arm around her. "Brides are supposed to be happy, sweetheart."

"I am," she said, standing on tiptoe to kiss him. "But how can I help being sad, as well?"

Her poignant expression haunted Nathan throughout his journey home. What was that phrase his mother was always coming out with? The bitter with the sweet. An apt description of Marianne's wedding day, he thought grimly. According to Sarah Sandberg, it epitomized the whole of life and you were lucky if yours was flavored with both in equal proportions. She viewed happiness as if it arrived by accident. Maybe it did, but too often it was design that snatched it away from you. The ruthless engineering of others.

A cheerful cockney steward popped his balding head around the compartment door. " 'Arternoon tea is now bein' served, ladies an' gentlemen!"

Nathan watched the portly man seated opposite heave himself up and lumber away to the dining car. A straw-hatted lady left close on his heels, smoothing her skirt over spreading hips. Nathan was tempted to follow them and comfort himself with the LMS Railway's generous carbohydrate repast, but resisted the urge. As you grew older, it was easy to take the road to avoirdupois, let sugar and starch appease hungers that had no connection with your digestive tract. As his brother David's burgeoning paunch all too amply illustrated.

He rested his head against the linen antimacassar behind it and closed his eyes, but his mother's bittersweet recipe for life had lodged in his mind and gave him no peace. He would have no cause for bitterness if his family hadn't made it so. And no gall would have diluted Marianne's joy today, but for them. To spare her the initial explosion that would follow their learning of her marriage, he had elected to drop the bombshell himself and had instructed her to arrive with Ralph at this week's *Shabbos* gathering. But not until it was almost over. After Nathan had said the things that must be said, which weren't for her ears, or her Christian husband's, he thought grimly.

He would not have any of the younger generation present to learn of the conniving of which some of their elders were capable, of the damage it had wrought over the years. That the grandmother they worshipped was a master puppeteer—and David, whom they respected, her chief assistant, though he had been manipulated by her himself. Why should the kids have to know their idol Sarah Sandberg had feet of clay? Let them keep their illusions, time enough to lose them when they grew older. He had lost his own too soon.

As the train drew nearer to Manchester, the scene that would be enacted in his mother's parlor on Saturday began to unfold in Nathan's imagination. But the trepidation with which he approached any kind of collision with the family had always affected him that way. When he'd contemplated marrying Mary, he had imagined the Sandbergs sitting *Shivah* for him, finalizing his severance from the tribe with the rituals performed after a death, as had been the custom in those days.

In his mind's eye now, he could see his sister Esther. Super-imposed on the stout lady who had just returned to her seat and was taking a packet of indigestion tablets out of a lizard-skin handbag. Beside Esther, Ben was mopping his brow and his mother and David standing imperiously on either side of them. How would you like it if we took such a thing upon ourselves with your daughter? he could hear his sister shrieking. It will never be necessary, he would reply. With quiet dignity. His home truths would have been delivered before then. Because I'll never stand in the way of my daughter's happiness, he would declare finally. And that about summed it up.

The images flickered out abruptly and Nathan transferred his gaze from the stout lady's pink tongue curled around a heartburn tablet to the newspaper he had not yet unfolded. How many days had he been away? Out of routine, he'd lost track of time. He noted it was Wednesday, July 30th. And that the strife in Palestine was escalating.

The inner conflict such headlines aroused in him made itself felt, but he stamped it out. What could the English Jews do about it? Except feel embarrassed. You got hot under the collar when you read what the Irgun were doing, but your own troubles took precedence over things that didn't affect you directly.

Now, Nathan had shouldered Marianne's, too. And would reap the consequences of his complicity. Why did the prospect no longer fill him with apprehension? A moment ago, when he was rehearsing his side of the confrontation, he'd been sick with it. Practically shaking in his shoes, like the time he'd faced David about not wanting to study medicine. But the dread had suddenly left him. Been purged from his spirit as if by some cathartic exercise.

Could it be that what he was doing for Marianne was, in effect, also for himself? For which he had not found the courage years ago? No matter. He had found it now. His fear of the family had been switched off with the images that had accompanied his final bout of it. He would never be afraid of them again. Nathan Sandberg had just been reborn. On a train speeding through the dingy perimeter of his native city. What was that his *alter ego* was saying? Albeit too late.

Chapter Six

The day after Nathan's return home, the world awoke to the news that two British Army sergeants had been hanged by the Irgun Zvai Leumi.

"The Government won't give in and move out the troops because of this," David prophesied to Bessie over the bagels and jam for which they had just lost their appetite. He pushed his plate away and drank some tea. "How would it look if they did? The UN Assembly's had a special session about Palestine. The whole world is waiting to see if Mr. Bevin can get the better of Menachem Begin."

"Don't mention that name to me!" Bessie exclaimed with revulsion. "I get the creeps every time I hear it."

David was no less appalled than his wife. But this did not blind him to the Palestine situation in its entirety. "Which of the two names I've just mentioned do you mean?" he asked, though he knew. "The British sent three Irgun lads to the gallows the day before yesterday, don't forget. They weren't the first and the Irgun warned there'd be retaliation in kind if it happened again."

"Two wrongs don't make a right," Bessie retorted.

"Have I said they do? But I have to ask myself what the British are doing there. It's time they got out and left Palestine to the people it was promised to. And not just by God. You'd think there'd never been a Balfour Declaration the way Bevin's behaving. And now he's afraid to admit he's bitten off more than he can chew. It was a bad day for Jewry when he became Foreign Secretary!"

"I can do without a lecture, thank you! My head's aching," Bessie said sourly. "And I'm not looking forward to the dirty looks I'll get from the *goyim* when I go shopping this morning. Take the morning to work with you, I don't want Lizzie to see it."

Bessie's sentiments epitomized the feelings of the Jewish community. They shared their Gentile neighbors' horror about the hangings, but for them there was an additional dimension. The act had been perpetrated by their own brethren against soldiers of the country of which they were loyal citizens.

The gruesome, full-length picture of the two sergeants strung by their necks, that filled the front page of the *Daily Express*, was all too graphic evidence.

"Jesu, Mary'n Joseph," Bridie whispered, crossing herself when she saw it.

"But it isn't my fault, is it?" Leona said to her defensively.

Bridie removed her stricken gaze from the picture. "However cud it be, peteen?"

Leona refolded the newspaper with page one hidden inside, but this did not erase the hideously dangling figures from her mind. Why did the *Express* have to print it? *The Manchester Guardian*, which the family also took, hadn't. "Some people will behave as if it is," she answered Bridie. "Just because I'm Jewish. There's a girl in my class I don't get on with very well and once, when we had a bust-up, she accused me of killing Christ." Why had she suddenly remembered that? Because it was the same kind of thing.

Bridie was clearing Nathan's end of the breakfast table and clattered the toast rack on to her tray indignantly. "I nivver heard anythin' so daft in me whole life! Anyone who'd lived wi' ye since ye were born like I have'd know ye couldn't kill a fly!"

"You're like one of our family, Bridie. But—forgive me for saying this—most Christian people lump all Jews together. We all get the blame for everything." Leona stared pensively through the window at the blaze of marigolds bordering the lawn. "I'm glad it's the summer holiday and I don't have to go to school today."

"Why's that?" Rebecca inquired, entering the room in her housecoat. "Make me a pot of coffee, will you, Bridie dear? I took a sleeping pill last night; that's why I overslept. You didn't answer my question," she said to her daughter.

Leona unfolded the *Daily Express* and showed her the front page.

"Oh my God," Rebecca breathed, avoiding Bridie's eye.

But the shock and shame combined that summed up English Jewry's feelings did not prepare them for the anti-Semitic backlash that followed.

Nathan and Lou emerged from their surgery that morning to find that their car tires had been slashed. And Sigmund Moritz had an experience that left him trembling.

"We're full up," the conductor barked when he was about to board a bus to the city center. "Why don't you get on a boat to Palestine instead?"

Sigmund abandoned his errand and went to share his indignation with Sarah.

"Me, I didn't have to go out of the house to get it," she said after he had told her. "The window cleaner gave me a taste of it here! He doesn't know how much longer he can go on cleaning Jewish windows, he said to me. "A pane of glass has a religion all of a sudden?" I asked him. But my heart was thumping fifty to the dozen."

Sigmund sipped the lemon tea she had made to calm his nerves and her own. "Only last year they finished trying the criminals at Nuremberg," he reflected. A long sigh escaped him. "The holocaust outraged the whole world, Sarah. But the instinct to take it out of us is still there."

Sarah put down her glass of tea and busied herself preparing to make her *gefilte* fish. "Isn't that the reason Jews stick together? Who else dare we trust? It's what I told Marianne when she said it isn't right that we do."

Sigmund snorted irascibly. "Marianne is another Hannah! Until we stop sticking together, our troubles will never end, my daughter-in-law says. Intermarriage she believes in, even."

"And a few generations from now there wouldn't be any

Jews!" Sarah exclaimed tartly. "A solution like that to our young machinists entered.

Trouble met David the moment he entered his factory. He had called to see his accountant en route and did not arrive until mid-morning.

"Myrna and Joyce are waiting to give you their notice," his secretary greeted him. "I'll give you three guesses why."

"I'm not in the mood for guessing games, Rita."

"In that case I'll let them tell you. I might gag on the words if I tried to." Rita knocked on the glass partition and beckoned the two girls, who were standing sullenly in the workroom.

David sat down at his cluttered desk. Why did he have an uneasy feeling? Because of the way he'd started the day. And as a rule, notice wasn't handed in until Friday evening.

"What's all this about?" he asked when the stony-faced young machinists entered.

"Me brother's in't regular army," Joyce informed him.

"I beg your pardon?" It took a moment for the implications of what she had said to sink in.

"But I won't work fer Jews anyroad after what's bin done by 'em t'our lads," she added defiantly adjusting the purple scarf that did not quite hide her bangs of steel curling pins.

"Nor me neither," the other girl declared.

"Suit yourselves," David answered curtly. But his innards were churning with something akin to distress. Joyce and Myrna had worked for him since they left school. It was like finding out you'd been nursing a couple of vipers in your bosom for four years.

"Good riddance is what I say," Rita told them.

"An' we'd say t'same if you lot went back ter wherever it were yer come from," Myrna retorted.

David felt as if he was having a bad dream. His tongue had cloven to the roof of his mouth and he could not speak.

"So now yer know," Joyce said cheekily.

"Make up their pay packets," David instructed Rita. "With an extra week's money in lieu of notice. They can leave right now. I don't want to see them again."

He got up and went to the pressing room to make sure he would not have to, thankful that Shirley and Peter were away on holiday. His daughter might have torn the two girls apart.

"Oy," Abraham sighed when David recounted the distasteful incident. "So what can you do?" he added inevitably.

"I'm beginning to think there's nothing we can do," David answered. He watched his father hang up a coat that was one of the new autumn range. The room was large and airy and equipped with modern presses. But the atmosphere was steamy nevertheless and did not help Abraham's chronic bronchitis.

How many years had he watched this stubborn old man labor? Listened to the phlegm rolling around on his chest? Since David was a lad and they'd worked together in Isaac Salaman's filthy workshop. Factory conditions had changed since then, as had the family's fortunes. But for David, the journey over the years seemed in retrospect all uphill. He had clawed his way to something better. And until a few minutes ago had thought things that had nothing to do with material achievement had changed for the better, too. But some people were still only too ready to turn on the Jews. As if it was bred in them and that, nothing could change.

He stared through the window unseeingly. The petty anti-Semitism he had experienced as a child in Strangeways had not gone away. It had only been lying dormant.

"You don't intend doing any work today?" his father inquired. "My assistants neither," he added caustically.

David glanced at the idle presses at the other end of the room, which ordinarily would not have escaped his attention. He returned to his office and saw the absentee pressers talking with Eli and Issie beside the cutting benches. But he could not bring himself to go into the workroom and break up the group. The two newly-vacated places among the sewing machines had the same sickening significance for them as for himself.

Rita was leaning against a filing cabinet, studying her coral fingernails absently, but he did not prod her into activity, either. Today was no ordinary day.

"They're not all like Myrna and Joyce," she said. "And we've got to be grateful for that."

The things Jews had to be grateful for!

"The other Christian machinists didn't behave any differently from how they always are with me, when I said good morning to them," Rita went on. She stopped studying her nails and managed to smile. "So I don't intend to dwell on it."

But it was difficult not to, David thought. "You always were a sensible girl," he said.

"That must be why I've never got married."

David glanced at her lush figure, enhanced by a clinging, black dress. She still modeled coats for him and since the war had taken to garbing herself for that role, instead of her secretarial one. How old was she now? Nearing thirty. And no man had found her alluring shape sufficient compensation for her ugly face. But she had never lost the capacity to laugh at the cruel joke Nature had played upon her. Nor David his compassion for her.

"The chaps don't know what they're missing," he smiled.

"Me neither," she quipped. "And I'll probably go to my grave without finding out." She sat down at her desk and picked up a pencil and her shorthand notebook. "Meanwhile, let's do some work, Mr. Sanderton."

David had grown accustomed to his new name, but this morning it had a hollow ring. Why had he bothered? Jews were thought of as foreigners whatever they were called! He shifted his mind to his correspondence and was halfway through his dictation when Moishe Lipkin rang up.

"How is it in Manchester?" Moishe inquired when the business part of their talk was over.

"It isn't raining."

"We should worry! If I wake up in the morning and the sun's shining, instead of asking God to arrange for a cloudburst, like I used to, I bless your Shirley for designing garments women'll wear even when it isn't wet. I wouldn't like to go back to the days when we sank or swam according to the weather," Moishe said. "But I wasn't referring to the weather. I wondered if you'd seen any anti-Semitic slogans chalked on walls. I've seen some in Leeds."

A leadlike feeling settled in David's stomach. "I haven't been round looking."

Later, he learned in telephone conversations with customers that slogans of this kind had appeared on walls elsewhere.

This was not all he learned. "They're at it again," Izzie Klepman, who owned a string of rainwear shops in London, said hotly when he rang to inquire why an order had not been delivered. "You'd think they'd had their lesson, but no!"

"Who are you talking about, Izzie?"

"Who do you think? Mosley and his pal Arnold Leese,

of course. Even sticking them behind bars during the war because they had the same kind of ideas as Hitler hasn't
stopped them. The moment they're let loose the Jews know
about it!"

"I thought the British Union of Fascists was disbanded."

"It was. But a rose by any other name can still do damage if its thorns are poisonous. Leese was the leader of the
Imperial Fascist League and they say he's the biggest Jew-
hater of them all. Now, there's something called the British
ex-Serviceman's Movement—"

"I've never heard of it," David cut in.

"What are you? A greenhorn or an ostrich? They've already been tub-thumping on a bomb-site in Hackney. The
same old stuff the Blackshirts did before the war."

"I didn't know."

Izzie snorted down the phone. "Because all you ever
think of is Zionism. I give my whack to the JNF, too. But it
doesn't shut my eyes to what's going on nearer home."

"Are you saying the Fascists are behind what's happening at the moment?"

"Too true I am."

David's disquiet deepened when his errand-boy, whom
he had sent to buy cigarettes, returned in an agitated state
and told him that a gang of thugs had charged up Cheetham
Hill Road chanting, "Out with the Jews."

The lad stood pale-faced in the office doorway, the
yarmulke he wore atop his crinkly hair because he came
from a devout family askew, as if he had been running. "I
didn't get your cigarettes, Mr. Sanderton. They were breaking
the Jewish shopkeepers' windows and I was scared stiff."

"It's all right, Harold. I'll get them myself."

"I never expected to see anything like that in England,"
the boy muttered. "I can't believe it." He gave David a dazed
glance then turned away and went into the workroom.

David, too, found it difficult to believe. He pulled himself together and saw that Rita was staring down at her
typewriter with a confused expression on her face.

"I'm going to see what's happening," he said to her
brusquely.

By the time he reached the main road, the mob was receding in the direction of the city center. He surveyed the
broken windows. How could you not believe what you had
seen with your own eyes? The traders were sweeping up the

glass. Like Sigmund Moritz had had to do in a ghetto in Vienna at the turn of the century.

"For this I lost a grandson in the war!" one of them exclaimed to David.

David put a hand on his trembling shoulder, wordlessly.

"That nothing like this should ever happen again, he thought he was fighting for," the man added emotionally.

David walked slowly back to the factory. It was happening again because those who were determined it would have been let out of jail and were making sure it did. What Izzie Klepman had said was right. Political forces were behind it. The personal animosity directed at David by the two young machinists was the kind of ill-feeling that would blow over. But there were those who didn't want it to. Whoever had organized the riot on Cheetham Hill Road—and a mob that size would have had to be organized—was using the gruesome incident in Palestine to fan the flicker of anti-Semitism it had sparked to life in England.

That evening, he heard there had been rioting in other Jewish districts. And that the local branch of the Union of Jewish ex-Servicemen and Women had called an emergency meeting.

"Why aren't you going to it, Dad?" Ronald demanded over supper. "Uncle Nat is. And if Peter wasn't sunning himself in Lugano, he'd go."

Bessie eyed Ronald reproachfully. "Do you want your dad to get hurt in a brawl with the Fascists? It isn't for him, at his age, to start taking them on. I'm ashamed of you, Ronald."

"And I'm ashamed of Dad!" Ronald retorted, stalking out of the room.

"Pay no attention to him, David," Bessie said dismissively. "And don't take it out on me," she added when he did not reply. "My head's aching."

"When isn't it?"

"And a lot you care!" She, too, removed herself from his presence, slamming the door shut behind her.

David lit a cigarette and stared at the half-eaten dessert his wife and son had abandoned, beset by a sudden desolation. Was this what he had come to? After a life of striving for others? A careworn, middle-aged man who felt lonely in his own home? He ground out the cigarette, which tasted more acrid than it should. But why should his sense of taste be spared the bitterness presently permeating everything else? Did anyone ever get back from life what they put into it? he wondered. In business, maybe. Hard work brought its reward. But in personal relationships—the less said the better! He didn't want to think about it. Only how could he not, when the son he idolized had said he was ashamed of him.

This generation of youngsters spoke their minds to their parents as David's had never done. He had not exactly been ashamed of his own father, but in some ways had been unable to respect him. It had been hard for a go-ahead lad like David to accept Abraham's total lack of ambition. But he had kept his opinions to himself. A father was a father and you made allowances because you loved him.

He heard Ronald leave the house and roar off in his car, without saying goodbye. To the father who had provided the car—and everything else he thought of as his. Yet Ronald was always comparing him with Nat, from whom David had received the same treatment. Which amounted to a kick in the arse, though he had supported Nat, too. And hadn't he got the same from Miriam? Despite all he had done for Sammy, from which she had benefited. Thanks he didn't want from any of them, but he didn't deserve what was meted out to him. Why was it that those for whom you did most were the ones who turned against you?

Bessie popped her head around the door. "If you want to go to the ex-Servicemen's meeting, don't let me stop you," she said in a surly voice. "So you'll get landed by a thug, I should worry!" she added before she withdrew again.

As usual, she had escalated the situation in her mind and could see the Jewish men and lads scuffling in the streets with Fascist bruisers. The meeting had been called to discuss strategy. But would what Bessie foresaw eventually happen? As it had in London in the thirties? The possibility made David shudder. He'd been sitting here feeling sorry for himself, but his personal problems were insignificant by comparison.

The thought of Jews who had worn British uniforms battling with bricks and fists against Gentiles who had been nominally their comrades in arms during the war was nothing short of horrific. And that it should be necessary was even more so. War was a great unifier, but afterwards, it seemed, people resumed the attitudes that were theirs previously.

David recalled the soldiers with whom he had stood side

by side in the trenches in Flanders. They had come from all walks of life and some had been rough types; but he couldn't imagine any of them terrorizing a neighborhood as the Fascists had done today. It took a special kind to lend themselves to mob violence. The kind in whom Man's basest instincts were never far below the surface. But if it came to it, the Jewish ex-Servicemen would give them no quarter; they had not fought against the Nazis to stand by and watch the worm eat away the apple again.

Bessie returned to the room and sat down on the sofa. "I only said what I did because I love you," she said, playing with her pearls. "I love you too much."

That this was the root cause of all that ailed her, David had decided long ago. Her moodiness and jealousy were side effects of it.

"Are you going to that meeting, or aren't you?" she asked.

"No, Bessie." David smiled ruefully. "As you said to Ronald, I'm past the age when I'd be any use if it came to fisticuffs. Let's hope it won't. But there'll be no shortage of able-bodied volunteers."

This was confirmed by Nathan at the Sabbath gathering. David noticed that his brother seemed edgy, but who wasn't with what was going on? There had not been a recurrence of the rioting; but the lads would be ready for it if there was, Nathan told the family. Observers had been posted and everyone was on call.

"Who would have thought, after beating the Nazis, we'd be sitting down talking like this?" Sarah sighed.

"Anti-Semitism is a bestial instinct," David declared.

"Nonsense!" Hannah said in her brisk way. "Nobody's born hating Jews; it's something that's planted in them. It's a carefully engineered tactic, David, that makes use of people's need for a scapegoat."

"And why is the scapegoat always us?" he retorted.

"Because those doing the engineering know we're sitting ducks. Jews became the whipping-boy because they've never been prepared to renounce their beliefs. What were the pogroms but attempts to make people like your parents accept Christianity? Modern anti-Semitism isn't motivated by religion, as it was then. It's a political weapon pure and simple these days. That's why it's always at its worst when the economic climate is bad—why it thrived in the thirties when the unemployed needed an outlet for their anger, someone to blame and hit back at."

"Meanwhile it's the forties and not too many people are unemployed," Abraham reminded Hannah.

"But there's the Palestine situation, isn't there?" she replied. "And the Fascists have hung their hat on that. Opportunism is their middle name."

The family fell into a contemplative silence whilst Sarah poured the tea.

"The room is half empty today," she remarked, glancing around at the vacant chairs.

"It's the holiday season," David said.

"So far as I know, Ronald isn't on holiday," she answered rebukingly. How dare he not attend his grandmother's tea party? her tone had implied.

Nathan defended his nephew. "Ronald called to see me this morning, Mother, and mentioned he was doing ward duty today. For one of his Christian pals who was invited to a wedding."

David's lips tightened. Ronald had reached the final stage of his medical training and was working on the wards at the infirmary. This was supposed to be his weekend off, but David had had to learn from Nathan that his son was doing a duty-stint!

Nathan saw David throw him a sour glance and wondered what he had done to deserve it. But more than sour glances would come his way when he dropped the bombshell about Marianne. Which must wait until Esther and Ben arrived from the shop. It was August Bank Holiday Saturday, one of their busiest days of the year, and he hoped they wouldn't come later than usual because of this.

Hannah put down her cup and saucer. "We'd better be off," she said, prodding the twins, who were seated by the window reading. She rumpled their hair, one head with each hand. "Nobody would think these two boys were going on holiday! Other kids get excited about it, but not them."

"How can anyone get excited about Blackpool sands?" Henry asked. "I'm long past the stage when I enjoyed digging holes and making castles."

"I don't think you ever did," Hannah laughed. "You were never normal."

"He still isn't," Frank declared. "As Leona would have said if she'd been here."

"And that's another thing," Sarah said, eyeing Nathan. But he remained silent and she said no more.

The Moritzes made their usual noisy departure. Sigmund had maintained a pensive silence throughout the afternoon, but now began protesting that he did not need a holiday.

"He's been saying that ever since we made the arrangements, but we're paying no attention to him," Helga smiled.

This would be their first vacation since the war and was to be spent in the same rented flat they had occupied during bank holiday week for several years before then. They could not set off until evening, the bookshop where Carl was employed now opened on Saturday afternoon, but would have been unable to do so in any event. Nothing short of a life or death emergency would have induced Sigmund to ride on the Sabbath.

"Enjoy it," Sarah smiled when she saw them to the door. Abroad, in a posh hotel, like some of her grandchildren now went to with their families, it wasn't, and for them never would be; the twins had the same disinterest in the good things of life as all the other Moritzes. Which seemed a pity, when they were both brainy and could probably end up rich if they wanted to. But, as she'd had cause to ask herself too often in recent years, what were riches if you weren't content in other ways?

"So why did your wife take it into her head to visit her mother in London this weekend, Nat?" she asked apropos of her final thought when she returned to the parlor. "All of a sudden and taking Leona with her?" She transferred her attention to David. "And Bessie's in bed with another headache?"

"It's a pity Sammy's in America, or you could give to him the third degree, too," Abraham said tetchily.

Sarah ignored the interruption and awaited her sons' replies. That things were going from bad to worse between Nat and his wife, even a blind man could see. And Bessie had pleaded a headache too often lately.

David was not sure if the headaches were real or simulated. He sometimes thought they were just Bessie's newest way of manifesting her anxieties and irritations. "It's probably her age," he said to his mother. "You know. The change of life."

And when I went through it, my husband didn't even know it was happening to me, Sarah thought. In her day, women had not made what was natural into an excuse for this, that and the other.

"This isn't the first time Rebecca's gone to visit her sister at a minute's notice," was the only answer Nathan was prepared to give regarding his wife.

And it won't be the last, Sarah sighed to herself. What sort of home life did these two sons of hers have? She eyed Nathan's hair, which wasn't entitled to so much silver at his age. And the deep furrow, that came from frowning, above the bridge of David's nose.

"So," she said, hiding her distress behind a smile. "For once, there's nobody here but us Sandbergs."

"One of us isn't a Sandberg any more," Abraham said with an acid glance at David.

"Don't start on that again, Father," Nathan interceded.

"All of a sudden you're on his side?"

Nathan noted David's surprised expression. "I don't believe in what you call sides, Father. Any more."

"It must be because you've joined the Reform *Shul*," Abraham retorted with sarcasm.

"It isn't, as a matter of fact. It's because I don't think what a person does is anyone else's business."

David gave him a look that harked back to the past. "It depends what about. And how it's going to affect other people."

Nathan held his gaze. "That's the whole point, David. There are some things that ought not to affect other people."

The arrival of Esther and Ben cut short the exchange.

Nathan wished they had been there when it took place. From that point, he could have gone on to talk about Marianne.

"Such a day it's been! We've been run off our feet," Esther said, sinking on to the sofa and easing off her shoes. "Harry sends his love. He got into his car and drove straight to Southport. It's a pity his wife couldn't have come to help at the shop, instead of spending this weekend at the Prince of Wales Hotel," she added, airing her disapproval of her daughter-in-law. "I said so to Harry, but he said he wouldn't expect it. Neither would I, I thought. Ann Klein she is now, but she's still one of the stuck-up Smolenskys."

"So what can you do?" Sarah shrugged.

Esther smiled sourly. "Go on working myself into the

ground with my husband and son, so she won't go short of her luxuries!"

Nathan surveyed the permanently miserable expression on Esther's aging countenance. Which her younger son's defection had put there. Arnold was guilty of treason, in her eyes. Ben's, too. But, in effect, they had betrayed him. No son or daughter should be cast out by parents who purported to love them. But Esther and Ben had been ruled by religion, not by love and the whole of life had lost its savor for them as a result.

If they had let themselves come to terms with things, what a different picture they would present from the one they did now. Arnold and his child would be bringing them joy, instead of heartache. And Esther would have a daughter-in-law worthy of respect. She had accepted Harry's marriage to a girl she did not like. Accepted her because she was kosher. Nobody could fail to like Arnold's Lyn, who was sincere and unaffected. As Mary Dennis had been as a girl. This was what made the situation not only tragic, but ludicrous.

"What're you staring at Ben and me for, Nat?" Esther asked him.

"I'm thinking what damn fools you are."

Esther stopped nibbling a piece of strudel. "I beg your pardon?"

She was seated on the sofa with Ben beside her. David and Sarah were standing on either side of them. Exactly as Nathan had seen the group in his mind's eye, when he anticipated this moment, on the train. His father was behind him and this was uncannily right, too. Abraham had not been part of the imaginary scene. Only the strong ones had flanked Esther and Ben. His mother and brother. Who no longer intimidated him.

"Hasn't it occurred to you how stupid it is to try to dictate your children's lives?" he said calmly to his sister and brother-in-law. "You'll end up with only Harry. Unless you do something to interfere with his happiness, too. In which case you'll be a lonely old couple, crying into your tea because you're all on your own."

Esther looked at David. "Has our Nat gone mad?"

"It sounds like it."

"As a matter of fact, I've never been saner," Nathan declared. "Something's happened to make me see straight, which I'd never done before. I hope it will have the same ef-

fect on all of you. I have something to tell you. And please
don't say anything until I've finished."

The request was unnecessary. Learning that Marianne
had married a Gentile reduced his listeners to silence.

"How could Marianne do this to us?" Esther whispered.

"She wouldn't have had to if you hadn't done what you
did to her," Nathan said.

"What is he talking about?" Ben asked confusedly.

"That's the root of the trouble. That you don't know."

Esther began weeping. "What is there to know? Except
that we cherished her and she's let us down."

"It serves you right," Nathan said ruthlessly. "For putting her—and Arnold—in a position where they had to." He
eyed his mother, who was clutching her brooch as if it were a
talisman. And his brother whose expression was thunderous.
"Remember when I told you I was joining the Reform *Shul*
and you all set about me? I accused the family of molding
my life, but that doesn't only apply to me. We've all had a
taste of it in our time. Haven't we, David?"

He saw David flinch, but did not weaken. The things he
had decided to say must be said. He made his points swiftly
and sharply and watched them hit home, like arrows piercing
the target with deadly precision. "If we had a family tomb, a
suitable epitaph to be carved on the door would be, 'Here lie
the Sandbergs, who died of obligation—' "

"Shut your mouth!" David shouted.

" 'In their youth,' " Nathan went on. "And thereafter
only their ghosts existed. If David prefers not to admit it,
that's his choice. But I'm done with pretending it doesn't apply to me."

Sarah's complexion had tinged with gray and her eyes
were opaque with sorrow. "This is what you think your
family's done to you, Nat?"

"I don't think it; I know it. Maybe you're unaware of
your own power, Mother. It's the most dangerous and subver-
sive kind there is, because it's fueled by maternal love which
children accept naturally. But not for a moment do I think
David is unaware of his."

"Oy," Abraham sighed eloquently.

Nathan had forgotten he was in the room. But how often had that been the case? If his father had been a strong
enough character to make his presence felt, his mother's

materialistic designs for her children might not have been allowed to dominate all their lives.

Esther dried her eyes. "What do we do now?" she asked David.

The way she always had, Nathan thought. Though her husband was right beside her, it was David whom she consulted. Ben was regarding David helplessly, too. They never moved a muscle without his advice. He watched his brother take a silk handkerchief from his breast pocket and hand it to Esther, whose own was soaked with tears.

"Get the marriage annulled, of course," David said tersely.

As Nathan had anticipated he would. But the trump card was still up Nathan's sleeve, saved for this moment. "You'll have a job, with a baby on the way."

The silence that followed was terrible. Nathan could find no other way to describe it. As if he had dropped a great stone into a lake without producing a single ripple, or so much as a tiny plop.

He saw two patches of red appear on his sister's sallow cheeks. Then his mother lowered herself into a chair.

For once, Abraham was the first to speak. But it was God whom he addressed. "All my life I've been Your obedient servant and this is the thanks I get for it," he said, raising his eyes to the ceiling. "Your ways are weird and wonderful, somebody, I can't remember who, once said to me. Weird, I agree."

Nathan put a comforting hand on his shoulder. It was shrugged off abruptly. Nobody had yet mentioned the matter of his own complicity, but that would doubtless come later. He glanced at the clock and saw that Marianne and Ralph were due to arrive shortly. Which he had so far kept to himself. "Something wonderful could come of this," he said vehemently. "If the people in this room were prepared to let it."

Esther sprang to life and glared at him. "Tell us what?"

"You could give Marianne your blessing and welcome her husband into the family."

"Over my dead body," she answered.

Sarah rose from her chair. "Which only one of your three children will be there to mourn over, if you don't. Nat is right about this, Esther."

"Have you gone mad as well as him?" Esther demanded.

"What you're saying goes against everything you brought us up to believe, Mother!"

"And many a time I've wanted to say it to you about Arnold, as well."

Nathan's surprise was such that he had to sit down. Was his mother really championing the cause of intermarriage?

Her next words put an end to any illusion that she was.

"To do something against what we believe doesn't mean we've stopped believing in it. Me, I'll never stop. But I have to try to put myself in Marianne's place. When I was a girl in Russia, who knew from anything outside our own way of life? Judaism was our be-all and end-all; to be Jewish was like living on a desert island and nobody went swimming in the sea of *goyim* around it."

Abraham contributed to the imagery. "They would have been frightened of being gobbled up by sharks."

"But here, there's no need to be frightened," Sarah said. "And both ways you can't have it. We'd only been in England a few years when I found that out. My eldest son rode on a train to Alderley Edge, on *Shabbos*—to visit a Christian school friend."

"You can hardly compare that with marrying-out!" David exclaimed.

Sarah agreed; it was the kind of misdemeanor that these days ranked low on her list of sins. "But it was the beginning," she declared. The first installment of the price of freedom, it seemed to her now. "Since then my children and theirs have traveled a long way on the path away from Judaism. And after a while, I stopped protesting. What they can't do in front of your eyes, they'll still do behind your back—that I had to accept. Only a fool wouldn't accept it. And protesting will only drive them away, my commonsense told me." She allowed herself a long sigh. "What is the use of fighting a battle you know you can't win? Only the quality of Jewish life is still the same, the part that has to do with our hearts. The faith my generation has is less so with my children's and even less with my grandchildren's."

"Because they're moving further and further away from religious observance in their daily lives," Abraham said in a grieved voice. "Do my sons and my son-in-law still lay *tefillin* and say their prayers in the mornings, I wonder?" He eyed their expressions and knew the answer was no. "And *shul*, except on *Yom Tov*, they don't bother with any more, either."

"I do," Nathan informed him. "I enjoy the service, now. For the first time in my life I understand it."

Abraham snorted derisively. "The *shul* you go to doesn't count. Every word you said was right," he told Sarah. "And for what their children do they have only themselves to blame."

Nathan was watching the clock. Marianne and Ralph would be here any minute. "Which returns us to the point," he said brusquely to Esther and Ben. "What about your daughter? And your unborn grandchild?"

"I'd like to throttle the man who's got her in the family way!" Ben blazed. It was the first time he had spoken since learning Marianne was pregnant and his words sounded like the sudden eruption of a volcano.

"He's now her husband," Nathan reminded him. "And she wouldn't have slept with him out of wedlock if you hadn't made marrying him seem impossible."

The red patches appeared on Esther's cheeks again.

"Such matters we won't talk about," Sarah said delicately.

A taxi pulled up outside the house, but only Nathan noticed it. "Well?" he demanded.

Esther and Ben exchanged an agonized glance.

"Are you going to deal with this like you dealt with Arnold?" Nathan asked them.

"I won't let them," Sarah declared. She rose from her chair, wearing her Queen Victoria expression. "Marianne is my granddaughter and I don't intend to lose her." She cast a glance at Abraham. "Like I said to you about Arnold, I want my family to get bigger, not smaller. And I don't stop loving people because they make mistakes."

David hesitated, then spoke decisively. "I agree with Mother. If we go on cutting people off, we could end up with a family half the size."

"You always do agree with Mother," Nathan said. "But in this case I'm delighted." He waved through the window to Ralph, who was opening the garden gate.

"Who is it?" Ben asked.

"Your son-in-law. A big fellow, isn't he? That's why you can't see Marianne standing behind him. I hadn't yet mentioned they were coming."

Marianne ducked under Ralph's arm and preceded him up the path.

"Thank God her pregnancy doesn't show yet, Ben," Esther said.

But Ben was no longer at her side. He had rushed to open the door and embrace his daughter.

Chapter Seven

Marianne's son was born in the spring of 1948. She named him Martin, which did not surprise the family. But the way the whole clan traveled to London for the baby's *Brith* astounded Ralph.

"The circumcision was over in no time, then they just had some cake and wine and left. I wouldn't have thought they'd consider it worth coming," he ruminated to Marianne that evening.

Marianne smiled. "Because you still don't know my family. And most Jewish ones are the same. All you've learned so far is that everyone's business is everyone else's."

"You can say that again!" Ralph grinned from the armchair into which he had sunk, exhausted, after his clamorous in-laws' departure.

"You'll find out that goes for joys and sorrows, too," Marianne informed him.

She was curled up on the window seat of their new home, watching the rush-hour traffic crawl along Hammersmith Road, with a potpourri of the expensive perfumes most of her female relatives wore lingering in the air to remind her of them now that they were gone And of some of the things they'd said, she thought as a whiff of Shirley's Chanel Number Five overpowered all the others.

"I don't know how anyone can live in a flat," her exquisitely turned-out cousin had declaimed, standing with her hands on the "peplum" of her New Look suit.

Marianne had not known until today that there was a New Look. Or that a few inches of jacket, flaring over the hips from a tight-fitting waistline, was called a peplum. She had put on the navy-blue frock she had bought for her wedding, thankful to have regained her normal shape immediately so she could wear it and look dressed up. But it seemed something had happened to feminine fashion recently. Including a drop in the hemline to only a few inches above the ankles.

Auntie Bessie had only removed her critical gaze from Marianne's Old Look in order to survey the living room and pronounce her opinion of it. In one sentence. "There's no space to swing a cat round."

"And no garden where the baby can lie in his pram, in the fresh air," Ann had said, sounding horrified.

"I hope my darling grandson won't feel sick riding up and down in the elevator," Marianne's mother had moaned.

But her grandmother had had the last word. "A person has to make the best of what they have. And Marianne takes after me, she's the kind who's prepared to."

In Manchester, flats were a rarity, but Marianne's neighbors here had never lived in a house. Houses were more costly. This had not prevented Ben Klein from wanting to buy one for his daughter and son-in-law, but Ralph had refused the offer. Marianne was proud of his independence, which her family seemed unable to understand. Jewish parents, even those who had to scrimp and sacrifice to do so, always helped their newly married daughters set up home. And custom dating back to the days when a *perineh* for the marital bed was a girl's basic dowry, she thought wryly. Bobbie Sarah still had hers, stuffed with the original goose feathers. It must have been re-covered umpteen times since it traveled with her from Russia.

Customs and traditions were the warp and weft of Jewish life. But how far removed she felt from her roots. Seeing the family here today had made her feel more so. Removed, but not exiled. There remained a tenderness for the background from which she had sprung—and a new kind of tolerance for those who didn't see life as she did, who were content to be part of it.

Her son was beside her, swaddled in the shawl Helga had knitted for him, as she had for every new baby in the clan. A blue silk coverlet, crocheted by Lizzie Wilson, was thrown lightly over his cradle. The same cradle Marianne's nephew Howard had slept in last year, as Leona had once upon a time, and which Uncle Nat had stored away for future children. But looking to the future was a Sandberg quality, a Jewish quality—which was strange in a people for whom there had often seemed to be no future.

Martin was wearing the family gown, yellowed with age, yet still preserved in lavender and tissue paper, as it had been since Marianne's great-grandmother sewed it in Russia, for Uncle David. Would a grandson of hers wear it one day? she wondered, stroking the soft, black down on Martin's tiny head. But this was absurd! What had maternity done to her? Turned her into a Jewish mother thinking about grandchildren when her first child was only eight days old. Like Sarah Sandberg, who went on preserving the gown for the next *Brith*.

"What are you smiling about, Mrs. Dean?" Ralph inquired.

"If I told you, you wouldn't believe me."

He came to sit beside her and she rested her head on his shoulder. Sometimes she had to pinch herself to make sure this wasn't a dream. That Ralph was really her husband and they had a son. That everything had turned out as it had.

They had not yet lit the lamps, but Ralph had built up the fire and the leaping flames were casting an amber glow. On the silver 'tea service Uncle David had given them for a wedding present. And the twisted brass candlesticks that were her grandparents' gift. A small bookcase, from the Moritzes, held her most treasured literature and the leather wing chair was from Uncle Nat. The bed she and Ralph slept in had been bought by her parents and her household linens provided by Harry and her cousins. What was she doing? Counting her blessings? Yes, in a way. It was lovely to have all these things, but what they represented, being at peace with the family, was even lovelier.

When Sarah arrived home from London, she marched to the telephone without pausing to take off her coat and hat.

Abraham had no need to ask whose number she was dialing. Her expression had told him. "Again you're phoning Arnold? What makes you think he'll talk to you? When he's dropped the receiver in everyone's ear, including yours, fifty times? He's told Marianne and Nat he's finished with the family and you know what a stubborn he is."

"Four years the family left him out in the cold to get even more so," Sarah replied, listening to her grandson's phone ringing a few miles away in Didsbury. "But a person has to try."

Abraham sighed and took the electric kettle into the scullery to fill it. David had bought it for them, but it was rarely used. Sarah preferred to keep her old cast-iron one singing on the hob as she had done when electricity in the home was unheard of.

In many ways, people had been happier then, Abraham reflected as he turned on the cold tap. In Strangeways there'd been no hot one—water for baths and laundry had been heated on the fire. Now, people could switch on an immersion heater and make their household bills bigger. The more things that came along to make life easier, the more worries you had keeping up with them.

It was the same in the factory, where David had installed central heating and now had to employ a man to look after the boiler. Which ate up mountains of coke. The old-fashioned paraffin stoves Abraham had liked to warm his hands over had disappeared. And his children now had fancy electric stoves, with imitation coal that lit up when you plugged in, warming their living rooms instead of real fires. Sammy had written that his apartment had no fireplace, that all the blocks of flats in New York were centrally heated. Like a factory! Abraham thought with disgust.

In his view, a home without a welcoming hearth was not a home. But you couldn't halt the march of progress. More and more convenience was what everyone wanted. The simple life of old was looked back on with scorn. Modern gadgets left more time for pleasure, people believed. What pleasure? he asked himself. Was it the electric kettle that had set him thinking about this? Probably. But the feeling that the world wasn't what it was before the war had been creeping up on him for some time.

And what pleasure was right! Once, he'd enjoyed going to the pictures, but who wanted to see films about murder and adultery? Hollywood must be a different place nowadays from what it had been when Charlie Chaplin and Mary Pickford had made Abraham laugh and cry. And Malka Berkowitz's second cousin was one of the producers responsible for the change. What was the grandson of a *Hassid* rabbi doing making immoral films?

"Where are you with the kettle already?" he heard Sarah

call testily. Which meant Arnold had dropped the phone in her ear again.

Sarah watched him plug the kettle into the wall socket above the built-in dresser. "There's no such thing as undiluted joy, Abraham."

"News, she's telling me."

"What I've always said about the bitter with the sweet is staring me in the face again. Marianne, thank God, we didn't lose. But Arnold we can't get back."

They sat in pensive silence waiting for the water to boil. Then Sarah got up to make the tea, brewing it with an egg-shaped, metal infuser in the two, large, comforting cups they used when they were alone. "Did you ever think you'd get used to tea with milk?" she asked, adding some and handing Abraham his. "Instead of with lemon?"

"Plenty of things I didn't think I'd ever get used to," he declared. "And some of the new-fangled ones I never will. What America does today, England will do tomorrow, my son who's gone to live among the Yanks said in his last letter. Self-service grocery stores they've got there, Sammy said. What did he call them?"

"Supermarkets. You don't have to wait for anyone to serve you, so you get your shopping done quicker."

Abraham snorted. "Like machines put on the buttons and sew the buttonholes in the factory now. Instead of a person doing it. And those Hoffman presses do the job men like me used to take a pride in. Everything has to be quick, quick, quick!"

"You and those Hoffman presses!"

"But hasn't the human touch gone out of nearly everything? One day, these clever machines they keep inventing, and the groceries like Sammy mentioned, that don't need assistants behind the counter, will put everyone out of work." Abraham was trembling with wrath and had to put down his cup. A bout of coughing overtook him and left him limp and exhausted. "But why should I care? I won't be here when it happens," he said, replacing his handkerchief in his pocket. "And the simple things of life my great-grandchildren have never known they won't miss. A switch they'll flick and everything will happen by magic. So they can sit twiddling their thumbs, with nothing to do with their time."

Sarah eyed him anxiously. Giving vent to his feelings with such loquacity was not like him. The day trip to London had been long and wearisome, despite the comfort of David's car, and Abraham had dozed off on the return journey. At the *Brith*, he'd had the honor of holding the baby's legs during the ceremony, as he had for all his grandsons and great-grandsons. Except Arnold's Matthew, Sarah thought with a pang. Matthew, they'd learned from Nat, had been circumcised by a surgeon, without any prayers being said. No *mohel* would circumcise a boy whose mother was not Jewish, but Arnold had arranged the next best thing.

"Sammy and Miriam will be so happy there's now a name for their Martin," Abraham reflected with a poignant smile.

Sarah was thinking of this, too. But as she and Abraham had grown older, she had noticed that their thoughts often coincided. Perhaps it was because they'd lived together for so long that the inseparable quality that had always been the cornerstone of their marriage was, in their old age, making their two minds sometimes seem like one.

"Isn't that why Jews call the newly born after their departed loved ones?" she said softly. "What could be better than a living memory? Until David was born, my mother couldn't rest because nobody had yet been named for her father, though he'd been dead for five years."

Abraham stared contemplatively into the empty grate. "I wonder which of my grandchildren will soon name a child after me?"

Sarah's teacup clinked into the saucer. "So chilly it is in here without a fire," she said, reaching for her shawl and slipping it around her shoulders. Why didn't she tell him he was talking nonsense? Because they had never lied to each other. She eyed his frail figure, which for months she had tried not to notice was becoming more and more so. What a struggle it had been to stop herself from protesting when he dragged himself out of bed every morning to go to work. To let him shorten his life by laboring on. But that was how he wanted it. She hadn't expected him to reach the age he now was and sometimes wondered if God had decided not to take him because He admired a man with such a spirit.

Abraham saw the tears that had sprung to her eyes. His disenchantment had crystallized into the words he had just spoken. And he felt as if a great weight had been lifted off him now that he had uttered them. "Don't cry, Sorrel. The while I'm still here."

But Sarah knew in her bones it would not be for long.

The following morning Abraham rose early, as usual, to don his phylacteries and say the weekday morning prayer. They ate breakfast together as they had always done, with the ticking of the clock and the sound of Tibby lapping her milk emphasizing the homely peace.

Abraham dunked his bagel into his tea to soften it. His face had grown so gaunt in recent weeks that his dentures felt insecure. "I've made up my mind to retire, Sarah."

Sarah managed to smile. "Whatever you want is all right with me."

When David called to drive his father to work, Abraham told him, too.

"What will you do with all the time you'll have on your hands?" David joked.

"Some of the things I should have done years ago," Abraham replied.

For the next few weeks, Sarah existed in a state of heightened emotions, but revealed her feelings to nobody. Instead, she went about her domestic chores as usual, watching her husband put into practice what he had said to David. Oiling the hinges on the garden gate, which had creaked for years, and fixing new washers on the bath taps that had dripped for almost as long. Puttying the corner of the parlor window, where on blustery wet days rain seeped through. Removing the threadbare tapestry from her dressing table stool and re-upholstering it with the piece of chintz she had set aside for the purpose when new curtains were hung, after the war.

These and countless other tasks he performed one after another. As if he wanted to make sure they were done for her while there was still a man about the house. But to Sarah, it seemed as though he was gathering up all the loose ends of his life, too. Tying them together in a final knot.

One day, she found him planting seeds in the border that lined the front path. She glanced at the packet he had left on the doorstep and saw that they were nasturtiums, which she had once told him she liked. But his long-ago promise to put some in the garden for her had, she'd thought, been forgotten.

Don't! she wanted to cry out. By the time the blaze of color burgeoned from the ground, she knew he would be lying beneath it, in Blackley cemetery. What a torture this was. But she made herself smile when he raised his head to look at her.

That afternoon, he went to visit his old friend Shloime Lipkin, Moishe's father, whom a stroke had incapacitated. And Mr. Kletz, who had been the Sandbergs' neighbor in Strangeways and was now a widower residing in the Jewish Home for the Aged.

"When we were young, places to put old people in weren't necessary," he said sorrowfully when he returned. "Their children took care of them. But even family life is no longer what it was."

"Our children would never put us there," Sarah declared, stirring the milky potato soup she was making for supper.

"The best of children do it, Sorrel," Abraham answered pensively. "It's a different world these days. Everyone has their own separate life to lead. Me it won't happen to. But it could happen to you."

Sarah was so shocked she had to sit down. It was a terrible thought.

"I was thinking about Rabbi Lensky, while I was sitting with Moishe," Abraham said. "How he used to comfort us when we were out of work and give us tea. In that broken-down old house where his *shul* was in those days. One day, with our help, he'd have a better *shul*, with a *bimah* to stand upon, he said to us once. The first, he's got, though it's still only a converted house. The second, he's still waiting for."

"So tell Yankel Cohen the furrier, who was also there, out of work, when Rabbi Lensky said it, to have one made for him," Sarah said with asperity. "He's rich enough."

"Yankel doesn't go there to pray any more. Nor do the others who went in those days. Posher *shuls* they go to now, with their smart wives and daughters," Abraham replied.

"Like our children do," Sarah reminded him.

"Who after I'm gone will get together to endow a memorial window for me, so they can look at it the few times a year they attend a service! But you'll still be here to tell them a *bimah* for Rabbi Lensky is what I want. A memorial to the English beginnings of the Sandberg family."

"I'll tell David," was all Sarah could manage to say. But she would see that her husband's wish was carried out.

That evening, Abraham retired to bed immediately after supper. He had picked at his food listlessly and Sarah wondered if he would ever get up again. The brief upsurge of strength that had enabled him to do all the things he thought necessary had faded like an Indian summer.

She remained seated at the kitchen table, beset by a sudden loneliness. How would she accustom herself to all her evenings being like this? To living without him? Her children and grandchildren would visit her and go away again. Like Abraham had said, they had their separate lives. You brought up a family and never had a minute to yourself, but in the end solitude was your reward.

The telephone rang, cutting into her thoughts.

"It's me, Bobbie," her eldest granddaughter's lively voice said across the miles. "I was thinking about you while I polished my candlesticks, so I thought I'd give you a tinkle."

But when you had a big family, there was always someone thinking of you, Sarah comforted herself. "At night you do your housework, Marianne?"

"During the day, between Martin's feeds, I'm trying to finish my play."

"So when do you cook?"

"Ralph's very easy. He doesn't mind baked beans and things like that."

"So long as you're happy," Sarah said. "And your husband also," she added doubtfully.

Marianne laughed. "He loves me, Bobbie," she said as though this outweighed her domestic shortcomings.

"Take your grandmother's advice. Make Ralph a hot meal every night." When the Sandbergs had stayed with the Berkowitzes, Malka had been a slovenly housekeeper and Chaim had not minded. But if such neglect extended to a wife's culinary duties, sooner or later the most loving of husbands would. How could she be giving her attention to this, when Abraham was dying? When her married life would soon be ended? Because Marianne's was just beginning and Sarah wanted it to be as perfect as her own. "Set time aside for cooking, every day," she instructed. "Or get up earlier and put a stew to simmer in the oven. Like I used to do, when I spent my days sewing buttons on uniforms. At home, during the Great War."

"Did you really do that, Bobbie? I didn't know."

"All my neighbors in Strangeways did, too. Only we didn't call ourselves career women, like you and Hannah and Shirley. Or have help in the house, like your cousin now has.

We managed, and our husbands got a nourishing meal when they came home from work. To which a man is entitled when he is the breadwinner. Promise you'll do like I said, Marianne."

"I promise. How's Zaidie?"

Sarah hesitated, then made up her mind. "Not too good. Do you have any arrangements for the weekend?"

"Uncle Joe's asked us to lunch on Sunday. His son, my cousin Christopher whom I've never met, is paying a flying visit from California. He's a screenwriter out there. Why?"

"If you want to see your grandfather again, come to Manchester. Your cousin Christopher you can see some other time. And don't ring up your mother and frighten her with what I've said. You know how hysterical she gets and I can do without it. You, I can tell."

But the next morning Abraham surprised Sarah by rising as usual.

"Put on your best things, we're going out," he smiled to her.

"It's Thursday. I have to start preparing for *Shabbos*."

"You can fry the fish tomorrow morning. Or when we get home."

"Home from where?"

"I'm taking you to Southport."

Sarah did not argue. Making Abraham happy was more important than frying fish. But it felt strange to be putting on the gray silk dress she wore for weddings and *Bar Mitzvahs*. And the black coat with a velvet collar David had given her for her birthday.

"You should have let him buy you the one he wanted to," Abraham said.

"What do I need a fur coat for? Most of the time it would be hanging in the wardrobe. And he has better things to do with his money."

Abraham laughed. "I bet he wishes his wife thought like that!"

Abraham's light-heartedness raised Sarah's spirits. He had telephoned for a taxi to take them to the railway station and was laughing and joking all the way there. On the journey to the coast, they sat in companionable silence.

"You know what's just struck me?" Abraham said when the train was grinding to a halt at Southport. "The only other time we traveled by train in England was the day we arrived."

Sarah smiled reminiscently. "When our children were young, where did we ever travel to? And since they grew up and made money, they take us everywhere by car."

"Always with them we've been," Abraham declared. "When did we have even a day out on our own?"

"Never."

"That's what I thought when I woke up this morning," he said, helping her step down to the platform. "It's why we're having one now."

The resort was bathed in May sunlight and the Floral Gardens had never looked lovelier. Sarah watched a cabbage-butterfly dance a jig on a bed of scarlet geraniums and cast her poignant thoughts aside. For once, she would not think of the future. She would do what Abraham was doing, make the most of today.

They ate lunch in a kosher hotel and afterwards strolled along Lord Street, greeting Mancunian acquaintances who had retired to the seaside and admiring the elegant shop windows.

"Who is Christian Dior?" Sarah inquired, perusing the label on a suit. "That outfit is like the ones Shirley and Ann wore for Martin's *Brith*."

"For Dior originals they're not yet rich enough," Abraham replied. "He's a French designer, who David says has just turned the garment trade upside down. Everyone copies him."

"These new clothes remind me of what we wore when I was young. I said so to the girls. Except we didn't show our ankles. Seeing such styles again is like moving backwards in time," Sarah smiled.

"That, I feel today anyway," Abraham said, slipping his arm around her waist. "Just you and me taking the air together, like we did long ago." He pointed to a black taffeta coat, cut like a tent and with bell-sleeves. "There is a Sander-tyle."

"That's a raincoat?" Sarah exclaimed.

Abraham chuckled. "I said that to David in 1922, when he brought me his very first fashion sample to press. And compared to what he's producing nowadays, it was a raincoat! Over a ball-gown a woman could wear that fancy garment and Shirley says plenty do."

But Sarah was no longer looking at it. She had just seen their reflections in the glass. The stoop-shouldered elderly man with his arm around a little old woman. Could they really be the young lovers who had walked hand in hand on the banks of the River Dvina?

"It isn't respectable to put your arm around me in the street," she said to Abraham.

He smiled down at her. "So?"

"All right, I'll let you." What did respectable matter? It mattered a lot and always had, to both of them. But for some reason had temporarily stopped doing so. Just for today. He kept his arm where it was when they resumed walking, but Sarah did not mind.

"What are you going to buy me?" she joked when he halted outside a jeweller's shop and studied the glittering display.

"An engagement ring."

Sarah thought he was joking, too. Then he turned to look at her and she knew he was not. "After fifty-two years of marriage?"

"At the right time I couldn't afford to give you one. But late is better than never."

Was this another item on the list of things he had left undone and wanted to do before he departed? He had not suffered a bout of coughing since they left home. Or complained he was out of breath from walking, though Nathan had told her his heart was not strong. Nothing had happened to burst the bubble of happiness on which she had allowed herself to float and she would not let it now. She linked her arm through his and went with him into the shop.

"In a place like this, a ring will cost a fortune," she whispered, surveying the discreetly expensive decor.

Abraham smiled. "But diamonds I know you don't like." His voice thickened with emotion. "If you did, and I could give them to you, I would, Sorrel. Only the best is good enough for you."

An opal necklace in the display cabinet shimmered into a rainbow as Sarah gazed at it through misty eyes. It was as if, in that simple statement, Abraham had expressed everything she meant to him and there wasn't a jewel in the world the equal of that.

She emerged from the shop with a dainty cluster of garnets glistening beside her wedding band. The salesman had fitted a clip to the ring because her fingers were so tiny and she had refused to leave it there to be altered to her size. She wanted to wear it now, on this perfect day.

Later, they sat down to rest on a bench on the promenade, with Southport's silky, golden sands stretching for miles before them to the ever-distant sea.

"When I show my ring to the children, Bessie will say there's no accounting for taste," Sarah smiled. "And Rebecca will glance at it patronizingly and tell me it's the thought that counts. Esther, of course, will say it isn't an engagement ring because it has colored stones. Like she told Marianne about the turquoise one Ralph bought for her."

"And David and Ben will say they could have got it for you wholesale."

They shared a laugh.

"How well we know them, Abraham!"

"We shouldn't by now? Their good points as well as their bad. Which even my daughter-in-law Bessie has, I was surprised to discover."

Sarah watched a flock of seagulls descend upon the beach. Just like a family. It was the nature of all God's creatures to be together with their own. But, just this once, how refreshing it was to be where none of hers could reach her.

Sarah opened her eyes and looked at the clock. "Wake up, Abraham. We've overslept. The sea air must have drugged us!" Since he retired, she had not bothered setting the alarm. And would be an hour behind schedule with her *Shabbos* cooking, in consequence.

She was slipping on her dressing gown when she became aware that Abraham had not stirred. Her heart missed a beat. Then she went to look at him. The peaceful expression on his face was not of this earth. Her husband would never wake up again.

She wanted to take him by the shoulders and shake him back to life, and had to clench her fists to stop herself. Her hands fell limply to her sides. She must go downstairs and ring up the children. Instead, she sank on her knees beside the bed, her eyes riveted to Abraham's still countenance.

She could hear the loud tick of his pocket-watch on the bed table and the sound of the breeze rustling the net curtains at the open window. Distant traffic noises assailed her ears. And the clink of two milk bottles being set down in the

porch. Later, she heard the letterbox click and the thud of
the mail landing on the lobby mat. Her legs felt stiff. How
long had she been kneeling here? But she could not make
herself rise; grief had immobilized her. Where were the tears
she had expected to shed when this moment came? To un-
leash her sorrow would be a blessed relief. But who was she
sorrowing for?

Abraham had lived according to his beliefs. Known the
contentment only those who make no demands can know.
Seen the fruit of his seed unto the third generation and gone
to his Maker willingly. Sarah had never seen him happier
than he had been these last few weeks, when he had been
preparing for his going.

There was no cause to sorrow for Abraham and pitying
herself had never been her way. The iron-cast will that had
always been hers reasserted itself and she rose to her feet,
busying her mind with the things she must do.

After she had dressed, she slipped the garnet ring on her
finger. Everyone would look askance at a mourning widow
wearing jewelry. But Abraham would have wanted her to
wear it. She went to the bedside to kiss him goodbye before
David and Nat arrived and took over, after which she would
never again be alone with him. "Only the best is good enough
for you," he had said. Luxury he hadn't given her. But she
had had the best of marriages.

Marianne arrived with Ralph and baby Martin in the
early evening. Harry had telephoned to tell her their grandfather was dead and she found the family gathered in the parlor, where they had been all day.

She went to sit beside Sarah and took her hand. "There
has to be some significance in Zaidie dying the day Israel was
born," she said pensively.

"What is your wife talking about?" Sigmund asked
Ralph.

"It's the dramatist in her, she can't help it. But haven't
you heard the news?"

"Who switches the wireless on at a time like this?"
David said morosely.

His eyes were red-rimmed. Nathan's, too, Marianne
noted. She had not expected her uncles to weep; but maybe
losing their father had momentarily reduced them to small
boys again, reminded them of their childhood. "The Govern-

ment's withdrawing the troops from Palestine," she announced. "We saw it on the placards when we came out of London Road Station. They'd sold out of evening papers, but Ralph read one over someone's shoulder in the taxi queue. Mr. Ben-Gurion is Israel's first Prime Minister. He made the Declaration of Independence this afternoon."

"*Mazeltov!*" Ronald shouted jubilantly. He leapt up from his chair and went around shaking hands with everyone.

Shirley had rushed to hug David. If Abraham had been miraculously restored to life there could not have been greater excitement. At such a moment in their people's history, in the midst of their grief the family could not but rejoice, too.

"Our troubles are over," David said thankfully.

"What makes you think that?" Hannah asked him.

"This will be the beginning of another lot," Sigmund, the doom merchant, prophesied and a heated debate followed.

"How can you all sit here arguing about politics when you've just lost someone you love?" Ralph interjected.

"If it wasn't politics, it'd be something else," Nathan assured him.

Marianne sent Ralph to the kitchen to ask Lizzie or Bridie to feed Martin his bottle.

"It's like a crêche in there," he said when he returned.

"It always has been when the clan get together," Marianne told him. "And I expect it always will be."

"A little red-haired madam kicked me on the shin," her husband complained.

"Like her mother used to do to our Martin's namesake and me when we were kids. The little madam is Shirley's Laura."

Ralph gave his attention to something Hannah was saying about Egypt and Marianne glanced at her grandmother. Sarah had never seemed beautiful to her, but suddenly she did. How erect she held herself, seated in a high-backed chair with only her faded, gray shawl softening the starkness of her mourning attire. And her opaque eyes, which Marianne had inherited, mysterious dark pools in her proud face. Most people were diminished by age, but on Sarah Sandberg it appeared to be having the opposite effect.

"That's a beautiful ring you're wearing, Bobbie," Marianne said quietly. She had never seen it before, but it must mean something special to Sarah, or she wouldn't have worn it today.

Sarah read her thoughts and smiled. "I knew you would like it. And when I'm gone it will be yours."

"I hope that won't be for a very long time."

"Whenever it is, I won't argue. Like your grandfather didn't. He was a remarkable man. Only I didn't know it until lately." Sarah became aware that the room had grown silent. "The discussion is over so soon?" she inquired.

"You'll have to forgive us, Bobbie," Ronald said. "We got a bit carried away by the news from Palestine."

"Israel," Shirley corrected him.

"We ought not to have been making so much noise," David said.

"I should think not!" Esther, who had not contributed to it, exclaimed. "With Father lying dead upstairs."

"If the dead could hear and speak, your father would shout downstairs that he doesn't mind," Sarah told her. It had been almost noon when she telephoned David, too late for the funeral to take place today. With the Sabbath intervening, Abraham would not be buried until Sunday. "He wouldn't want everyone to sit here *shtum*, with long faces."

Little Laura Kohn wandered in from the kitchen, jangling the gold charm bracelet on her chubby wrist.

"Bless her heart," David and Bessie chorused adoringly.

The child climbed into Abraham's wing chair, which had remained conspicuously empty.

Shirley and Peter exchanged an uncomfortable glance.

"Now Gweat-gwanpa's gone to Heaven, Lawa can sit here," their daughter gurgled.

Esther burst into tears.

"Don't be upset, Esther," Sarah said, going to comfort her. "Nature arranged it that youth should replace age. Nobody's chair stays empty for long."

But before Sarah vacated hers she had a lot to do. Reuniting Arnold with the family was one matter. She must visit Sammy and Miriam in New York, too; it was unthinkable to go to her grave without seeing them again. And Nathan and Rebecca's strife was affecting Leona; something had to be done about that. Like Abraham. she had many loose ends to gather up and, God willing, would be around long enough to knot them together.

Glossary

Certain words and phrases have no precise English equivalent and the nearest possible definition is given. The original language is indicated by (*H*) Hebrew, (*R*) Russian, or (*Y*) Yiddish.

bagel (*Y*) Hard, ring-shaped bread-roll; adapted from the Russian "bublitchki."

Bar Mitzvah (*H*) Confirmation ceremony of a Jewish thirteen-year-old boy; also the term applied to the boy himself.

bershert (*Y*) Fated.

bimah (*H*) Platform in synagogue, from which prayers are led by ministers. Usually of imposing appearance and enclosed by a low railing, or panels of polished wood.

Bobbie/Bubbah (*Y*) Grandmother.

borsht (*R*) Beetroot soup.

Brith (*H*) Circumcision ceremony.

challah (*H*) Traditional Jewish loaf.

chalutzim (*H*) Pioneers in the land of Israel.

Chanukah (*H*) Described variously as "The Festival of Lights," "The Feast of Dedication," and "The Feast of the Maccabees." Celebrated for eight days (in December). Instituted by Judas Maccabeus and the elders of Israel in 165 B.C. to commemorate the route of the invader Antiochus Ephinanes, and the purification of the Temple sanctuary.

Chavurah (*H*) Group of young Zionists in the Habonim Movement.

chevrah (*H*) A small congregation.

cholent (*Y*) Butterbean stew.

chupah (*H*) Marriage canopy; a canopy supported by four poles, beneath which the marriage is solemnized, representing the home the couple will share.

chutzpah (*H*)   Cheek; audacity; brazen nerve.

droshky (*R*)   Low, four-wheeled carriage.

feinkochen (*Y*)   Omelet.
frum (*Y*)   Religious.

ganef (*Y*)   Thief.
gefilte fish (*Y*)   Fishballs, fried or boiled.
goy(im) (*Y*)   Gentile(s).

Habonim (*H*)   (lit. The Builders) A Zionist Youth Movement.
Haggadah (*H*)   The book containing the Passover Seder Service. (*see* Seder)
Hassid(im) (*H*)   (lit. The Pious Ones) Mystic Jewish sect founded in the mid-eighteenth century by the Ukrainian Rabbi Israel Baal-Shem. Hassidim seek God in everyday life, believe sadness hinders devotion and cheerfulness aids prayer.
holeshkies (*Y*)   Rolled cabbage leaves, stuffed with minced beef and cooked in a sweet-and-sour sauce.
Horah (*H*)   Traditional Zionist song, and group dance performed in a circle.

Kaddish (*H*)   The Mourner's Prayer, recited by immediate male relatives of the deceased.
kapora (*Y*)   A folklore curse invoked by the superstitious to ward off evil.
kazatsky (*R*)   A dance performed in a crouched position, stretching-out and bending first one leg and then the other.
Kiddush (*H*)   The benediction recited over wine.
knedl (*Y*)   Dumpling, usually accompanying chicken soup.
kosher (*H*)   In accordance with the Jewish dietary laws.
kuchen (*Y*)   Yeast cake.

landsleit (*Y*)   Fellow-townsman.
latke (*Y*)   Potato pancake.
liebchen (German)   Darling.
lokshen (*Y*)   Egg noodles.

Maoz Tsur (*H*) (lit. Rock of Ages) Chanukah hymn.

matzo(s) (*H*) Unleavened bread, eaten at Passover.

Mazeltov (*H*) Good luck; a congratulatory greeting.

megiyah (*H*) Conversion to the Jewish faith.

menorah (*H*) An eight-branched candelabrum used for the Chanukah Festival.

meshuga (*H*) Crazy.

mezuzah (*H*) Small, rectangular piece of parchment inscribed with the passages Deut. vi. 4–9 and xi. 13–21, written in twenty-two lines. The parchment is rolled and inserted in a wooden or metal case and nailed in a slanting position to the right-hand doorposts of orthodox Jewish homes (interior and exterior) as a talisman against evil.

minyan (*H*) Quorum of no less than ten males required to form a congregation for prayers.

mohel (*H*) The religious functionary who performs circumcisions according to Rabbinic rite and regulations.

nachas (*H*) Pleasure, pride and joy combined.

nosh (*Y*) Food; to enjoy food. Usually applies to sweetmeats and delicacies.

perineh (*Y*) Feather-filled bed roll in a white cover.

Pesach (*H*) Passover. The Festival commemorating the Jews' liberation from their bondage in Egypt. Lasts seven days, during which only unleavened bread and specially prepared foods are eaten. (March/April)

pisha-paysha. A card game introduced by Jewish immigrants. Probably Russian.

pogromschik (*Y*) (derived from pogrom) One of the mob perpetrating a pogrom.

Rosh Hashanah (*H*) (lit. Head of the year) The Jewish New Year. (Autumn)

Seder (*H*) The religious service conducted around the dining table in Jewish homes, recounting the liberation from Egyptian bondage. Is celebrated amidst festivity on the first two nights of Passover. (Reform Jews observe only one night.)

Sefer Torah (*H*) (lit. Book of the Law) The Five Books of Moses, in which are written the Law.

Shabbos (Yiddish for the Hebrew word "Shabbat") Sabbath.

Shalom Aleichem (*H*) Peace be unto you. A traditional Jewish greeting.

shatchan (*H*) Matchmaker.

sheitel (*Y*) Wig worn by ultra-orthodox Jewish married women.

shekel (*H*) Ancient Jewish silver coin. Pl. colloq.: money, riches.

shikker (*Y*) Drunk.

shiksah (*H*) Non-Jewish female.

Shivah (*H*) The ritual Jewish mourning.

shlemiel (*Y*) Fool; inept person.

shlep (*Y*) Drag: make a tedious journey.

shluff (*Y*) Sleep; snooze.

shmaltz (*Y*) Chicken fat, usually refers to the rendered-down form.

shmearer (*Y*) One who spreads the varnish (glue) on seams and hems in a waterproof-garment factory.

shmerel (*Y*) Dolt; stupid person.

shmooze (*Y*) Cajole; flatter; sweet-talk.

shmuck (*Y*) Twirp.

shnitzel (German) Thin slice of veal, coated in breadcrumbs and fried.

shnorrer (*Y*) Beggar.

shpeil (*Y*) Play.

shtetlach (*Y*) Back-of-beyond townlets.

shtum (*Y*) Dumb; silent.

shul (*Y*) Synagogue.

simchah (*H*) Joyous occasion.

Simchas Torah (*H*) (lit. Rejoicing of the Law) The Festival celebrating the completion of the reading of the Law. (Autumn)

streimel (*Y*) Large, fur-trimmed hat.

Succah (*H*) A booth, usually in the yard or garden, in which Jews are required to dwell for seven days during the Tabernacles Festival. Only the ultra-orthodox still observe this law, but all synagogue congregations erect, and adorn with fruit and flowers, a large, communal "Succah," in which to celebrate the Festival with sweetmeats and wine.

Succoth (*H*) The Festival of Tabernacles, commemorating

the Jews' departure from Egypt when tents sheltered them in the Wilderness. (Autumn)

tallith (*H*)   Prayer-shawl.
tefillin (*H*)   Phylacteries worn by Jewish men for weekday morning-prayers.
Torah (*H*)   Law; doctrine.
trafe (*H*)   Non-kosher (*see* kosher).
tsimmes (*Y*)   Carrot stew.
tsorus (*H*)   Sorrow; heartache; troubles.

yarmulke (Polish origin)   Skull-cap.
Yidden (German origin)   Jews.
Yom Kippur (*H*)   Day of Atonement. The holiest day of the Jewish year. A solemn Fast Day.
Yom Tov (*H*)   Festival.
Zaidie (Zaida) (*Y*)   Grandfather.

ABOUT MAISIE MOSCO

Raised in Manchester, England, MAISIE MOSCO was moved to write the trilogy that began with *From the Bitter Land* and *Scattered Seed* because she felt that the British Jewish experience was not being reflected properly in either theatre or literature.

"I wanted to remove all the myths and mysteries which surrounded the Jewish way of life and to show Jews as real people," she says. "I was angry with the tired old clichés about Jews. So my husband, listening to my complaints, said, 'Well, you're the writer in the family. Why don't you do something about it.' So I did." In *From the Bitter Land,* she began the story of "the English/Jewish experience told in novel form from the inside, which I don't think has ever been done before." The result was applauded in Great Britain by both fans and critics alike and was received with the same enthusiasm when it was published in the United States in early 1981.

Maisie Mosco was brought up in a traditional Jewish household and draws upon her own past to weave her fictional tales. Her grandparents were Russian and Viennese and they settled in Manchester around the turn of the century. Many of the events told in *From the Bitter Land* were related to her by her grandfather and other family members and friends.

Maisie Mosco began her career as a journalist, once serving as news editor for the *Manchester Jewish Gazette*. While raising her family, she wrote freelance advertising copy and then began working on radio, stage and screen plays. *From the Bitter Land* was her first novel, followed by *Scattered Seed*. The third novel in her trilogy will be published by Bantam in 1982.

Maisie Mosco feels that writing her trilogy has helped her to learn a great deal about her roots and hopes to share that education with her readers. "I think as far as Jewish readers are concerned, for older ones, there will be nostalgia, shared experience. For younger ones, like my children's generation, I think it's going to be a great revelation to know what their forebears went through. And for non-Jewish readers, of course, I think it is probably going to remove a lot of the myths and mysteries that surround the whole of the Jewish way of life, and perhaps explain why we are the kind of people we are."

Maisie Mosco is married to an accountant and has four children.